Sunset Run

William F. Carli

[handwritten:] WF Carli
To: Pete & Claire
St. Thomas VI
2016

Shooting Star Publishing

P.O. Box 2569
Friday Harbor, WA 98250

Sunset Run

ISBN: 0-9787311-0-7

Library of Congress Control Number: 2006905922

Cover illustrations by Robert Warren, Friday Harbor, WA

Cover and book design by Illumina
Friday Harbor, Washington, USA
http://www.illuminapublishing.com

Acknowledgments

This book is dedicated to Christy Marie,
the love of my life.

A special thank you to the people without whose help and support this book would never have been published: Sandy Paulus, Susan Stehn, Megan Connelly, Dolores Hollenbach, Ann Beaton, Jim Carli, Charles & Margaret Carli, Bruce Conway, Robert Warren, and Greg (Mondo) Taylor.

In loving memory of Frank Carli.

Prologue

Smokin' Joe was all that Mondo owned. He had never bought a house or a new car; as a matter of fact Mondo never really had much money. He didn't need it. He found earning money interfered with his life. Working at a job that his heart wasn't into just ate him up until it became too big of a compromise and off he went somewhere, someplace, it often didn't matter, just away.

Mondo tried college, even thought about law school, a fancy red Porsche and a three piece suit; it all went together in his mind. After two years he couldn't tell if it was boredom, lack of interest, or his conscience, but he quit thinking of law school and dropped out of college. It wasn't his dream. His dream was to see it all, to taste it all, to grab hold of this short amount of time that he had been given and to do something real with it.

He ended up in the British Virgin Islands, rebuilding after hurricane Monty tried to erase them and half of the Caribbean from the face of the earth. There was more work than people to do the job and Mondo was good at building. He was good at whatever he put his heart and soul into.

It was in the British Virgin Islands that he discovered sailing while working on the remnants of a winter home for a rich Nevada casino owner. The house was perched high on the hills overlooking Cane Garden Bay, sitting on the west side of Tortola. The island of Jost Van Dyke simmered in the heat four miles away, reflecting against a deep blue sea.

The afternoon trade-winds were up and blowing their usual twenty knots, which was refreshing in the heat of the day. Mondo saw the sailboat come out of Great Harbor on Jost Van Dyke, pull up its sails and head toward Tortola. He put his hammer down and watched. The boat was sleek, two sails pushing this graceful yacht towards its new destination, its next adventure. He couldn't take his eyes off of her. It was early in the cruising season and the yacht had the entire world to herself. This sailboat called out to him. He heard her on the wind. *Bring me your restless heart and I will show you the world. I can take you there.*

Mondo sat down and watched, embarrassed that something so simple could have such an impact on him, that it could speak so forcefully to his soul. He knew right then that this is what he wanted, this was the prize to work for, the goal worth the labor, a sailboat, his sailboat, to carry him wherever he desired to go.

That day Mondo put his carpenter tools down. He made his way home, showered and shaved, put on some good clothes, and within two hours was employed by Caribbean Sailing Service. He told them that he could learn fast, and would work for whatever they thought he was worth.

"Give me a week and then decide," he said. This wasn't about money—it was about life. From that day on Mondo became a sailor. It took almost the entire season for him to work from low man in the maintenance department to one of the head captains in charge of taking guests out sailing. He would meet the charter group on the boat, go over the important facts about sailing, answer whatever questions he could, then off they went sailing for the day, or longer, depending on their skill level. Even experienced sailors enjoyed their time with him, his enthusiasm was soo contagious. The guests loved him and more than a few young ladies wished they could get to know their blond-haired captain a little better.

The sailing season in the Caribbean goes from November to May, then it's hurricane season and most sailors leave. Many boats head south to Venezuela or north back to the states.

Smokin' Joe came to Mondo in a surprising way. Like so many things in his life, it all just worked out for the best. The previous owner decided that he wouldn't go home emptyhanded after spending the season "down island". He bought twenty pounds of marijuana and stashed it on board, a little profit down in the bilge. Unfortunately for him he was informed upon and never got out of St. John Harbor. He was arrested for drug possession, lost his boat, and a few years of his life. His boat was impounded by customs.

The owner decided to plea bargain, and so within two months of its impounding the sailboat came up for sealed bid auction. The bids came in late June when very few people were around. Mondo made a low bid (all that he had), was called a week later and informed that he had forty-eight hours to produce the money or the next bidder would be contacted. Mondo produced his hard earned cash and received title to a beautiful but rundown forty-four foot sailboat. He changed the name to Smokin' Joe in honor of the previous jailbound owner. It was the least he could do.

CHAPTER 1

Pacific Ocean

"This is Whiskey Charlie X-Ray 3381 sailing vessel Smokin' Joe, calling Soul-mate. Soul-mate, do you copy?" Mondo held the radio microphone in his left hand as he grasped the overhead grab rail tightly with his right hand. He listened for two minutes, with no reply. A cold shiver ran down his spine as he thought of the two of them out there. He hoped they were all right, but in weather like this, it was all he could do to keep his fear in check.

It had been beautiful sailing since he left Hawaii. The weather had been perfect, steady westerly winds blowing eighteen to twenty-five knots once he got over the Pacific high. Now, eighteen days out of Kauai and still four hundred miles from the Washington coast, trouble was brewing. NOAA weather had predicted that a low pressure zone in the Gulf of Alaska would make its way south. At first this didn't concern him. The storm didn't look too intense, and it was forecasted to veer east and hit the mainland of northern British Columbia. It wouldn't be within three hundred miles of his position. That forecast was for two days ago. The storm had stalled, then increased in strength. Yesterday it was upgraded to gale force winds thirty- five to forty knots. The front was still forecasted to turn east and hit British Columbia, but as Mondo continued to track its position he could tell it was coming right at him.

Last night he didn't sleep very well. The swells were increasing in size and he knew that he wasn't going to escape this storm. He hoped that his position was far enough south that he would only catch its outer edge.

Mondo was sailing by himself. At least he didn't have anybody else to worry about.

That changed yesterday afternoon when he received a radio call.

"This is Alpha Alpha Charlie 2459, sailing vessel Soul-mate, does anybody copy?"

It was a woman's voice and it held a slight edge of panic. Mondo had just finished plotting his position on the chart and he was standing next to the radio. If he hadn't been that close he probably would never have heard her.

"Soul-mate, this is Whiskey Charlie X-Ray 3381, sailing vessel Smokin' Joe, I hear you."

"Oh, good, our position is 134 degrees 59 minutes west by 48 degrees 30 minutes north, do you copy?" Still that tension in her voice.

"Roger, I copy." Mondo reached into his chart table, pulled out his notebook and wrote their coordinates down. He realized that they were fairly close to him.

"What is your position, Smokin' Joe?"

Mondo told her.

"Have you heard the weather forecast?" she asked.

"Yes, I have. Gale force winds blowing thirty to forty knots, over."

"That has been upgraded to strong gale to storm force winds. We're expecting gusts of over fifty knots. Our barometer is dropping like a rock and we're a little concerned, over."

Good, Mondo thought, *anybody out here facing fifty knots that wasn't concerned would be an idiot.*

"Soul-mate, how many people on board?"

"Two, my husband and myself. We're Mike and Sue, twenty-two days out of Honolulu, our boat is a thirty-eight foot Thines."

"Copy, stand by. I'm going to plot your position, you are pretty close to me. Hang on one minute, Sue."

Mondo hung up the microphone, reached across his chart table, grabbed his dividers and plotted their position.

"Sue, I have you about forty-five miles ahead of me and slightly to the north. I'm a single-hander, looks like we're going to be in some bad weather together."

"Roger that. Smokin' Joe, what's your name?"

Mondo laughed to himself. Out in the sailing world more people were known by the name of their boat than their first name.

"I'm Mondo."

"Mondo, we've never been in a storm like this before, Mike is concerned and so am I. We're pretty new to all of this."

A cold tingle ran down Mondo's spine.

"Not much I can say."

10

"I know."

"What preparations have you made?"

"Nothing, Mike can't quite seem to make his mind up, he's hoping the storm won't hit us."

Mondo sat down at his chart table, his mind going over what he would be doing in the next few hours to prepare for this coming storm. He knew that these two were out of their league. He also knew that if they panicked or made a mistake it could be all over for them.

"Listen, Sue, put Mike on the radio."

"This is Mike," that edge in his voice as well.

"Well buddy, we got some weather coming our way. Nothing that our boats can't handle, we just have to help them out. Know what I mean?"

"Yeah."

"Okay, here's what I think you should do. Strip everything off the deck that's not bolted down, remove anything that's windage. Then, hank on your storm sails. Do you have a storm tri sail?"

"No."

"No sweat. Pull your roller furling headsail down and store it below, and put the biggest reef you have in the main. Have you ever hove to?"

"No, just read about it."

Mondo just shook his head.

"Do you have a sea anchor?"

"What's that?"

Jesus Christ, what the hell are you two doing out here, he thought.

"Well, you have time to read about heaving to. If that doesn't work just drop your mainsail and head off downwind towing as much line as you have in a big loop off the stern. That should help keep your stern to the following seas. Got it?"

"Yeah fine, I'll start removing stuff from on deck, I think we should stay in radio contact."

"Good idea. For now lets contact each other at 0600, 1200, 1800, and 2400 hours. Once the weather gets bad we can make our contacts by the hour. Have your GPS coordinates so that way we can track each other. I doubt I'll be getting much sleep, but I'm going to try, so if we miss a contact just go to the next hour, okay?"

"Okay."

"Good, let me talk to Sue."

"Hi, Mondo."

"Sue, this isn't that big of a storm. You have a great boat and it will take care of you, just be smart and help her along. The best thing you can do is to prepare some warm food for later and try to get some sleep."

"All right, Mondo."

"I'm signing off. Let's start our radio checks tonight at 1800 hours."

"Mondo, thanks. You know, this is going to sound silly, but I'm really glad you're out there."

Mondo hung up the microphone and slumped back in his chart table seat. Those two could be in a world of trouble before this storm blew through.

In the next few hours Mondo prepared his boat. He did everything that he told Mike to do. Soon Smokin' Joe was ready for whatever the sea could throw at them; at least he hoped so. He had seen weather worse than this, but only once. One time sailing from Fiji to New Zealand it had blown over sixty knots for two days, creating the biggest waves he had ever seen in his entire life. The New Zealand Coast Guard had to rescue crew from five boats. Three people and one boat were never found.

By evening the swells were bigger than ever. They were still far apart so there was no immediate danger, but the growing conditions were a telltale sign of what was coming his way. Down in the trough of each wave he could see nothing but water, then up Smokin' Joe would ride to the top of the crest, and as far as Mondo could see all there was were mountains of lumbering white water, the tops of each wave blown into the air by the wind. He did get some sleep that night, wrapped tight in the lee-cloth that kept him from rolling out of his bunk if a big wave hit Smokin' Joe.

By noon the next day the wind was steady forty to forty-five knots. The seas were huge and growing by the hour. The swells were getting steeper, and closer to each other. Mondo knew that was the dangerous part. These huge rushing walls of water were now getting so tall that they couldn't support themselves, and over they would crash. If Smokin' Joe was hit broadside by one of these large breaking waves the boat would roll over and the trouble would start. At 1800 hours he made his first radio check with Soul-mate. They were all right, scared, but all was well at the moment. The wind was now blowing fifty knots with gusts even higher. Smokin' Joe was down to storm tri-sail and a heavy duty number two storm jib. The self-steering vane was working fine; all he had to do was hang on and let Smokin' Joe take care of the both of them. Mondo thought about changing his course and heading south. It would give him a better angle to the wind and the waves, and he could run before the towering seas. Still he had a nagging feeling about Soul-mate, so he stayed his course.

"Mondo, this is Soul-mate. Are you there?"

Her voice told him much. The fear he had heard earlier was still present, just amplified.

"Sue, I'm here, how are you two doing?"

"Not too good. We've taken two knock downs, one put our mast in the water.Soul-mate came up okay, we didn't lose our mast, but it's getting bad, Mondo, we're both really afraid."

Mondo had sailed for over two years all through the South Pacific and had never come close to having Smokin' Joe knocked down. Things were starting to come undone for Sue and Mike.

"Are you hove to?"

"Negative, Mike took all the sails down and we're just hanging on."

That was about the worst thing they could do. They were lying broadside to every wave that swept their way. No wonder they had been knocked down.

"You need to head down wind and run before it, trail out as much rope off the stern in a big loop as you can, that will help slow you down. You can't just sit there, it's too dangerous."

"Mike can't move. He's really hurt bad, he slammed his back into the stove on the last knock down."

Mondo looked at his watch. It was ten-thirty. He glanced out his port hole window. It was as black as black can be.

"Give me your position."

Sue read off her latitude and longitude, and he plotted it on the chart.

"You're thirty-five miles away from me. You have to hold on until morning. This should blow through in a few hours." He lied. He had no idea how long this storm would last.

"Sue, you need to.."

He was cut off by a scream from Sue, her terror echoing through the microphone.

"We're rolling over, Mondo, help!" Then nothing, not even the crackle of static.

"Sue, Sue, do you copy?"

Panic tried to race through Mondo's mind, but he held it back. He drew a circle on the chart at Soul-mate's position, then he slumped down into the seat at the chart table. He didn't know what to do. He was tired and the rough sea-conditions were taking their toll on him. Now he knew that Mike's and Sue's lives were in his hands, and he did not want that responsibility, not at all, especially in weather as bad as this. After five minutes of hearing nothing, Mondo plotted a new course toward Soul-mate. He struggled into his foul-weather gear, slid the companion way hatch open and reset the self steering vane on a direct course toward Soul-mate. Smokin' Joe's motion increased instantly as he changed course. It had been uncomfortable before, now it was down right wild. Smokin' Joe would fly off the back of a huge wave, slamming down into the trough, only to start once again climbing up the face of another monstrous wave. It would take Mondo over ten hours to reach them. It would be one hell of a rough night, and there was nothing that he could do but hang on and pray that he could somehow find them in this nightmare of a storm.

Mondo climbed back down into the shelter of Smokin' Joe's cabin. He pulled his foul-weather gear off, and threw it into a corner. He would need it again soon enough. He braced himself at the chart table, one hand clutching the overhead grab rail, the other hanging on to the bulkhead grab rail in front of the chart table. Suddenly his radio crackled. It was a very weak signal.

"Mondo, it's me, are you there?"

"Sue, I hear you, are you all right?"

"I'm on the hand held radio, we went completely over, Mondo. Mike is unconscious, the mast is down, and it's slamming against the hull. I think it's going to come crashing through any second. Mondo, we're going to die tonight."

"Listen, Sue, I've already changed course, I'm coming. I'll call the Coast Guard, maybe there is a ship close. Just hang on, I'm coming for you."

"Mondo, I am so scared."

"That's all right, wedge Mike somewhere, tie him to a bunk or something. I'll call you every half hour. Do you have spare batteries for

14

the handheld?"

"Yes."

"Okay, Sue, just hang on, I'll call you every half hour. I'm coming."

"Hurry, Mondo, please."

"Sue, I'll be there by 0300 hours. I'll call you in thirty minutes."

Mondo hung up the microphone. He had lied again to Sue. The earliest he could possibly arrive on the scene would be 0500. He grabbed the radio microphone.

"May-day, May-day, May-day. This is sailing vessel Smokin' Joe." His radio crackled with empty static.

"May-day, May-day," he shouted, this time giving Soul-mate's position.

"We are sinking, repeat we are sinking."

He listened for five minutes, but only endless static came back to him. The fatigue that he had felt earlier was gone, his adrenaline was pumping and his mind focused. It was up to him, and him alone to save Sue and Mike. They would be dead by tomorrow if he couldn't rescue them.

At 2300 he made contact with Sue. She was hanging on. Mike was still out, although she had somehow managed to tie him to the aft cabin bunk. The mast was still slamming against the hull. It sounded to Sue like it was going to come crashing through their fiberglass cocoon at any minute. He tried to picture Soul-mate riding up and down these huge waves. They were like a cork in a washing machine, but at least they were still floating.

At 0300 Sue told him that the main bulkhead was starting to come apart, and the mast was still slamming into the hull. Sue didn't think the boat could last much longer. Mondo was now fifteen miles away. At 0500 the call was even worse.

"Mondo, two port windows have blown out. The hull is flexing so much it feels like it's breathing. Water is coming in on every wave through the ports. I don't think we can make it."

"Are the bilge pumps running?"

"Yes, the bilge meter shows them coming on."

"Listen, Sue, it will be light in an hour. Have two life jackets ready. I'm only eight miles away. I should be there in an hour. Just hang on." He was getting tired of having to lie to her, but he had to keep her from panicking. It would take him at least two hours before he could get there. At 0630 the first traces of morning appeared. He opened his hatch and looked out at some of the biggest waves he had ever seen.

"Sue, give me your position."

"I can't, the GPS is smashed. Water is starting to float the floor boards up. The bilge pumps can't keep up. Where are you?"

"Close, Sue, real close."

At 0730, according to Mondo's calculations, he should be close to their position. He had calculated their set and drift and then had to make a guess as to how far the storm would push them. If he wasn't right on, he would never find them.

"Sue, are you there?"

"Yes, there's a foot of water in the cabin, Mondo. Mike is awake but he can't do anything."

"Listen, Sue, I should be at your position. I'm turning on my masthead strobe light. Look outside and see if you can locate it."

She was back on the radio in less than a minute.

"Mondo, I see it, hurry, my god Mondo, hurry!"

"Sue, what direction are you from me? I can't see you."

"I don't know, you're... God, Mondo, you're right there. Can't you see me?"

Mondo could hear the panic in her voice. She was about to lose it completely.

"Listen, Sue, look outside again. I'm turning on my mast head running lights, tell me what color you see."

"I see green, it's green," she said after sticking her head outside again.

Soul-mate had to be to his right. He pulled his foul-weather gear on and slid the hatch open, then closed it behind him. He crawled into the cockpit, disconnected the self steering vane, and grabbed the wheel. He looked to his right. All that he could see was mountains of white water rolling in every direction. Suddenly Mondo saw Soul-mate. For just one second the stricken boat lay at the top of a wave before disappearing. Mondo lined up his steering compass, got a rough fix and then grabbed the radio microphone in the cockpit.

"Sue, I see you, I'm a hundred yards away. I'm coming."

"Hurry, Mondo, the water is up to my knees."

16

"Sue, put life jackets on the both of you. You are going to have to drag Mike out into the cockpit. Take a short line and tie yourselves together."

"Okay."

Soul-mate rose to the top of another huge wave. She was sitting very low in the water, and her bow was down by at least twenty degrees. Soul-mate was doomed, no doubt in his mind. He just had to get Sue and Mike off.

"Mondo, we're both in the cockpit."

"All right, here's what we are going to do. I'm going to sail very close to you up wind. I will throw you a line. Once you get it, use it to tie a bowline around the both of you, under your arms, and make it tight."

"Okay, then what?"

"You have to get that line tied around you fast. The line is only three hundred feet long. You have to get it tied around the both of you before it comes up tight on my end. If you're not tied off I won't be able to hold the rope. There is only one chance."

"Got it."

Mondo put the wheel down and headed for Soul-mate. With one hand on the wheel he reached behind him and uncoiled the three hundred foot dacron line from the stern rail, letting it fall into the cockpit at his feet. He opened up his starboard locker and pulled out his tool box, taking a heavy pipe wrench out and putting the tool box back in its place. Smokin' Joe was now fifty feet away from Soul-mate and closing fast. This was absolutely crazy. If he made any mistake in these conditions it would be over for both of them before they knew it. Mondo could see the mast slamming into the hull on the starboard side.

"Sue, I'm coming on your port side. I tied a wrench to the line, don't try to catch it, just let it land in the cockpit."

He steered Smokin' Joe closer. He was now only twenty feet away, he would have to get ten. This was beyond anything he had ever attempted before.

"Sue, I'm counting down, watch for the line."

Mondo pulled Smokin' Joe even with Soul-mate. For one second their eyes met, then he threw the line, and it crashed into the cockpit. Sue grabbed it, untied the wrench and let it fall. Mondo turned away from Soul-mate trying to keep as close as he dared. The line was running out fast. He watched as Sue frantically tied the line around the both of them.

"OK, we're tied off, now what?"

"Jump."Mondo didn't even finish talking before he pulled on the line with all of his strength. Sue and Mike were swept right off of Soul-mate into the frigid water. Mondo pulled the line with everything that he had. He could see them coming closer, then they would disappear behind a huge wave before rising back into view. Mondo's body ached and his hands were frozen, but still he continued to pull handfuls of cold, wet line into the cockpit. He brought Sue and Mike up close, then in one rolling motion as Smokin' Joe slid down into a trough, he reached over and scooped them both on board.

The next afternoon the winds had decreased to twenty knots, the mountainous waves now no more than large rollers. Mondo hadn't been aware that when he sent his May-day it was received by the cruise ship Princess Star, which was heading north for another season in Alaska. The cruise ship tried to contact him but his radio wasn't powerful enough to pick up their signal. His May-day set into motion a large rescue attempt coordinated by the United States Coast Guard out of Seattle, Washington. Smokin' Joe and the Princess Star rendezvoused three hundred miles from the British Columbia coast late that afternoon.

Mike and Sue were transferred aboard the cruise ship. Mike was in stable condition, so it was decided that they would continue on board the cruise ship until it docked at Juneau, Alaska.

Two days after transferring Mike and Sue, Mondo pulled Smokin' Joe into the Coast Guard and Customs dock in Neah Bay, Washington. He had arrived in twenty-one days, sailing over two thousand, four hundred miles.

"You the guy that rescued those people off of the sinking sailboat a few days ago?"

Mondo had been escorted into the Coast Guard commanding officers private office.

"Yes, sir."

The commanding officer stood, reached across his large oak desk and shook Mondo's hand.

"That was one hell of a job, son, one hell of a job."

"Thank you." Mondo was escorted out of the office. Customs never even looked at his boat. Suddenly the voyage was over.

He walked to a pay phone and called Amy. He wanted to talk to her so badly. There was no answer at the condo so he tried the shop. No answer again, that was strange. It was early afternoon on a weekday. The shop should have been opened. Mondo was exhausted, but wired. He couldn't sleep so he started to put Smokin' Joe back in order. An hour later he called both numbers again, still no answer. He walked back to his boat, opened up his chart table and found his little address and phone book. He retraced his steps to the pay phone, this time calling Christy's cell number. After two rings she answered.

"Christy, it's me, Mondo, I can't get hold of your sister. Where is Amy?"

"Oh, Mondo, thank God you called. Amy's in trouble, big trouble."

Mondo's heart sank like a rock in a mill pond.

"What?"

"Listen, Mondo, I'm at a bed and breakfast on Salt Bay Island, its called the Baker Street Inn, it's only about sixty miles down the Straight of Juan de Fuca from Neah Bay. Amy was here until just a few days ago. I just missed her."

"What are you talking about?" Mondo interrupted.

"It's so confusing, Mondo. Amy disappeared. Then she called my cell phone very late one night. Her message and the number that she called from were recorded in my missed messages. I've been here for a few days, and I don't know what to do. I knew you would call me on the cell. You need to get here, Mondo." Christy's voice held that same panicked edge that he had listened to for so long from Sue. What was going on?

"Okay, Christy, I'm on my way to Salt Bay Island. I'll find it on the charts. What did Amy's message say?"

There was a long pause from Christy before she continued.

"All she said was help me."

"Jesus, Christy, this sounds crazy."

"You have no idea, Mondo."

"I'm on my way."

CHAPTER 2

Genoa, Italy, 1930

For Edwin Hawkins the gods had truly looked upon this last year with favor, unbelievable favor. A year ago he was just one of many seekers, searchers, charlatans, and hoaxes who had moved from around the world to Genoa, Italy. He hadn't come for the seashore or the fine Mediterranean weather. Edwin came to receive power, to find enlightenment, to study the most ancient of arts. In the early 1930s Genoa was the center of the world for the occult and mysticism. Teachers and teachings flourished, from the magic of ancient Egypt to the dark evil magic of Aleister Crowley. Power was to be found here for the man who knew what to look for.

Edwin arrived from London in May, 1929. He was fascinated with the occult, with the power of magic, and how it enabled him to entertain and captivate others. For the last six years he had supported himself by performing magic in and around London. Edwin understood magic, now what he wanted was the power to use it.

To Edwin the key to magic, to getting his audience to believe what he wanted them to believe, rested in the persuasion of speech. The key to magic is communication, mental and verbal, he knew. The mood was set through the voice, and the magic through the mind. In his early years he had been afraid to use his mind during his magic shows. To him magic lay in the trick, the sleight of hand, the pre-packaging of the act. This was all true, but as he continued to grow as a magician he realized there was so much more. Edwin wanted to control the audience, not just trick them. To make the crowds believe what they saw was easy compared to making them believe what they felt. The spectrum of human emotions lay before him as he did his magic. Learn to control this, he knew, and everything else would be easy. How far would he go for this power? He didn't know. He thought little of the price that he might have to pay to receive what he coveted above all else. He believed in magic, he knew it was real, he had tasted the power of it.

Many who came to watch his magic shows became captivated by his speaking. Edwin would discuss the plight of mankind, the emptiness and sorrow that many felt. He would tell all who would listen that mankind was living in a dark shadow of itself, had forgotten the true light that we all once lived in. Wasn't there more to life than the struggles and fears that we face? The greed and envy that we all feel is because we are living in a spiritual void. He would always end his shows with the good news that once again wisdom was about to shine upon mankind. True knowledge would again be available for all who would listen, to all who would become as children at the feet of the master.

It was in Edwin's mind to become that master. The power that he felt on stage once he had the audience in his grasp, in his mental control, was beyond description. It was lust for more of this power that brought him to Genoa.

Edwin rented a small flat one block from the sea on Via S. Lorenzo. It was located in an area where he could walk the city safely at night. It was close to many of the teachers that were of interest to him. He would travel the city listening to many, enjoying their teachings, but he would never join them. Edwin was destined to teach, not to be taught.

Edwin continued to do his magic shows and slowly he started to attract a following, a small group that would show up whenever he would perform. Still, he could never reach the heights that he knew he was destined for by being just another street performer in a city of street performers. It soon became apparent that the best way to rise above the crowds was to be selected by the gods. Was this possible? Would the spirit world reach out to a mortal human? Many of the great religions of the world thought so. If the spirit world would reach out, why would they reach out to him? These were the challenges that he faced as he thought more and more about his calling. Could he use his magic to make others believe? Could the power that he so desperately sought be enough to create what he desired? Self proclamation wouldn't work, he must be chosen.

He decided that the written word was the answer. He stole away to his flat and started writing his small book simply called *Yehla Has Spoken.*

It began:

I was awakened on the night of July 14 by the spirit. I was in deep sleep when I awoke to find all of the candles in my room lit, and an old man standing at the foot of my bed. I felt no fear......

"I am Yehla," he said.

"I am here to teach you the wonders that you have been so faithfully seeking. You will become wise, then you will become the teacher. You will be given knowledge beyond this world, even beyond time itself. You must use it to help your fellow man. Judgment is soon to come. Each evening I will come to you, I will teach you. Fear not, Edwin Hawkins."

After Yehla left, fear and doubt overwhelmed me. Was I mad? Did this just really happen? Why would the gods choose me? I am a nobody, just an honest seeker of the truth. Now a responsibility has been given to me that can crush me. I am afraid.

Edwin knew that he would have to portray all of his human emotions, his own weaknesses and fears, to make people believe. He was given a task, not of his choosing, not because of any abilities that he had, he was called, that was all he knew. He was the reluctant teacher, fearful of failure and fearful of his fragile human nature. He would do his best, teach what he was taught, share with all who would listen. There was nothing more he could do.

Night after night Yehla appeared to me, giving me more truths than I could comprehend. More than I could ever put down with pen and paper. What I could be taught by the master in one night would take years for me to learn on my own, if ever. One night I forced myself to ask the question that had been on my heart since his first visit.

"Why have you chosen me, and will I fail you?"

"Fear not, Edwin, for I know you. You who call yourself in this lifetime Edwin Hawkins, you have lived in the great white throne room with us in the past. It was your decision to return to where you find yourself now, to allow us to teach through you. You have forgotten where you came from, forgotten who you are. You knew this would happen before you decided to return. I have returned to you as you yourself asked me to. You are the 9th brother of the great white throne. It is your time to reveal to all who will listen. You will not fail."

"I am not worthy of this task."

"Worthy of this task? You are the 9th brother of wisdom. Eight have gone before you to different nations, to different people, in different times. All have gone with the same message. The battle between good and evil is real, and either side can be victorious. The hearts and minds of people

are what decide the outcome. The war of good and evil is fought in the heavens, but the battles are fought on earth. Look and see, Edwin, what are the hopes of the nations at this time? I tell you this now. People need to hear your words. Look at the emptiness most live with. They have been fooled into believing that this physical world is all there is. Many may talk of the spiritual side of life but do not live in the power that it has to offer. Greed, corruption, lust, and envy, all are tools of evil to make people lose heart, to lose their focus on what matters in life. There have been times in the past when goodness was victorious. Nations lived in harmony with all that was around them. There was no war, no concept of war, no hatred, there was peace and harmony and the heavens and earth rejoiced. People lived their lives with their hearts, not their minds. Times of such joy are short lived. Evil does not rest. Evil will always struggle to tear down what goodness has built."

As the weeks went by I realized I must speak these truths with a boldness far beyond my abilities. There is so little time left. I must tell all who will hear my words, that a cataclysmic battle between good and evil will soon be fought. Nations will rise against nations until the whole world is once again at war. Millions and millions will perish in this evil madness. New weapons of unbelievable power will be unleashed. Nothing can stop it from coming, and it will come soon. It will destroy all that we know, love, believe in, hope for. Nation will turn nation into dust. Terror and tragedy will fill the entire world.

I must also tell you of a hope that is to be found. Fear not, my true believers. There is a place for all who hear my words and heed them. Not all will perish in this insanity. There is a stronghold, a fortress of good, which evil will not be able to enter. We must flee, all who hear my words, we must flee to an island kingdom located in the wilderness of British Columbia, far across the sea. Yehla has told me exactly where this island fortress of good will be created, and we will create it. Together we will live in peace and harmony while the rest of the world burns in destruction. Yelha and his spiritual army will protect our city. It will be up to us to rebuild this shattered world once this madness ends. That is our hope.

Edwin continued to write, filling his book with twenty-four pages. He had one hundred copies printed. The first day on the street was the last day that he ever had to peddle his book. They were gone overnight. Now his audience came to hear him speak of Yehla, his magic forgotten for his new message. The little sidewalk cafes and bars that he once had trouble filling now couldn't support the crowds that came to listen. He printed another five hundred copies; they were gone in a week.

Edwin threw open the curtains in his room, then opened the door facing the water and walked out onto his patio. The vast Mediterranean Sea lay a hundred feet below him. His house was high on a cliff, built into the rocks over three hundred years ago. He had moved three times since he printed his book, each flat nicer, and more expensive, until two months ago when he left Genoa completely. His new home was in a small village sixty miles south of Genoa. It took over two hours by train to reach it. Santa Maria was old, built upon the ruins of an earlier village that had been destroyed by Moroccan pirates over four hundred years ago. Five small seaside villages were perched on the rugged cliffs, all interlaced with footpaths. All five villages acted as one, sharing resources and keeping a constant vigil out for pirates and marauders. In the days of old the only way to reach these villages was from the sea, the foot paths the only link between them. The old-world charm of these villages appealed to him. Since he had written his book he had found no refuge, nowhere that he could be off guard. His book had become so popular that everywhere he went people flocked to him. He could find no peace. His writing had enabled him to rise above the rest. It had given him what he had so desired, but it came with a price. Now his followers would come to him at his choosing, to his sanctuary, his fortress high above the sea.

The sun warmed him as he looked back into the house and saw Latina still in bed. She had become his favorite. Latina had a quality about her that many other women didn't have. She could picture herself at his side, sharing his power. He knew this and it excited him. She could be very useful, she was a woman that understood power. Latina had latched onto Edwin after one of his teachings. She had seduced him that very night. Latina, dark haired, with deep brown eyes, had a radiance about her that captivated Edwin. She was Italian, and she was beautiful, with a hint of gypsy in her face, her eyes were able to look deep into a man's heart. Many men were afraid of her, but not Edwin. He knew she couldn't look into his heart.

Edwin sat in his chair, café in hand, thinking of this day. An important meeting was coming up this afternoon. Mrs. Arthur J. Bouthrum was coming for tea at one o'clock today at his home.

Mrs. Bouthrum had sent her request by her personal secretary one week ago. Her noted simply stated:

I wish the pleasure of meeting you. If possible, can you please come to Villa Charbeau at your earliest convenience? Cordially, Mrs. Arthur Bouthrum

Edwin made her personal secretary wait long enough that she missed the next train out of Santa Maria, almost missing the last train back to Genoa that evening, before he had decided how to handle her invitation. He would invite her to his home. Villa Charbeau was a palace and he wouldn't be at the disadvantage of walking into her domain. Let her come to his. He had written his invitation asking her to come this afternoon, at one o'clock, for tea. He signed it,

Your Servant, Edwin

Mrs. Arthur J. Bouthrum was very well known in Genoa. She and her husband had come to Italy nine years earlier, following their passion for the occult and mysticism. With the family name and the wealth of old money, doors opened smoothly for them. Many said Arthur was a weak-minded, sixty-year-old man and that Jenina Bouthrom, his wife, twenty years his junior, was the true spiritual seeker in the family. It didn't really matter what they thought, Edwin knew. Arthur had the money and the influence to open whatever doors his wife chose to have opened. They were extremely wealthy. This fact hadn't escaped Edwin.

He walked back into the house, leaned over Latina and woke her.

"You need to be out of the house by noon. You can return tonight after seven or you can stay in the boat house, whichever you prefer."

There was no warmth in his voice; he hadn't started to give her that.

She sat up in bed, swung her long dark legs to the floor and walked naked to the bathroom. By noon she had left. He made the bed, finished cleaning his house and made himself ready for Mrs. Bouthrom. He did this by meditating. In his quiet mind he could see her coming in the doorway, dressed in her finest, with an air of self importance. She would arrive as one who was used to being in charge, used to having others seek out her wisdom. Edwin knew that he would seduce her this afternoon. He would take what she had and he would show her something new, servitude. She would submit to him with pleading for more on her lips. He could see it all so clearly in his mind, and his mind was always correct. His magic was growing. He would be very gracious, so pleased that she had chosen to come this afternoon. Small talk would last for a short time. She had come to see the 9th brother of wisdom, and he would not disappoint her. He could visualize her after she entered his house, commenting about the lovely ocean view, sitting in the very chair that he now sat in. His meditation lasted forty-five minutes. Five minutes before she knocked on his door Edwin knew she was coming. He stood, changed into his finest clothes, and waited.

"Mrs. Bouthrum, I am so delighted that you could travel such lengths to visit me, in my humble home. I am honored."He bowed, reached for her white gloved hand and brought it to his lips in one sweeping motion.

She had come alone and in her finest.

"Thank you, Edwin, may I call you that? That is how you signed your invitation."

"Of course."

He took her coat that she had been carrying and hung it on the back of the bedroom door. When he returned she was standing looking at the sea.

"The view, Edwin, it's so wonderful, it... it's spellbinding."

"Please sit anywhere."

Mrs. Bouthrum sat in the chair he had vacated five minutes earlier.

"Please, allow me to bring you a cup of tea. The water is hot."

Edwin brought two steaming tea cups out, handed one to her and sat down in another chair facing the sea. They both drank their tea in silence. He could feel her apprehension, her nervousness. Good, he thought.

"I am so pleased that you accepted my invitation to visit me here. I would have liked to come to Villa Charbeau but…" he paused, letting her think he was at a loss for words.

"I do better here. My spirit is at home here. This is where Yehla has chosen for me to do my teaching."

He put his tea down on a small end table next to his chair, turned and looked directly at her.

"You are a very special woman, Mrs. Bouthrum. You have powers that you do not know you possess."

He could see her take it all in.

"Please, Edwin, in this room call me Jenina."

He stood, walked over in front of her and knelt down before her. He took both her hands and looked deeply into her eyes, his mind power melting away any doubts or fears she might have had.

"I will call you Jenina until I have given you the name I have been instructed to give you."

He stood, grabbed his chair and brought it before her. He sat down right in front of her, disregarding her personal space. Again he looked deep into her eyes.

"Jenina, I have so much to tell you, you who have been given so much but are not sure of yourself. I will teach you, I will show you all that will be."

At first she didn't move, just stared into his eyes, trying to take it all in. Then slowly she reached her hands down and wrapped them around his.

"I have dreamed of this day, for I knew you would come to me. Yehla told me so. You are so much more than Mrs. Arthur Bouthrum. You and I have lived together in the spiritual houses of the heavens. I have known you for a very long time."

He stared into her eyes. She didn't blink, her mind captured by his.

"You know the vision given to me by Yehla. I am the only one who can do this work, but I need your help. Together we can do great things, reach and touch so many, save so many. We have been as one in the heavens, now again I need you at my side."

He leaned forward and brought his lips to hers; there was no resistance, only hunger.

"I need you by my side. Together we can build our great city, our great hope for mankind. I need what the gods have given you."

With that he kissed her again. He raised her up to her feet and slipped her dress from her. He gently led her into his bedroom and showed her the magic that he had learned.

Mrs. Bouthrum caught the last train out of Santa Maria for Genoa. Before she left, as they stood together in Edwin's house, she grabbed hold of his hands, wrapped them in hers.

"Edwin, Arthur will always be my husband. I will always be Mrs. Bouthrum. I will not let anything get in the way of that. I believe in your vision and I know that Yehla is real. I know your vision is pure and that money is the tool that you need now. I will see what I can do. I can

28

open doors for you, Edwin, that you never dreamed could be opened. Be patient with me."

She drew him to her, kissed him hard; still she held such passion. Then Mrs. Bouthrum opened the door and walked out.

He walked to the patio and sat down on one of the two outside chairs, his mind playing over the afternoon.

"Yes," he said out loud, he would be patient with Mrs. Bouthrum, she had much to offer.

CHAPTER 3

Edwin rented a large abandoned boat house by the pier. With Latina's help he converted it to a meeting hall capable of seating fifty people. He let it be known that every Tuesday and Thursday he would be teaching from noon to four for all who would come, and people came. The train from Genoa would be full of people hoping to gain a seat. It was so easy for him to teach. He knew what they wanted to hear. They all wanted to be special, to belong to a higher calling. All wanted some sort of meaning and purpose for their lives, they wanted something to believe in. They wanted to feel empowered, and he could do that.

After a month of his teaching the boat house could no longer seat enough people, and he had another problem that he had to deal with. Too many were coming that had no money. He knew he couldn't charge for his teachings. The donation jars that were passed at the end of the meeting by Latina and two of her girlfriends were as close as he could get to charging. The donations brought in good money, money that six months ago would have seemed like riches to him, but not now.

He had opened a bank account in Genoa and also an account in Zurich, Switzerland. Most of his money went to Switzerland, where he had it converted to gold. Gold and himself were all that he truly believed in.

Mrs. Bouthrum came to his aid. She would often come to his teachings. He would show her no special favor. No one would ever guess of their affair. One afternoon he dismissed his class early and asked Jenina to stay after. Once all the other students had left he sat down beside her.

"I have a problem. I would like your advice."

"I am honored, tell me what your problem is."

"I haven't enough room for the true believers. Many come that haven't the faith to belong to our higher goal. I have wondered what you think of issuing passes for these meetings. Making just fifty available for each teaching and putting a small price on them to discourage those who waste my time."

He looked at her. He had gotten close to the line, money and the prophet; can they be compatible?

"I think, dear Edwin, that would be a great idea. If you would allow me, I would like to take this responsibility upon myself, if you would trust me in such matters."

"My dear Jenina, I have trusted you with my soul. This is of little consequence to me, please, I am happy to leave this matter in your capable hands. Thank you."

He stood and escorted her to the door.

"You will be very pleased with my work." She smiled and left, walking for the train station.

He knew she was hungry for him, but why would he risk another affair when already she was doing his bidding? He had hoped that she would ask for the responsibility of handling the tickets. If anyone would be able to get a good price for them, she could.

Money started to pour into Edwin's account. Mrs. Bouthrum had indeed risen to the challenge. Besides seeing that each ticket brought in a fair amount of money she also took it upon herself to see that they were not wasted on those unworthy. That meant socially or financially unworthy. She never told Edwin what each ticket sold for. They never discussed money, but he could do the math. At times she would deposit over three thousand dollars a week into his account. At times large donations would be deposited, never with any names, just cash deposits, some for over five thousand dollars.

The crowd of students changed as well. In the beginning of the boat shed teachings most had been young, free spirits, eager to learn but with little to give in return. Many spoke of joining the migration to the new city in British Columbia, many said yes, I will follow. Few had the means to even pay their way to Canada, let alone help the cause. Now most of the new students were older, more successful in business and in life. Mrs. Bouthrum had given Edwin's teachings the validity that he needed.

Students who a month ago would not attend were now trying to follow his words, trying to make their hearts and minds believe. No matter what she charged for the tickets, the boat house was always full to capacity. Many would spend over four hours on the train only to be turned away, or at best have to stand outside and try to hear. The limited capacity and the hours of train travel had many upset.

Mrs. Bouthrum asked Edwin to return to Genoa for a special night of teachings. She would rent out Garibaldi Hall, the large opera hall in Genoa that had seating for twenty-five hundred people. She told Edwin, "Now is the time to get Yehla's message to the masses. I can fill Garibaldi Hall for you, if you will speak. Think of the people who could hear your words, think of those who would believe."

He had been hesitant. In his private world that he had constructed for himself he had never doubted his abilities, now he did. To speak to over twenty-five hundred people at one time, in one setting, was more than he thought he was capable of. His enemy was fear and self doubt. He had come so far in such a short time. Each step he took was based on earlier successes. Now he wondered, did he have enough power to accomplish a night at Garibaldi Hall? He knew that if he accepted this invitation his life would never be the same. What would he tell such a large audience? Somehow the same old teachings would not be enough. He would have to give the most powerful words of wisdom that he had ever spoken. Could he do it?

Latina gave him his answer. They had been living in Santa Maria for six months. One evening after supper as they stared out at the sea she looked at him.

"Edwin, I am four months pregnant."

He turned to her, not knowing what to say.

Silence hung over them as they watched the sunset. He was at a loss for words, indecisive about speaking at Garibaldi Hall, and now this revelation. It was all too much for him.

"Latina, I need to speak with Yehla. Will you please spend the night in the boat house?"

He was surprised by the tone that he used. There was a touch of warmth in his voice. That night, alone in his house overlooking the sea, Edwin made one of the most important decisions of his life. He would speak at Garibaldi Hall. He would introduce Latina and their soon-to-be-born son to the world.

"Jenina, I accept your offer to speak at Garibaldi Hall. I am sure that you need time to organize such an undertaking and I need more time with Yehla."

She smiled, held his hands in hers. It was after another one of his teaching sessions in the boat house.

"I am glad, Edwin. The world needs your message, and this is the best way to get it out to them."

"Won't it cost a lot?"

"My dear Edwin." She paused, looking into his eyes.

"Please don't concern yourself with money. I will arrange all. You prepare your message, leave the rest to me. How much time do you need to prepare?"

"I need three months to finalize my message. It will be my last teaching in Italy. Then I will depart to British Columbia and prepare for the faithful who will follow."

"Edwin, I want to come and be by your side there."

"You are too important to me here. Your work, is something only you can do. Before the end comes, once our city is built, I will send for you and Arthur, and we will be together for our new beginning."

"I don't know if Arthur will come."

"He will."

"Arthur leaves for England tomorrow for business. He will be gone for two weeks." She left her words hanging in the air, her intent implied but not spoken.

"Jenina, you who are so special to me, you are my spiritual soulmate. Come the day after tomorrow, at noon we will share what the gods have given us."

The twice-weekly boat house sessions continued. Edwin spoke with more urgency as his time to speak at Garibaldi Hall drew closer. He would shout at his students.

"Open your eyes, look and see the world around you, the madness has already started! Nation will rise up against nation."

The darker his message, the more people believed.

"How much time do you think you have? Now is the time to flee. All that you hold so dear will be torn from your grasp. Flee with us to our island fortress, our refuge."

He continued his boatshed teachings until two weeks before he was to speak at Garibaldi Hall, then he stopped. He had only one more lesson to teach, one more opportunity for the people to hear his words. His night at Garibaldi Hall would be the greatest night of his life. His power was ready.

One week before speaking at Garibaldi Hall, Mrs. Bouthrum had sold all twenty-five hundred tickets. She also held three different fund raisers at Villa Charbeau. In the last month over seventy-five thousand dollars had been deposited into his account. Edwin spent the remainder of his time in meditation. He could see himself on stage at Garibaldi Hall. He could see the confidence that had brought him to this very moment. It made no difference anymore if he taught in front of fifty or five thousand. It was Yehla who had chosen him in the beginning and it was Yehla who would prepare him. Fear and doubt left his mind and soul.

Two days before his appearance, he and Latina traveled to Genoa and stayed at Villa Charbeau, guests of both Arthur and Jenina. The city was full of gossip and speculation. Hundreds had signed up with Mrs. Bouthrum and her workers to move to Canada and be part of the building. Some had sold all and donated the money to the cause, to Edwin's cause. Mrs. Bouthrum had now raised over one-hundred thousand dollars for Edwin, and more was coming in.

The day of his appearance Edwin awoke early and went to the hall. He was allowed inside, everything was ready. He studied the empty seats that tonight would be filled for his greatest performance. He looked to the upper balcony, looked to his left and right, then he walked down the main aisle and up to the stage. He turned and looked out over a sea of empty chairs, the silence echoing in his mind. He studied the rich interior. In less than ten hours this hall would be full to capacity for him. He had seen himself back stage waiting. He could see Mrs. Bouthrum walk onto the stage in all her glory, and speak into the microphone. She would ask the crowd for silence. It would take ten minutes. Then she would talk about Edwin, how she had first met him such a long time ago when many hadn't heard his message. She would share her doubts in the beginning, then as she listened more and more to his teachings and studied his book *Yehla Has Spoken* the more she believed. The more her heart and soul told her that this man's message was for all who would listen.

He had seen himself walk on stage, the crowd momentarily silent, then a roar of applause. It would take five minutes for silence. He saw himself standing in front of them all. He saw himself saying, "Good evening." Then he could see no more. He knew that from then on Yehla would speak through him as he had never done before.

He returned to Villa Charbeau and met with the Bouthrums, and, they spent an hour in conversation. Not teaching, just social conversation, enjoyable, nothing more. At two in the afternoon he asked to be excused and went to his room.

"Tonight I want you back stage. I will need you, be ready, pay attention," he told Latina.

Poor Latina, her belly bulging, seven and a half months pregnant, she had no idea what her part in this very special night would be. He told her nothing else of what he had planned, just be back stage, be ready.

He entered Garibaldi Hall through a side door near the stage off of a back alley. He had been guided there by a friend of Mrs. Bouthrum. The street was a sea of people waiting to show their tickets and to be ushered in. He could see people dressed in their finest. This was to be a gala evening for a gala performance. He was dressed casually. No top coat, no hat, just slacks and a white shirt.

Mrs. Bouthrum arrived backstage and, spying Edwin, she rushed up to him.

"I am so excited and nervous. I hope I..."

He put a finger to her lips, then he reached for her hand and brought it to his lips. He kissed her hand. His lips lingered there, and then he moved her hand to his heart, before letting go.

"You will do fine, we will do fine. This isn't our message. We are but the voice people will hear. We will say what is needed to be said, the rest is beyond us."

At eight-fifteen Mrs. Arthur Bouthrum walked out onto the stage to an explosion of applause. She walked to the microphone.

"Ladies and gentleman, I am so pleased this evening..." she went on for five minutes just as Edwin had seen.

"Lastly," she continued, "this evening is unlike any other at Garibaldi Hall. Please, before I introduce Edwin Hawkins, I ask for one thing from all of you." She paused, waiting.

She is good, Edwin thought to himself.

She waited for thirty seconds, the last few seconds becoming uncomfortable, a theater of twenty-five hundred people all quiet in silent anticipation.

"I need you to listen, not just with your ears and your mind. I need you to open your hearts as well. Open them as you never have before.

Let your soul tell you if this teaching, what you will hear tonight, is real and is of importance to you. Don't judge, be open, listen with all of your being. I bid you a wonderful evening. Now I ask Edwin Hawkins the 9th brother of wisdom, I ask him to come and share his words with you."

She turned and walked off the stage, passing Edwin as he walked into the lights. There was a moment of silence as he had foreseen, then a thunderous applause. On and on the crowd clapped. It took five minutes before he could speak.

"I thank you for being here. I ask you all to remember that I am just the messenger. I pray that this evening, this message is for you and that it takes hold in your heart. If it is not for you then so be it. I make no excuses to those who listen but do not hear. Open your hearts and your souls.

"I am here to tell you that good and evil still fight over mankind. That heaven and hell still wage war on each other. That goodness will win in the final hour but a conflict is coming that will shatter the world.

"Yehla has taught me much. He has explained his beginning to me. He told me that since time began he has been here. I've learned that our world has lived for millions of years, but time has only been here for fifty centuries. For eons and eons earth knew no time. Time has been created for us, the children of earth.

"He has taught me that the dead are alive, that they affect our lives. That prayer is power. That there are more dimensions around us than we could ever believe. Mostly he has taught me that evil is jealous of goodness. That goodness chose mankind in all our wretchedness such a long time ago. Goodness chose to love us, to care for us, to raise us, to nourish us, the children of planet earth. Goodness brought us forth because she loves us. Evil is a jealous lover of goodness. Before time, goodness and evil were one. Evil wants goodness back for itself, has no desire to see goodness share herself with us. Evil watches as mankind betrays all that goodness has given us, all the wonders of life and this planet. We humans have betrayed goodness, and evil seeks to put an end to us.

"That is the war that is waged in the heavens, a war of jealousy, of love and a sense of betrayal. Goodness hasn't betrayed evil. She has only opened her arms wider to embrace us. I..."

He stopped speaking, for suddenly no words would come from

Edwin's lips. His knees grew weak, his pulse started racing, his breath coming free and floating from him. He collapsed on the floor. The audience sat in stunned silence. Mrs. Bouthrum started to get up and run to his side but Latina held her back.

Edwin lay on the floor for two minutes, then arose. He brushed his hair back with his hands and opened his arms wide to the crowd.

The voice that spoke was not Edwin Hawkins'.

"I will tell you what you need to hear. I am Yehla." His voice echoed through the hall. It was a voice beyond human capacity, a voice with such power and depth that all who heard it were mesmerized. None had ever heard a voice like this before.

Not a sound could be heard from the crowd. Every human sense was riveted on the speaker on stage.

"What do you want from me, cheap magic tricks so you will believe?"

He raised his arms to the crowd and suddenly balls of fire flew upwards from his open palms, up to the roof, then died out.

"Do you want the heavens?"

He cast his hands apart and a universe of stars flew out over the crowd, upwards, flashing, spiraling, before disappearing at the roof.

"I will not make you believe by magic. Listen. A great calamity is soon to descend upon this world. It seems to you as the madness of men. It is not. It is the wickedness of evil that arrives. This world will enter a time of such bloodshed and war that the very fate of mankind is still unknown. I say to you, flee to the great white city that will be built by your hands and my wisdom. This city and all who live there I will protect. Flee young and flee old. Young people, you will be needed to re-seed this world. The old, your knowledge will be needed to guide this new generation. Evil will lose this battle and a time of peace and joy will descend upon the earth and her inhabitants. A time of peace that has not been seen since the beginning of time. Yes, purification will come through fire. You who hear, it is your mission to survive the coming terror. Enough of you must survive or else evil will be victorious.

"I leave you with a great joy. Latina, come."

She walked out on stage, her mind in complete confusion and filled with fear. She walked up to his side, and stopped, looking out into the lights.

38

"I give you a son, a leader to carry on. This child will be the first born to inhabit our great new city. Around his wisdom and strength your new city, your new world will grow. I give you a son."

With those words Edwin or Yehla collapsed once again to the stage floor. Latina knelt at his side, raised his head up and kissed his face, her tears streaming onto him.

"Come back to us, Edwin, come back!"

The crowd was silent as the grave.

Edwin slowly rose to his feet. In his heart he knew what had happened. Yehla had come. He reached for the microphone, his strength gone and his energy sapped.

"I know that Yehla has spoken. I have nothing else to add. Those who believe my words, now is the time to follow to British Columbia, now is the time to leave and build our island city."

He turned and walked off the stage, supported by Latina. The stunned crowd started chanting Yehla, Yehla, Yehla, but to no avail. Yehla was gone. He had spoken what he needed to say. Edwin Hawkins was finished speaking.

Edwin and Latina decided to stay in Genoa until the baby was born. They lived at Villa Charbeau; the Bouthrums were so hospitable. Edwin and Latina could do nothing for themselves.

Edwin felt trapped. It was funny, he thought. When he had first arrived in Genoa he was almost a pauper, but he was free. Now he was worth so much and yet he felt trapped in a mansion of luxury. Days dragged on. Latina went into labor at eight months. She was rushed to the hospital. Her labor was hard. All worried for her and for the baby's safety. After nineteen hours of hard-labor Edwin Hawkins was presented with a baby daughter.

His son, the first born of his new world, the son proclaimed by Yehla to all at Garibaldi Hall was a girl. Yehla was wrong.

CHAPTER 4

A week after the birth of Edwin Hawkins' daughter he fled Genoa in the middle of the night. He left daughter and Latina behind, never to see them again. His master plan, his purpose in life, lay in a shattered ruin.

Yehla had failed him, Latina had failed him. He had only himself and his riches. Edwin lost track of the fact that he had created Yehla for the purpose of getting rich. At that he had succeeded beyond his wildest dreams. What bothered him now was the fact that he had tasted the power of Yehla, and he now believed in his creation. His life and his destiny with Yehla were far from over.

Edwin headed south to Florence.He rented a small inexpensive flat near the Dumas Square. It was a time of great turmoil for him. He explored the city, the fine art and museums, taking in all of the Renaissance culture that he could. It did little to ease his soul.

He meditated night after night, using the same mental power that had worked so well in Genoa and Santa Maria. He would not surrender the magic that he had held in the past. He would call out to Yehla from the innermost darkness of his mind.

"Yehla, where are you? I am here, I am your servant."

He had been in Florence for over a month when Yehla returned to him. It was late in the evening; the city was quiet. He was in deep meditation when he suddenly awoke to find himself sitting at the small table in the kitchen with Yehla sitting across from him.

"What do you want, Edwin?"

"I want to know what went wrong. Where is my son?"

"Yes, it did go wrong. Goodness was stronger than I thought."

"I thought you were goodness?"

Yehla laughed.

"No, Edwin, I am neither evil nor goodness."

Edwin felt no hesitation.

"I want more of you, I want more of your power."

"Do you? Can you live with the cost?"

"Yes, I can."

"You don't even know the price!"

"What is the price to be your servant?"

"More than you know."

"I have tasted your power, I cannot go back."

"So be it. The true magic that you want is not mine to give you. It is not tricks, it cannot even be called magic. What you want is ancient. It has been on earth since goodness first raised mankind up. She gave power to her chosen people to tame this world and to fight against evil. For in the early days evil used its powers in an attempt to destroy man. Without the true magic that goodness bestowed, mankind would never have survived. But mankind did survive, and as he grew in strength and populated the world, goodness pulled her magic back. She hid it. Yes, Edwin, she hid it.

"As the masters of this true magic died, she took what they knew and buried it with them. True magic doesn't die, it sleeps. It sleeps in many different places in the world. It sleeps, and only one with power can awaken it. Is that what you want, Edwin, the power to awaken true magic?"

"Yes."

"So your sojourn begins. Here is what you are to do."

CHAPTER 5

Amy Wilson and her older sister Christy couldn't have been more different if they tried. Christy, who was the wild one in her earlier days, now at age twenty-eight had become the responsible one, constantly giving Amy advice on how to live her life. Amy, at twenty-three, didn't want any of it.

The two sisters had been close growing up. They shared the joys and sorrows of growing up in Malibu, California, the lifestyle of the rich. Their parents were both extremely successful business people. Their father was vice-president of Mayflower Oil & Gas, one of the largest west coast distributors of energy products. Their mother was an accomplished artist who spent more time at fundraisers and social events than at being their mom.

The girls knew they were loved and cherished, knew the safety and comfort of their home. They were indulged and spoiled, and grew up thinking it was normal.

It was so important to their mother, Julie Ann, for the girls to have the best that she and her husband Chester could offer. Julie Ann knew she was adopted, knew that she and her parents came from France after the war. She had no brothers or sisters. Her parents told her very little of her life before they came to America. Her biological parents were never discussed and Julie Ann never felt the need to know more. She remembered her parents as loving and wonderful people who worked hard, had very little to show for it, and died early in life. Julie Ann was determined to offer her girls more.

The two sisters loved each other. At one time they had been so close, Amy was destined to grow and follow in Christy's footsteps. That all changed when Amy was fourteen years old. The family decided to take a vacation to Fiji. Christy at age nineteen would have none of it, and after much argument and frustration the family went anyway, leaving Christy home alone for the first time.

The vacation destination was a small island twenty miles south of Suva, called Mbengga Island. This pristine jewel of an island recently had a world class fishing resort built on it. The resort was so exclusive that the local inhabitants were not allowed on the property, except to work. Now a flood of rich tourists came who expected everything and gave nothing back. It had become the domain of the rich, paradise for a price, a big price.

It bothered Amy so much that the native people were so mistreated that in a fit of young teenage defiance she refused to accept any of it, and that meant going fishing as well. She refused even to go out on the boat when her parents went fishing. One day she took off by herself and started to walk around the island. Soon she met a small group of girls, in sparkling clean uniforms walking home from school. They sang and giggled and laughed with such joy that it was surprising to her. They invited Amy to their village a few miles away. When she entered, all eyes were upon her, friendly and smiling eyes, eyes that held no judgment or malice.

The village was small, about fifteen houses made of concrete cinder block and tin roofs. A large red roofed church dominated the village. The beach was gentle as it led to the sea and the group of brightly colored fishing boats. Amy spent the rest of her nine days on the island at the village. Every morning she returned and stayed until late in the afternoon. She never once went fishing.

Never did it feel right to her when she returned to the resort at the end of each day. The resort that her new friends, people who grew up on Mbengga Island, were not allowed to even visit.

The contrast was amazing to her. The resort catered to every guest's desire, with a waiter or servant always ready to fill the half empty wine glass. The overabundance of food piled high, and then thrown into the garbage after the guests had picked their way through the second or third helping, sickened Amy. The resort had an air about it of nervous tension. The village, on the other hand, had a sense of peace, of joy, of quietness, and completeness. The villagers seemed to have a constant smile on their faces, they laughed, they hugged, they shared. It seemed to Amy that the little children were always in somebody's arms. There seemed to be a respect and a sense of well being and belonging that they all felt, a feeling she had never really known.

On the flight home Amy couldn't get over how much the people of the village had touched her. They gave her a new insight into life and what was important. These people who had so very few worldly possessions, who lived in such simple homes, who ate fish and fruit and spent a lot of time doing nothing, seemed to have a joy for life she had never known. She remembered when the young girls who had first brought her to the village would sing in Fijian, so beautiful and with such natural harmonies. Amy remembered them bursting into laughter as she tried to sing along.

The family fell right back into their regular lives, but Amy couldn't return to life as it had been. She had tasted something on Mbengga Island that had changed her forever. Amy promised that she would write and that her friendship with the village would never end. All through high school she wrote them, she sent care packages and birthday presents. At times her best friends in the world were her big & little sisters on Mbengga Island. She wrote and told them the truth about her life, about the teenage pressures that she felt, about America and how fast everybody went. Her sisters would write back. Some of the letters were signed by the whole village. She loved them and they loved her.

After high school she entered college. She had no goals to fulfill, no direction, she didn't even want to go, she just went because she was the good daughter and she was supposed to. Christy was out being the party princess and Amy was stuck in college.

Still she corresponded with Mbengga. Many of her sisters had married, some had children, and she could watch from afar as they lived their lives.

After four years in college and a degree in archeology Amy did what she had wanted to do for years. She returned to Mbengga Island.

She decided to arrive unannounced, just get off the boat and walk into the village. Amy flew into Nadi, and no one was there to greet her. She almost wished she had let them know she was coming. She knew if she had, the whole village would have met her at the airport. She took the bus to Pacific City, then caught a local water taxi out to Mbengga Island and the village. Word must have gotten out because as the water taxi rounded the point and the village came into view, every single inhabitant, over fifty people, were lining the beach to greet her. The water taxi pulled up to the beach and stopped.

"Sister Amy! Sister Amy!" the villagers shouted, jumping up and down, unable to control their happiness and excitement, the whole village in tears of joy. As soon as Amy stepped out of the boat the whole group swarmed forward as one, surrounding her, hugging and kissing her. The group kept edging forward, pushing her backwards into deeper water until she lost her balance and fell just as a large wave appeared and rolled right over the top of her. The villagers laughed and laughed, some laughing so hard they collapsed into the water holding their sides. Amy stood up, her hair dripping wet, clothes soaked, laughing and crying and feeling such a joy she thought her heart would explode. Some of the men grabbed her few bags and carried them into Sara and Patamo's house, a home that she remembered so well.

"Sister Amy, why you not write and tell us you coming?"

So much joy and confusion.

"Sister Amy, come!" They all wanted to drag her to their homes. She felt like she was being drawn and quartered, pulled apart at the seams. She walked out of the water and sat down on the beach, the exhaustion of the long trip hitting her. Her tears had stopped, but the joy she felt continued. The happiness of the village filled the air. Children ran up to her.

"Hi, I'm Michael," or "I'm Suzy, my sister brought you to our village so long ago," on and on it went.

"You stay with us, our home is ready for you," or, "You come for dinner tonight, we have the whole village over."

Or the one she heard more than once while she sat there soaking wet on the beach.

"What, no husband, why, what's wrong with you?"

She just sat there taking it all in, the ocean, the warmth of the sun, the sound of the surf, the delicious smell of Mbengga Island.

The chatter continued, so many talking at once that she couldn't really hear any of them. She glanced down the beach and half a mile away in the small cove that ended the village beach sat a sailboat anchored all by itself, riding smoothly up and down the gentle swells.

"Who is that?" she asked no one in particular as almost the whole village still sat around her on the beach.

Sara's sister Lenna answered.

"Oh Amy, a very cute young American. He is helping us fix our outboard motors, maybe you should marry him."

The whole group burst once again into laughter. How easily they could laugh.

Amy sat there for a while, her jet lag continuing to catch up with her. She was exhausted. Twenty minutes later she excused herself from the group on the beach and went to Sara and Patomo's house. They greeted her again with hugs and kisses. She knew they would give her their house. She couldn't discourage them from doing so.

Amy walked out to the one and only shower in the entire village. It was outside, with four walls of corrugated tin for privacy and a two-foot-wide entrance way. She took a long shower in some of the softest water she had ever felt. She never even ate dinner that night. Arriving back at Sara and Patamo's, she found them gone. She lay down on their bed and fell asleep. Her dreams were dreams of joy and happiness.

She would always remember meeting Mondo the next day. Up the beach walked this tall, sun-tanned young man, with his blonde hair long and blowing in the breeze. He walked barefoot carrying a small backpack over one shoulder. He was one of the most handsome men she had ever seen, his mannerisms so relaxed, so effortless. He was dressed in shorts and a tee shirt, wearing sunglasses and a baseball cap. She was sitting in front of Sara and Patamo's house. He walked right up to her, knelt down in front of her and in one of the nicest voices she could ever remember hearing said, "These people really, really love you. Hi, I'm Mondo, I'm on the sailboat."

Amy couldn't find the right words to say. Nothing came out.

He sat down next to her and looked at her with a smile that helped set her at ease.

"Well, it's my pleasure to meet you. Any person who is half as nice as these people tell me you are... and I have heard nothing else since I got up this morning but about you... well, if these people think you're great, then so do I."

"Thank you," she managed to say.

They stared out at the sea for a few minutes.

"Tell me about yourself, Amy."

She laughed.

"About myself, please, I don't want to bore you."

"I doubt you would."

"Oh, I think so. I'm just a regular California girl, twenty-three years

47

old, trying to figure my life out."

It was Mondo's turn to laugh.

"See, you're far from boring," he said with another smile that helped her to relax even more.

"Want to know what I think?" he asked.

"No, not really," but she did.

"I think you have to be a very special person. You have stayed in touch with these people for years, sent them gifts, written them letters, remembered birthdays. Why would a boring twenty-three-year-old California girl do that?"

"These people have given me more than you could ever imagine," she said softly.

"That's right, they have. They've given you what I have felt from all of the native people I have met since I started sailing the South Pacific. They gave you who they are."

Amy was so touched. A tear came to her eye. She had never been able to explain to her family, especially her sister why she loved these people so much. Mondo had just explained it perfectly to her.

"You're right."

They smiled at each other.

"I'm still trying to fix Patamo's outboard motor. I think I have the parts that I need, I hope anyway. Want to come along?" he said as he stood up and reached his hand down to her.

"Sure."

That was the beginning of their friendship, and of their romance. Amy spent the next three months sailing with Mondo. They explored much of Fiji, the primitive Yasawa group, then down to Kandavu, which has some of the best-skin diving in the world. Then on to the outer islands of Mango, Tuvutha, Navau. It was a time of wonder for both of them. Amy fell in love with Fiji even more. What she had experienced on Mbengga Island, she felt everywhere she went, wonderful people and wonderful adventures.

She tasted a freedom she had never known. She was also falling in love as she had never done before.

It was getting close to the end of the sailing season, and it would be a long trip back to New Zealand for Mondo.

"I want to come with you," she pleaded.

"I know, I wish you could, but it's too dangerous of a trip. Last season was bad. Let me sail to New Zealand, you fly home. Once I get settled we can touch base again."

Mondo was falling in love with Amy and it scared him. He needed time for himself. He had never felt this way before.

It was the end of September when they arrived back at Nadi. It seemed like a life time ago to Amy since she had flown into this city from California. They spent a few days anchored out, Amy getting her things ready. It was an uncomfortable time for them, both caring so much for the other yet realizing that in a few days they were going their separate ways.

At the airport they were both in tears.

"I love you, Mondo."

"I love you, Amy."

As Amy walked to the boarding gate she turned, looked back at him.

"Don't forget me."

"Never."

CHAPTER 6

The first few weeks back home away from Mondo were the hardest in Amy's life. She constantly relived the last three months aboard Smokin' Joe. The wonders of living aboard a sailboat in Fiji, the freedom, the sea, the sun, the sand, the whole experience was magical. Amy kept thinking about it over and over, all the wonderful people they met, the wonderful places that they explored together, the joy that they felt for each other. Now she struggled, wondering what she should do next. He should have called by now.

Mondo was in her heart and soul and she could do nothing to get him out. She started to expect his call after her first week home. She knew it was over one thousand miles from Fiji to New Zealand. She knew it could take a week or longer for him to make the trip. After three weeks she couldn't believe he hadn't called.

Did he fall overboard and drown? Did he fall in love with somebody else? Did he not want to call her, maybe he'd never call? Did he lose her phone number? (That was ridiculous, she knew.) Suppose he never did call, what would she do?

She was living with her sister in Malibu. Christy had been trying to help Amy snap out of the depression that she was in. Christy never had any patience or tact when it came to Amy.

"You have to get out of the house and get a life, Amy, quit thinking about Mondo. At least you can help me in the shop."

Christy was no longer living off of mom and dad. She owned a small clothing boutique down on Riverside Road, two blocks from the ocean. She had her own two bedroom condo, three blocks from work. She was making it on her own. Amy started helping her sister at work. At least it took her mind off of her heart.

Amy wanted to go to New Zealand. She would have left tomorrow if she thought she could find Mondo.

The day after Amy flew home, Mondo was sitting on Smokin' Joe getting ready for his trip to New Zealand. He missed her terribly. He knew he really cared for her, maybe he even loved her. He didn't realize how much until he climbed back on board after taking her to the airport. Smokin' Joe without Amy felt as empty as a tomb.

Mondo pulled out his charts. He dug through them until he found the one that he wanted, a chart showing the entire Pacific Ocean. He studied it hard. He looked at where he was in Fiji, then looked at New Zealand a thousand miles south. He looked at Los Angeles where Amy was. Did it make sense for him to head south when his heart told him to head north? If he went to New Zealand then decided to sail north to America, it would add another two thousand miles to the trip, plus he would have to wait six months for hurricane season to end before he could leave New Zealand. It seemed like the wrong way and a lot of wasted time.

He could sail from Fiji to Hawaii. That was the right direction at least. He knew that he would be sailing at the beginning of hurricane season, and he would have to be lucky, but so far he always had been. It was over three thousand miles from Fiji to Hawaii. It would take him at least twenty days and he had better plan on thirty just in case.

Mondo sat in his cockpit, his mind in turmoil, his heart a mess. It was early afternoon before he realized that there was no way he could sail south away from Amy. He would sail to Hawaii.

Mondo brought Smokin' Joe into the marina at Nadi and started his preparations. He stocked up on supplies, filled his water tanks, topped-off his fuel tank with diesel, and also filled his two spare six gallon diesel jerry cans that he lashed on deck. He checked his emergency and survival gear. He went over his boat with a fine-tooth comb. He was hauled up to the top of the mast, checked all lines and standing rigging, checked all sheaves and halyards. He had to prepare so that nothing could go wrong, even though he knew anything could.

One of the things to do on his three page list was to call Amy and tell her of his change in plans. In all the confusion of getting Smokin' Joe ready for sea and the unbelievable amount of paper work that it took to check out of Fiji, Mondo forgot to call. He was two days out from Nadi racing along at eight knots when he remembered that he never did call her. He had twenty more days before he could.

"Amy, get the phone," Christy hollered over a pot of boiling water. She was making spaghetti.

Amy ran into the living room.

"Hello."

"Amy, it's me, Mondo."

Amy burst into tears, her breath fleeing from her. Her knees flexed, and she thought she was going to fall.

"Mondo, God, I thought you'd never call! Do... I thought..."

"Amy, listen, I really miss you."

Amy tried wiping her eyes dry, tried to catch her breath.

"Mondo, I miss you so much, I really do."

"Amy, I'm in Hawaii."

"What?"

"Yeah, I'm in Hawaii, I just couldn't head off to New Zealand. I tried, but Smokin' Joe wouldn't let me go that way, he turned around when I wasn't looking and I ended up in Hawaii. I was going to call you before I left Fiji but, well, I just spaced it out."

"You idiot."

"I know, I thought about you every day for the last twenty-two days. I'm safe and I want to see you."

Those eight words were the words that Amy wanted to hear more than anything else in the world.

Tears came back to her. She fought to hold them in check.

"Mondo, I am so glad to hear from you! I was so worried. It's been such a long time since I talked to you."

"Listen, Amy, I could come to Los Angeles and see you, but I feel about as comfortable in a big city as Howard Hughes in a flop house. Why don't you come to Hawaii?"

"Yeah, for what?" She was teasing him, and they both knew it.

"To see the flora and fauna, why else?" he jabbed back.

"Mondo, I'd go anywhere to see you."

"I'll call you tomorrow, let me know your schedule. I love you, Amy."

He hung up.

Christy had put the boiling water on hold and she was leaning against the wall, looking at her sister sitting on the couch. Christy was so happy for her. Amy sat there holding the phone, then she looked up at Christy.

"He really missed me, he wants me to come to Hawaii. God, I really do love that man."

The two sisters hugged, Christy felt the joy that Amy had and it made her so happy. Amy couldn't shut up, she talked about Mondo this and Mondo that, going on and on about the adventures that they shared in Fiji. Christy hadn't seen her sister so wired in years.

A week later Mondo met Amy at the airport in Honolulu. He showered her with a beautiful flower lei, draping it over her neck, then gave her a huge hug and held her close to him.

"Mondo, I am so glad to see you," she said, then kissed him.

"Amy, Amy, Amy, you are a little heartbreaker."

They strolled out of the airport arm in arm to a rusted and battered old Nissan pickup truck that Mondo borrowed from a cruising friend.

They talked constantly driving from the airport. They headed north on highway H-1. Soon they were past Pearl City, then past the Pearl Harbor War memorial. The air smelled sweet to Amy, and the sun warmed her heart. She was so at peace at the moment. Soon they left highway H-1 and hit highway 93. They were driving on a narrow road with the ocean on their left and the tall mountains of Nanakuu forest reserve on their right, the rugged green mountains piercing the dark blue sky.

Besides Fiji this was the most beautiful place Amy had ever seen.

"Where are we going?" She asked.

"A surprise, do you trust me?"

"No!" They both burst into laughter.

Makaha is a small surf town at the end of the paved road. Highway 93 rambles on a few more miles but it becomes a dirt road, best for four-wheel-drive vehicles. Just before Makaha, Mondo turned right off the main road, drove up behind a few houses, and pulled into a rutty dirt driveway that went back a hundred feet before stopping at a small cute cabin. The cabin had a metal roof and a large screened-in porch. There were so many plants and trees growing around it that Amy thought it looked like it was inside a terrarium.

"What's this?" Amy asked with a cute little smirk on her face. She was sitting sideways looking at Mondo. He turned the truck off and turned looking at her.

"This, dear, is home."

"What?"

"Yeah, I moved off of Smokin' Joe."

They both climbed out of the truck. Amy took a deep breath; the air was like perfume. She looked to the west and could make out the ocean through the towering mango trees that lined the property. Mondo was leaning back against the truck, taking it all in. Amy walked around to him and brought her body up close and tight, and gave him a kiss like he hadn't had in a very, very long time.

"Why did you move off of Smokin' Joe?"

"The only anchorage on this whole damn island is in Keehi Lagoon. It's right under the airport approach and it's a derelict mess. Some friends from New Zealand are there and they said they'd keep an eye on Smokin' Joe. I rented this yesterday. I hope you like it."

They held hands as they entered. It was small but beautiful. The ceiling was open-beamed and exposed the rich dark Koa wood that had been used to build the roof. A small five-bladed fan hung down low from the rafters. The west facing wall was almost completely windows, the broad expanse of the Pacific Ocean shining before them.

"The sunsets must be awesome," Amy said.

Her heart was once again full of the joy of the moment. This house was so Mondo she couldn't believe it. The house had one small bedroom and one small bathroom. The kitchen had been recently remodeled with nice wood cabinets, and a large skylight over the sink. Amy would have been happy in a trailer, but she didn't tell that to Mondo. This place is perfect, she thought.

Amy brought herself up close and tight against Mondo, and kissed him again.

"I really missed you, Mondo."

Mondo reached out and grabbed hold of her hand. He kissed her, then led her into the tiny bedroom. The passion that they shared was like nothing they had ever experienced before.

CHAPTER 7

It was hard for Amy to be back in Malibu. She and Mondo had shared the most wonderful five months together. Their little house overlooking the ocean had become the most memorable home she had ever lived in. Mondo had started doing carpenter work, and she worked in the local surf shop. They saved money and talked about future plans. Mondo found himself constantly busy between work and getting Smokin' Joe ready for his next voyage.

Mondo talked often about sailing to Alaska. It was someplace that he really wanted to see. Amy could tell as their months together rolled on that he was getting anxious. It wasn't that he didn't feel committed to their relationship, she knew he cared so much for her, it was just his restless heart. He had started collecting charts and books about Alaska, and started asking her what she thought about a summer up north.

"Sure would be different than Hawaii," was her reply.

After a few months of listening to him talking about Alaska she knew that he would go, with or without her. She had to accept that part of him. That was the part that made him who he was. He had an enthusiasm for life that she didn't find in other people. For some reason he was able to let go with both hands and reach for what he wanted. Mondo was so different from most. He craved new horizons, he longed to experience all that life could offer.

"You can never see it all, Amy, never taste it all. Life is such a short ride."

He often told her that and she knew it was true. At times she thought he couldn't be contented, that his restless heart was a curse, and maybe at times it was. The more she grew to know him, and to love him, the more she realized that much of what he felt was right. Life is short, you will never taste it all. Amy often thought that Mondo should have lived in the sixties.

So in early March they packed up their belongings and moved away from their little cabin in Mahaka. Amy would have sailed with him to the northwest but he didn't invite her. She had asked about going along but she could tell that he wanted to do alone. She couldn't understand why he loved to sail upon the ocean by himself. Did he like his own company that much? She thought that it had more to do with the freedom of being in complete control of one's life, of having no responsibilities but to oneself. She realized that it was a time of personal growth for him, a time for Mondo to recharge his batteries, for him to be able to stand back and reflect undisturbed upon his life and those that he loved and cared about.

Was he a selfish bastard, she asked herself? No, she loved him too much to ever hold such malicious thoughts. He wasn't selfish at all. He was a very caring, giving person. He just had to isolate himself at times from a crazy world to see how he fit and what he wanted out of his life.

It was so different this time for Amy being back at her sister's.The last time she was here she didn't know if she would ever see Mondo again, now she knew that in a month they would rendezvous up north somewhere near Seattle, and together they would spend the summer sailing up to Alaska and back.

After Amy left, Mondo moved back on board. It seemed such a long time ago that he had lived on Smokin' Joe. His numerous visits to Smokin' Joe weren't the same as cutting his ties with land and once again moving back home. He would be leaving early in the sailing season. He knew that he could expect some bad weather. The only way that they could spend the summer in Alaska was to get an early start from Hawaii. He would sail up to Kauai, make his way north to Hanelai Bay and wait for a good weather forecast. Mondo liked to get the first few days at sea underway in good weather. It made it easier to readjust to life aboard.

By mid-March Smokin' Joe was provisioned with supplies.On March 20th he filled up his water tanks, topped off the diesel, and headed north to Kauai. It was about one hundred and thirty miles, and should take about twenty hours. He left Oahu at five in the afternoon. The trade winds tend to die down at night and build to their strongest in the early afternoon. Mondo knew it could be rough sailing in the Kauai channel.

It felt so good to be back onboard and out sailing. The wind was from the northwest, making for a wet beat-to-weather, but it didn't really matter. Smokin' Joe could go anywhere.

The next afternoon he tucked into Hanalei Bay. He dropped the anchor and sat in the quiet lagoon just enjoying life. The weather forecast was a go, twenty to twenty-five knots from the northwest. That was about as good as it got for this time of the year. Mondo ended up spending a week in Hanelai Bay. It was just so nice to be back on board, anchored out in the tropics.

In the five months that Amy had lived in Hawaii, Christy had relocated her clothing store to a larger space only one block from the beach. Amy was happy for Christy. Her life seemed to be coming together. Her business was successful and she had a great condo just a few blocks away. Christy had no one special in her life and that was sad for Amy. She thought what her life would be like without Mondo. It was a depressing thought. Amy wondered about setting her sister up with someone but she couldn't quite figure out who that someone was.

"All right, I'll work for you Tuesday as well, but I need a day off soon," Amy hollered through the bathroom door as Christy was doing her makeup. Amy had been working long and hard helping her sister. She needed a day for herself. She wanted to go to the beach and just sit, read a book, and do nothing. It seemed like her time back in Malibu had become a frantic mad dash.

Christy hurried out of the bathroom, knowing she would be late to open if she didn't get a move on.

"Thanks, Amy, you're great. Listen, come in at noon today and work Tuesday and enjoy yourself on Wednesday and Thursday. I promise, take the time off, you deserve it."

"Deserve it, I earned it, I've worked eight days in a row for you."

Christy gave her a kiss on the cheek as she went for the front door.

"You're an angel, sis."

Christy charged off to the boutique.

Amy sat down and reached for her lukewarm, half empty coffee cup.

Her sister was the perfect southern California woman. Able to rush around at lighting fast pace, and drive even faster, Amy wondered if she could jump over a building in a single bound.

Amy woke up early Wednesday, to a glorious sunny day. An off-shore wind had blown yesterday, clearing the sky and taking the smog somewhere else. Amy knew she was going to the beach. She showered, had breakfast, threw a beach towel, her sunglasses, sunscreen, favorite book, a bottle of Cascade drinking water, and some food all into her large beach bag and walked out the door. The bag weighed ten pounds. She needed a wheelbarrow for all her stuff.

The beach was empty, which made it all the nicer for her. She walked about a half mile down the beach and found a protected spot that she just liked for some reason and decided this was her spot for the day. She rolled her towel out, peeled her clothes off down to her two piece bathing suit, lathered herself with sunscreen and started to catch some rays.

It all felt so nice. The gentle slapping of the small surf a hundred feet away was like music to her ears. It was a beautiful day.

Amy started daydreaming of the first time she met Mondo. She could see him walking up the beach, walking right up to her. No hesitation in his steps. If she had only known how that chance encounter would change her life. Meeting him had been the best thing that ever happened to her.

Amy read for an hour, getting lost in a thriller. After reading she put her book down and closed her eyes, the sun was so sensual on her. She lay there for a half hour when she suddenly felt a cold shadow pass over her. She opened her eyes and looked around. An anxious feeling overcame her, then it disappeared.

She got up, and for some reason decided that it was time to head back to the condo. She put her things back into her bag, walked out from behind the dune, and almost bumped right into a middle-aged man.

"Excuse me," she said.

He laughed.

"Excuse me, I haven't been bumped into by a beautiful woman for a very long time."

He reached down and grabbed her beach bag from her.

"Allow me, please, we seem to be heading the same way."

"Sure," Amy said hesitantly.

They walked a few feet before he said. "I thought I would enjoy the beach, but it's so different from Fiji, I find it rather sad here." She looked at him.

"Fiji," she said. She felt a chill for a moment, then it passed.

He smiled back.

"Yes, I lived in Fiji for a few years, worked for the government down there. I just returned to Los Angeles and, well, I just had to get out of the city and see the ocean again. I thought Malibu would do it but I don't think anyplace will."

Amy was drawn right into his conversation.

"I spent some time in Fiji," she said.

"Really, what a coincidence, where?"

"Mbengga Island."

He stopped walking, took his sunglasses off and looked at her with the most penetrating black eyes she had ever seen.

"Mbengga! Why, I love Mbengga, you must know Sara and Patamo?"

Amy's knees went weak.

"Why, of course, how do you know them?"

They continued walking up the beach towards the parking area and the restaurants.

"They are such wonderful people, those two, I have been trying to get work permits for the both of them to come to America. We have a sponsor in Colorado, a sailor who spent time with them. It's just all bureaucratic paperwork, it's disgusting really."

Amy was completely confused, this wasn't real. You just don't bump into somebody on the beach and start talking and find out that they are friends of Sara and Patamo. One part of her wanted to reach down, grab her beach bag and walk away from this stranger as fast as she could. For some reason she just couldn't do it. At the parking area they stopped. He had been talking about Mbengga Island and what a shame the fishing resort was, and how it had such a negative influence on the whole island.

He put her beach bag down on the ground then reached his hand out to hers as if to shake her hand goodbye. His touch flooded through her body. She had never experienced anything like it. He looked deep into her eyes, smiled and said, "My name is Edwin Hawkins. Let's get lunch, my treat."

Amy couldn't say no. Somehow the thought entered her mind that she should get to know this guy, she could set him up with Christy.

He picked up her beach bag and they walked up to the Reefnet bar and grill. They took a seat outside overlooking the ocean. They ordered gin and tonics, watched the ocean and talked—he did most of it. Amy was drawn along by his words. At times she would become so engrossed by what he was saying that it seemed to her some part of her being would disappear, then come rushing back from somewhere. It was like losing oneself in a good book; you are there physically reading but your thoughts are somewhere else. It's only when you come back that you realize that you were gone.

He was the perfect gentleman.

By the end of lunch she had given Edwin her phone number and address and asked him to call her as soon as he could.

CHAPTER 8

Edwin thought long and hard about Amy Wilson and her sister Christy. He wondered which one of them was more important to him. He thought of taking both but he only needed one and he knew it would be harder to control the sisters if they were together. Whoever he took would have to grow to rely solely on him for everything, if his plans were to succeed.

After much thought he decided it had to be Amy. He felt an attraction to her that was to strong to ignore. Edwin knew why he felt this attraction, understood where it came from, and he could do little to push it away. This attraction to her was a human emotion that he did not need or want, it was a weakness to overcome. In his mind Amy was the picture of female fertility, the essence of the mother goddess who brings forth new life. It was now once again possible for Edwin to bring forth a male child from the lineage of Latina.

It had taken Edwin decades to find the girls, his great granddaughters. Only from them, from the line that was Latina, could his son be born. It was destined; no other woman, no other female lineage could bring forth the first-born of Edwin's new world.

The last known record of Latina was in 1934, her shaky signature giving all control of her child Agnes, his daughter, to the nuns of Saint Gabriel's Hospital outside of Paris. Agnes was committed to the hospital for the insane for her entire short life. According to her file, which was extremely difficult for Edwin to obtain, in August of 1943 Agnes was raped by a janitor who worked at the hospital. Nine months later she gave birth to a baby daughter. The child was whisked away by the nuns and given to a family living in Paris. This daughter was named Collette.

In November of 1945 Agnes had another daughter. The father was never mentioned in any of the records. This daughter was named Saertae. She was given to an Italian family living in Paris.

After the birth of Saertae there were no more records of Agnes. She disappeared into the dark void that was the end of World War Two.

By 1948 both daughters and families had immigrated to America.

Collette's name was changed to Julie Ann. The family moved to Los Angeles, where at age 23, she married Chester R. Wilson. Julie Ann Wilson had two daughters of her own, Christy and Amy.

Saertae's family moved to New York City. They changed her name to Margaret. At age 19, Margaret married a small time gangster named Antonio LaMartina. A year after their wedding they moved to Los Angeles. Daughter Isabella was born shortly after.

All three of Edwin's great granddaughters lived in Southern California. How convenient, he thought.

That evening back at the condo Amy waited for Christy to come home. She poured two glasses of wine and set them out on the counter to breathe. Somehow in her heart Amy knew she needed her big sisters help.

"Hey Amy, did you have a nice day?" Christy said as she rushed in and headed for the kitchen with a sack of groceries in her hand.

Amy didn't respond. Christy put the groceries down, took one look at her sister and knew something had happened.

"What happened, sis, did Mondo call with bad news?"

"No."

Christy saw the wine glasses, brought them out, and they sat at the kitchen table.

"I had the strangest experience of my life today," Amy said.

Christy could see the fear and confusion on her sister's face.

"What happened?"

"I met a man on the beach."

"So worse things have happened." Christy was trying to be light, but it didn't work.

"He knew me, he knew Sara and Patamo. He knew Fiji, he knew Mbengga island. We had lunch, it was impossible for me to think my own thoughts clearly. He was like no other person I have ever met."

"Did he scare you?"

"Not then, but now I am scared. It wasn't real, Christy, it was something more."

They each finished their glass of wine. Christy got up and filled them again.

64

"Okay," Christy said.

"I gave him our phone number, our address, I asked him to call us as soon as he could."

Christy put her wine glass down and looked hard at her sister. She knew Amy was wise enough to never do what she had just done.

"Why?"

"That's just it, I don't know. I thought that maybe you would like to meet him but that wasn't the reason. I don't know the reason. There is no reason and that is what has me so afraid."

The girls finished their wine in silence, Christy trying to fathom what her sister had just told her.

"Do you think he's dangerous?" Christy asked.

"No, I don't think he is physically dangerous at all. Somehow I know he isn't. But that doesn't mean I think he is harmless. I just don't know."

"What's his name, what does he look like?"

"His name is Edwin Hawkins. He's about fifty, seems well off financially. I think, anyway. He seems like such a gentleman. He acted with such charm and poise. He reminded me of some hero from a 1930's movie."

"What do you think we should do?"

"I don't know. I just needed to tell you about this. I really don't know at all."

The girls tried to put Edwin out of their minds, but it was difficult.

Two days later, after dinner, Edwin knocked at their front door.

"Hello, Christy, may I come in?" He walked in and closed the door behind him. Christy was speechless, her mind a sudden blank. Amy looked up from the sink and gasped.

"Edwin."

"So nice to see you again, my dear," he smiled.

That same confusion of feelings swept over Amy. She looked at Christy, her face flushed, and her expression one of shock.

"Why don't you sit down, Christy? You look rather faint," Edwin said as he led Christy to the couch where she sat down, aided by Edwin's hand.

Amy wanted to shout, to scream, to tell Edwin to leave and to never come back, but nothing came out.

"I so hope you were looking forward to my return."

He walked up to her, took the dish rag from her hand, and kissed her on the cheek.

"I was really hoping we would have a chance to talk. I have something very important to discuss with you."

Christy was still sitting on the couch, looking at them but not moving or saying a word, her mind was somewhere else.

"Edwin, please don't," Amy was able to say.

"My dear, please, we have so much to share, please sit down next to Christy."

He led her over to her sister and sat her down.

He sat down across from them and for five minutes said nothing. Nobody spoke. Edwin was in their minds. He was calming their fears, reassuring the two sisters that all was well. His mind was telling them that he was an important person to them, that he was one to be trusted and embraced, a person that they could share themselves with.

It had taken Edwin longer than he thought it would to accomplish this. Both girls had resisted his thoughts. It was futile, he knew, and he enjoyed their struggle. The human mind is so predictable, he thought. After five minutes the sisters came out of the fog.

"Edwin, so nice to meet you. Amy told me of your chance encounter on the beach a few days ago," Christy said.

"It was such a wonderful coincidence, I find it hard to believe."

"Edwin, I told Christy what a nice person you are. I think you two should go out."

They all laughed, each girl treating Edwin as a long lost friend.

"I had been hoping to make some female friends since I returned from my travels. I would be honored to count you two as my dear friends."

"Oh, please do," Amy said, as if she were speaking for both of them.

"I really can't stay, but I wanted to ask you both something that is very important to me. I am taking a road trip up north into Canada. I have a nice motor home and I would love your company. I will be leaving in a week and I want you both to come along."

Edwin had already suggested to Christy's mind that she would be too busy to leave her store. Christy would say she would love to come but just couldn't get away. He had suggested to Amy that she would love to take the trip.

"Oh, Edwin, that would be great!" Christy spoke first, then her thoughts returned to her store.

"Edwin, I am so sorry, I just don't think I can get away. Oh, I want to so bad. I need a break."

"I can go," Amy replied.

He looked at her with his jet black eyes, melting any of the last doubts that she had.

"Are you sure? We might be gone for a month or so."

"Yes, I would love to go."

Mondo was not even in her thoughts.

"Splendid, I would like to leave in a week. Could you be ready by then, Amy?"

He knew she would be.

"Sure, that sounds great. Christy, can you find somebody to fill in for me? This is such a wonderful opportunity."

"No problem."

"Great," he said. "I will see you in a week, I'll call first to confirm the day."

He knelt down in front of each girl and kissed her, his magic entering into every fiber of their being. He filled them each with desire and a longing for him.

"Edwin, are you sure you must leave?" Christy said hesitantly.

He smiled.

"Oh yes, I must go. I will see you in a week."

He walked to the door, turned, and looked back at both girls who were still sitting on the couch. Neither had moved. Both were filled with passion for him.

"It will be such a nice trip, Amy, you will never forget it."

He opened the door, walked out into the evening, and closed the door behind him.

CHAPTER 9

Antonio "Sunny" LaMartina held the gun to the punk's head.

"One more time, Jimmy, and it's over, one more time you dick around with Mr. Concenta, with his time, money, women, whatever, I will personally put you six feet under, got it?"

The punk was huddled on the floor, surrounded by Sunny and two other big goons he had never seen before. He knew death was at the door. Sunny didn't play around.

"I swear to God, Sunny, you will never have to deal with me again, tell Mr. Concenta I will never, ever deal him wrong."

"Get the hell out of my sight."

Sunny leveled a boot at the punk's head, sending him reeling over backward, blood dripping from his scalp. Sunny turned and started to walk away, changed his mind, returned to the punk and kicked him again, this time in the mid-section.

"That's for taking me away from my daughter's homecoming, you shit."

The punk lay sprawled on the concrete floor.

Sunny walked out of the dark warehouse into the waiting car and drove off.

Antonio "Sunny" LaMartina worked for the mob. He didn't see himself as a gangster; he was in business, and his business was taking care of Mr. Concenta's problems. In return he was paid enough to live the good life in Los Angeles, the really good life. Sunny (nicknamed after his sour disposition) had it all, the big house in an exclusive gated community, the cars, the boats, the women. Sunny had everything he wanted except for the one thing that mattered most to him, his daughter Isabella. She wanted nothing to do with her father. Isabella, nineteen years old, sharp-witted and beautiful with a dark complexion and a hint of mischief in her eyes, had grown up with the abuse and pain that Sunny had caused her mother. Her mom, who after twenty-three years of marriage simply had enough, filed for divorce and was killed in a car crash three months later. The accident was investigated and ruled a simple case of being in the wrong place at the wrong time, involving a semi truck, California highway 101 and a two-hundred-and-fifty-foot cliff. Still, Isabella had her doubts. She idolized her dead mom and the more she loved her mom's memory the more she blamed her dad.

Sunny acted as if he had it under control, but he didn't when it came to Isabella. He just didn't know what to do. In his professional life people treated him with respect, either because they were scared to death of him or because they were on his side. It really didn't matter to him, just as long as the respect was there. The one person he wanted it from the most, his only child, didn't even like him, let alone respect him.

Isabella had flown to Los Angeles that morning, arriving for a few days to get her belongings out of the house and then return to Washington State. She had a summer job working with a wildlife conservation group. The program took interested young people and for a two month commitment used them in wildlife rehabilitation or habitat programs. Isabella had volunteered to work with the Whale Museum's Orca Whale research program based out of Salt Bay Island in the northwest corner of Washington State. Her first day there she fell in love with the beauty of the islands. These island jewels were like nowhere else she had ever been. No traffic lights in Salt Bay Village, no neon, no horns blaring, no people screaming. Salt Bay Island and Los Angeles could not be on the same planet, she thought.

Her plans were simple. Return to Los Angeles, get her stuff, see her dad, and get back to Salt Bay Island. She wanted no confrontation with her dad, she wanted space from him. She needed air to breath whenever she was around him. She knew he loved her but he didn't know how to show it, didn't know how to respond to her. She was no longer the young daddy's girl she had once been.

Sunny had been out most of the evening and returned after she was in bed. The next day she did her thing, Sunny did his, and besides a few words at breakfast they didn't see each other at all. The next day she flew north. Sunny took her to the airport, he tried to have a conversation, tried to tell her he loved her, tried to see if things were all right with her, if she was doing well.

"Do you need money?"

"No dad, not your blood money."

They did hug and kiss at the airport saying goodbye. Isabella gently closed the car door, turned and walked into the airport lobby, no turning back, not a glance. Sunny's heart broke.

"Shit," he muttered to himself.

He had hoped for so much more, hoped to start mending broken fences with her. He was so good at breaking other people, but Isabella was beyond his abilities to deal with. The more distant she grew, the more it broke his heart.

"Someday, dear, you will need me, and I will be there for you," he thought as he left Los Angeles International Airport.

Isabella was glad to return to Salt Bay Island. Her second day back she was once again out on the whale watch boat, the small six person zodiac inflatable, zipping through the waves as she counted Orca whales. Isabella's job was to photograph each whale and then try to identify them back at the research center by their distinctive dorsal markings.

"Isabella, look to your right."

Johnny Mason, twenty-six years old and the main driver for the research center, hollered at her over the roar of the outboard engines. She swung her camera around and snapped three quick photos of a mother orca whale and her brand new calf.

"That could be J-48," Isabella yelled back.

"With the newborn we heard about. I hope you got a good shot."

Isabella liked Johnny Mason, liked him a lot. He was as different from her as possible. He was from the Midwest, he had grown up in a suburb of St. Louis. This was his fourth season in the program. His upbringing sounded so normal, regular parents with regular jobs, living the regular life, in the regular suburbs. He had an honesty about him that made Isabella comfortable, something so foreign to her upbringing. Hers was a childhood of pretenses. She grew up spoiled, she knew, the only child, the only daughter of a heavy-handed Italian father. Italian men trust only their mothers and their daughters, and maybe the Blessed Virgin, she had been told.

Isabella went through life not really thinking anything was amiss until, when she was twelve, her father was arrested and charged with murder. This traumatized her and her mother so much that it drew them close, closer than most mothers and daughters. Her father was acquitted, all charges dropped, but for the first time Isabella's eyes were opened. Her mother never recovered from the shock of Sunny's arrest and the time he spent in jail. The two found comfort and refuge in each other; at times it seemed Isabella was the adult, her mother's confidant.

"Let's spend another hour before we go in. There are reports of more whales up by North Beach," Johnny shouted.

Isabella glanced back over her shoulder and smiled, leaning her weight on the two restraining belts that kept her in the middle of the inflatable.

"Ok, you're the driver, don't crash," she said.

They raced north, ever vigilant for the tell-tale spray that was often the first sign of the Orca whales. Isabella loved it out here, the wind, the waves, the smell of the ocean, the freedom she felt when she was on the water. There was only the moment, and that was the greatest freedom that she had ever known. In the distance, the Olympic Mountains rose up from the sea. To her right as she glanced north were the mountains that created Vancouver Island. These mountains formed this inland sea, so protected from the ravages of the cold Pacific Ocean some eighty miles to the west. This was the most beautiful place she had ever seen.

They spent the next hour searching for more whales, but had no luck. On the way back to the research center Isabella unhooked her harness and moved to the back of the zodiac to talk to Johnny.

"Those photos of J 48, I bet, are the best I have taken."

"What are you betting?" Johnny smiled.

"What am I betting? Why, I don't know," she started laughing.

"Let's see your pictures," she said.

"I drive, you're the photographer."

"I know you don't have any, just a dumb driver."

They laughed and laughed, teasing each other all the way back to the center.

Johnny pulled the inflatable into its slip and turned the motor off.

"Ah, the quiet, my God, how did we even think with that racket?" Isabella said.

Johnny glanced up at the parking lot.

"Who's that?"

Isabella turned and saw a man about fifty years old standing next to a silver colored Mercedes Benz.

"I don't know," she replied.

Together they walked up to the parking area. It was very unusual to see anybody here except for staff members.

"What's up?" Johnny said, not too friendly, but not hostile.

"What's up?" the man mimicked back, a small smile on his face.

"What's up? Well, I am a friend of Isabella's mother, a very good friend, and I was hoping for a chance to talk to you, Isabella. I've come a very long way."

Isabella went weak in the knees.

"My mother?" It was a question as well as a statement.

"Yes, my name is Edwin Hawkins." He extended his hand; she didn't even bother trying to reach for it. He didn't extend it to Johnny.

"Isabella, maybe I should leave," Johnny said as he started to walk away.

"No, stay."

"Let me drive you to your center. I know it's only a short walk. Please, climb in." He motioned for them to climb into his car.

Edwin was dressed stylishly, his hair combed straight back, clean shaven with a very expensive looking suit on. He didn't look like he belonged on Salt Bay Island.

"Isabella, I was hoping we could get together and talk. I know your mother would want us to meet. I don't know what your schedule is, maybe dinner, tonight?"

Isabella was numb in the back seat. She had no idea what to make of Edwin Hawkins.

He pulled his car in front of the research center, turned the engine off, and turned around to look at Isabella. He completely ignored Johnny.

Isabella looked into his face, his eyes, and suddenly a thought entered her mind.

"Okay, dinner," she said weakly.

"Splendid, how about tonight at the pub, the Whale's Tooth I think it's called. I can pick you up here or we can meet there, whatever is best for you."

Johnny didn't like this guy at all. It had taken him less time than it took to drive from the parking area to the center to realize that.

"You're sure, Isabella?" he said, glancing from the front seat to the back.

"Yes, I'm sure." She turned her glance back to Edwin. "I'll meet you at seven-thirty."

"Wonderful," Edwin replied.

Johnny and Isabella climbed out of the car and started walking up the pathway.

"Isabella, your camera."

"Oh, my God."

She rushed back to the Mercedes just as it was leaving.

"Mr. Hawkins, wait, I can't believe I left my camera."

She opened the back door, grabbed her camera bag, and slammed the door closed. She was so embarrassed that she could have forgotten her camera, it wasn't like her.

"That guy gives me the creeps, Isabella. You sure about meeting him?"

"I don't know, something just made me think it's all right."

"I could go sit in the bar and keep an eye on you both."

Isabella looked up at Johnny as they walked into the research center.

"I'll be all right, it's just dinner, spend an hour and find out what he can tell me about my mom. She never mentioned Edwin Hawkins, not once. That's what bothers me. Even if they were having an affair, she would have told me about him, said they were friends or something."

"I wish you weren't going, I really don't like that guy."

Johnny liked almost everybody and everybody at the Whale Research Center thought the world of Johnny. For him to not like somebody in less than two minutes said a lot.

"I'll be okay," she said. Isabella removed the film from her camera, and left it for the development crew. She had no plans for the evening before meeting Edwin, but now somehow she felt at a loss, like something important was slipping by her.

"I'm going to lie down for a while. See you later, Johnny."

She gave him a smile, but he could tell it was half hearted.

Edwin Hawkins had gotten to her somehow, and Johnny knew it.

Isabella left the center at seven, getting a ride into town with one of the female interns.

Johnny made dinner, read a boring book that he was trying to stay

74

with, played his guitar and finally watched T.V. It was after eleven-thirty when she returned.

"God, Isabella, I was going to call the police, I thought maybe you got beamed up or something."

Isabella looked at him. There was no smile or warmth. Johnny knew her, knew she would have come right back at him with a one-liner.

"You shouldn't have stayed up, I'm okay, goodnight."

She walked into her room and closed the door.

Johnny's heart sank. Something wasn't right with Isabella. Who was this Edwin Hawkins?

Three days later, Isabella resigned her position at the center. She sent her dad a short letter saying she was going on a trip for a while, so don't worry, and I'll call you soon.

Johnny didn't know what to think.

"Isabella, what is going on?" he said to her the day she resigned.

"Johnny, I'm going away, something has come up."

Her face was drab, colorless, she wore no make up, her voice held no enthusiasm.

They were sitting in a small café overlooking the harbor, Johnny holding her hands, looking deep into her eyes.

"Isabella, I know you love this job, you would never just resign. Please tell me why? It's all about Edwin Hawkins, it has to be."

"Yes, it is, but…well, I'm taking a trip with Edwin. I'll keep in touch. Don't worry."

"Isabella, I'm terrified, this is not you."

"Yes, Johnny, this is me."

The next day she packed up her belongings, called a cab and left the center without saying goodbye to anyone.

Johnny called the taxi cab company and found out that they had dropped her off at the Baker Street Inn, a bed and breakfast in Salt Bay Village. Johnny didn't know what to do. He could tell that Isabella didn't want to see him. She had become a different person after she had met Edwin Hawkins.

CHAPTER 10

By the time Edwin came to pick Amy up for the trip north, both girls were full of excitement. Neither felt the least bit of concern regarding the trip. Christy actually thought of closing her store down and going, but something stopped her from doing that.

Neither girl called their parents to let them know what was happening. It all seemed so normal; Amy was just taking a motor home trip with Edwin. He had called and said to pack lightly, that if she needed anything he would buy it on the way.

It was a very nice, new motor home that pulled up in front of the girls' condo that evening after work.

Christy had closed the shop an hour early so she could make dinner for all of them. When he knocked on the door, both girls greeted him like a long-lost friend, with hugs and a kiss from both.

"Please, Edwin, I insist, stay for dinner."

"I would love to."

They sat around and talked while drinking a wonderful bottle of wine that he had brought.

It felt like old times, the three of them enjoying each other's company, the conversation flowing so easy and freely. Edwin told stories of his travels around the world. He had seen and done so much. Christy felt like she needed a new life after listening to some of his adventures. Amy talked about Fiji, and the time that she spent living in Hawaii. She even talked about Mondo, but her voice carried none of the emotions that she had felt for him. Mondo was just a name that kept coming up in her conversation.

A part of Christy was envious of her little sister. She wanted Edwin for herself; she didn't really understand why and she fought that feeling, but it was there.

After dinner they carried Amy's few bags out to the motor home. Edwin gave Christy a hug and a passionate kiss goodbye. Then Amy and her sister hugged.

"Call me, I wish I was going."

"I'll call you, don't worry. Thanks, sis."

Edwin and Amy climbed into the motor home and pulled away. Christy's heart turned sad as they drove around the corner. She wasn't sure if her sadness was because she would be missing her sister or that she would be missing Edwin. She couldn't quite figure it out.

Edwin and Amy pulled out of Malibu, made their way to Highway 5 and started driving north. He knew that he would have to keep a close watch on her. It took effort on his part to keep her thoughts where he wanted them to be. He also knew that Christy would slowly come out from under his influence the further north he drove and the longer he was away from her. It was inevitable that Christy would start to wonder about this whole encounter with him. She would remember it all, her first meeting with him, the dinner, the enjoyable conversation and her sister leaving with him in the motor home. None of it could be blocked out of her mind. It would take her at least a week before she became alarmed, and by then it wouldn't matter what she thought.

The two of them enjoyed their drive north. To Amy it felt like she was with an old boyfriend, someone she had shared so much with once upon a time. She felt such a closeness to him. She wondered if they had ever slept together. Did she like him that much? She couldn't remember ever making love to him but it seemed that they must have for her feelings to be so strong.

It was at night when she slept that terror filled her. She would wake up so afraid, one terrible nightmare after another. She could never remember her dreams, but it was so real to her. She was sleeping in the main bedroom. He was sleeping on the bed over the cab. She would lie in bed, to afraid to go back to sleep, too afraid to enter back into this dream that she knew was waiting for her.

"Edwin, I don't understand, I am too afraid to sleep, I just lie there knowing that if I fall asleep, this dream is waiting for me. It's the same dream over and over. It's haunting me, Edwin, something is wrong."

"My dear Amy, I am so sorry, I have no idea what could be causing these nightmares. I can get some sleep medicine if you like."

"I don't know, Edwin, I don't think that will help. I can't remember my dreams, but I know they're there, just waiting. I am going crazy."

Edwin was so sympathetic, so understanding. He constantly tried to reassure Amy, trying to make her not afraid. Each morning took longer and longer to bring her out from the influence of her nightmares. Except for her dreams, it was such a pleasant trip. Amy was enjoying herself, relaxing, feeling so comfortable with him. She never thought for one moment about the time she had first met Edwin. She couldn't remember her fears, they were locked out of her memory, replaced by feelings of warmth and trust. He had planted himself into her subconscious memory as a true friend, maybe even a lover. Edwin was someone that she could count on; hadn't they been close for years?

For Edwin, it was taking more effort than he had thought to maintain her thoughts of well-being. His problem was her nightmares. He knew it was her mind fighting to come out from under his control. It was something that he hadn't anticipated. Each morning would drain him in his attempt to lay her fears to rest and to bring her back to him. Each day took more of a toll on him and he realized that he was losing the battle. His energy was not able to keep up with the demand of keeping Amy under his control. Her mind was stronger than Edwin had anticipated but he didn't worry. He knew that in a few days he would be leaving Amy behind. She would go and stay at the bed & breakfast. Once she was there, his power would be able to handle her with little effort. The bed and breakfast was one of his energy points. It didn't have anywhere near the power that he felt on his island, but it held magic for him. She would be fine there until he returned. Many different places around the world held magic for him.

By their fourth day they were heading north of Seattle, and Edwin was drained. Amy's nightmares had gotten worse. Her subconscious mind was fighting sleep at night, knowing what lay there for her.

They pulled over for the evening at a beautiful waterfront travel park nestled on the quiet shores of Puget Sound. It felt good for them both to get out and stretch.

Edwin grabbed Amy's hand and they walked out to the beach and sat on a large driftwood log. The sun was just starting to set, the evening so still and peaceful. She was filled with the wonder of it all.

"Tomorrow I need to go take care of some business for a few days. I have arranged for you to stay at a wonderful little bed & breakfast that I know. Does that sound nice?"

"I'll miss you, but if that's what you want."

"This business is important to me. I have taken care of all the arrangements. I stay there often when I am in this part of the country."

"Fine."

The next day Edwin pulled his motor home up to the ferry landing in Anacortes. It was the central hub for the Washington State ferry that ran out to the different islands, including Salt Bay Island. He parked the motor home in the oversize parking area and grabbed her bags, then they walked into the small terminal building.

"When you arrive on Salt Bay Island I want you to walk up two blocks on the main street, then turn left at the church and walk another two blocks. The bed and breakfast is on your right—it's called Baker Street Inn."

"Ok, how long will you be gone?"

"Only a few days, I'll call you as soon as I can. There is another woman there. Another special friend of mine, does that bother you?"

Amy thought that it should, but it didn't.

"No, is she nice?"

"Isabella LaMartina is her name and you two have more in common than you might think. She is a wonderful young lady and a very good friend of mine. I know you two will enjoy each other. You both are so special to me."

Edwin paid for her ticket and walked her to the waiting room.

Twenty minutes later Amy walked onto the ferry heading for Salt Bay Island. Edwin walked back to the motor home, exhausted. He knew she would be fine for the next few days, even longer if necessary. Amy and Isabella would become the best of friends. Their spirits were already intertwined with his. His mind had made them kindred spirits before they ever met. They will be as sisters. He laughed to himself as he drove away from the parking area. He knew that they would spend the rest of their short lives together.

Amy arrived, found the bed & breakfast, and checked in. She felt so at home there. It was such a cozy wonderful little bed & breakfast. She never wondered why she liked it so much. She and Isabella became great friends the moment that they met. Each knew she was there waiting for Edwin, but neither felt any jealousy. They shared one room upstairs. Edwin had called twice while he was away, just to say hello and to see how they both were feeling.

It was in the middle of the fourth night at the bed & breakfast when Amy once again awoke from another terrible nightmare.

She lay in bed, her heart racing, her thoughts trying to reach back into the dream.She got up as if sleepwalking, her movements not necessarily her own. She walked down the stairs to the entry way and picked up the guest phone. Without even thinking she dialed her sister's cell phone number. It didn't dawn on her that Christy never had her cell phone on at night. She wasn't really thinking any of this. After getting her sister's voice message all she could say was, "Help me."

CHAPTER 11

Amy and Isabella didn't think anything was wrong when, at three o'clock in the morning, Edwin arrived, and fifteen minutes later the three of them left the bed & breakfast without any of the girl's belongings. They walked the three short blocks to the harbor. Each girl felt so glad that he had returned for them. They walked down to the main breakwater and climbed aboard a large, creamy white power boat. Two men were on board, an asian man that they were introduced to as Mr. Chein. The other, the captain just gave the girls a smile and a nod; no introductions were given. The boat pulled away from the dock and headed out into Humphrey Channel.

The powerboat reached its normal cruising speed of twenty-five knots. Both girls were sitting close to Edwin on the large comfortable couch in the main cabin.

"I am sorry for this late night departure, but my business had taken longer than I had hoped. I am sure you enjoyed your accommodations."

"Oh, Edwin, we're just glad you're back," Isabella said.

"That's right, Edwin, please don't leave us again," Amy said as she snuggled close to him.

They headed north. Twenty minutes later the boat entered into Canadian waters. The girls had fallen asleep on the couch. Edwin gently laid them down and covered each one with a blanket as he got up. The steady hum of the twin diesel engines was having the same sleepy effect on him, but he resisted the temptation.

"All is ready at the island, I presume," he said to Mr. Chein as they were sitting at the dining table.

"Yes, all is ready. I have the girls' accommodations finished. All the food and medical supplies have been taken care of, over a years worth. The medical team is available whenever you need them, if you need them, by radio. All communications systems are a go and the surveillance system is finished as well. I think that you have thought of everything ,

Edwin."

"I hope so. I feel confident in our timeline. We can keep both of the girls on the island indefinitely. I doubt anybody will come looking around our island for two missing young American girls. If we do have uninvited company we can place the girls in the underground living quarters. Nobody will ever find them there."

"I see no problems with your planning. It all seems to be coming together."

"Yes, I think you're right."

"Edwin, I know we have discussed this before, but I still think you risk complicating matters by having two girls, instead of one. They will find comfort in each other and it will be harder to control them."

"I realize that, although I see no real problem. You know the difficulty I had trying to decide between Amy and Isabella. Both are so beautiful and young. Let an old man enjoy some of the pleasures of life, Mr. Chein."

"As you wish."

"It has taken quite a toll on me to get both of these girls here. I can't continue this. Once we are secure at the compound I will start to release them, slowly at first, but I must completely release my control over them. That is the only way that we can proceed. I know it will cause some difficulties for us. They will both react. It will take time for them to grow used to their new situation. Are we ready, Mr. Chein, for this difficult time ahead?"

"That, Edwin, is up to you. They cannot escape, but I think that it will be hard to live with them until they accept their situation. We have our ways to help encourage them to come to our way of thinking. Though I fear it will be harder than you think."

"It will be hard, I know."

Edwin was thinking that it would be enjoyable to watch the girls slowly come out from under his spell. Each girl would remember all that they had been through, but neither would be able to recall why they thought it was fine to leave everything behind and follow him. In the next few days both of the girls would go from blindly loving Edwin to questioning why they loved him, to fearing him like they have never feared anybody else. That didn't bother Edwin, fear was one of the greatest tools that he used.

"What about our surveillance of the bed & breakfast?" Edwin

asked

"As planned."

The large powerboat pulled up to a private dock at eight-thirty that morning. Edwin, Mr. Chein, and the girls walked down the boarding ladder, then up the ramp, and through an open gate to the parking area.

Both girls were fully awake and filled with excitement. All climbed into a red jeep that moments before had come over the ridge and parked before them. They left the dock area behind as they drove over the hill and towards the compound.Neither girl thought too much of the large open gate that they drove through, nor even noticed the eight foot high fence that surrounded the entire compound area.The fence was covered with military camouflage, making it impossible to see without really looking for it.

"Welcome, ladies," Edwin said, as they pulled up to the main two-story house.

The entire fenced area area was two acres. It sat on level ground with four small cabins, a few outbuildings and the one large two-story house. A pond lay off to one side away from the driveway. The buildings all looked new and the whole area had a clean, orderly sense to it. They followed Edwin into the house.

"This is home for a while, ladies. Mr. Chein will take you to your rooms. I do trust that you will enjoy your stay here and that we will continue to be the very best of friends. I will come visit each of you soon."

The girls followed Mr. Chein. They had their own bedrooms with doors across from each other in a narrow hallway that was to the right of the living room. Each room had a small private bathroom off to one side, through a sliding door.

Ten minutes later Edwin walked into Isabella's room just as she was stepping out of the shower, her naked body wet and glowing. Edwin was surprised at the lust that he felt for her. She made no effort to hide her nakedness.

"Isabella, you know that I love you so much, that you are so special to me."

"Oh, Edwin, I feel the same," her voice full of tenderness.

"Please, let me continue."

"All right."

She slipped into a tight pair of jeans and pulled a dark blue sweater over her head.

Edwin sat down on the bed as she walked over and stood before him. She longed for Edwin Hawkins.

"I want to tell you that you are home now, you are safe here. You will soon start feeling different emotions, you will become confused and you will doubt my sincerity. Please don't. We, you and Amy and I, we are all here for a very special purpose, one that I will share with you as the days go on. Don't doubt me, Isabella. Let us grow together as long as we are here."

He reached for her hands and pulled her onto him as he fell backwards on the bed. How he wanted to take her right now, his lust burning deep for her. He cupped her face with his hands and brought his lips to hers, his kiss conveying not only passion but care and concern. This was not the time, he knew. She returned his kiss with all of herself.

"Edwin, make love to me," she whispered in his ear.

"Oh Isabella, our time together will soon come. Be patient with an old man, my love."

He kissed her again, then rolled out from under her and stood up. She looked so innocent there on the bed. Edwin feared how she would feel in a few days, once her thoughts were her own. Maybe he should take her now, just for pleasure. No, that must wait.

He walked to the door, opened it, and looked back at Isabella on the bed.

"Remember, Isabella, I will always love you."

He turned and closed the door behind him before she could say anything.

He walked across the hall and entered Amy's room. She was brushing her hair, standing in front of the mirror over the bathroom sink.

Edwin walked up behind her, and wrapped his arms around her waist. He pulled her back into him, both looking at each other's reflection in the mirror.

"Amy you know that I love you and I always will. Do you trust me?"

Amy gave Edwin a funny glance in the mirror.

"Edwin, what kind of question is that? I love you. I will always love you."

86

Amy turned in his arms and faced him as she brought her lips up to his and kissed him with all of her passion.

God, Edwin thought.

"You and Isabella will live here for a long time, all three of us will live here for a long time. I fear that you might grow tired of me and want to leave. Do you think that will ever happen?"

"Edwin, you are my love, why would I want to be anywhere but with you?"

How much easier it would be if I just kept them under my mental control, Edwin thought. But he knew that was not possible. The girls must be themselves when he took them on the Altar of Life.

"Amy, you will soon start to feel confused, different emotions will run through your mind. You will soon start to doubt me. I want you to remember one thing. You are safe here, we all belong here, you are mine and I am yours."

"Edwin, that is so dumb."

"Well, maybe so, but I hate to think that anything could cause me to lose you." He kissed her again, then walked out of the bathroom and left Amy's room.

CHAPTER 12

Marshall had always been an asshole! As long as he could remember, way back into the glimpse of his earliest childhood, he had been mean. In his forty-three years of life he couldn't remember anytime that he enjoyed being nice. Maybe he blotted those memories out of his mind, too painful to keep. Marshall had been big for his age, when he was young, which works great if you're a bully. If he couldn't intimidate someone with his attitude he could always beat them up; barbaric but easy. High school was hard for him simply because a lot of kids were bigger than him. He learned fast, and became a diplomatic guy. This lesson ended up being invaluable for Marshall his entire life. Realizing who to intimidate, who to beat up and who to kiss up to, helped him to become well-rounded. After high school it was the service. He had the good fortune of not being sent into any military conflict and the misfortune of being a bully on the low end of the military totem pole. He did his time and got out.

Marshall found bully, hillbilly heaven, when he became deputy sheriff in Bodega County, in sparsely populated northern California. He couldn't wait to start work everyday. One of the joys of his miserable life was to stand in his uniform in front of the full length mirror in his office and admire himself. He was good friends with his boss, Sheriff John Michaels. If two peas were ever from the same pod it was these two. Marshall was happy to play second fiddle to John, he had so much to learn. Bodega County is large, and Marshall worked the eastern half of the county out of a two-cell, one-man sheriff's office. Marshall became a complete sleaze bag. He got laid on more than a few occasions by arresting women for public nudity (skinny dipping in the Wilcox River), taking them to jail, and then giving them an easy way out. If they refused, he could get really upset and intimidate them and if that didn't work he would just arrest them and let justice be done. Damn hippy chicks anyway.

Lots of people hated Marshall, but the sheriff loved him, and who was going to raise the torch to get rid of him? So life just went on.

Then things got even better for him. The continued influx of counter-culture, pot-smoking, pot-growing hippies and tree huggers got the attention of the federal government. Soon, besides his boss loving him, the DEA also loved him. They found their man to fight the "war on drugs". Marshall was being flown all over his county in DEA helicopters in search of marijuana growers. He organized busts, kicking doors in remote backwoods cabins at three o'clock in the morning, SWAT teams surrounding him. His biggest rush, the greatest thrill of all was to see the fear, the terror in the poor hippy's eyes. What a job for an asshole! He would have worked for free, but he never mentioned that to anyone.

All good things come to an end even for a guy like Marshall Sandbourn. His demise was the quick-thinking daughter of the Bodega County head administrator, home for spring break. Marshall pulled her rental car over for speeding late one night. She was half drunk, but still in control, yet they both knew she would fail the breath test. Marshall never even ran her name, never even more than glanced at her driver's license. He told her all the trials and tribulations that would come upon her for a DUI, or there was another option. She could give him a little something right then and there. She told him to walk to the passenger side of the car and to open the door, anything was better than a DUI. He obliged, opened the car door with his pants down around his knees, when she took two rapid pictures of Sheriff Marshall Sandbourn with his pecker as hard as a rock. Marshall was so stunned that he fell over backwards, tripping over his pants, and landed butt ass naked in the rose hip sticker bushes that lined the road. Before he could react, she threw the car in gear and raced for the nearest town. The second photo was the best. Mr. Sheriff, pants down to his knees, falling into the rose hips with the most god-awful stupid expression on his face.

He was fired three days later.

Things never did improve for him after that. He ended up in San Francisco hanging up a Private Detective shingle, placing a few ads in the local paper, and sitting in his office reading cheap paperback detective novels, hoping his phone would ring. He spent the next three years barely surviving, mostly following married men or women around with his camera. It was hell. Marshall could hardly afford the rent in a cheap boarding house in the cheap part of the city.

He may have been stuck there forever if not for one night while walking along the EL Camino Real. That night, some Hare Krishnas got to him so bad that he lost all control and beat up three of the robed beggars. He ended up in San Francisco county jail for seven days.

The newspaper account of private detective Marshall Sandbourn and the Hare Krishnas fight was printed in the bottom corner on the next-to-the-last page in the San Francisco Herald.

Within one week of returning to work, his phone rang, and a male voice spoke.

"Mr. Sandbourn, I see that you do not like strange religious cults. Good. Please check your mail for an envelope that I will be mailing for my employer which will have $2,500 cash as a retainer and a few simple instructions for you to follow. My employer is a man of power and for some unknown reason has chosen you to help him with a rather difficult problem that he has. I am sure that even you will be able to follow his instructions." The voice paused, then continued.

"Mr. Sandbourn, no more embarrassing photos of you with your pants down around your knees. Have a good day."

The caller hung up. Marshall tried to stand up, tried to get out of his chair, but his knees buckled and he fell right there on the floor, a heap of asshole wondering who just called.

The envelope arrived three days later, with no return address. There were twenty-five one-hundred dollar bills enclosed with a note that said for him to do nothing, to go nowhere, but to simply be available by phone every day. That was it.

For four days Marshall went nuts. The few calls he received put his adrenaline in overdrive and none of them really wanted to hire him for anything. Marshall was going crazy. He couldn't even read his detective novels any more.

On the fifth day his call came through.

"Mr. Sandbourn." Marshall recognized the voice at once; the caller didn't bother to introduce himself.

"Please arrive at San Francisco International airport for a flight on Alaska Airlines, departing ten-thirty this coming Tuesday morning. Your pre-paid ticket will be waiting for you under your name. You will receive more information when you need to know. Bring no weapons of any kind and dress warmly."

The phone went dead, and Marshall didn't even try to stand for five minutes. His mind reeled and his adrenalin pumped; he finally got up and rushed to the bathroom.

"My God," he thought, over and over.

"Welcome to Seattle/ Tacoma International airport," the stewardess said over the loudspeaker. Marshall really didn't hear the rest about checking overhead luggage and all that have a good day stuff. His ticket was for a connection with a commuter plane that would take him to a small town he had never heard of before called Salt Bay Village.

Oh well, he thought. He was just following orders, kind of like the military, and he was just as confused by the whole affair as he had been back then. The small eight-passenger twin-engine commuter took off on time, and a short twenty minutes later he was landing.

After collecting his small bags he walked into the lobby. A tall, gangly-looking fellow who looked like he was duly impressed walked up to Marshall.

"This way, Mr. Sandbourn," and without another word grabbed his luggage and walked out of the lobby into a waiting taxi.

Marshall mutely followed and not a word was exchanged between the two of them until the cab pulled into a driveway a few minutes later.

"Here you are, sir, enjoy your stay and welcome to the Baker Street Inn."

CHAPTER 13

Mondo sailed through the night, arriving at Salt Bay Island an hour after sunrise. He swung Smokin' Joe inside the breakwater, past a long row of commercial fishing boats, down to the end of the main dock, and tied up. He knew it was too early to go to the bed & breakfast. Fatigue flooded through his body, but he was too wired to sleep. It was such a clear beautiful spring morning that he didn't want to stay on the boat so, as tired as he was, he grabbed his jacket, climbed off his boat, and headed up town.

Salt Bay Island is part of an island chain that starts north of Seattle and stops somewhere in Alaska, over eight hundred miles of water-way wilderness. That was what intrigued him so much about this area. This island archipelago consisted of literally thousands of islands and bays. It held some of the last remaining pristine wilderness in the world. Deep, dark forest filled with life, running down to the sea, almost all of it only accessible by boat. Orca whales, the wolves of the sea, lived here year around. Mighty humpback whales, following ancient migratory routes, traveled from Hawaii to Alaska each year. He had studied it all for a long time, spent hours looking at his charts, marking places of interest. The more he looked at this area the more it impressed him. A person could spend a lifetime exploring this maze of islands and waterways and never even come close to seeing it all. Some of the deep fiords cut by glaciers over twelve thousand years ago ran fifty miles into the heart of the British Columbia Coastal mountain range. Snow-capped peaks over a mile high, and one over two miles high, dominated the distant vistas. After the years in the South Pacific, Alaska held the promise of new adventures for him and the magic of new places, new people, and of scenic beauty that had changed little in the last ten thousand years. Salt Bay Island should have been his gateway to this wonderful new world, but now he was filled with fear and apprehension as he thought about the telephone call that had brought him here.

The streets were empty. He found one restaurant opened for breakfast. It was obviously the locals' favorite place, and the volume was loud. Fisherman types and construction workers seemed to dominate the restaurant. A haze of cigarette smoke hung in the air. Mondo found a seat at a table, and a few minutes later ordered coffee and breakfast. The caffeine did little to shake the tiredness from him; his body ached. It had been a long trip from Hawaii and a very short rest before leaving Neah Bay and heading out again.

Mondo's breakfast arrived and he consumed it. After paying his bill he walked out into the fresh air. God, that place stunk. It reeked of cigarettes and human sweat, of greasy food and burned coffee. He hoped he wouldn't smell like an ash tray when he met Christy for the first time.

Salt Bay Village seemed like a tourist trap of a town. Real estate brokerages dominated the main street. There were clothing boutiques, nautical souvenir shops and restaurants. The main drag was five blocks long. He walked up two blocks and turned left. Christy said the bed & breakfast was on Baker Street. It was quiet; he saw nobody walking and only a few cars drove by. He walked by old houses dating back to the turn of the century, most in good repair. One old house stood back from the road, surrounded by large old trees. It looked like a mansion. It must have been gorgeous in its time, and what stories could it tell, he wondered. Now it looked run down, it even had plywood nailed over one part of the roof. The yard was filled with wrecked cars and used fishing gear. Two small fishing boats were tucked under a large fir tree. This was the kind of place that he would try to buy if he ever settled down, a place with lots of work to be done and lots of history to tell. One short block past the run-down mansion he found the bed and breakfast. He didn't know if it was too early for him to knock on the door. He had no idea if Christy would be up, he would just have to check it out.

He saw the sign next to the road: Baker Street Inn. There was a long driveway on his right leading back to a large Craftsman designed house. The house looked charming and inviting. The yard was full of flowers and plants. Whoever took care of this place loves yard work, he thought as he walked down the driveway. The house was freshly painted, an off-white with green trim. Flower boxes full of blooms hung down from the windows on the main floor. It was a two-story house, built with knee braces and gabled ends. The house looked well-maintained and loved by somebody. Mondo wished he were coming here with Amy for a romantic getaway, not because she was in trouble. He walked up to the front porch. A beautiful wood door with stained glass at eye level greeted him. A small hand-written note on the door said, "Guests please ring the door bell and enter."

He thought about ringing the bell but it was early. He knocked once softly and twisted the door handle. It turned in his hand so he opened the door and walked inside, closing the door behind him. He was standing in a small entry way, a registration desk to his left. A computer and a telephone sat on the desk next to a dish full of chocolates, a small note written in beautiful calligraphy said for guests only. He was looking up the stairs that led to the second story. A small velvet cord was stretched across the bottom of the stairs, closing it off. No lights were coming from the second story or the stairway. It was definitely off limits. Soft music floated through the house; at least somebody was up. He turned to his right and walked into the living room. It had such a warm feeling to it. Not too crowded with things, nicely furnished, and tastefully done. The house smelled like grandma was baking cookies. It was very pleasant. He had worried what he would say if the owner asked him what he wanted but he didn't have to.

A dark-haired woman in her late twenties, slim and very cute, sat on the sofa drinking a cup of coffee. Even though they had never met, they knew each other.

"Christy?"

"Mondo."

She stood up, walked over and put her arms around him and held him close. He could feel the trembling in her body.

"It's so nice to meet you finally. I've heard so many wonderful things about you."

"Thanks, you look a lot like your sister."

Mondo wished there was time for small chit chat conversation, but he couldn't stop thinking of the last time he had talked with Christy. What the hell was going on?

"Do you want a cup of coffee?" she asked.

"I'd love one."

Christy got two large steaming cups of coffee, and handed one to

Mondo, then they walked outside, Christy quietly closing the front door behind them. He followed her around the back of the house to a patio area. They sat down at a small bistro table, with more flower beds full of blooming flowers and a small fountain setting the mood. It would have been so peaceful had his heart not been so full of apprehension.

"You know, Mondo, Amy really loves you."

He smiled. Those words meant more to him than Christy could have known.

"Thanks, I feel the same way. What's happening, Christy?"

"It's such a long story, I don't know where to begin. Just remember as I tell you this that Amy really does love you, and you alone."

Mondo felt like he was getting set up for a sucker punch.

She sipped her coffee, trying to get her thoughts in order. Where to start? God, she didn't know.

"Amy met a man on the beach about two weeks ago. It was completely unreal. I met him a few days later. He came over to visit us both."

Mondo could see the tension in her face, sense her voice struggling to maintain composure.

She looked at him. He could tell she wanted to go on but didn't quite know what words to use. She was trying to protect him from what she was about to say.

"Listen, Christy, just tell me."

"This man, Edwin Hawkins, he took over both of our minds, I swear to God he did. A week after he came to our condo, Amy left with him in his motor home for a trip north. He said something about going to Canada and being gone for a month. I wanted to go. I had never even met him before and I wanted to go. I would have gone but I had the shop. I never believed in mind control, but I do now."

"You heard nothing from Amy after they left except for the message on your cell phone?"

"That's right, nothing. If she hadn't called that night I would have no idea where she was, even if she was alive. My cell phone recorded her number as a missed call. She would have just disappeared from the face of the earth without that one call. You should have heard her voice on the phone, it wasn't her. It was haunting. She sounded like she was in such trouble, like she was so afraid of something, terrified of something. It sounded like she was talking in her sleep."

96

"So you retrieved the phone number, found that the call originated from this bed and breakfast, flew up here, and she was already gone, right?"

"Yes, but that's not all. There was another girl here as well. Her name is Isabella. She and Amy shared the same room upstairs. Amy had never even met this lady as far as I know, and suddenly the two of them are roommates? They disappeared together the day before I arrived. I've been here four days. I have no idea what to do, Mondo."

"They disappeared?"

"Right, they just vanished. The innkeeper told me she got up early to make breakfast and the girls never showed up. It was after ten in the morning when she finally went upstairs to check on them and the girls were gone. All of their things are still in the room. She told me she even called the police, but they said it wasn't something that they would get involved with. They told her the girls probably skipped out on their bill, which isn't true. This whole thing can't be true, but it is."

Mondo sat sipping his coffee, taking every word in. He could tell Christy believed everything that she told him.

"How many other guests are there staying here?"

"Just one, a guy named Marshall Sandbourn. He gives me the creeps. He just sits around all day doing nothing. It's not like he's a tourist or something exploring the island, he just stays here. Honest to God, I think he is spying on me. He watches my every move. He was here when I arrived, said he got here late in the afternoon the day the girls left, claims he never met them, didn't know what I was talking about."

"Jesus, Christy."

"I know, Mondo, we have to find her. I think she is in real danger."

Mondo sat in silence, taking it all in, trying to think of something. It seemed like a complete dead end.

"Where do we go from here, Christy?"

Christy burst into tears. She was trying to hold them back, but they just came. A wave of pent-up emotion, of fear, and frustration that she couldn't contain any more flooded from her.

"I was hoping you could answer that," she said, struggling to speak.

Mondo sat there looking into his empty coffee cup, unconsciously shaking his head, his mind drawing a blank. What could they do?

"You said their things are still upstairs?"

"That's what the inn-keeper said. I asked if I could go look and she told me no. I got so mad, but for some reason she doesn't want anybody upstairs. Marshall and I have the two rooms downstairs. I don't think she will even rent the upstairs rooms. I don't know if she is part of what's going on around here or not."

"Okay, we need to get into that room and look around. That is the first place to start. Does this innkeeper person have a schedule? Does she leave at any certain time every day?"

"She does leave around one in the afternoon and comes back about an hour later with a bunch of groceries. I think it's a daily occurrence."

"Good, I'm going back to Smokin' Joe. I need a few hours sleep. I'll be back up here a little after one. If she's gone we'll go have a look in their room."

"How? I'm sure it's all locked."

"Leave that to me."

He stood up, and smiled at Christy. He wanted so much to reassure her, he almost lied and said something encouraging, but he couldn't think of anything to say.

CHAPTER 14

Mondo was back at the bed and breakfast by one-fifteen. The innkeeper was gone; no one was there except for Christy and Marshall. Marshall was sitting in the living room reading a book, but his eyes followed every move that Mondo made. Mondo knew exactly what Christy meant when she said there was something wrong with this guy.

They walked back out to the patio and sat down.

"I've been thinking about what you said about mind control. Do you really believe that"?

"Mondo, he did it to me. I believe it, and I know it's true."

"Why would Edwin want two girls who never even met each other, who seem to have nothing in common? And why would they vanish?"

He already knew the answer.

"I think Edwin returned for them and he wants to make sure they can't be found. He wants nobody to be able to follow them. We're lucky that no cars can drive on or off Salt Bay Island except by using the ferry or it would be impossible to figure out how they left. The fact that they couldn't drive off the island any time they wanted to helps us more than you think. I bet he took them from here on a private boat. If he took the ferry, too many people would see them. He couldn't fly on a commercial flight for the same reason. I guess he could have flown on a private plane, but I think they are supposed to log their flight plan, plus he would have to be a pilot or hire one. I think the girls went from here on a private boat. There would be no record of it. It could leave any time it wanted. Why he wants these two, what they have in common, it's impossible for us to know. Time will tell us, when we find them, but I don't think he just randomly picked them. It sounds like he went through a lot of effort to bring Amy this far."

Christy looked at thim and said softly. "Great, so what do we do? We have my sister and some lady named Isabella leaving here five days ago in the middle of the night on a small boat going north, south, east or west."

Mondo could hear the panic in her voice as she spoke. She was close to losing it completely.

"We have no idea where they went! We have no idea why this crazy guy wants them! What can we do with that?"

Christy laid her face in her hands, tears streaming through her fingers.

"We need to go look in the girls' room, Christy. It's all we have."

"What about Marshall?"

"The hell with Marshall."

"I feel so weird breaking in, it doesn't seem right."

"It's not right, but it's all we can do."

He stood up, reached his hand down and gently pulled her up. There was nothing else they could do but search the girls' room.If they turned up nothing, they would have nowhere else to go. Amy and Isabella would be lost to them until Edwin Hawkins decided it was time to release them, if he ever did.

They walked into the entry and closed the door behind them. Marshall put his book down and stared at them. Mondo stared right back, not intimidated at all by him.

"Let's go." He unhooked the velvet cord that closed off the stairway, pulled Christy behind him and up the stairs they went.

They came to a hallway with three doors. Mondo flipped on the lights and reached for the door on his right. It opened. The room was completely made. This wasn't the girls' room. He closed the door and walked back to the door at the end of the hallway and tried it. It was locked. Mondo turned and looked at Christy but said nothing.

He reached into his jacket pocket, and pulled out a small leather case. He opened it and took out two small pieces of flat brass, each piece looking like a wide toothpick, and in fifteen seconds had the door opened.

"Where did you learn that?" Christy whispered as they entered.

"Not telling."

He closed the door behind them.

This was their room. The two twin beds were not made, sheets and blankets were thrown in a heap on the floor. A small pile of clothes was sitting in one corner, a jacket thrown over a chair. It looked like the occupants of this room were out for the afternoon. Two suitcases were opened and full of belongings.

"Look through the suitcases, Christy. I'm going to look in the bathroom."

The bathroom counter was filled with miscellaneous female products: make up, a blow dryer, a curling iron, a hair brush and a large hand-held mirror, even two toothbrushes and a tube of tooth paste. One small hand towel was lying on the edge of the counter. It was hard to believe that the two girls would leave everything and go. Towels were piled in a corner next to the shower. Mondo reached out and grabbed the large hand mirror that was sitting face down on the counter and turned it over.

"Christy, come look at this."

She rushed in.

He showed her the mirror. In lipstick was written the numbers 493012415.

"What do you think, Mondo, is that anything?" she whispered.

"The numbers certainly look out of place. Do you have a pen and a piece of paper?" he asked.

"Yes, in my purse."

"Good, write these numbers down. Did you find anything?"

"Nothing."

She pulled a pen and paper out of her purse and wrote the numbers down.

They both stood in the bathroom looking for anything else that could possibly help them understand what happened to the girls. Nothing jumped out at them. They walked out into the bedroom and stood. Were there any clues that they were missing, anything saying dear Christy and Mondo? They knew there wouldn't be.

"Let's go," Mondo said.

They walked out of the room and locked the door behind them, Christy flicked the hall lights off and they walked down the stairs. Once he hooked the velvet cord back in place, it all looked just as they found it. Marshall was still sitting on the couch, his book in his lap, watching them. Mondo took one quick glance his way just to acknowledge that he saw him, then they went out the door.

"Let's go back to Smokin' Joe. I need to look something up. I have a hunch about those numbers."

"Really, what? Do they tell you something?"

They started walking down the long driveway from the bed and breakfast.

Mondo smiled at Christy. He put his arm around her and pulled her close to him.

"Christy, I think I know where they are."

They walked back to the harbor and climbed aboard Smokin' Joe.

"God, Mondo, I've heard so much about this boat, I feel like I know it. It seems so small to sail across the ocean! I can't believe this is where you and Amy spent so much time together."

"We spent so much wonderful time together here. Our time in Fiji was one of the greatest experiences in my life. This boat is home, and it's not complete without Amy."

They walked down into the cabin. Mondo was glad he had put some things back in their place and that Smokin' Joe wasn't a complete mess, though it probably looked like one to Christy.

Mondo went to the navigation station and pulled out some charts. He looked through them, sorted them out, and then grabbed one.

"Sit down, Christy." He motioned for her to sit at the chart table. He leaned over her and spread the chart out.

"Here is what I think." He folded the chart over once, helping it to fit on the chart table.

"Amy spent a lot of time doing navigation when we were in Fiji. She knows how to do it. Navigation is simply being able to go from point A to point B on the planet. But you have to be able to identify those points. That is done by using a set of numbers called latitude and longitude.

"Crossing latitude and longitude on a chart gives you a position, a place. It tells you right where something is. Every spot on the planet has its own latitude and longitude numbers. It's like taking a piece of paper and drawing a line straight down the middle of it, then drawing another line right across it. Where those two lines meet, where they intersect, is a position. Now if you do that on a chart, you can put numbers to that position.

"I think Amy wrote those numbers for me, hoping that somehow we would discover the bed and breakfast, discover their room and be able to get inside and find that mirror. It seems to me she was casting a bottle with a note in it into the sea, hoping against all odds that we would find it. I think that those numbers will tell us where she is. I hope to God they do. She also knew that if anybody else saw those numbers, they couldn't make any sense out of them. Those numbers were written for me, Christy. If I'm right we will know in about thirty seconds."

Mondo reached into his chart table and took his dividers out.

"Look, here is 49 degrees 30 minutes north." He pointed to the left side of the chart, about half way up the page.

He drew a thick line across his chart from left to right.

"Now here is 124 degrees 15 minutes west," he said, this time pointing to the bottom of the chart.

He drew another heavy line from the bottom of the chart upwards. They both stared at the chart. The two lines intersected on an island about one hundred miles north of Salt Bay Island, in Canadian waters. On the chart, right where both of the lines met, was located Penderville Island.

"That, Christy, is where I think the girls are."

Christy sat there staring at the chart. She had been at a complete loss as to what to do next, and the first day Mondo shows up he figures out where the girls are. At least it made sense to her. At least it was something.

Mondo also stared at the chart. He knew he would leave Salt Bay Island tomorrow and sail north to Penderville Island. What he would find there he had no idea.

If there was mind control, if both of these girls were under some sort of spell from some crazy guy, then heaven help us all, he thought.

"I'm going to leave tomorrow and sail up there. It should take me two days to get there. Do you want to come?"

"I don't know, I have to call back home. I just don't know what to do."

Poor Christy, she was so confused by this whole affair. Her emotions completely drained. Mondo thought she should go home and rest.

"If you don't make it, no problem, I'll call you at home and let you know what's going on. I'm leaving here at six in the morning. If you want to go, just be here by then, okay?"

Christy smiled at him. She completely understood why her sister loved this man.

"All right."

"Christy, I'm exhausted. I haven't slept a good night's sleep in over twenty-two days. I need time to put Smokin' Joe back together and plan my trip."

"Sure, no problem. I'm heading back to my room. I want to go, Mondo, I just can't say for sure."

"Christy, you look so wiped out, you should just take it easy."

"I know I should, I just don't know if I can."

Christy stood up and walked up the companionway steps into the cockpit. At the top of the stairs she turned around and looked down at him.

" Mondo, I see whyAmy loves you so much."

Then she turned, and walked off Smokin' Joe.

CHAPTER 15

As Christy walked from the docks to the bed and breakfast, she made her mind up that she was going to leave with Mondo in the morning. As exhausted physically and emotionally as she was, there was no way she could return to Malibu without seeing her sister and knowing that everything was all right.

Could her sister be on Penderville Island? It seemed too simple, but it had made such sense back on Smokin' Joe. It amazed Christy how Mondo had been able to put it all together. He walked into the bed and breakfast after she had spent four days there wondering what to do next, and in an hour he figured out where the girls were and had a plan to follow them. At least it was something to go on. He was so convincing, and it made sense how those numbers lined up. It was almost as if whatever had forced Amy to call her late that night had also compelled her to write those numbers down on the mirror. Something deep inside Amy was reaching out for help.

Christy walked into the kitchen of the bed and breakfast. The owner was mixing a bowl of flour and some other ingredients for breakfast.

"I won't be here for breakfast. I'll be checking out bright and early. I would like to take care of my bill now if I can?"

"Sure, no problem, give me an hour and we can settle up."

Christy walked into her room and started packing.

The bed and breakfast had three rooms upstairs and two downstairs. The downstairs rooms were separated by a large hallway closet. Christy's room was on the left and Marshall's was on the right. Their doors were only ten feet apart from each other.

Marshall was sitting in the living room on the couch, pretty much in the same place as when Christy and Mondo had left an hour ago. Christy could feel his stare on her as she walked into her room.

Marshall had listened to her conversation with the innkeeper, and after five days of sitting around he finally had something to report. He got up off of the couch, flipped open his cell phone and walked outside.

"Yes." It was the same male voice that had called him the first day.

"A lady named Christy, her sister was one of two girls who supposedly disappeared from this bed and breakfast before I got here, well, she's checking out bright and early tomorrow morning. Some guy came to the bed and breakfast this morning and the two of them went outside. I couldn't hear what they were talking about. They came back this afternoon and they went upstairs and looked through the girls' room."

"What did they find?"

"I don't know, but they left in a hurry and went downtown or someplace. Now an hour later she's back and says she's checking out early tomorrow. Thought you'd want to know."

"Did you check out the girls' room?"

"Nope, not causing any trouble."

"Okay, I will call you back shortly."

Marshall walked back into the bed and breakfast, grabbed two beers from the guest refrigerator in the entryway, and walked back to the patio to wait for his call. The call came before he had a chance to open his second beer.

"It's time for you to become creative, Mr. Sandbourn. If Christy leaves, then I want you to know where she is going."

"How the hell can..." He was cut off by the voice on the cell phone.

"If you cannot do this then there really is not much that you can do for us at all. If she leaves you find out where she is going, and you call me back."

The voice on the cell phone hung up without another word.

"Shit," Marshall said out loud.

Marshall popped open the other beer and thought, thought hard. Thought back to all of the dime store detective novels he had ever read. What the hell could he do?

If she walks out the door and meets lover boy then the two of them would be long gone and he would never be able to figure out where she went. Marshall would have to buy some time. Somehow he would have to disrupt her plans, make it so she couldn't leave early tomorrow morning. How? Handcuff her to the bed post, gag her, slip her a mickey and send her to wa-wa land?

She didn't even like him and he knew it. So forget *lets go have a few drinks and tell me what you're planning.*

She said she was leaving bright and early. What the hell time is bright and early? What could he do? Stay up all night waiting for her to leave? Follow her in the morning, sneaking behind bushes as she left? If she called a cab, he could find out where she was going. Suppose she just walked on the ferry and took it back to the mainland. It was impossible for him to figure out where she was going without just asking her, and he knew that was out of the question.

Marshall's mental dialogue continued as he got up off his chair and started walking around the house. He walked past the fountain and down the walkway behind the house. On his left was the owner's cottage, on his right was a door part-way opened that led into a small room. He peeked inside. It was the laundry room. There were two washing machines and two dryers against the far wall; bedding and towels sat folded near by. On the opposite wall in the corner he saw the electric panel. He turned and walked away. He knew how to disrupt her early departure.

Christy spent an hour packing most of her things. A few items she left out for the morning; a change of clothes, some make-up, and her tooth brush. By late afternoon she was ready. She felt herself all wired up, she was chomping at the bit. At least now she had a plan, she knew what her next move was going to be.

She walked downtown and went shopping for a few hours but didn't buy anything. Then she went to the movies and watched some stupid love story and walked home. It was eleven p.m. when she set her alarm clock. She double checked it, then turned the radio on to make sure it worked. Christy slid the bed out from the wall and double checked the plug, making sure it was good and tight. She would be at the dock before six. She set the alarm for five and turned off the light. Five minutes later she got up and checked the alarm again, making sure the alarm was set to a.m. not p.m., making sure the clock was p.m. Satisfied, she turned off the lights once again, rolled over and went to sleep. She didn't wake up until after eight.

Marshall spent an equally unproductive day. He wandered through the two book stores in town, spent an hour at each looking at detective novels, then walked down to the marina and strolled around the boats. He had a great dinner and was home by ten. He heard Christy come home, heard her scurrying around in her room, and then quiet.

Marshall had a plan. He set his own portable travel alarm clock for four-thirty, put it under his pillow, and went to sleep.

At four-thirty his alarm went off. He reached under his pillow and turned it off. He stayed in bed for five minutes listening for any noises. The house was quiet. He got up and dressed, then grabbed his small pocket flashlight and walked out of his room to the back porch, and down the steps. He opened the door to the laundry room, closed it behind him and opened the electric panel. He shined his light on the written columns next to each breaker. The writing was old and he couldn't tell what circuit breakers would turn the power off downstairs in the main house. Finally he held his breath and flipped the main circuit breaker off. The house was without power, all was turned off. Marshall wondered if any alarms would go off, smoke alarms or something, but all remained quiet. He walked back upstairs into his room. The only difference from when he had left was the night lights were out. Otherwise it all felt the same. He took his clothes off and climbed back in bed. He was proud of himself.

"Wake up early now, Christy," he thought.

Christy woke with a start. She knew it was late. She rolled over and looked at the clock. Nothing, no time, no blinking lights, nothing. She jumped out of bed and opened the blinds. She didn't know exactly what time it was but it sure was after six a.m.

She threw her clothes on and rushed out into the dining room just as the owner was rushing up the back stairs.

"Oh, I'm so sorry, the power went out last night, I don't know what happened, it's never..."

She looked at Christy standing there.

"You were leaving early this morning. I'm so sorry. I don't know what happened."

Christy pulled a chair from the table and sat down. The wind-up ceramic clock on the wall said eight-fifteen.

"Let me get some coffee going. I am so sorry, this has never happened before. We must have blown a circuit or something, I'll go check."

The innkeeper walked back out the door and in a minute the stove started flashing, the microwave started beeping, power was restored.

Christy's heart sank. Now what?

"The main circuit breaker tripped," the innkeeper said as she slammed the back door behind her and walked into the kitchen.

"I've had this house for eight years and that has never happened. I'm so sorry if this goofed up your plans. What are you going to do?"

Christy was thinking the same exact thing. What could she do? Mondo was gone by now. No doubt about it.

"Coffee would be good," Christy said.

The two of them sat there waiting for the coffee. After it was poured the innkeeper sat down at the table next to Christy.

"I don't know what your plans are. Everything is so crazy since those girls left. Please feel free to use my phone long distance, I don't care, if I can help let me know."

Christy's heart was crushed. After four days of doing nothing, waiting, looking, searching for some sign of what to do next, in walks Mondo, and suddenly it's all there, the next step. It was the right next step and she knew it. How could the power go off? It wasn't right, it made no sense. If this hadn't happened in eight years then it sure didn't happen last night on its own. Somebody switched the power off. She knew it was either the innkeeper or Marshall; it didn't really matter that much at the moment. What mattered was that Mondo was gone. She didn't know what to do.

Marshall lay in bed smirking to himself. He could hear their conversation through the walls.

After her second cup of coffee Christy got up and walked into the entry way, sat down at the desk, and pulled out the phone book.

"Island Air, one moment please."

Christy felt so impatient, just talk to me, but she knew that it made no sense. Whatever her next move she had plenty of time.

"Hello, may I help you?"

"Yes, I want to fly to Penderville Island."

A pause.

"Where's that?"

"Its up north somewhere, someplace in British Columbia, I'm not sure exactly."

"One moment please."

A few minutes later Island Air returned to the line.

"We don't fly there direct. The best we can offer you is a flight to Campbell River. From there you can take a ferry if they have one or charter a boat. Sorry."

Christy wasn't sure what to say.

"We have two flights a day to Campbell River," Island Air continued. "One has already left and the other leaves at three-thirty, arriving Campbell River at four forty- five."

"Okay, I'll book it."

Christy gave her all her information, credit card number, yes she had a passport.

Christy hung up. She was booked. She had a plan. Problem was, it was so damn thin.

CHAPTER 16

Things were starting to come undone around the compound, as both Edwin and Mr. Chein had foreseen. The second day the girls were there, all was fine, both were still so captivated by Edwin. Neither girl questioned being on the island or the boat trip. No thought was given to family and friends or loved ones they had left behind.

By the third day, both were feeling confused, Amy more so. Thoughts of Mondo were entering her mind. She knew this man was so special to her, she could picture his face, but she could feel no emotion for him. Her feelings were numb and she knew this was wrong.

Isabella was struggling with her emotions as well. She remembered her dad and the way they parted the last time they saw each other. She felt bad and knew she should call him; she also thought about Johnny at the Whale Research Center. When she thought about the joy that she had felt there, a flood of feelings came back to her, her mind suddenly recalling so much all at once. She walked out to the living room, where Amy was sitting on the couch reading a book.

Amy looked up as Isabella very slightly waved her index finger her way. Amy got up and followed Isabella outside.

"What is going on?" Isabella asked. She couldn't think of any way else to say it.

Amy knew what she meant.

They walked over to the pond and sat down beside it.

"Amy, what are we doing here?"

"Isabella, I am wondering the same thing. Why did we come here with Edwin?"

"I don't know."

"Do you think we can leave?" Isabella asked.

Amy said nothing. Both girls were sitting there with their thoughts, trying to remember back to when this all started, trying to remember why they had followed Edwin. There were no answers for them. Neither could recall what had made them do what they did.

Amy looked over the compound, as if seeing it for the first time. The gate had startled her, then she saw the fence. There was no way out except through the gate.

"Look around, Isabella, we are prisoners. See the fence?" She pointed it out.

"God, this can't be happening."

"It is."

"What does he want?" Isabella asked.

Neither girl could answer. They sat there for an hour mostly in silence, trying to take it all in, both wondering what this could possibly be about. Sometimes one of them would say something, mostly short words of comfort to help support the other. In that hour they became closer than if they were born sisters. Both girls knew that they were in trouble and that Edwin had no intention of letting them go.

"Is he a sex pervert, are we his sex slaves?" Amy asked.

"No, I don't think so. I told him the day we arrived, when he came to see me in my room that I wanted to make love to him. He kissed me and just flooded my senses with passion, I never felt such desire before, I wanted him so much, he told me to wait, that the time wasn't right. God, I can't believe I felt like that," Isabella confessed.

"I felt the same way. He could have seduced me any time from when we first met, I would have willingly given myself to him," Amy replied.

"We have to stay together. I have no idea what this is about, Isabella, but I promise you, I am here for you. We are stronger as two than as one. I have a feeling we will soon be having a very terrifying conversation with Edwin."

Edwin and Mr. Chein were upstairs in the communications room. They were listening to every word the girls were saying. Miniature microphones were placed throughout the compound and the house. Each girls' room had a microphone and one small camera. Nothing was going to be missed.

"I think it is time for the first of many conversations with these young women. I tried to tell them their feelings for me would change. It was so nice to be so loved by them both."

"We have the other problem to consider as well, Edwin."

"Yes, I know. First, I must congratulate you on your insight regarding the bed and breakfast. I would never have thought they would be able to trace the girls there. I still have no idea how they did it. It was something that I did not forsee."

"At least we can track what is going on. We know that Amy's sister arrived there only to be followed by some guy a few days later. That is a complication that is too big to be ignored. Also we must assume that something was found in the girls' room that led Christy to leave the bed and breakfast. I do believe we will find out her destination soon. Edwin, we must also assume that the location of our island could be compromised."

"The girls were under my control. I am certain that both girls were not capable of reaching out. I knew better than to stay away so long, but certain things could not be rushed."

"I know, Edwin. We must keep our surveillance up. If others somehow find this island we must be prepared to make them disappear."

"We could always keep Christy, make it three girls. I think they used to call that a harem."

Mr. Chein smiled and shook his head.

"Edwin, I cannot share the sense of humor that you have."

"Right, I feel at the moment that two girls is one too many. Maybe, Mr. Chein, I was foolish to not listen to your words more carefully. I think I will go have a talk with my girls."

"Better you than me, Edwin," Mr. Chein replied.

Edwin walked downstairs and outside. He watched as the girls seemed to freeze in mid-sentence when they saw him walk out the front door. He could sense their panic when he walked over to them and sat down beside them.

"My dear, dear ladies, have you both forgotten how much we care for each other?"

Neither said a word.

Edwin shook his head.

"I am heart-broken that you have changed your feelings towards me. I know you both are afraid. Do you each remember me telling you the day we arrived, that you are safe here? Do you remember me telling both of you that we will be spending a long time here?"

"Why, Edwin?" Amy asked, the words getting choked in her throat.

"Why, Amy, because there is so much that neither of you know. So much that you are helpless to control. You have been destined to be mine for much longer than you could possibly guess; before you were born you both were destined to be mine."

Neither girl could speak. What madness was Edwin saying? Both of them looked at each other, then glanced at Edwin trying to make some sense of what he was saying.

"Edwin, I just want to leave," Isabella said, her voice cracking as she spoke.

"My dear Isabella, Amy too, I want so to please you both. I would give you almost anything that you ask for, but unfortunately, your freedom is not something that I can give. Let me assure you we will be here for a very long time. You both will grow to trust me, with your own minds, not with my help. You will grow to need and depend on me. We, ladies, are a family created in the heavens. We will have dinner tonight at seven. I have taken the liberty of having something special laid out for you to wear. I know you will think this all rather silly, but please wear what you find on your bed, and I will tell you why we are here. I would ask you both to trust me, but I believe that we are past that."

He stood, giving them both a long smile, then turned and walked back into the house.

The two sat by the pond the rest of the afternoon. Neither felt like returning to their rooms. The house, the whole compound had suddenly turned into a prison. Somehow sitting outside made them both feel better.

Finally the chill of the evening drove the girls inside. Neither Edwin or Mr. Chein could be seen. Each of them walked into her room to find a luxurious long gown laid on her bed, long white gloves and satin shoes as well. Laid across each gown was a beautiful long pearl necklace. Both girls ran back out into the hallway to find the other, laughing at the ridiculous gown that they each had to wear. They walked into Amy's room.

"This is right out of the 1920s. Look at this, it's made for a princess," Amy said as she held the gown up to her. It was exquisite. The material felt like silk. Both knew that these gowns were worth thousands.

"He's crazy," Isabella said.

"He is, but I think we should wear these and I think we should play along. For one thing we have no choice at the moment, but I don't think he means to harm us. I felt that from the first moment I ever met him. Let's play along. If what he wants is proper ladies to join him for dinner, then I think we should oblige."

"God, Amy, I don't think I can. He's nuts, he has kidnapped us, brought us to his island, and says we were destined to be a family before we were born."

"What else can we do, Isabella?"

Both girls decided the best course of action was to give Edwin what he wanted. They stayed in Amy's room helping each other dress. Neither wanted to be alone. They could hear noise coming from the kitchen and soon the house had a wonderful aroma to it. They both admired themselves dressed as they were. Each looked so beautiful, they felt like princesses.

"Did you ever see the Bride of Frankenstein?" Isabella laughed.

"I feel like her," Amy replied.

At seven o'clock they walked out of their rooms into the dining room. The lights were turned down low. A soft Bach concerto played, filling the room with music. The table was ablaze with candles all in a large candelabra.

Edwin was standing looking out the window, watching the sun set. He turned and looked at them, bowed and smiled. Edwin was dressed just as wonderfully as the girls were. He had a tuxedo jacket on, a white billowing shirt open part-way down his chest, dark slacks and polished dark shoes, his entire demeanor that of royalty.

Amy felt like she had entered a mad hatter's ball.

"I am enchanted," he said.

He walked over and took Amy by the hand. He brought her hand up to his lips, kissed it so gently, then led her to a seat at the table. Isabella stood frozen. After seating Amy, Edwin turned, walked up to Isabella and kissed her hand, then led her to another seat at the table. Then Edwin walked to the head of the table and sat down.

"Ladies, I know you feel so confused and fearful right now, but please, just for this evening, if possible, might we enjoy each others company as we have in the past? I am so enchanted by both of you. Please, I know I have promised you that tonight I will tell you more of what we all are doing here and I will, but first."

He rang a small silver bell not two inches high sitting on the table at his right hand. Mr. Chein appeared from the kitchen with a bottle of wine. Silently he poured each glass full, then departed. Amy and Isabella almost burst into laughter but both were too afraid.

"I know you will find this difficult to believe, but I am at a loss for words at the moment. Your beauty has captivated me. Shall we toast to beauty?"

They all raised their glasses and toasted. Soon Mr. Chein brought dinner out and he kept the wine flowing. A fire roared in the fireplace, the soft music filling the room. Each girl felt this was the most romantic setting they had ever been in. The terrifying part was that they were sharing it with Edwin.

The food was delicious. Mr. Chein brought out course after course. Both girls were watching their alcohol intake; neither wanted to lose control. Edwin did most of the talking. He was such a gentleman. He told them about his travels around the world. Much of it didn't make sense to the girls. His dates were all wrong. He would talk about the Queen and about England and his years before the war as a young man. He seemed to forget what decade he was living in.

It was wonderful to listen to Edwin speak, his words, his mannerism from a distant past. Both girls were drawn into the splendor of the evening. Once they had finished dinner Edwin again rang the little bell, and Mr. Chein returned, pushing a small rolling cart, and started clearing the table.

"Shall we go and sit by the fire?" Edwin asked.

"Sure." Both girls were fighting as hard as they could to not get drawn into the magic of the evening. If this night had been shared with any one else, they would have cherished it for the rest of their lives.

They stood and Edwin escorted them to a couch sitting in front of the fireplace, then he took a chair facing the fire. There was an awkward silence for a moment before Edwin spoke.

"Today I told you I would share with you why we are here. I had hoped to have more time to spend with you before we got to this point."

He spun his chair around so that he was now facing both of them.

"I will not tell you all tonight. There is much for you to learn and, unfortunately for you both, much time for you to learn it in. I want you both to know that you are completely safe here. My home, my island, my domain is here for you. I hope you will grow to enjoy it. Are you sure you want me to continue?"

Each girl nodded yes. Both were feeling the sincerity that Edwin was speaking.

"Amy, do you know much about your mother's childhood?" he asked softly.

Amy thought that was a very strange question for the moment.

"I know she was adopted after World War Two and that my mom and her parents came from France."

"Isabella, what about your mother?"

Isabella's heart reacted to Edwin's words regarding her mother. Tears filled up in her eyes, ran down her cheeks.

"I know my mother loved me."

"Oh yes, she did," Edwin replied.

"Did you really know my mother? You told me you did the first time I ever met you, Edwin."

"Isabella, I speak the truth, I knew your mother. There is more, though, that you both need to hear. Isabella, your mother never told you this, but she was adopted as well. I don't know if she was ever told.After the war both of your mothers and their parents came to America from France."

Edwin looked at them both, studied their faces. Each girl knew his next words would be so important.

"Your mothers were sisters. Both were born in the Hospital of Saint Gabriel's in Paris. Amy, your mother was born in 1944; Isabella, your mother was born in 1945."

Both girls sat there aghast, their minds not being able to take it in.

"What I am going to tell you next is beyond reason, beyond what your mind is capable of understanding. Try not to reason with it, just listen. What I tell you is the truth. I will explain later how it all came about.

"The woman who gave birth to both of your mothers was named Agnes, Agnes Hawkins. She was my daughter."

CHAPTER 17

Mondo was up and ready to go by five-thirty. It was another beautiful, crisp, northwest morning. The sun was just starting to break through the low-hanging mist that was suspended in the mountains surrounding Salt Bay Island. It reminded him of a Chinese painting in his favorite restaurant back in Hawaii. The dock was quiet, nobody else stirred. Mondo made coffee, had breakfast and was ready to go by six-fifteen. He hoped that Christy would show up. She reminded him of Amy and he needed that connection with her. After twenty-two days of sailing by himself he was ready for company.

By seven he was wondering what he was waiting for. He still hoped that Christy would come racing down the docks, her long hair flying, and climb aboard.

At seven-thirty, he untied Smokin' Joe from the dock and motored out past the breakwater. He took one last glance back, hoping to see her, but she was nowhere to been seen.

He steered up Humphrey Channel, a mile-wide body of water bordered by high forested mountains, and set his course north.

His first stop would be Mackay Harbor just on the other side of the border. He would have to check into Canada by clearing with Canadian Customs and Immigration. He doubted that whoever took the girls north bothered with such formalities. Mondo settled into a leisurely trip. Mackay Harbor was nine miles north of Salt Bay Island. The currents would be running against him at almost two knots for most of the trip. It would take a few hours.

Untying the dock lines and casting off from land was one of the biggest thrills for him. He found a sense of magic when Smokin' Joe was released from her bonds and he guided her out into the blue. All of the preparations, worries and concerns of shoreside life vanished. What was now important was the moment, the freedom of doing the task at hand. Life was much easier at sea, much less complicated than the real world.

On shore there were just too many things to deal with. Rent, insurance, bills, jobs, what most people considered normal life was bondage to him. His spirit called out for a sense of freedom and adventure, and he found it taking his boat wherever his heart desired.

The motor purred on, pushing Smokin' Joe at an easy six knots. The water was like glass, parting before the bow, and then slowly returning to caress her stern with barely a ripple.

Mondo hoped that the wind would come up. Normally in this area the wind, if there was any, would start in late morning and blow until evening.

Mackay Harbor was plotted into his G.P.S. and he had a paper chart before him in the cockpit. His compass course was 350 degrees, almost due magnetic north. There were no other boats on the water; as far as he could see it was all his. Except for a few houses tucked here and there, it must look as pristine as when the Indians had it all to themselves, he thought.

Soon the mountains of Canada came into better focus. He could see the headland that was the prominent landmass before entering into Mackay Harbor. He had another half hour to go.

Checking in and out of different countries, the legal paperwork that it often took, drove him crazy. If he only had a dollar for every carbon copy he had signed in his life of cruising he would never have to work again. All countries were different, some much easier than others. Mexico was a legal nightmare, with different rules everywhere he went. He remembered in Costa Rica, the customs agent apologizing because he would have to take a three hour bus ride one way to the airport to check into the country. The local customs agent had gotten drunk the night before, crashed the official customs car and was in the hospital, sorry. It was all part of the adventure of cruising, but still at times it stretched him to his limit. In many third world countries it was up to the officials in charge to supplement their meager income by demanding bribes in one form or another. At first this really bothered him. To his way of thinking it was wrong that these officials abused their powers. Only after he realized how poor they were and how rich he appeared to them did he no longer allow himself to be troubled by it. Now he looked at these bribes as gifts; it made it so much easier. He would always have some fishing lures and fishing line to give away. Paper products that were so cheap in America were extremely expensive in the tropics. The greatest gifts that he could give, the ones that would bring tears to many officials' eyes, were clothes for their kids and wives. A Michael Jordan tee shirt was worth more in many parts of the world than cash. Often, after he gave his gifts, he would be invited to the official's home. It amazed him how many family members could live in a two-room house. These people had so little financially, yet at times their life seemed more blessed and richer than most people he knew.

Mondo pulled into Mackay Harbor and up to a small dock reserved for Canadian Customs, jumped off Smokin' Joe and tied her up. He climbed back on board and went to the chart table, grabbed his Federal Documentation papers, his passport and his wallet and walked up to the customs office.

"Good morning, may I help you?" a gray haired woman with a nice smile said.

"Yes, I'd like to check into Canada."

"Fine, please fill out these forms."

She handed Mondo a short stack of papers.

Mondo was busy filling out the pages when she asked.

"Where to, how many people, and for how long?"

"Not sure, just myself, and not sure."

She looked up from her computer screen, studying him for a second, trying to decide if he was a smart ass or cute. She decided that he wasn't a smart ass.

"OK, that's an honest answer," she laughed.

"Cruising permits are good for one hundred and eighty days. After that you need to leave Canada and then check back in again."

After fifteen minutes of paper work, Mondo was finished.

He turned, and opened the door to leave when he heard her say, "Don't get into any trouble, son."

He laughed, looked at her. "Who me?"

As he walked down the ramp and back to Smokin' Joe, he wished that lady had never said that.

Mondo pulled out of Mackay Harbor heading east. He would have to travel for a few miles before he could turn north and head out into the large open waters of the Strait of Georgia. If there was going to be any wind today it would start out there.

He had studied the charts, and knew he would sail or motor for most of the day and try to get the anchor down in Clam Bay, an hour before dark. The bay was halfway to Penderville Island and looked like a well-protected anchorage. Smokin' Joe had been motoring ever since they left Salt Bay Island, but once they turned north a nice fifteen knot breeze started to blow. Mondo steered his boat into the wind and pulled up the mainsail. Once it was set he let the bow fall off the wind and Smokin' Joe heeled gently, then he reached down and pulled the fuel cutoff valve, killing the engine. Silence, the only sound was of wind and waves, the steady hum of the engine was gone. Next he unfurled the head sail and sheeted it in. The wind caught both sails and heeled Smokin' Joe over, then she dug her shoulder into the waves and gained speed. His boat charged her way north, spray flying over the bow, her deck rail inches from the water.

Smokin' Joe was in her element, driving through the swells, heading whereever Mondo drove her. She came to life when the wind filled her sails.

The wind was blowing from the east down the tall snow-capped mountains of the British Columbia Coast Range. Mondo relaxed, taking it all in. Never had he been bored while sailing; scared, nervous, apprehensive, yes, but never bored. The absolute peace and harmony, the joy of it all, filled his senses. He had been sailing the world on Smokin' Joe for the last five years. He still loved it.

It was later than he had hoped when he got the anchor down in Clam Bay. He had fought an adverse current for most of the trip.

The bay was large with a great mud bottom for anchoring. Mondo had to thread his way through a very narrow passage not fifty feet wide between two large cliffs before the bay opened up before him. It would have been very easy to miss if he hadn't studied his charts well beforehand. There were no other cruising boats anchored. If not for a few rustic cabins nestled in among the trees it would have looked like it must have looked a thousand years ago.

Mondo got the anchor down, looked around and made sure he was satisfied. It was now time to unwind. He poured himself a glass of wine, a luxury that he never let himself have when he was underway, and sat back in the cockpit. After finishing his glass of wine he cooked dinner, cleaned up and made ready for an early departure the next morning.

Once he finished the dishes, he climbed out on deck, carrying a detailed chart showing Penderville Island and the surrounding area. He also carried two of his favorite pillows and a wool blanket from down below with him. The air was turning crisp outside, a chill setting in on the evening. The first stars were just beginning to make their way through the heavens. It was going to be a beautiful night.

Mondo flipped on the outside cabin light, lay back on his pillows, wrapped himself in the blanket, and spread his chart out before him. This was his destination. What he would find there he had no idea. One part of him hoped that the girls wouldn't be there, wouldn't have been kidnapped and whisked away by some mind-controlling madman. Then if they weren't there, he reasoned, he would have no idea what to do next. It seemed to him that the lesser of two evils was to find the girls on Penderville Island.

Penderville Island was shaped like a pair of lungs. It was divided into East and West Penderville. If not for a thin, mile-wide landmass at its northern end it would be two parallel islands.

The two sides of the island were separated from each other by Penderville Sound, a body of water over a mile wide. The island looked steep on the charts, the shoreline running deep into the surrounding waters. He could see one bay on East Penderville that could be a good anchorage, but according to the charts it was filled up by a fish farm. All of West Penderville looked too deep to anchor.

The island was located at the northern end of the Strait of Georgia. The deep, wide-open waters of the Straits turned into a maze of islands and waterways, as if the hand of God had thrown mountain tops into the sea to land wherever they fell. This was a wilderness. The charts showed no roads or power line crossings, no docks, hardly any signs of civilization. The nearest town was Campbell River, and it was over twenty miles away. Mondo felt a chill run up his spine as he studied the charts. If someone wanted to disappear, this was sure a great area to do it in.

CHAPTER 18

Christy checked out of her room and put her things in the entry way of the bed and breakfast. She brought only two small carry on bags. She had packed in haste, thinking she would be gone from Malibu only for a few days. Now she wished she had brought more. She thought it should have been so easy. Fly up here, find Amy, discover what was going on with Edwin, tell him to go to hell if she had to, and fly back the next day with her sister. It sure didn't work out that way.

Christy called the local taxi cab company, arranging a ride to the airport for that afternoon. Once that was taken care of she walked out of the bed and breakfast and walked downtown. She was heading for the docks. Mondo would be gone by now, but there was no place else she could think of to go. Even if Mondo had waited for her, he wouldn't have waited this long. He probably thought she was on her way back to Malibu. She walked down to the marina and down to the slip that Smokin' Joe had been tied up to. It was empty. Her heart turned sad, then angry; she tried to push the anger away but it had nowhere to go. Who had turned the power off? Somebody had deliberately sabotaged her plan to meet Mondo. She knew it had to be Marshall. He just didn't fit into the whole picture. He certainly wasn't a tourist. Was he at the bed and breakfast as a spy for Edwin? She hoped that she would never have to find out. She hoped never to meet Marshall Sandbourn again.

Christy left the vacant slip and walked back up town, feeling empty and lost.

There was no place that she wanted to go, she was sick of Salt Bay Village, sick of the confusion and fear that she had felt since she arrived. At least now she had a plan and an airplane ticket. She would go to Campbell River and see what she could find out. Hopefully, she could meet Mondo at Penderville Island in a few days.

Marshall had coffee and a small roll for breakfast. So far so good, his next move was formulating in his mind. He had bought some time, now he would hang around and find out where she was heading. With lover boy out of the way he might even be able to get her to trust him. Stupid woman! Still, suppose she would, maybe together they could rescue the girls, unless that stupid bastard on the other end of his cell phone had a different idea.

Marshall walked into the entry way and saw Christy's bags. He took out a small note book and wrote down her address, copying it from the airline baggage tags. This might come in handy someday, he thought. He had the hots for Christy. It didn't matter much how she felt, if she liked him, great, but if not —oh well, he could still have fun with her.

He couldn't sit still. He was too wired from his overnight ordeal. He felt great about himself, and how he had been able to make Christy miss her early morning rendezvous. Maybe he really was cut out for this kind of stuff after all. Marshall found the detective novel that he was reading, plopped himself down on the couch and waited for Christy to show up.

Christy arrived back at the bed and breakfast at two. The taxi arrived at two-thirty and took her to the airport. She didn't even say goodbye to Marshall. He was sitting there on that damn couch reading another one of his damn novels, staring at her the whole time she was getting ready to leave. God, that guy gave her the creeps.

Marshall dialed the cab company a little after three.

"Hello, this is Michael James." He could have used his real name, but he felt better using an alias.

"A good friend of mine was just picked up at the Baker Street Bed and Breakfast. She left some papers in my room. I need to get them back to her. Her name is Christy Wilson. Can you contact the driver?"

"One moment, sir, while I put you on hold."

Marshall sat at the desk drumming his fingers, feeling his excitement growing.

The operator came back on the line.

"She is at the airport. She has a three-thirty flight on Island Air. You might still be able to get there in time. Should I send a cab for you?"

"No thanks, I'll drive. Thank you."

He hung up.

At three-forty-five Marshall called the airport.

"Island Air."

"Hi, my girlfriend Christy Wilson left some important papers with me by accident. I need to get them to her. Is she still at the airport?"

"I'm sorry sir, her flight has already departed."

"Damn, oh sorry, this is really important. Where was she going?"

"Her flight ends in Campbell River, sir."

"When is your next flight there?"

"Tomorrow morning. It leaves at eight a.m."

"Good, I want to book a ticket."

Marshall hung up. He walked outside, flipped his cell phone on and called the number.

"Yes, Marshall."

There was no warmth in this guy's voice. He was really irritating Marshall.

"Okay, here's what's going on. Christy left a half hour ago flying north up to Canada. She's landing at Campbell River, from there I don't know where she is heading, but at least we know she's going to Campbell River."

There was a long pause on the other end of the cell phone. Marshall continued.

"I have an eight a.m. flight up there tomorrow morning, thought I'd see what she is up to, unless you don't want me to do that."

"That's fine, Marshall, good work, I'll be in touch."

Marshall hung up, put the cell phone back in his pocket and walked downtown.

He was getting sick of this cute little town. He had seen it all the first day. There was nothing for him to do. He wandered around looking at tourists and finally made his way into the main book store on the island. He spent another hour sitting in the small reading room, glancing through a pile of detective novels. None of them grabbed him. He was doing the stuff that these books were about. Maybe it was time for him to write his own damn novel.

Christy arrived in Campbell River on time. She gathered her few bags and called a cab. Twenty minutes later she was checked into her room at the Harbor View Bed and Breakfast. She had asked the cab driver to bring her to a nice bed and breakfast that overlooked the harbor. She told him that she liked boats, but what she really wanted was a room with a view in case Smokin' Joe arrived.

After Christy got herself situated she started walking along the waterfront. There were a few restaurants, a couple of micro brew pubs and a few fishing charter companies. This town didn't have the huge tourist influx that Salt Bay Village had, and it showed.

Christy walked into the first fishing charter company that she came to. An older gray-haired, weather-beaten fisherman was sitting behind the desk playing with a VHF marine radio. He saw Christy enter, and signed off from whoever he was talking to.

"Hello there, can I help you?"

"Yes, I'm interested in going to Penderville Island."

The old man changed his look when she mentioned the name of the island. He stared at her a moment longer than was polite and Christy suddenly felt very uncomfortable.

"Why do you want to go there?" he asked.

There was no way Christy was even going to start trying to explain what brought her to Campbell River and her interest in Penderville Island.

"That's not really your concern."

She tried to be nice when she said it but it came out harsh. She didn't know what else to say.

"Well, lady, you're right. That's none of my damn business. But Penderville Island, it's not a place people normally go. As a matter of fact, since the island sold a while ago, nobody goes there."

"Why?"

"Why don't people go there?" The old man shook his head, scratched his beard as if he didn't really want to get into it as well. "Because they're not welcome, how's that?"

"I want to see it. Do you want to take me there?"

"Listen, lady, I sure don't know why you want to go to Penderville Island, but I'm gonna tell you something. There ain't nothing but trouble on that island."

Christy glanced around the small shop. There were lots of fishing supplies and pictures plastered on the walls of happy smiling faces holding trophy-size fish.

"You take people out fishing?"

The old man shook his head; he knew where she was going with this. "You don't look like the fishing type, my dear."

"I'm not, but that doesn't matter. I want to see Penderville Island. Do you want to take me there? We can always go fishing along the way if it makes you feel better."

"Nothing's gonna make me feel better about Penderville Island. Why don't I take you to Jones Island, Jackals Bay, South Point? Lady, there are about a thousand places better than Penderville that I can take you. Why, you can't even go ashore on that damn island."

Christy was at a loss. This guy knew what he was talking about, he was trying everything that he could to change her mind. Christy could feel his apprehension, she could see it written all over his face.

"Listen sir," she said. "I need to see Penderville Island, I just need to drive by and look at it. How much would you charge me for that?"

The old man was getting curious, but he was still scared to death of Penderville Island.

"My rate is three hundred dollars a day." He figured that would scare her off. His normal charter rate was thirty-five dollars a person with a two person minimum.

"Okay, great."

"Jesus, lady, there ain't no stopping you, is there?"

"Sorry, where is Penderville Island?"

The fisherman walked out from behind the counter, over to a wall map by the front door and pointed it out. Christy followed him over and studied the map. Could her sister really be there? She didn't know whether to hope she was or to hope she wasn't. The way this guy tried to make her change her mind made Christy feel very uncomfortable.

"Here's Campbell River," he said as he pointed to the map.

"Here's Penderville Island, it's about eighteen miles from here. Should take us about two to three hours to get there depending on the currents. You really want to go?"

"More than you could ever guess."

"All right, be here at nine tomorrow morning, we'll take a look at Penderville Island for you."

"Thanks, do you want me to pay now?"

Nobody ever paid a day in advance.

He walked back behind the counter and ran her credit card, all the while wondering what in the hell this woman was up to.

Christy left the fishing charter company and started walking down towards the docks.

She knew she was pushing things by going out there tomorrow. She knew Mondo couldn't get there until the next day at the very earliest, but still she had to see Penderville Island.

Christy walked along the busy docks. Fishermen were scurrying all over, and more than a few whistles were directed her way. Large fishing boats, many with big rust streaks running down their sides, were docked here. This was such a different place than Salt Bay Village. Here boats had names like *Lucky Lucy* or *Fish Killer* or *Arctic Storm*. She wandered along not really thinking of much, just letting her mind ramble on, trying to get a picture of the whole situation that she found herself in.

Here she was in a different country, in a little fishing town she had never even heard of until today, looking for her lost sister on an island that scared the hell out of at least one local, and would probably scare the hell out of most of these men on the docks.

As she wandered along the waterfront, she realized that except for the boat ride tomorrow she didn't have a clue what her next plan was going to be. If she couldn't find Mondo she didn't know what the hell she was going to do.

CHAPTER 19

Marshall was at the airport early the next morning. By seven-thirty he was all checked in and ready to go. He had done a little homework yesterday afternoon about Campbell River. He found it mentioned in a few guide books about fishing in British Columbia. The town was smaller than Salt Bay Village. Good, he thought, Christy won't be too hard to find.

He arrived in Campbell River on time, departed the airport by nine and had the taxi drop him off at the Blue Dolphin, a local breakfast hangout. It was crowded. Marshall ordered coffee and breakfast. A dense cloud of cigarette smoke hung in the air, while he ate.

After breakfast Marshall walked to a pay phone and looked up taxi cabs.

"Cutch cab service."

"Hi, my fiancée flew into Campbell River yesterday around four-fifteen. Christy Wilson. Did you pick her up?"

He could hear the person on the other line call to someone else.

"Did you have a pick up at the airport yesterday around four?"

"No, sorry not us."

Same response at the second company. The third and last company answered the phone. "South Beach Taxi." He explained that he was looking for his fiancée who had arrived yesterday afternoon, had they picked her up?

"Sir, all I can tell you is we did have a pick up yesterday afternoon at the airport."

"Great, where did you drop her off? I want to send a present."

"Sorry, sir, that information is private."

Marshall started to get mad. Don't give me this shit, he thought.

"Okay, sure, I understand, but it's really important, and I can understand your point of view. I'm calling from New York City, can't really cause much trouble from here. How about this? Just give me the place's phone number, you're not revealing much, then I can go from there."

"Well, I..."

"It's really important to me, please." He cringed at having to be so kiss ass, but this operator could just be dumb enough to go for it.

"One moment." In thirty seconds the woman was back on the line.

"You didn't get this from me, the number is 589-2030."

"Thanks, you saved my engagement, I owe you." He hung up, then dialed the number.

"Harbor View Bed & Breakfast."

"Sorry, called the wrong number."

Marshall walked down to the waterfront, found a luggage storage bin just like in a big city airport, and stashed his carry-on bags. Now he could easily blend in; he was no longer a tourist with his bags, wandering around looking lost.

There was a small circular park at the end of the one and only street that ran through the middle of Campbell River. The park looked out over the water and the distant mountains. Huge trees grew around the edge of the park. It reminded Marshall of a little fort in the woods. He sat down and waited. He was hunting now, just like when he lived in Northern California. The best way to find your prey, he knew, was to sit in one place and let it come to you.

He pulled out his latest detective novel, kicked his shoes off, and started enjoying the day.

Christy was at the fishing charter company at nine. The old man was waiting inside for her. She walked in and closed the door behind her.

"Good morning," she said.

The old man shook his head.

"Was hoping you had changed your mind. I can still refund your money."

"Not a chance."

"Well, let's go, boat's fueled up and I'm as ready as I can be."

They walked out the door, the old man locking it behind them.

"This way," he said.

They walked in silence down to the dock and climbed aboard a small fishing boat. Her name, *Norma Jean,* was painted on the bow. The old man started the engine, then turned and looked at Christy as she sat on the gunnel.

"My name is Jack Basey. My friends call me Captain Jack, and you can call me that if you like," he smiled at her.

"I'm Christy Wilson."

"Yeah, I know, from your credit card."

Captain Jack cast off the lines and they headed out past the breakwater and out into the sound. The motor rumbled on, quieter than Christy had thought it would be. The gulls flocked after them and the sea was a gentle swell. Christy thought that it could be so beautiful if she weren't so afraid of what she would find. Captain Jack seemed nice and Christy could tell he was still trying to figure her out. Trying to figure out why this woman was so damn interested in Penderville Island.

Christy knew the earliest Mondo could arrive was sometime tomorrow. In a way, this trip was a waste of time and money but she couldn't sit in Campbell River and do nothing. She needed to see Penderville Island, and size it up for herself.

They worked their way through narrow passages and around different islands, into a large open waterway, then through narrow little cuts. They motored on. Christy didn't want to talk, she just wanted to take it all in and be left alone with her fears. How could she explain her reasons for going to Penderville Island? Would Captain Jack believe her? Did she believe it?

Captain Jack offered her coffee, which was very good and hit the spot. For most of the trip they traveled in silence.

"Around this bend and we'll see Penderville Island," he finally said.

They rounded the bend and headed up into a wide channel, land on both sides.

"Which side is Penderville Island?"

"Both, this is one island that connects up at the head of the bay."

On her right Christy could see an older house, some run-down docks, and a large group of red floats.

"What's that?"

"That's Sharon Jackman's place. She's been here a long time. She's good people."

That can't be what she was looking for.

"Let's swing over to the other side of the bay." She pointed towards

West Penderville.

"Okay," Captain Jack said, still shaking his head.

Soon a large dock came into view.

"Slow down, please."

"Here, look through these." Captain Jack handed her a pair of binoculars.

Christy could see a new dock with a road leading up to a level parking area. Two large no trespassing signs were hung on a metal gate, which had barbed wire stretched around it where it connected to a fence that surrounded the entire dock area. This was what she had come to find. In that very moment she believed the whole story. Christy knew her sister and Isabella were here against their will, held for what purpose, she had no idea.

"Pull closer, please."

It went against Captain Jack's better judgment but he pulled his boat to within one hundred feet of the dock and put her in neutral.

"Take a good look, Christy, there ain't nothing but bad there."

Christy took it all in, then she slumped down in a chair next to Captain Jack. A wave of despair overcame her. She had hoped beyond hope that Mondo was right, that her sister was here. Now, looking at the dock, noticing the two video cameras that were following their every move, she knew that getting her sister and Isabella out would be impossible.

"We can go," she said weakly.

"Okay."

Captain Jack spun his boat around and headed off, but not before the two video cameras captured them being there. The image of Captain Jack, Christy and the fishing boat were picked up by the high resolution cameras and sent by microwave transmitters across the sound, to a relay that could send the images anywhere within a five hundred mile radius.

After they left Penderville Sound, Captain Jack asked her.

"Want to tell me about it?"

She looked up into his face. He smiled and his eyes held a warmth and honesty that made Christy feel better.

"You wouldn't believe it if I tried."

"Well, I can tell you this much, Christy, I hope you don't have anything to do with West Penderville. There really is evil in this world and right now some of it lives on West Penderville Island."

By two-thirty they had returned to the dock and finished tying up *Norma Jean*. Christy followed Captain Jack up the docks and back to his office.

"Tomorrow a friend of mine is sailing his boat up to Penderville Island. I'd like for you to take me back out there to meet him. Is that possible?"

Captain Jack sat down on his chair behind the counter. He gave Christy a long hard look, trying to size her up. What the hell, he thought, could she be up to?

"All right, you give me an hour's notice. Here's my card, call me, I'll have the boat ready to go."

"Captain Jack, thank you."

Marshall watched the two of them as they walked up the boat ramp from the docks and into the charter office. He put his book down and watched as Christy came out of the office five minutes later, turned to her left and started walking along the waterfront towards him. Then she turned into the Crow's Nest restaurant.

He gave her ten minutes, then followed her into the restaurant. She was sitting on the outside deck overlooking the waterfront. It was busy and most of the tables were full. Good, he thought, too many people for her to make a scene. Her back was towards him as he walked up to her table, pulled out a chair and sat down right in front of her. Her eyes bulged, her mouth dropped, her face turned ashen and before she could say anything he said. "Hello Christy, I've been wanting to talk to you. Mind if I join you?"

Christy was stunned.

Marshall looked over at the waitress.

"I'd like a menu when you get a chance, thank you."

Christy was speechless.

"Listen, Christy, we're here for the same reason and I'm on your side. I'm here to find out what happened to the girls and to get them back. I'm a private detective hired out of San Francisco. I'm a professional, this is my business and I do it well."

He glanced at his menu when it arrived.

"Okay, I know you don't like me, but you don't know me. At the bed and breakfast I had to keep my distance from you, keep you off guard.

I couldn't let you see the nice guy that I am. It's just business and that's how my business is done."

Christy was still too stunned to even think.

"So I know all about the girls, know about your boyfriend. I don't know what he can do but I have connections and I can get stuff done."

He was bullshitting her now, and he knew it, but she looked so defenseless, and it was fun to make shit up on the spot.

"So what's it going to be? You can scream at me, throw your plate of food at me, and storm out of the restaurant," he said, as he thought that would probably be her best move.

"Or we can put aside our differences and work on this thing together?"

He looked back at his menu, looked up at the waitress, ordered a cheese burger and didn't say a word. It was up to Christy now.

"How'd you find me?"

"Look, I told you this is my job and I do it damn well. I'm good, Christy, so what's it going to be, you want some help or not?"

Christy felt so confused she didn't know what to think.

"What do you want from me?"

"Want from you? Nothing. Just let me inside, work with me, together we can get this done. I don't want nothing else and that's it."

Christy played with the food still on her plate, her appetite gone the moment Marshall sat down.

"I went and saw Penderville Island today and it looks really scary. There's cameras, barbed wire, a big dock, it looks all locked up like a fortress or something."

She was just about to tell him that Mondo was on his way but decided to hold that piece of information back.

"Captain Jack said that evil lived on Penderville Island. I could see that it scared him."

"Shit, evil, these people around here. Listen, why don't I get a room at the Harbor View Bed and Breakfast and we can sit down and work out a plan. I have people that I can call and bring into this situation."

"You know where I'm staying?"

"God, you're dumb. I told you I'm good at this, this is what I do. What room are you in?"

"Garden room."

"Good, let me finish my lunch. I'll see you in an hour or so."

Christy got up, walked to the register, paid her bill, and headed back to her room. Her mind was spinning out of control. She would play Marshall as best as she could. She knew her hope rested on Mondo. Marshall was just too much of an asshole to be trusted.

Marshall finished his lunch and thought back to the last ten minutes. It had gone better then he had hoped. She didn't like him or trust him, he could tell; at least she wasn't that dumb. But she had nowhere else to go and he knew it. He was right where he wanted to be. He flipped out his cell phone and punched in the number.

"Yes, Marshall."

"I'm in Campbell River, just finished having lunch with Christy Wilson. She likes me, I can tell. She went out to Penderville Island today on a fishing boat and it shook her up, whatever she saw out there. How do you want me to handle this? It's your call."

"Enjoy your time with her. I'll call you back."

Marshall had decided when this was all over, he hoped he could meet the guy on the other end of his cell phone. He wanted to punch his lights out.

He retrieved his bag from the locker and walked up to the Harbor View Bed & Breakfast. He had no trouble booking a room. Marshall flopped on his bed, kicked his shoes off and wondered what his next move should be. If that asshole on the cell phone didn't call him back, then it was his decision to make. He thought about chartering a boat and having a look for himself at Penderville Island. He knew that he had to get there one way or another. He could find some cove or something, go ashore and really find out what was going on. Maybe he'd just rescue the girls while he was there. Why not? He thought. How hard could it be? He wished he had his gun with him. He lay in bed thinking and thinking until he finally fell asleep.

CHAPTER 20

Sharon Jackman was fifth generation Canadian. Four of those generations, dating back to her great-grandfather, were on Penderville Island. The family log cabin was long-gone, replaced with a home built in the early 50s. The homestead still nestled on the only protected bay in Penderville Sound. Her family were survivors, hanging on to a living and lifestyle that was getting harder and harder to maintain. From logging to commercial fishing there seemed to be enough, but never extra.

With no brother, the homestead had fallen to her and her husband, John Jackman. John was a good guy. They had met at the University in Vancouver. They became friends, then lovers, and married after graduating. There was no place that Sharon was going to live but Penderville Island and she told him that. John was a city boy from Toronto. He gave it his best try but after two years he couldn't handle the remoteness of Penderville Island any more. Their marriage broke up and now Sharon lived there by herself, just her and her fish.

Sharon farmed fish. Aquaculture, it's called. It had become big business and some people were making lots of money. Sharon wasn't, but she was able to keep the family homestead and that was the most important thing to her in the world. The British Columbia government had offered great financial incentives for Aquaculture. They praised the future of it, called it the new renewable resource, just grow them and eat them. Sounded simple. Sharon hated it. After three years she knew what was happening. She sure as hell wouldn't eat her fish, not with all the poisons that she had to feed them.

There wasn't much she could do about it all. At least she could live on Penderville Island, things weren't too bad. That is until last year. The rumors proved to be true. Somebody bought all of West Penderville Island. Sharon didn't even know it was for sale. The sale was hushed up until it was finalized. No names given, no previous address for the new owners. Nobody even knew who the new owners were. But Sharon knew one thing, they weren't good. A few months after the sale, a crew of workers appeared and built a ten foot high fence along the entire narrow mile-long corridor that separated West and East Penderville. A steel cyclone fence with one gate, and barbed wire strung along the top of the entire fence. The fence was built massively strong; it was no ordinary country fence. When she saw the strands of razor sharp barbed wire atop the fence she broke down in tears. Was that fence built to keep people in or out? She had no idea, but she knew in her heart that evil had moved next door.

She watched as they built a big dock and a landing area. Soon trucks, people, and building materials swarmed the island. One road was punched in from the landing area over the low-lying hills and into the island. Hustle bustle and people everywhere. Not once did anybody come over to introduce themselves. Not once did the work boats swing by for a better look, maybe a wave, anything. She felt invaded and she knew trouble was coming.

Nothing could soothe her fears. She hoped that maybe the new owner was some wealthy recluse that wanted a hideaway. Sharon tried to convince herself that everything was all right, but when she thought about that mile long fence with razor sharp barbed wire, she realized that she knew all she needed to know. Whoever bought West Penderville Island had secrets and those secrets were not going to leave that island, ever.

The construction was over in six months, then nothing. Occasionally she would see a boat pull up, one that she didn't recognize. Sometimes it would stay for days, sometimes for hours. Still no contact. She thought of going over there and seeing for herself what it was all about, but fear stopped her.

Don't mess with evil, she thought.

Somehow she knew that, even when no one was on the island, nothing escaped the owners. There were large *No trespassing* signs on the dock with a large metal gate and more barbed wire, more *trespassers beware* signs, one sign even said *caution, fence and gate electrified*. It was a prison. Sharon couldn't tell for whom, or why, but she knew it was a prison.

Life was best for Sharon when she didn't think about her new neighbors. She just continued on as her family had for over eighty-five years, making a living and being thankful that she could still live here.

Mondo had two good days of sailing. The wind held and it was late afternoon when he pulled into Penderville Sound. He knew from looking at the charts that finding a shallow anchorage was going to be hard. The chart showed a bay with an aquaculture farm in it, no anchoring there. He pulled the sails down and turned the motor on. The mountains reached to the sky and seemed to plunge straight into the sea. He studied the shore line as he motored up the sound. He saw a few small nooks that he might be able to back into and tie a line ashore but the depth was too great. He was surprised to see a large dock on West Penderville Island. It wasn't on any of the charts. He swung Smokin' Joe across the channel for a better look. He realized instantly that this was what he was looking for. He also knew that he couldn't tie up at the dock. He doubted he would last five minutes before something bad would start to happen.

The bay ended about another mile up the sound. It should have had an anchorage there but the charts showed depths of one hundred and thirty-five feet just off the shore. Mondo was starting to worry. It would be dark soon and he had better get the anchor down before then. He circled up to the end of the Penderville Sound, swung around and headed back down the channel. Nowhere could he find a cove to anchor in.

The aquaculture farm appeared on his port side. A cute old house with a few rundown outbuildings made up the landscape of the fish farm. He could see large pens outlined by red buoys that floated just above the surface. These floats were about twenty-five feet apart and ran in a row for about a hundred feet. Mondo could make out six rows of these pens. There was a dock to the left of the house with a few small boats tied up to it.

He swung in closer for a better look. He couldn't see anybody around but he had a feeling that someone was watching him. There weren't any *no trespassing* signs on the dock, and he thought about trying to tie up there, but he continued on.

At the south end of the bay away from the house and the floats was a small cove that he would try to anchor in. If he could get the main anchor down he might be able to back close to shore, row his dinghy to land, and tie a stern line to a tree. He slowed the boat down, untied the rowing dinghy from the cabin top and placed it overboard tied up tight behind Smokin' Joe. Next he pulled out two hundred feet of line and uncoiled it in the cockpit.

Slowly he made for the south end of the cove; the depth read 125 feet as he got closer. It seemed to stay right there, then slowly started to recede, 100 feet, 90, 80, 65. The problem was he was getting too close to shore. He slowed Smokin' Joe down even more and swung her around so that he was backing toward land, then he ran to the bow. He had a feeling that there wasn't going to be a second to spare in this anchoring attempt. In his mind he went over the procedure and it came to pass just as he thought it would. About fifty feet from shore the bottom raised up to forty-five feet. He dropped his bow anchor as his boat continued backing towards land. When he had played out eighty-five feet of chain, he snubbed it off and ran back to the cockpit. The weight of the chain dragging from the bow caused Smokin' Joe to slow down. He tied off one end of the two-hundred-foot rope to a stern cleat, then threw the rest in his dinghy and, while Smokin' Joe was still slowly backing towards land, jumped in the row boat. He dug hard at the oars, reached the shore, scrambled over the wet slippery rocks and threw the line around a large Madrona tree some ten feet back from the water, then he raced back to his boat. By now his boat had stopped her backwards movement but was starting to swing sideways in the current. Mondo threw the remainder of the line back into the cockpit and tied it off to the stern cleat. Smokin' Joe was suspended between her bow anchor and the line ashore. She was good. As long as a strong wind didn't blow, Smokin' Joe could stay where she was for a while.

The banging on the hull came early. Deliberate, not a timid knock, but three sharp bangs. He had expected it. He knew he was too close to the fish farm. Mondo slid out of his bunk, threw a shirt on, opened the hatch and peered out. Sharon Jackman was there. Mondo glanced at his clock on the bulkhead. Seven-fifteen in the morning.

"Good morning," Mondo said.

"What are you doing?" Direct and to the point.

"Trying to wake up."

"No, buddy, I mean what are you doing anchoring in my cove?"

Mondo paused, not sure what to say.

Sharon stood in a small aluminum workboat, one strong hand on Smokin' Joe's rail, the other on her hip.

A fighting posture, Mondo thought.

"This is private property, and I don't like trespassers."

Mondo didn't know what to say. He thought of telling her to come back later but didn't think that would work.

"Well, if I told you the truth it would take too much of your time, and I haven't even had a cup of coffee yet, and... " he paused. "I don't know your name. Mine is Mondo."

"Sharon Jackman." No warmth.

"Well, Sharon, what would work really well for me would be to go back to bed, but I doubt that will happen, so how about I make myself some coffee, get some clothes on and in twenty minutes I'll pull my dinghy up to your dock and tell you why I am here."

"You gonna bullshit me, Mr. Mondo?"

"Sharon, I don't bullshit." It was a statement, a fact.

Sharon felt that he meant it.

"Okay, Mr. Mondo, you come up to the dock. I'll meet you there and we can have our little chat."

She pushed off from Smokin' Joe, kicked the outboard in gear and headed for home.

Mondo went back down below, started the stove, and made himself a cup of coffee.

It was another beautiful Northwest morning. It was so quiet here. In all of his travels he had never found an area as peaceful, serene, and beautiful as the Pacific Northwest.

He wondered what to tell Sharon.

How about, I'm here because my girlfriend and another lady were kidnapped from Salt Bay Island, smuggled into Canada and are being held hostage on West Penderville Island by some crazy, mind-controlling madman?

He wasn't sure if he could believe it and he knew it was true.

For all he knew Sharon could be the watch keeper for the whole group.

Mondo finished his second cup of coffee and rowed over to the dock. Sharon was there waiting, dressed in a yellow rain slicker and rubber boots.

"Mr. Mondo, follow me up to the porch, we can sit."

He followed a few steps behind. They walked in silence to the front porch. She pulled out a chair for herself and sat down; Mondo followed her lead. They sat looking out over the bay towards West Penderville Island. He could sense that some of her hostility had left.

"Thanks for the anchorage last night. I thought about asking permission but it was getting dark and I needed a place to drop the hook. I went up and down this whole channel and yours was the only anchorage I could find."

"You're the first person to ever anchor there. Pretty good the way you rowed that line ashore, doing it all by yourself."

Mondo knew he was right, somebody was watching him yesterday.

His stare drew him across the sound to West Penderville Island. How to feel her out? He thought. What is her take on all of this?

"Sharon, mind if I ask you how long you have lived here?"

"My whole life, except for the last two years of high school and four years at the University. My great-grandfather homesteaded this bay, and we've been here ever since."

Mondo didn't know what to say. Sure, he thought, just tell her. His mind went on like an actor on stage thinking two sentences ahead of the script, what next?

They both sat there in silence. He knew it was up to him, he could sense Sharon waiting for his story, no bullshit. Finally Mondo just started talking.

"Sharon, what do you know about your neighbors across the bay?"

He watched her face as he said it. She flinched. Most people wouldn't have noticed but Mondo did; her eyebrows raised, her forehead wrinkled, eyes focused, all in a moment, then composure again on her part. He knew he hit a button.

"Why?"

"Because that's why I'm here, and I'm not sure if you want to hear the story, or if you're going to believe it. It might be best for me to just walk back to my dinghy and row home and not get you involved."

Sharon looked into his eyes, and Mondo could see the fear and pain that she couldn't hide.

"Tell me," she said her voice a small flutter.

So he did just that. He told her about Amy and Isabella, how they had disappeared from the bed & breakfast. He told her about the lipstick sign on the mirror, the whole story. He even told her about Christy Wilson and Marshall Sandbourn.

There was silence when he finished. He didn't know what Sharon was going to say but at least he told her the truth, no bullshit.

"There's evil over there, Mr. Mondo."

"What do you know?"

"Not much, but I know evil when I see it. Ever since West Penderville was bought I knew trouble had moved to my front door. They never came around and I never went over there, but a person's heart doesn't lie, and I know that no good is going on over there."

"These two girls would have arrived in the last week. Did you see anyone over there?"

"I can't say that I did, but that doesn't mean they're not over there."

"Sharon, I'm starting to believe this more and more, and now that I'm here, I don't know what to do."

"Well, Mr. Mondo, you feel free to stay anchored where you are for as long as you want."

She stood up. Their meeting was over.

"You just stay here and I hope you find your friends. If you need any help you can count on me."

She turned and walked into the house. Mondo knew he could trust her. He also knew that she was scared to death of whatever was on West Penderville Island.

He rowed back to Smokin' Joe. He needed time to think, he knew that he had to make the next move and he had one chance of getting it right. Any mistake and there would be trouble.

CHAPTER 21

Marshall asked Christy out for dinner after waking up from his nap.

"No thanks," she replied.

"Why not, what's wrong with me?" He asked so innocently, shrugging his shoulders.

They were sitting in the living room of the Harbor View Bed and Breakfast. No other guests were there.

"I don't feel good."

"Bullshit!"

"I've felt like throwing up from the moment you sat down at my table today."

"Oh, well, must have been something you ate."

He got up and walked outside.

That bitch, he thought, *talk about a bad attitude*.

Marshall walked down to the waterfront. All the shops were closed but he continued walking along the docks looking for a boat. He had decided that his next move was to go charter his own boat and head for Penderville Island. That would give him the freedom that he needed. He didn't know what to expect. Just go there, check it out, and see what happens next.

He finished dinner and was back at the bed & breakfast by ten. Christy wasn't around and he didn't feel like being subjected to her bad attitude any more. He set his alarm for eight and crashed.

Christy didn't know what to do, but she knew that Marshall was now part of whatever plan she would come up with. At breakfast she and Marshall and a young couple from Ohio ate together. Christy was glad the couple was there. She would have hated to have it be just her and Marshall. After breakfast, as they were all getting up, Marshall looked at her, made eye contact.

"I'm chartering a boat today, going to do some sight seeing, maybe head out to some of the other islands around here, want to come?"

"Sure, what time?" Not much enthusiasm in her voice.

"In about an hour, meet me at the gate by the head of the dock. Dress warm."

Marshall walked to the waterfront, found the fast, twenty-seven foot boat that he had seen last night and chartered it for the day.

"You know your way around boats?" the owner of the charter company asked him as he filled out the forms.

"Know my way around boats? Shit, I grew up in Florida. I've spent more years around the Keys than Jimmy Buffett."

The boat owner looked at him.

"Well, just remember there's a $500 deposit on your credit card if anything bad happens."

"Don't worry, nothing bad ever happens to me."

He walked to the store just up the block from the docks and bought a six pack of beer. Might as well make it a picnic, he thought. After buying the beer he walked upstairs to the marine store and bought a nautical chart that would get him to Penderville Island and back.

Christy met him at the gate by the docks.

"We're ready to go," he said with a smile.

She followed him down to a candy-apple-red, hot-rod-looking boat.

"Hop in, and fasten your seat belt."

Christy did and a few minutes later they were racing out of the harbor causing at least three people to yell something at them about slow down! Your damn wake! One guy flipped them off. Marshall didn't care. He was out for a joy ride.

They raced along, bouncing over the water. The sun was warming up the day. This would be really nice, Christy thought, if she was with anybody else but Marshall.

"Can you slow this thing down? I can't even see."

"What the hell do you need to see for? Shit," Marshal replied, but he did slow the boat down.

"Okay, here's what we're doing. I want to see Penderville Island and this dock and gate and all that stuff that you told me about. I bought a chart just in case you can't remember how to get there. You know, Christy, you really have a bad attitude about me. You're so, I don't know, you're so hostile."

148

"Sorry, I've got a lot on my mind."

"I guess that's an apology, good. You know we could be good friends, I know it. You could use a boyfriend like me."

He glanced at her, caught her attention.

"I'm an Italian stallion, you know," he said, smiling to himself.

Christy almost threw up.

In the fast boat they reached Penderville Sound within forty-five minutes.

"All right, where is this dock?"

Christy pointed where she remembered the dock to be, and Marshall hit the throttle. In ten minutes they were a hundred yards off the dock, the hot rod boat idling.

"They sure don't want any guests, do they?" Marshall said looking through the binoculars. He could see why Christy had felt the way she did about it. It sure looked locked up. Marshall gave everything a good looking over. The large empty slip, it could hold a seventy-five foot boat he thought, all the no trespassing signs and barbed wire, this wasn't going to be as easy as he had hoped.

"Let's drive along the shore and see what else we can see," he said.

He engaged the throttle and the boat started heading along the shoreline, the video surveillance camera recording their every move.

He brought the boat closer to the shore and they continued to head up the sound. Marshall kept the speed slow; he was enjoying this. He was on his third beer, a beautiful woman by his side, driving his hot-rod boat along a gorgeous shore line. Life is good, he thought.

They came to the head of Penderville Sound, turned around and started their way back. They slowed down again when they got to the dock. By now Marshall was on his fifth beer.

"Maybe I should just park this thing at the dock, and walk up there and see what's going on. What do you think?"

"I don't think they want any guests. Might be better to do it at night, where you could sneak around, play ninja warrior or something," she said, sarcastically.

"Jesus," Marshall said.

They left Penderville Sound, heading back to Campbell River. It was early afternoon. Marshall wasn't driving very fast. He was enjoying himself too much to rush. He was even thinking of anchoring the boat, if they gave him an anchor, and see how far he could get with Miss Christy Wilson.

They entered a narrow channel. Marshall remembered it from when they had come this way earlier. It was about a mile long before it opened up again. He also remembered thinking it wasn't big enough for two large boats to pass through at the same time They were about half way through the channel when suddenly, coming the other way, was a large powerboat, creamy white, about fifty feet long.

"Shit," Marshall said, spilling his last beer as he sat up and got a better grip on the wheel. Marshall pulled his boat over to his right, getting closer to the rocks than he wanted to. He had to make room for this other guy. He slowed the boat down. The other boat was coming up the channel at a good clip.

"Slow down, buddy," Marshall shouted.

The cream-colored power boat pulled over closer to the shore to make more room for the two boats to pass. The large powerboat was sixty feet in front of them and Marshall was just starting to relax. He realized they could pass each other without any problem when suddenly the power boat turned sharply into their path and started heading right for them.

"Shit! What are you doing?" Marshall shouted, as he was taken completely by surprise.

The powerboat was now only thirty feet from crashing right into them. Marshall hit the throttle and spun his boat hard to his left, digging the propeller in, hoping to make a turn inside the narrow channel. The large powerboat was slowing down but still coming straight at them. The opposite shoreline raced in front of him. He couldn't make the turn, he slammed the boat into reverse, the engine still racing, and spun the wheel the other way. He backed his hot-rod boat up, almost ramming the large powerboat then threw his boat in gear. He turned and looked behind him, watching as two men came out onto the front deck, each holding a high-powered rifle. Marshal was terrified. He pushed the throttle all the way forward, spun the wheel hard and headed for where they had just come from. Before he even heard the shots he knew they hit his engine. He threw his head forward and down as fast as he could. His engine coughed, then sputtered. He looked behind him and saw smoke coming from under the engine cover. He glanced at Christy; she was frozen in fear.

The large powerboat was gaining on them, racing closer. It looked like it was going to drive right over them. Marshall pushed the throttle all the way forward, trying to get everything out of it. Their boat was doomed, Marshall's mind was in a panic, the large powerboat now only fifteen feet away from them. They both heard the next two shots, rapid explosions, the sound reverberating off the narrow walls around them. Marshall spun the boat over to his left, hoping to get out of the way. His engine gave a last gasp, then stopped, flames shooting out of the engine cover.

The powerboat had backed off and was now about twenty feet away.

"Jump!" The words weren't even out of Marshall's lips before he jumped overboard, Christy followed moments later.

They came up sputtering, each on different sides of their burning boat. The large powerboat slowly started to make its way towards them. Marshall reached the shore and started to climb out, trying to race up the hill. A bullet smashed into the rocks two feet in front of him. He stopped, turned around and put his hands in the air.

The powerboat pulled alongside Christy and she was hauled up on deck.

"Two choices," a loud speaker from the powerboat said.

"Swim back and climb on board, or die. We have the girl." Marshall jumped in the water and swam back. He had never been this scared, ever.

He was pulled aboard by two large burly men. Neither spoke, just looked at him.

All of Marshall's bravado was gone. He was dripping wet, looking at two of the meanest looking guys he had seen in a long time.

Christy was sitting on the cockpit floor. Shaking and shivering, her hair a tangled wet mess.

"Smart choice," said a voice over the loudspeaker.

Christy was escorted by one of the two men that had just helped her on board. She was brought downstairs to a small cabin. A set of clothes were on the bed.

"There's a shower behind that door," the man said, pointing to the only other door in the cabin.

"Clean yourself up and change into these." He pointed to the bed.

"Just sit here, don't even think of opening this door."

The man turned around and closed the door behind him, locking it.

The powerboat pulled up close to the burning boat. Two crew members jumped aboard with fire extinguishers and raised the engine cover. They had the fire out in a minute. Marshall looked on, freezing, not saying a word. Next a large rope was thrown down to the speed boat and it was tied off behind the larger boat, and then they started up the channel, the power boat towing the still-smoking go-fast boat. Marshall was too terrified to even think of trying to escape. When the two boats came out of the channel into the sound, one of the crew climbed back down to the smoking speedboat, taking a large sledge hammer with him. He smashed two holes into the bottom of the burned out speedboat then climbed back on the large powerboat. Marshall watched as the speedboat slowly sunk without a trace. He knew that they wouldn't find any traces of him, either. He was way in over his head.

A middle-aged Chinese man walked down from the top deck of the powerboat, looking down at where Marshall lay on the deck.

He didn't say a word at first, just stared at him. Marshall was freezing, his teeth chattering, his fingers numb and his heart full of fear.

The Chinese man smiled, then in perfect English, with no hint of an accent, he said, "So, Marshall, we finally meet. You are such a dumb shit."

Marshall recognized the voice instantly.

It was the voice on the other end of his cell phone.

CHAPTER 22

All through breakfast Mondo wondered what he should do next.He knew he had to get to West Penderville Island and see what was there. The best chance for rescuing the girls was under the cover of darkness, but success or failure would depend on what he accomplished today.

He grabbed his backpack, tossed in his binoculars and a small hand-held compass, then threw it over his shoulder. He rowed his dinghy to shore and tied it to an overhanging Madrona branch. Mondo scurried over the rocky shoreline and up a hill until he was one hundred feet inland, then he turned to his left and started walking around the fish farm. The forest was thick, making walking in a straight line difficult. He could have walked along the rocky cliffs but he would have exposed himself to Sharon and to whoever could have been watching from West Penderville Island. He wanted no one to see what he was up to. Mondo took a bearing on his compass and kept walking, the forest hindering his every move.

From yesterday's trip up Penderville Sound he knew that he would have to walk over a mile before he would reach the narrow land bridge that connected the two sides of Penderville Island together. Mondo remembered from the chart that the land was about a mile wide, with steep cliffs plunging into the sea on each side. He walked on, occasionally stopping and taking his binoculars out to study West Penderville Island. One time he spotted a very small cove, not even big enough to anchor Smokin' Joe in, so small that he didn't remember it on the chart. It was half a mile up the channel from the boat dock. He studied the distant cove as best he could from where he was. It was hard to pick out details, but it looked to him that it was a steep rocky cliff right down to the water. It looked like there was no place he could pull his dinghy out and secure it.

He walked on, using his compass to head in the right direction. The forest was eerily quiet. No birds, nothing, just an unnatural silence. Mondo wasn't enjoying himself. This was not a walk in the park; he had too much at stake. The fear of failure hung over him. This was like

153

nothing he had ever attempted before.

Soon he could make out the curve of the land to his left that led to West Penderville Island. He was still blazing a trail, trying to keep himself a hundred feet back from the shoreline, trying to keep a steady compass bearing. He was halfway across the land bridge when he was stopped dead in his tracks. Stretching as far as he could see in front and to either side of him was a huge fence, cutting East and West Penderville Island in half. This fence was not made to keep forest creatures in or out. This fence was meant for people. It looked like it came from a Russian Gulag. The fence was ten feet high, made of steel mesh. Upright steel I-beams supported the fence every four feet. These I-beams were buried deep in a concrete base. At the top of the fence, welded to each upright beam, were two three-foot long narrow pieces of steel angled out ninety degrees from the fence in opposite directions from each other. Six strands of razor sharp barbed wire were stretched tight, supported by these angled pieces of steel. This fence was for a prison, meant to keep anyone from crossing in either direction. Fear filled Mondo. Whoever built this monstrous fence meant business.

The ground was cleared on both sides of the fence for twenty feet. Any trees that could have been used to climb over were now just cut-off rotting stumps. Mondo took a deep breath and turned to his left, following the fence line. He walked for over ten minutes before the fence reached a steep cliff. The fence continued down the cliff for another twenty feet before it ended, overhanging a fifty foot drop down to the water below. Even if he used rope, he doubted he could climb down and get around the fence and climb back up. It would be impossible for the girls to make it. Mondo turned around and started walking the fence line going the other direction. He walked past where he first encountered the fence and continued on. Soon a gate came into view. The gate was three feet wide and built even more securely than the fence. It was made of heavy gauge steel mesh at least a quarter of an inch thick. The mesh was welded to a heavy steel frame that was connected to a support I-beam by four huge, welded-in-place hinges. Barbed wire was stretched tight across the top of the gate. Two welded reinforcing steel plates about three inches by three inches, one at eye level, the other three feet off the ground, were welded to the other side of the gate. Mondo reached his hand between the gate and the upright I beam and felt a large deadbolt lock on each

154

pad. He studied the gate. His little trick that had gotten him into the girls' room at the Baker Street Inn wouldn't help him here. The two locks each had a deadbolt that looked like a solid one-inch steel bar. There was no way through this gate without a key. Mondo shook his head and started walking past the gate. He followed the massive fence until he came to the end of the land bridge. He stared out over Wycliffe Sound. The crashing surf was over one hundred feet below him. This fence ran twenty feet over the side of the cliff and terminated at a large rock outcropping that dropped straight to the sea below. Mondo grabbed hold of the fence and leaned himself out over the cliff's edge to get a better look. The cliff ran straight down for forty feet before it went back under itself and then plunged straight into the water. This side of the fence looked impossible. It was more secure than the other side and he knew he couldn't get around either.

Mondo turned away. He was completely defeated. He walked back to the gate and stared at it. This was the only way in. How in heavens' name could he open this door? He looked closely at the gate, and at the very top he saw two sensors, one on the gate the other on the overhead support beam, making an electrical connection. It was part of an elaborate security system, he knew. If he opened the gate it would break the circuit and let somebody, somewhere, know he was coming. He scoured the area, looking for any signs of cameras or other monitoring devices, but he could see none. The grass around the gate was growing tall and ragged; at least nobody used this gate. Someone felt very comfortable with this massive steel reinforced fence and gate. It looked impossible to get through.

Mondo started walking back to Smokin' Joe. He walked slowly, letting his mind race with different thoughts about what to do next. He could row over to the little cove that he saw and use that as a base to begin his search for the girls. If he could rescue them, he could row back across the sound under the cover of darkness. The biggest problem with this plan was that there were no second options if something went wrong, and he knew things always went wrong.

Mondo untied his dinghy and rowed back to his boat. It was early afternoon. He made lunch and studied West Penderville Island. He took out his small handheld compass and took a bearing on the cove and then on the dock. He wrote those two bearings down and then figured out the reciprocal bearings back to Smokin' Joe and wrote them down as well.

Mondo lay down. He was too anxious to sleep but he knew that he should try. Tonight he would need all of his mental and physical strength. He lay on his bunk half asleep, thinking over and over about this whole crazy business.Why hadn't he just let Amy sail with him to the Northwest? He struggled to find rest but he couldn't. He tossed and turned for over an hour, when he suddenly heard the faint noise of an engine transmitting through the water and into Smokin' Joe's hull. He knew a boat was coming. He climbed out of his bunk, grabbed his binoculars and stuck his head out of the hatch. Mondo watched as a large creamy-white powerboat, at least fifty feet long, pulled up to the dock on West Penderville Island. He focused his binoculars for a better field of vision and studied the boat. Two crewmen jumped off the boat as it reached the dock. Lines were thrown down to the waiting dock hands and the boat secured. A set of stairs rotated out from the side of the boat and down to the dock. Out stepped two middle-aged men. Suddenly Mondo's heart fell to his knees. He couldn't believe what he was seeing, as Christy and Marshall followed next. One last crew person walked off the boat after them.

The group walked off the dock and part way up the hill to a level parking area. Two minutes later a jeep pulled up, and they all climbed in. Mondo was in shock as he watched the Jeep drive away in a cloud of dust. What the hell was going on? What were Christy and Marshall doing here? He had left them on Salt Bay Island.

Mondo climbed down the companion stairs and threw himself on his bunk. My God, things were going the wrong direction already. His whole plan just disappeared. There was no way he could get three girls and himself plus Marshall in his little rowing dinghy, even if he could free them all. Even if they all could fit in his dinghy, what bothered Mondo was the powerboat. His hope of being able to escape from the island under the cover of darkness just disappeared. That powerboat would have enough on board electric systems to pinpoint them in the dark in a heartbeat.

His mind went back to the gate. What if he could somehow unlock it? What then? He and Marshall could make a run for the gate while the three girls went for the dinghy, then they could rendezvous back at Smokin' Joe and head out. Even if they all could make it back to his boat, which was a really big if, he still had a problem he couldn't figure out. Smokin' Joe's maximum speed was seven knots. He bet that the powerboat could easily do thirty. Even if they could escape the island, they could never outrun that powerboat. They would never make it to the safety of Campbell River, the closest place to run.

Mondo knew he would have to start thinking out of the box, there were just no answers there. He walked over to the center of Smokin' Joe just before the mast, knelt down and pulled up a teak and holly floorboard hatch. He reached under the floor, five inches to his right, and flipped on a light. This was his treasure room. Inside were three plastic bins, each with a lid firmly attached. All of the things that he might need someday were stored down here. Each bin was sorted into different belongings. One held tools, one held parts, and the third held whatever wouldn't fit in the first two. There were many miscellaneous things; even a length of standing wire rigging was rolled up and stored there. Mondo never threw anything away when he was sailing. The first time he threw something away, the next day he would need it.

He knew what he was looking for. He opened his tool bin and took out a heavy five-pound sledge hammer, the handle shortened to eighteen inches so it could fit in the bin. Next he opened the third junk bin and took out two cans of Freon gas. This was the gas that he used to recharge his refrigerator system. When Freon gas was discharged it has a temperature of thirty degrees below zero. He once had to break a lock on his dinghy in Panama after his keys fell overboard. By freezing the lock, then hitting it with a hammer, he had been able to shatter the frozen tumblers. He had no idea if it could work on the locks at the gate, but he had nothing else to try.

He grabbed his daypack, threw in the two cans of Freon and five rubber bungee cords, then grabbed the sledge hammer and rowed back ashore.

Mondo retraced his steps to the gate. It was late afternoon, and the evening chill was starting to descend, the sky was already slowly darkening. He walked up to the gate and knelt down in front of it. He had been thinking of his next move all the way here. If he didn't freeze the lock long enough the metal wouldn't become brittle and break. If he used too much gas on one lock and couldn't get the second one frozen it would accomplish nothing. He laid his mallet down at his knees and took the Freon out of his backpack.

Mondo steadied his breath, tried to calm his nerves. What would he do if this failed? He had no idea. He unscrewed the cap from one of the Freon cans and screwed in the five inch slender discharge tube. He slid the can between the gate and the upright I-beam and placed it on the ground, then he grabbed his sledge hammer and leaned the handle up against the gate, making it easier to reach. Mondo slid his left hand between the gate and the I-beam and grabbed the Freon. His fingers found the key hole and he slid the Freon tube into the lock, then he hit the release button. He held the can tight, keeping the tube in the lock as he slowly climbed to his feet. The Freon was blasting back into his hand, freezing his fingers, but he didn't let go. The instant the can emptied he grabbed the sledge hammer and slammed it into the back of the steel backing plate. The tumblers shattered inside the lock, the keyway exploded out of the lock and landed five feet in front of the gate. Mondo reached down and slid the steel deadbolt back from its locking counterpart on the I-beam. He grabbed the other can of Freon and repeated the process, making sure that he held the gate tight as he slammed the sledge hammer into it. Breaking the lock was as important as not breaking the electrical connection and setting off an alarm. Mondo held the gate tight as he slid the second dead bolt back. He opened the gate an eighth of an inch, then he closed it tight.

Son of a bitch, he thought. Mondo made sure the gate was as tight as possible, checked to make sure that the alarm sensors were making good contact. Then, holding the gate closed with his left hand, he reached down into his backpack, pulled out the five bungee cords, and wrapped them around the gate and the steel I-beam. He gently pushed on the gate. It wouldn't budge. The first step of his plan was a success. He would need a lot more success tonight, or he might end up dead.

CHAPTER 23

Mondo returned to Smokin' Joe, and tried to fall asleep, but his restless mind wouldn't turn off. He knew he needed to rest if he was going to function at his best, but his mind just wouldn't stop spinning. There were more questions than he had answers, and the questions just kept coming.

After two fruitless hours of trying to sleep, he got up and started preparing. He put new batteries in his flashlight, then covered the flashlight lens with a thin piece of red plastic. He used duct tape to hold the plastic in position. The red light would help him keep his night vision. He made an electrical connector using a three foot long piece of fourteen gauge wire and crimped an alligator clamp on each end.

He stood in the cabin of his boat trying to think of anything else that he would need. He grabbed his skin-diving knife, his binoculars, the flashlight, the electric cable, and his small illuminating hand-held compass. He put them all in his backpack. At the last minute he put on his wrist watch, then he dressed in his darkest clothes, climbed into his dinghy and rowed ashore.

He once again skirted around the fish farm and continued walking. It was easy for him to find the gate. He was able to do most of the trip without using either compass or flashlight. Mondo had a great sense of direction once he had been to a place. At the gate he opened his pack and took out the electric connector. He connected the alligator clips to the top and bottom of the sensor pads, creating an electric circuit, and then removed the bungee cords. He opened the gate just enough so that he could slip through. Once on the other side he used the bungee cords to secure the gate closed and removed the connector, putting it in his backpack. Now it was new terrain for him. He had a fairly good idea of the direction that he wanted to go. By studying the nautical chart of West Penderville Island he was able to get a compass bearing from his estimated position at the gate to the boat dock. From there, he figured, he would skirt around the road and follow it to wherever it led.

He walked twenty feet back from the cliffs that dropped steeply into Penderville Sound. A mile after he left the gate he found the little cove that he had spied with his binoculars. It was steep down to the water, not a cliff, although it would be hard to climb up or down without a rope. It looked to be about thirty feet down to the water. He made a mental note of it all and continued on. Another ten minutes brought him to the hill that overlooked the dock. The entire dock area was deserted, the large white powerboat securely tied up. There were no lights on anywhere. No sign of any crew or surveillance equipment, except the two monitoring cameras that were mounted on either side of the gate that led down to the ramp. Mondo knew that the dock would have more security than just the cameras and a gate. His dealings back at the fence made him think about pressure sensitive pads connected to an alarm system. The dock could be full of them and one wrong step could trigger alarms. His worst fear was that the alarms were probably silent at the dock. He would never know if he tripped one until the bad guys came running. There was no way he could risk walking out to the large powerboat.

Mondo followed the road up and over the ridge. He was walking ten feet back in the forest picking his way around trees, rocks, and scrub brush. It was slow going, but it didn't matter much to him. He was making progress, he had all night. He could not afford one mistake.

He knew that at the end of this dirt road he would find Amy and Isabella. The scary part was that he also knew he would find the people that took them. As he walked down the backside of the ridge, the road curved to the left and then straightened out for a few hundred feet before turning to the right. As he swung up above the right turn he looked down and saw a cluster of buildings about a hundred feet away. He brought out his binoculars and studied the entire compound. A large two-story house dominated the area, surrounded by four small one-story cabins and a few little outbuildings. There was a pond off to one corner about sixty feet away from the road. Mondo studied the road and the well-lit gate before seeing the fence that wrapped its way into the darkness. He couldn't see the entire fence, but he had little doubt that it enclosed the whole area that he was looking over. It was a prison.

The lights were on in the main house and two of the cabins as well. Mondo sat down and hit the illuminating switch on his watch. It was ten-forty-five.

Now what? He really had no idea. He had made it through the gate, checked out the little cove and the dock as best as he could and found a fortress where he assumed Amy and Isabella were. He would go check out around the fence, follow it in the shadows and see if he could find a way under it. He decided to wait until it was very late and everybody was asleep. He set the alarm on his wrist watch for two-thirty. He tried to wiggle his way in between some rocks for comfort, then he pulled his jacket tight around his head and fell asleep.

Edwin and Mr. Chein were in the upstairs surveillance room, the door closed behind them. Amy and Isabella were both asleep in their rooms. Their worst fears had come true. Their island stronghold had been discovered. How many people knew of it, they weren't sure. Marshall Sandbourn's call telling them that Christy was on a flight to Campbell River had started their fears. If she was coming to Campbell River, then she must be coming because she knew of their island. Marshall had more than earned the retainer they had given him. Then the surveillance cameras had picked up Christy and another man on the fishing boat "Norma Jean", cruising very slowly past their island inspecting it. That boat was registered to South Town Charters out of Campbell River, operated by Captain Jack Basey. Captain Jack was already dead. He had a sudden heart attack that very night in his house. It was convenient that he lived alone, it made his murder much easier to commit. They just had to hope that Captain Jack hadn't mentioned their island to anybody else.

Then there was the rental boat that Marshall and Christy were taken from. The evidence was destroyed, nobody would ever find any part of that boat, but still it caused more problems. People would soon start searching for it and its missing occupants.

Now they had Marshall and Christy in two of the underground living areas. Marshall had become a pain since finding out that Mr. Chein was the person that he had been talking to all along. They finally chained Marshall to his bed, his right foot connected to five feet of chain, his toilet a small portable bucket.

"Let him go hungry for a few days, he will come around. He could scream forever down there and nobody would hear him," Mr. Chein said.

Christy was locked in another underground living area. This all posed a big problem for Edwin and Mr. Chein.

"What do you think we should consider doing, Mr. Chein?"

"Edwin, I was hoping that you would be able to see through this and find the best course of action."

"I am so surprised that I did not see this coming. One small shortfall somewhere while the girls were at the bed and breakfast has led to this entire problem. We will either have to kill Christy or let her be united with her sister and Isabella. If we do unite the girls, then Christy will never be allowed to leave. We can eliminate Marshall anytime. I don't think he can be of use to us anymore. So for now, let us bide our time. I think we should wait to introduce the girls and we should keep Marshall isolated. This is just a short term solution to our problem."

"Are you able to kill Christy if necessary?" Mr. Chein asked, although he already knew the answer.

"I will do whatever is necessary to see the fulfillment of this vision. Christy is dispensable as is one of the other girls. We need only one child."

"I understand."

Mondo slept right through his wrist-watch alarm. He awoke suddenly cold and confused. Daylight had already appeared. His body ached, his mind at first unable even to identify where he was. Then it came back to him. He could see the compound clearly now. He knew he had slept through his alarm; he also realized that he couldn't leave his hiding area. Mondo was trapped for the day. He took a better look around at his location. It was high on a ridge above the compound and it gave him some visibility of the entire area, but he felt exposed. He saw a large group of rocks thirty feet off to his right. They seemed to offer more protection from being seen from below, and also better visibility of the area. He crawled on his belly over to the rock formation, then slowly stood up. This was a great observation place. He slowly looked around, making sure he could not be seen. There was deep forest to his back and around each side. He would spend the day here hungry, thirsty, and at present very cold. There was nothing else he could do.

Around ten he watched as the front door opened and out walked

Amy and another girl Mondo thought had to be Isabella. His heart raced at the sight of them. They seemed in good health and were talking as they walked. They headed over to the pond and sat down alongside a group of large flat landscape rocks. He had no idea what they were saying, but he felt better just seeing them. He watched them for two hours. He had to control himself to keep from working his way down the ridge and trying to get their attention. His goal was to get them off of the island, not let them know he was here. He watched them and tried to form a plan. His only chance was still under the cover of darkness. Somehow he had to find Christy and get them all out, but first he would have to get himself into that fortress. It didn't look any easier in the daylight than it looked last night. The fence did enclose the entire area and there were two strands of razor sharp barbed wire stretched tight above it. Mondo wondered if he could cut the fence. Was it electrified? Could it have some sort of alarm system?

All through the day he watched. He saw a man he assumed to be Edwin Hawkins come and go out of the house a few times, watched him walk over and talk to the girls. He wished he could have read the girls' facial expressions but their backs were facing him. He saw a few other people walking around, going from one building to another. He saw no sign of Christy or Marshall. Somewhere in this island fortress they were hidden. He guessed that Amy and Isabella didn't even know Christy was here.

The girls seemed to favor sitting on the rocks, the sun hitting that area for most of the day. He watched as they went back into the house around noon, then came back out an hour or so later and spent the next three hours sitting on the rocks talking. He knew they had much to talk about.

Mondo was hungry and thirsty, and he had hours to go before he could even think of returning to Smokin'Joe. He knew that before he left tonight he would have to crawl down and inspect the entire length of the fence. He would have to find a way in. His fear was that even if he could get in, could he get to the girls without waking somebody up?

At dusk the air turned cold and Mondo watched as the night descended. Once it was as dark as it was going to be, Mondo left his hiding place and continued walking to his right. He wanted to be able to see into the main house. Just before he passed out of sight of the front door he saw it open, and watched an asian man walk out with a large plate covered in foil. He was bringing dinner to somebody. Mondo hid in the shadows and watched as the man walked across the compound to the cabin nearest to where he was hiding and entered. Mondo reached into his backpack, pulled out his binoculars and followed his every move. He saw one light flick on as the man entered the cabin, then another. The curtains on the window facing Mondo were open. He watched as the man walked down a hallway, unrolled a carpet and lifted up a trap door. Then the man descended and disappeared from view.

That must be where Christy or Marshall or both were being kept hidden. If they had let Amy know her sister was on the island Christy would have been in the house with them.

Finding Christy or Marshall's location gave Mondo hope. One answer to the many questions he would have to answer before he could accomplish this insane rescue.

He watched as five minutes later the man reappeared without the tray and returned to the house. Mondo walked on, keeping his profile low and himself in the darkness. He was now looking into different parts of the main house, and he could see through a large picture window into the dining area. He watched the girls having dinner with the man he assumed to be Edwin Hawkins. He watched their demeanor, trying to get a sense of what was going on inside their minds. With the help of his binoculars he could see that both girls ate mostly in silence, that the man did most of the talking. The food looked good and he remembered his hunger.

Mondo watched as they finished dinner, watched the table being cleared, and then the girls walked out of his line of sight. A moment later he saw a light turn on in what must be a bedroom window down from the dining room. This must be one of the girls' rooms. If Edwin and the asian man stayed in the main house it would be almost impossible for him to get the girls out.

Mondo walked around the perimeter of the entire compound. Only in one small area was he not on high ground and well hidden. He kept his distance from the fence and worked his way to his right, finally crossing the road and returning to his rocky outcropping. He was able to get a good picture of the entire area in his mind. There was one small locked gate, only big enough for a person to walk through opposite from the roadway. A path led away from the gate but he didn't follow it. It was now eleven. All the lights except for the two bright lights at the gate were off. He worked his way down the hill to the fence. The pond was five feet away from him. Slowly, ever so slowly, he started crawling again to his right, searching the ground before every move. He was afraid of trip wires or pressure pads, he was afraid of a lot of things that could go wrong. It took him an hour to make it back to the pond. He found no easy way in. The fence ran deep into the ground. Mondo had taken his knife out at one well-hidden location and dug down twelve inches and still the fence was there. He had no idea how deep it was buried.

It was twelve-thirty when he turned away and started back to Smokin' Joe. He knew that sleeping through his alarm and being able to see what was going on had worked in his favor. Mondo would have to go back to his boat, eat, sleep, repack and make it back to his rock formation before daylight. He had to get a sense of what was going on there before he could do anything else.

CHAPTER 24

It was after one-thirty when Mondo climbed back aboard Smokin' Joe. He would have to leave by four to give himself enough time to get back to his hiding place above the compound. There was no way he could let his exhaustion win, not yet. He ate two peanut butter and jelly sandwiches and washed them down with a glass of wine. What things did he need to bring with him when he returned? Would he try to contact Amy and Isabella? It would only make sense to contact them if he had a plan.

He sat down at the chart table, thinking. His best bet would be to somehow let the girls know that he was there and find out if they could free themselves from the house. If they could get outdoors without being caught then he would have to get them through the fence. Once through the fence they would race like hell back to the dinghy, back to Smokin' Joe, head out and make it to Campbell River. There were too many chances for something to go wrong. Way too many, he knew.

Mondo dug back down in his treasure chest and pulled out a small short-handled shovel.

"What else?" he said. He was so tired he was starting to talk to himself but he couldn't allow himself to rest. When he awoke early this morning he must be ready to go. He reached down into one of his bins and brought out a small fishing box. He also pulled his casting pole and reel out. The pole was the breakdown type, three pieces inserting to make one long pole. He threw some spare line and his small tackle box in his backpack. Mondo pulled out a piece of paper from his chart table and wrote a note to the girls,

Don't react/ don't discuss/ hidden cameras & microphones/ can you escape from house? If so, meet me tomorrow night by pond after midnight/

Love Mondo

Next he wrapped the note in two water-tight plastic freezer bags, and sealed the edges, then he took a tube of fast drying sealer and ran a small bead along the edge for extra protection. He made some more sandwiches and put them in his pack along with two plastic bottles of water, and the note.

He opened his chart table and took out a small stapler and put it in his backpack as well.

It was after two-thirty when Mondo set both of his portable travel alarm clocks and hit his bunk. He had no trouble falling asleep this time.

A few short hours later, both of his alarms went off six inches from his head. There was no chance of sleeping through these. He jumped up, ready to go. He had slept in his clothes so he didn't even have to dress. He threw one of his alarm clocks in his pack and climbed out of the hatch. It was beautiful, a million stars shining bright in the moonless night. The air was cold but it didn't make much difference to him. He rowed ashore and started making his way back to the compound. He had no problem getting through the gate. He walked past the dock and the boat, making a mental note to do something to stop that boat from being able to come after them. He made it to his rock outcropping with still some darkness left. Taking his backpack off, he laid it on the ground next to him. Then he found a small tree limb and broke off the last twelve inches of it. He pulled his stapler out and stapled the plastic freezer bag with the note for the girls to the branch. Next he connected his casting pole together and ever so carefully made his way down to the fence and the pond. Mondo tied a small eight-ounce lead ball to three feet of fishing line and stapled that line to the branch right next to the freezer bag. Holding his breath, he cast the branch and note over the fence into the pool. The splash sounded like an explosion to him, but it was just that the night was so quiet. The branch drifted over next to the rocks right where he had seen the girls sitting for most of the day. He hoped the lead weight would keep the branch from drifting around the pond. He cut the remainder of the fishing line and made his way back to his protective rocks. Twenty minutes later, dawn came. He nestled himself in between the boulders and made himself as comfortable as possible. All he could do was wait, and pray that it was the girls that found his note and not somebody else.

Amy and Isabella were starting to fall into a routine and that scared both of them. They talked at length about how they needed to stick together and help each other get through all of this. They had to be ready to protect each other mentally, physically, and emotionally from Edwin. Neither girl could afford to give up hope that somehow they could escape from this island fortress.

Both had decided that they needed to confront Edwin and find out what was really going on. They couldn't sit here day after day not knowing what this was all about. The fact that they were cousins confused things even more. It made this whole situation that much more difficult to understand. Was Edwin trying to live in the past? Was he trying to resurrect his lost daughter by keeping them? What did their family history have to do with their situation? They had no idea, but both knew that it was the reason that they were here. This connection to their grandmother, Edwin's daughter, was the key to this whole mystery.

It was possible that Edwin's daughter could be their grandmother, but then it was impossible for Edwin to be the age that he seemed. He would have to be close to a hundred years old for it to all add up. Edwin didn't look sixty. Unless he had discovered the fountain of youth, this made no sense.

Both girls felt very helpless. Nobody knew that they were here. Amy didn't remember calling her sister late that night from the bed & breakfast. With nobody knowing their location, they knew that no one was coming to rescue them. It was up to them to escape and that looked impossible. Would they really have to live here for a very long time, as Edwin had told them? What, they wondered, is a very long time? Would their families give up on them and assume that they were dead and try to put their memories behind them? Would they be left alive whenever this madness was over? It was just too insane for either of the girls to consider. The greatest thing that they had on their side was that they had each other. Neither girl could imagine what it would be like to be here alone. They were both trapped on this island with a mad man and no way to get off unless Edwin decided to let them go. Amy thought that her family must be worried sick by now. She thought of Mondo and her heart broke; what was he doing? Isabella thought more and more about her dad. He was the only real family that she had in the world. He must know by now that something was wrong. The whole world could know something was wrong, but nobody would know where to look for them.

They walked out of the main house after breakfast and started walking around the compound, circling inside their cage. Neither felt like sitting at the moment.

"Isabella, I don't think any help is going to come."

"Did you do anything with the information that I gave you about the island?"

Amy laughed. She remembered Isabella telling her that Edwin had said something to her about an island paradise up north called West Penderville Island. She had told Amy about her conversation with Edwin regarding the island late one night when they were sitting in their room at the bed & breakfast just before they went to bed.

"West Penderville Island, what's that?" Amy remembered herself saying.

"That's a place that Edwin told me about, said he owned it and that I should see it sometime. I don't know why he even mentioned it to me, he was just talking away," Isabella had replied.

Amy remembered the island's name. The next day when the two girls had gone downtown, Amy walked into the marine supply store and started looking for the island on a Canadian chart. She didn't have much difficulty finding it, and she had no trouble writing down its latitude and longitude.

"I wrote the location down on the hand-held mirror in the bathroom five minutes before we left with Edwin. I really don't know why I did it. It seemed stupid to me when I did. Nobody is going to find it and I don't think anybody will know what a bunch of numbers mean if they did find it."

"Yeah, you're probably right. Are we just going to live here forever? He still hasn't told us what he wants from us. I don't know if I believe his story about our mothers, do you?"

"I do. I don't think Edwin has told us a lie yet," Amy said.

They walked in silence and finally made their way back to the pond and sat down on the rocks. The sun was out and this was by far the nicest place for them to sit and talk. It felt like this little spot was theirs, and they needed something to hang on to.

"I think we need to press Edwin again and ask him why we are here. He seemed to like us all dressed up. Maybe we should make him a deal. We'll dress up if he'll tell us what is going on."

170

"I am afraid to ask him. I want to know, but I am scared to know. What do you think he wants from us, Amy?" Isabella asked

"I don't have any idea, but we must be very important to him. Just look at all he has gone through to set this place up and to get us here. If he is crazy, then he is the Einstein of the crazy department."

They both laughed.

Mondo studied the two girls. They seemed to be doing fine, they talked and laughed, neither seemed misused or abused. Neither of the girls saw Mondo's branch with his note hanging underneath. The girls spent over an hour by the pond, his branch not two feet away from them. With horror he watched as they got up and walked back into the house. He could see his stick floating there, looking out of place on the pond. If anybody else found it, all was lost. There was nothing that he could do. He thought about throwing a rock into the pond near them; that would get their attention, but it was too far away from his hiding place and it would expose him more than he wanted. His hope rested on the chance that the girls would return after lunch and see the branch.

It was close to three in the afternoon when the girls came out from the main house. They started walking the area like they did earlier in the morning. Both were talking a lot, their hands waving about as if they were trying to get a serious point across. The two walked for an hour. Mondo thought that they wouldn't return to the pond, but finally they did. It was Isabella who saw the branch. He was watching them both through the binoculars. The branch and the bag hanging underneath it must have caught her eye for she looked at Amy, motioned with her head, and then looked carefully around the compound. Nobody else was about. Isabella reached in and pulled the branch out of the water. She tore the plastic bag off and put the stick down. They looked at each other, looked around again, and then Isabella opened the bags. Both girls read Mondo's note. Amy grabbed the bags and the note and put them under her shirt, tucked tight in her waistband. Slowly both girls looked around. Only once did they glance his way, and he didn't move. After five minutes they went back into the house.

Mondo rolled over on his back. His muscles ached from lying prone so long watching the girls. They had found his message. The second part of his plan was a success. Now he would have to wait and see if they could figure a way out of the house. He prayed that they took his warning seriously about microphones and cameras. They couldn't afford to underestimate Edwin Hawkins.

The girls walked back to Isabella's room and went into the bathroom. They studied the entire bathroom looking for a camera or microphone. They could find neither. Both hoped that they would have some privacy in the bathroom from Edwin's cameras. Amy turned the shower on and pulled out the message. She had almost died the first time she read it. Mondo was here, that was beyond belief! How he had found them, she had no idea, but he must have a plan to get them off of this island. They needed to find a way out of this house in the middle of the night. Was it possible? The girls had such a hard time controlling their excitement.

Amy returned to her room. Her heart was exploding. Mondo was here.

CHAPTER 25

The room was small, with no exterior windows. It was painted a soft white, an attempt to give it some sense of comfort. At least that was what Christy thought as she looked around her surroundings. The room was about fifteen feet long by twenty feet wide, with narrow steps leading up to the ceiling with the trap door that she had been forced to walk through earlier. There were no pictures, no décor, just a closet, a bathroom and a bed. Christy lay on the bed thinking. She had hoped by now to see Amy and meet Isabella and to find out what was going on. She wanted to talk to Edwin as well. Since her arrival she had seen nobody except for the asian man that had brought her dinner, and he said little. When she demanded to see Amy, he simply told her to wait.

There was nothing that Christy could do to get herself out of here. She was a prisoner. She was also an emotional wreck and she knew it. To have gotten this close to her sister only to end up like this made her physically sick. This nightmare was more than any fiction writer could imagine, it was not possible, it couldn't be real, but it was.

Suddenly she heard footsteps near the trap door. She glanced up and watched as the doorway opened, and Edwin came down carrying a tray.

Edwin set the tray on the floor and looked at her. Christy thought she could see pity in his eyes, but if any was there it lasted only a second.

"Christy, my dear, here is breakfast, coffee as well. I do hope you find your accommodations comfortable?"

"Comfortable, Edwin, for a prison!"

"My, my, my, have I fallen out of favor with you also? Tell me, Christy, what should I do with you? You really weren't supposed to be here, you know."

He was leaning against the stairs, looking at her with those incredibly dark eyes, a small smile on his face.

"Edwin, you're a bastard! I want to see Amy now." Christy was forgetting her situation, she was just so angry.

"That's not a very good way to get things done around here. You see, you are a complication to me, Christy. I have had more than enough complications in the last few days. It really would be easier for me if you just died."

With that he turned around and climbed the stairs and slammed the door behind him. Christy sat on the bed stunned, Edwin's words haunting her.

It was late afternoon before Edwin returned. Christy was lying on the bed half asleep, the other half of her mind going crazy. Edwin entered carrying a small folding chair with him. He opened it and sat down. Christy knew she could not let herself get angry.

"Edwin, I am sorry for calling you a bastard. I'm scared and I don't know what is happening. Why is this happening, Edwin? Please," she let her voice trail off, her tone a plea for help.

"Christy, I still am at a loss about what to do with you. I want you to know that Amy and Isabella are both fine, and they are here. They don't know that you are here, and that is my first decision; do I let the three of you reunite? It will make my plans harder. You will make things harder for me, Christy, and I don't know if I want that."

"Edwin please, I just want to see Amy, I want to know that she is fine. I won't cause you any trouble."

Edwin reached into his jacket pocket, took out a small remote control device and pointed it at the far wall. The wall separated, revealing a TV screen two feet high and three feet long. It showed the inside of a house somewhere. Christy could see the man that brought her dinner last night in a kitchen cooking, then the TV screen divided into four small pictures. The top two pictures showed empty bedrooms, the bottom two pictures showed Amy and Isabella, sitting on a couch reading. The girls looked comfortable, looked like they were enjoying a leisure day. It could have been a typical Sunday afternoon anywhere in America, but it wasn't.

"Christy, I have no intention of harming either girl, they are too important to me. They are part of my plan; the problem is that you are not."

Christy again felt that deep fear in her innermost being. Edwin could kill her, and nobody would ever know. Christy hadn't told another soul where she was going, nobody knew she was here.

Edwin pushed the remote again and the TV screen went blank, then the wall closed back upon itself. Christy could see no signs that the TV monitor was there.

"Edwin, please."

"Christy, I plan to have Amy and Isabella both carry my child. Each of them will bear me a son. Then after that I will decide their fate."

His words stopped Christy's mind in its tracks. Any thoughts that she had about her own safety, or Mondo, or seeing her sister, froze in time.

"You see, Christy, why these two are so special to me."

Christy couldn't say anything.

He stood up, walked over to her bed, and sat down next to her. He ran his fingers through her hair, then he grabbed her face hard, and brought her eyes up to meet his.

"I really only need one woman and one son, but now I will have two sons from two different women. I don't think I need three. Do you understand me, Christy? If you live, you will also bear me a son."

She looked up at him. She was absolutely helpless and she knew it.

"Think about it, Christy, you and me together, my seed growing to fulfillment inside your body. That is the only offer I give you, and I may not even give that, new life for your life. I will have to make my decision soon."

Edwin got up, grabbed his folding chair and left without saying another word.

Christy was in shock. She lay there on the bed unable to move, fear controlling her every function, her breathing rapid, her pulse racing, her mind going out of control. Christy knew that Edwin wouldn't offer her a life for a life, he would kill her. She could see it in his eyes. What could she do to convince him that she wanted to live above all else? What if he did offer her a chance to live, could she? What choice would she have? She would have to give her body to him, then be his prisoner for at least the next nine months. Then what? What about Amy and Isabella, did they know what their fate was? She doubted it. They looked too composed sitting there reading. They must be completely oblivious to the dangers that were soon to come.

Christy didn't want to die, she would do whatever she could to stay alive. Could Mondo save them? Probably, she thought, if anybody could, but where was he? She hadn't seen Smokin' Joe anywhere, besides he wouldn't even know she was here. Even if Mondo rescued Amy and

Isabella he would never know to look here and find her. He would think she went home to Malibu and was waiting for his phone call. *God*, Christy thought, *I'm in the biggest trouble of my entire life.*

Marshall was fifteen feet away from where Christy lay. His room was exactly like hers, his situation different only because he was chained to his bed.

When they had brought him breakfast he threw it against the wall, and demanded that he be set free and told what the hell was going on. Mr. Chein thought the man was extremely rude and barbaric and asked Edwin for the opportunity to teach Marshall a few manners. Edwin thought that would be enjoyable to watch.

Ten minutes after Marshall threw his breakfast against the wall, the same two thugs that pulled him from the water came into his room.

"Get up, asshole, follow us," one said.

Marshall didn't say a word; he just did as he was told. He followed the two up a set of stairs, then out into the daylight. They walked up to the main house, entered and walked into the living room. Amy and Isabella had been ushered into their rooms a few minutes earlier.

"This way," one of the thugs said.

They walked to the opposite side of the living room and down a flight of stairs. At the bottom of the stairs was a long hallway. Halfway down on the left was a door. The thugs opened it, pushed Marshall inside and closed it behind him. They didn't enter. Marshall looked and saw Mr. Chein and Edwin sitting in portable chairs at one end. The room was a large rectangle with a low ceiling. There was no furniture in the room except for the chairs that Edwin and Mr. Chein sat on. On the far wall from him he could see five rings, each four inches wide, connected to the wall at three foot intervals. The rings were two feet off of the floor. Connected to each ring was a short chain with handcuffs at the end.

"Marshall Sandbourn, you have the manners of a pig and neither Mr. Chein nor I feel like dealing with you anymore. It would be very easy to just dispatch you and be done with you, but we feel some sense of loyalty seeing as how you have been of use to us," Edwin said. Marshall was scared shitless.

"So why don't we do this? Mr. Chein, if you please."

He reached his hand out and Mr. Chein stood up and walked to the center of the room.

"I will let you go free, Mr. Sandbourn. I will personally escort you to our boat dock and put you aboard our boat for Campbell River. I do trust you would never mention us, or our island, to anyone, but first things first. Mr. Chein has been offended by your tirades and thinks that you need a beating. So to be fair to you both, why don't you come and try your hand with Mr. Chein? If you succeed I will set you free."

Marshall was frozen with fear. His body wouldn't move, his mind was too numb to think. Mr. Chein was much smaller than Marshall, but he looked incredibly strong. He reminded Marshall of an English bulldog in a Chinese body.

"What if I don't?" Marshall asked.

"Then you will lose, which I think you will anyway," Edwin replied.

Marshall slowly controlled his breathing, tried to force the fear from his mind. He counted to three and charged Mr. Chein. Marshall was three feet away from his opponent, running full speed, when Mr. Chein back-stepped, turned his body sideways and exploded a side kick out at Marshall, catching him completely unprotected in the midsection. Marshall was flung back with such force that when his head hit the floor he went out cold.

"So much for taking your time and enjoying the process, Mr. Chein," Edwin said, shaking his head.

"Have two of the crew return him to his room, keep him chained. I don't think Mr. Sandbourn will cause us any more troubles. That is, if we let him live."

CHAPTER 26

Edwin's demeanor had changed. Both of the girls picked up on it the moment they walked into the dining room. Edwin was staring out the window looking as if he was lost deep in thought. He turned and looked at them as they entered, then slowly returned his gaze back to the window. He didn't say a word.

The girls sat down at the dining table, glancing nervously at each other, neither speaking.

Did Edwin know about Mondo, they wondered? The girls suddenly felt very uncomfortable and wished they had stayed in their room. It seemed rather awkward to them to get up and leave so they sat there, looking at each other and Edwin, nobody speaking. They had never seen Edwin in such a somber mood. He had always been the perfect gentleman towards both of them. Now as they sat at the table they knew something wasn't right. His mannerism was cold, his face looked sullen. He looked like somebody they didn't want to be around.

Edwin had been struggling with his emotions and it surprised him. He had decided to kill Christy. He didn't need her and he didn't need the complications that she brought with her. The emotions that he was struggling with infuriated him. He had killed many; never did it bother him before, but the thought of killing Christy did. He realized that it had more to do with Amy than Christy. Was he letting himself become too emotionally involved with these girls? Was it foolish for him to try and develop a relationship with Amy and Isabella? They each would have his child, that he knew. Did it really make much difference to him what they thought? He realized that it did make a difference, and that was an unacceptable human emotion.

He would have to distance himself from the girls. They were his, and it was his plan that needed to come to fruition. Once the children were born he hadn't foreseen letting either of them live anyway. Why should he?

Edwin turned and looked at each of the girls. "What do you want?" he asked, as he looked at them with his haunting black eyes.

Neither girl wanted to speak. Fear filled them.

"Edwin, what's wrong?" It was Isabella who spoke.

"You want to know why I have brought you here. You want to know what the future holds. I will show you, now you will know the truth."

The girls' minds were frozen with fear. His tone was so menacing, so evil, this was not the Edwin Hawkins that had cared for them and told them they were safe here, this was another person.

Edwin walked to the door leading upstairs and opened it.

"Mr. Chein, can you please come here?"

The asian man walked down the stairs and out into the living room.

"Yes, Edwin."

"Bring the girls to our chapel. It is time for them to learn what we are doing here."

"As you wish."

Mr. Chein walked over to Amy, grabbed her arm, and pulled her up from the chair. His grasp was incredibly strong and her arm hurt. He pulled her around to where Isabella was sitting, grabbed her arm and jerked her up forcefully.

He pushed them toward the front door.

"Open the door," he said. Amy opened it.

He manhandled both of the girls outside. The girls were in incredible pain, Mr. Chein's grasp digging deep into their muscles and cutting off circulation.

"Please," Amy said, her voice reflecting the fear she felt.

"Quiet," he replied, although he did loosen his grip ever so slightly.

He pushed the girls toward one of the small cabins, the one nearest the road and gate. When they walked up on the porch he released his grip and opened the door.

"Follow me."

He closed the door behind them as they entered a small cozy cabin. He pushed the girls past the living room and part way down a hallway.

"Stop here," he said.

Mr. Chein walked to the back of the hallway, and rolled up a narrow carpet, revealing a trap door. He opened the doorway, looked at the girls.

"Down."

The girls walked down into a dark room. There were no windows; the only light was shining down from the hallway and the trapdoor. Neither girl could see ten feet into the room.

Mister Chein followed the girls' down the steps, then he grabbed Amy and dragged her into the darkness. Amy could feel herself being thrown in the air and landing on a bed, then Mr.Chein reached out and grabbed her right hand, and locked it into something that felt like a handcuff. Mr. Chein brought his face right next to hers. She could hardly see him in the darkness.

"Scream all you want to, no one will hear," he whispered, his voice the voice of evil.Then he came back and grabbed Isabella, dragging her into the darkness. She was thrown on a bed, and her right hand locked in a handcuff. He walked to the foot of the stairs. Both girls could see him in the light. His face looked twisted, and he seemed to be gloating over them as the shafts of light streamed down around him. Mr. Chein stood there for a minute, as if savoring a beautiful sight, then without a word he bounded up the stairs and slammed the trap door closed behind him. The girls were thrown into complete darkness. They both screamed, burst into tears, neither could see anything. Now this truly had become their worst nightmare.

Mondo had watched the entire episode from when the front door opened and the girls were dragged out of the main house and into the cabin. The Chinese man looked like a brute, Mondo thought. He could see the fear and anguish on the girls' faces as they had been dragged along. It was all Mondo could do to stop from charging down the hill and climbing the fence and attacking. If he had a gun he would have. He watched in horror as the girls were pushed into the cabin and the door slammed behind them.

Five minutes later he watched as Mr. Chein left the cabin alone.

The girls must be in an underground room like the one he saw last night. Mondo couldn't take his eyes off the cabin. His heart ached. What must be going through their minds? Mr. Chein's treatment of them had shocked Mondo. The cruelty that he inflicted on the girls as he brought them to the cabin was evident even from where Mondo was. He watched their faces through his binoculars as they walked across the compound. It seemed to Mondo as if he was watching some scene from the prehistoric era, from the caveman days. The successful brute dragging his two new female captives home from the hunt. He knew that tonight he would have to rescue the girls.

After ten minutes of screaming and crying, both girls lay quiet and exhausted in the dark.

"I'm here, Isabella, are you hurt?"

"I am so scared, Amy. Did you see his face, did you see Edwin's face?"

Isabella was near hysterics, her breathing coming in great gulps, her eyes trying to see anything in the blackness.

"Are you hurt?" Amy asked again.

"Just my arm, he's so strong, I thought my arm was going to break. What about you?"

"I'm not hurt, just scared. What do you think happened to Edwin?"

"I don't know, I don't think we want to know what he has planned for us. I thought things were bad here before this, now I am terrified. I don't think we will ever get out of this alive," Isabella said.

"I'm here for you, Isabella."

"I know."

The girls lay there in the complete darkness with only their thoughts racing through their minds. There was no sense of time.

Three hours later Edwin entered the cabin that the girls were in. He walked over to the far wall next to the hallway and switched on two wall switches. The lights in the girls' room flashed on. The sudden rush of light caused both girls to scream and cover their eyes with their hands. Edwin sat down in the cabin upstairs. He would let them see their surroundings before he would proceed.

It took five minutes before the girls could completely open their eyes and look around. What they saw scared them more than the darkness.

They were in a long narrow room. Each lay on a bed with her right hand cuffed to a chain that was connected to a heavy bed frame. They looked at each other, their beds only ten feet apart. The entire room was painted black. No windows, no lights except for the few overhead lights that had just flashed on. The far end of the room was lost in darkness. They could see the trapdoor stairs that they had walked down. The wall

182

behind the stairs was empty. It had no paintings, no furniture, nothing. On both of the walls that ran lengthwise along the room hung huge tapestries, suspended from the ceiling and just touching the floor. The tapestries looked rich and old and they looked haunting. The entire room had only the large tapestries hanging from the wall, and two beds. What was lost in the darkness at the end of the room they couldn't imagine.

Suddenly the trap door opened and Edwin walked down and into the room. Both of the girls were sitting on the edge of their beds looking at each other, looking at him, hoping to God that the Edwin who appeared was the gentleman that they had known. Neither of the girls could hide the fear that shone from their faces. Edwin saw the terror that they revealed, and it didn't bother him. He enjoyed feeling their fears.

Edwin reached up and flipped two wall switches. The lights over the girls went dim and three spotlights shined at the far end of the room. The girls both turned their gaze towards the lights. They saw three steps leading up to a large platform that had a massive bed sitting on it. Two very large candle stands were sitting on each side of the platform at the top of the stairs. A narrow carpet flowed down from the bed, down the steps and out ten feet into the room. It looked like a throne but it was a bed not a chair. The headboard of the bed was a large tapestry suspended between two upright posts. The tapestry weaving depicted the sun and the moon entwined together with rays from the sun shooting off to the edge of the tapestry. The whole setting was a stage.

Edwin walked over without saying a word and sat down next to Isabella. She cringed back, trying to slide to the far side of the bed. Edwin grabbed her hand and pulled her to him. He looked deep into her eyes, the fear on her face exciting him, driving his passion and lust. He reached into his pocket and pulled out a key and unlocked her handcuffs. He dragged her up to her feet and pulled her towards the far wall and the bed.

"No, Edwin," Amy screamed.

He glanced back at her.

"Your turn soon, my love," his voice not the Edwin that they knew.

At the foot of the stairs he reached down and swept Isabella up into his arms. She was too scared to resist. He carried her up to the bed and gently put her down. In one swift movement he reached for both of her hands and handcuffed her again. She lay on the bed, her arms stretched out over her head, her hands locked to the massive bed.

Edwin stood back and looked at her. This was what he had seen in his meditation, the moments leading up to when he would take both of them. Soon he could give into his lust and desire. The altar of life was all but ready. Only one last ingredient must be added. The actual fabric of his power, the blanket that would blind goodness, must be laid atop the bed before conception. This magic fabric was woven in ancient days, giving power to whoever controlled it. This was Edwin's secret to power, this fabric, the gift that Yehla told him he needed, and told him who to kill to attain it. The fabric had been created by evil such a long time ago. Used by only the greatest of sorcerers in the past, its power unstoppable, the magic more powerful than any other. This was Edwin's, it belonged to him, and only he controlled it.

Edwin stared at Isabella. He was consumed by the power and lust of the moment. His senses so alive, his imagination running wildly, racing away from his control. He sat down beside her, looking deep into her face. Isabella was so scared she was shaking uncontrollably, tears streaming down her face, her heart exploding deep in her chest. Edwin brought his face down close to hers.

"Soon we will lie together on this bed. I shall enjoy your body to my fullest pleasures. I will take everything from you that I desire and then I will give you life, you will conceive me a son, together we will bring forth new life, you will bear me what is mine."

He reached down and grabbed her face and drew her lips to his. He kissed her long and deep, filled with his own passion. He used no magic this time; there was no need. He cared little about how Isabella felt. Isabella was so filled with fear she felt none of the passion that she had in the past from Edwin's kiss. This was terror filling her being. She tried to scream but her mind refused to obey, her eyes staring deep into the sinister eyes of Edwin Hawkins. He lifted his face from hers, a deep smile across his lips. He had tasted her terror and it filled him with more lust. He stood up turned and walked away from her. He walked down the three steps and over to Amy.

Amy's fear was mixed with anger. What had he just said to Isabella? What was he planning to do to Isabella?Amy's thoughts weren't just for her safety, but for Isabella's as well.

"Goddamn you, Edwin!" she hollered as she kicked out when he reached the side of her bed. Edwin was taken aback by her outburst as her foot crashed into the side of his leg. He stood there looking at her then burst into laughter, a haunting evil laugh that filled the room, driving panic into Amy.

"You bastard, Edwin."

"That's exactly what your sister called me."

"What?" Amy's voice broke.

"Yes, poor Christy. She was here, but I am afraid she is no longer part of the living."

Amy burst into tears. Inbetween sobs of hysterical crying she screamed out, "Christy! Edwin, no! What did you do?"

"She should never have come here. That stupid bitch, she came to rescue you. No one will rescue you, you both will be mine."

He sat down on her bed and grabbed her face. He brought it up close to his, just as he had done with Isabella. He looked deep into the fear in her eyes, feeling the helplessness that she felt at this very moment.

"When I am finished with Isabella on the altar of life, I shall bring you forth. I shall ravage your body, taking all of the pleasure that I want from you. Then when I have tired, when I allow myself, you will conceive my son. You will gain life from my seed. You and Isabella both will conceive and both will bear me a son. That, Amy, is what this is all about, the son that your great grandmother should have given me so long ago. A son! Not Agnes, not a daughter. My son should have been born decades ago. Latina, your great grandmother, the woman chosen to bear forth my son, was weak. We were both tricked by powers stronger than mine at the time. I will not be tricked again. You and Isabella are the only women living who carry Latina's bloodline and I need that bloodline to resurrect my son with the power that is destined to be his. There will be no more treachery this time, no more deceit as in the past."

"Christy! God, Edwin, tell me you didn't kill her."

Edwin rose up from her bed, looked deep into her eyes, his human emotion trying to rise up for Amy. Why did he feel this weakness for her? At the bottom of the stairs he turned and looked back at them. Both of the girls stared at him. He would never let them go. He switched off the light, listening to their screams, and climbed the stairs.

CHAPTER 27

Mondo sat with his back to the large rocks that made his hiding place, his heart and mind racing. He truly feared for the girls' lives. He didn't know who was in the first cabin that he saw the asian man bring dinner to last night, but he hoped to God it was Christy. Marshall could take care of himself as far as Mondo was concerned. His only thought now was to get the three girls and escape from this evil island. If the girls were moved back into the house it would be impossible for him to rescue them. Edwin must be feeling very comfortable at the moment. *May his overconfidence be his downfall*, he thought.

Mondo had such a thin strand of hope to go on. Everything would have to go perfectly for him to succeed. He was up against incredible odds, and he hadn't forgotten what Christy had said about mind control and evil, and it scared him. This whole crazy situation scared the hell out of him, but there was no alternative. He would rescue the girls or die trying, simple as that.

He waited until an hour after dark, then slowly started making his way back towards Smokin'Joe. He stayed to the woods, walking carefully, slowly, trying to see all around him. He walked past the dock with the large powerboat, then on through the fence. He walked around the fish farm; a few lights were on in the house but he saw nobody. The dinghy was right where he left it. An hour after leaving the rock fortress he was back on board.

Mondo made something to eat and washed it down with a large glass of water. It was taking its toll on him, all of this. Not getting enough sleep, his diet, the constant trekking to and from the compound, the fear that he felt so deep inside. He sat at his chart table thinking of what he would need. He knew if he forgot anything there was no chance to return and get it.

He still had to figure out how to stop that large powerboat. He went to his galley and took out a large jar of sugar. He poured the entire contents into two plastic freezer bags and put them in his backpack. His plan was to pour the sugar in the fuel tanks of the powerboat. He remembered hearing somewhere that sugar would cause the cylinders to glaze up and freeze an engine. Next he pulled out his junk treasure box and removed the sheet of red plastic that he had used to cover his flashlight. He cut another lens cover and duct taped it to his spare flashlight. The girls would need their own.He threw the extra flashlight and the roll of duct tape in his pack. Next he reached down into his treasure box and pulled out his small handheld hydraulic rigging cutters. He had prayed that he would never need to use these to cut away a broken mast on Smokin'Joe. Now they were the only tool that he had that could get him through the fence. Mondo put the wire cutters in his backpack. He opened his chart table and removed a small leather pouch that held the tools he had used to break into the girls' room at the bed and breakfast. He put those in his pack as well. What else did he need?

He tried to think this night through. His first step was to cut through the fence and get inside the compound. Next he would have to get inside both of the cabins. He hoped that they weren't guarded or rigged with any sort of alarm system. Then he would have to get the girls out of the cabins, out of the compound and back near the boat dock. Once close to the boat dock they would split up. He would go and disable the large powerboat while the girls would have to find their way to the little cove and his dinghy. He hoped that it wouldn't take very long to pour the sugar in the fuel tank and that he could get back to his dinghy without the girls starting to worry. Once back in his dinghy it was a race for all of them. Race back to Smokin'Joe and race as fast as they could to Campbell River and safety. How long would it take Edwin Hawkins and his crew to discover the girls missing and come charging out after them? Long enough, he hoped.

It was nine-thirty. Mondo felt that he was as ready as he would ever be. If he forgot something then he would have to improvise or do without. He wanted to sleep but he feared not being at his rock hiding place and seeing what was going on. Suppose they moved the girls while he was away. Mondo looked around the inside of his boat, thought about all of the adventures, the joys, the struggles and hardships that together they had endured. Tonight would be like nothing else he had ever done. He hoped that he wasn't looking at the inside of his beloved boat for the last

188

time. He climbed out the hatch and into his dinghy. Mondo started to row away, then remembered the rope that they would need to get down the cliff. He rowed back, grabbed a coil of rope off of the transom and started rowing for West Penderville Island.

Mondo was glad that he had written down the compass course for both the dock and the cove. He needed them. Without the compass bearing he would never have found the cove. There were no lights from West Penderville Island and he was rowing in the darkness and fog with no sight of land. A few times he stopped rowing and just sat; it was so quiet, not a sound to be heard. The silence became too eerie so he started rowing again. It took him over an hour to row across Penderville Sound and land at the cove. He took the short rope that he used to tie his dinghy up and tied it to the line that he had grabbed from Smokin'Joe, creating a hundred-foot-long dinghy line. Next he climbed ashore, holding one end of his long dinghy line, and scrambled up the steep rocky cliff. It was a hard climb, and a few times he felt himself starting to fall backwards, but he made it to the top. He took the line and secured it to a large tree that hung over the cove, then he turned and started making his way back to his hiding place. He kept to the woods as he walked back; he could take no risks. The pathway was getting easier for him to walk, and it didn't take him very long to once again be at his rock outcropping. The lights were on in the main house and two of the other cabins. Mondo hoped that the girls hadn't been moved. Now he would have to wait. He knew he wouldn't allow himself to sleep. He needed to be ready and to have all of his senses sharp the moment he decided to go. The time slowly dragged on. One of the cabin lights switched off, then another. It was after eleven before the main cabin's lights went out and all the compound was in darkness except for the two lights at the closed gate.

Adrenaline was pumping through his body. It was hard for him to keep himself behind his rock hiding place and wait. All of his senses were so heightened and alert, his mind was razor sharp. Mondo knew he would have to use all of his mental and physical abilities tonight. If he succeeded, he would be able to rest for as long as he wanted. If he didn't succeed, then it made little difference.

It was after one when he left his hiding place and started making his way down to the compound. He already knew where he was going to go through the fence from his inspection the night before. Once he reached

189

the pond he got down on his belly and started crawling to his right. He dragged himself until he reached the point where he could no longer see the front door, but before he could see into the main house and the dining room. He had to keep putting the thought out of his mind that Edwin had found the note and that he was walking into a trap. There was nothing he could do about that, and his constant fear was a distraction that he could not afford. He had inspected the fence very closely last night and found no evidence that it was electrified or had any alarm. He pulled his backpack off and laid it down beside him, then he reached in and pulled out his wire cutters. These cutters could cut through half inch stainless steel cable. They should be able to cut through the fence without any difficulty. He reached up to the first strand to cut it; the cutters wouldn't fit. Sudden fear filled him when he realized that he couldn't get the cutting teeth around the first wire. The round head of the cutter was too large to fit between the wires of the fence. He rolled over on his back as he forced fear and panic from his mind. Already his plan wasn't working as he had thought it would. He reached down and grabbed his short handled shovel and started digging into the earth next to the fence. This was where they could have put an alarm system, he thought. He dug down deep trying to find the end of the fence so he could get his first cut going. Every time he dug down he feared hitting some sort of wire that would sound an alarm. He continued digging. There was nothing else he could do. After a foot he still hadn't hit the end of the fence. The ground was hard and he was afraid that he was making too much noise, but still he had to dig on. He had to get through the fence. That was only the first of many obstacles that he faced tonight.

He finally hit the end of the fence at eighteen inches. He cleared away the dirt so he could get his cutter in position. He brought the first strand of fencing into the jaws of his cutter and pulled the trigger. The cutter sliced through the fencing without a sound or any hesitation. Mondo worked his way up the fence, cutting a single line until it was two feet above the ground. Next he pulled the fence out and started another cut across the top. He cut a foot on each side, then he reached up and pulled the fence out towards him and folded the cut pieces back on themselves.

He left his shovel, put his cutters back in his backpack, and, pulling his backpack behind him, he crawled through the fence. He lay there for only a few seconds before he crawled to the first cabin that he had seen the asian man enter. He pulled himself up to the door, and tried to open it; it was locked. He pulled out his leather case and jimmied the lock open in under a minute. The cabin was dark and he didn't want to use his flashlight, so, very slowly, he made his way through the living room and down to the hallway. He reached down and found the carpet, and pulled it to him. Still with no light he got down on his hands and knees and started crawling down the hallway, feeling for the trap door. He found the door and slowly opened it, and peered down. It was pitch black.

"Quiet, it's Mondo," he whispered.

He turned his flashlight on and walked down the stairs. His light caught Christy sitting on a bed. She looked like a deer caught in headlights. She was too afraid to even move, her entire body was trembling with fear. Mondo walked over to her and hugged her. Thank God he thought.

"Let's get out of here," he whispered as he held her tight. "Follow me. I am going to turn the flashlight off before we leave this room. Keep one hand on my shoulder. I am going to take you outside of the fence, then I am going to come back for Amy and Isabella. No sound, please, Christy."

Christy just nodded her head in understanding. She couldn't believe that Mondo had found her.

He flipped the flashlight off and they made their way up the stairs and out of the cabin. Then they both crawled over to the hole in the fence. Mondo motioned for her to crawl through and to wait for his return.

He kissed her on the forehead, then he turned and started crawling back to the other cabin. He hoped to God the girls were still there.

He pulled himself up to the second cabin door and checked it. It was locked. Again he jimmied open the door in less than a minute. This cabin was laid out the same as the other one so he had no trouble finding the hallway or the trap door. He reached down and lifted the door up just a few inches.

"Amy, Isabella, it's me, Mondo, quiet."

Then he opened the trapdoor, flipped his flashlight on and walked down. His light caught Amy sitting on a bed, her hand chained to the bed post.

"I'm here, we're getting out," he whispered as he walked over to Amy.

He brought himself to her, reached down and wrapped his arms around her. Both he and Amy were in tears, Amy trying to fight back the deep sobs that wanted to rush out from her.

"I love you, Amy." He reached up and cut her handcuffs.

"Where's Isabella?"

Fear rushed through him as he thought that she wasn't here. He wouldn't leave without all three of them.

Amy brought her index finger up to her lips and motioned him to follow her. He kept his light shining down, pointing just a few feet in front of their steps. Amy led them into the darkness, then up three steps to another large bed. There lay Isabella. Mondo reached out and cut her chains.

"Isabella, so nice to meet you, let's get the hell out of here."

They started walking back to the trap door, each girl supporting the other. At the bottom of the stairs Amy reached out and grabbed hold of Mondo. She whispered to him, fighting to hold back her tears.

"He killed Christy, she was here."

Mondo pulled her tight to him. He could feel her heart beating wildly as he held her.

"She's fine, I've already rescued her. Follow me keep, your hand on the shoulder of the person in front of you. We must be quiet."

Mondo flipped the flashlight off and they made their way up the stairs and out the door of the cabin.

The girls followed his lead as he got down on his belly and started crawling for the fence. At the fence it was all that Amy and Christy could do to control themselves. The emotions that they felt at that very moment were the strongest that they had ever shared together. They would love and cherish each other for the rest of their lives. They held each other in a long deep embrace. Amy felt like her heart was going to leap from her chest, as if she was about to have a heart attack right then and there. Her sister was alive!

As soon as all four were through the fence they followed Mondo up the hill and away from the compound. They stayed in the woods just as Mondo had for the many times he had walked back and forth from the compound. Everybody wanted to talk, but nobody did. They all knew that they were far from safety, and this evening was far from over.

CHAPTER 28

The four of them stopped at the top of the ridge overlooking the dock. Nobody had spoken since they left the compound behind. The night was dark with no moon to show the way, and fog hung low over the entire area. Visibility was reduced to seventy-five feet. Mondo had led the girls to this spot, knowing that here they would part company. He gathered them into his arms, each girl feeling the warmth and security that his touch gave.

"I have one more job I have to do tonight. Listen, I want you to follow the shoreline past the dock. Stay right next to the cliff, as close as possible. Half a mile past the dock you will find a little cove. It will be easy to miss, so be aware. There is a rope tied to a large overhanging tree. Use it to get down to the water. My dinghy is there. Wait for me."

Mondo pulled his backpack off and searched through it. He handed Amy a flashlight and the hand held compass, then hit the glow button on his wristwatch.

"It's almost two. I want you to wait for me at the dinghy until three. If I'm not back by then get in the dinghy and head on a compass course of 095 degrees. That will take you to Smokin'Joe. Wait there for me until five. If I'm not back by five, take off and head for Campbell River. It's the closest safe place there is."

He reached down and pulled his watch from his wrist and put it in Amy's hands and wrapped her fingers over it. It was his way of telling her to keep this for him. He would be back soon to reclaim it.

The girls looked at him in the darkness. He could make out the fear on their faces; none of them wanted to be away from him.

"I have to do this. You need to go, and I'll meet you at the dinghy."

He hugged Isabella and Christy, then pulled Amy's face to his and gave her a kiss filled with care and passion.

He turned and started walking for the dock. He looked back and saw the girls hesitate for a moment before they headed off towards the cove, the red beam of the flashlight leading them on.

Mondo made his way down to the edge of the road, still hidden in the trees and brush. He was thirty feet from the locked gate and the dock. The night was cold, the air brisk; fortunately, there was no breeze or it would have made his next move even harder. Mondo walked past the gate and fence, then turned and walked to the water's edge. He stood in the cold only for a moment before he stripped his clothes off and forced himself into the freezing water, holding his backpack high over his head. There was no safe way that he could get to the dock and the boat besides swimming. He knew the entire dock area would be very well protected from shore side. The water took his breath away. His entire body ached the moment he entered the water. He never even became cold, he instantly went to a bone chilling pain. He struggled to swim as he tried to catch his breath. His entire body demanded that he turn around and climb out of this freezing water. The temperature of the water was forty-eight degrees. A human body in water this cold has about ten minutes before hypothermia takes over and the body starts to shut down. Twenty minutes and a person is dead. Mondo forced himself onward towards the boat, his mind driving him forward, his body sluggishly responding to the commands that his mind forced him to obey. He reached the powerboat and pulled himself up and over the side, landing with a crash in the cockpit. He stood up shivering, his breath still coming in great gasps. Mondo knew he had little time. His mind would continue to shut down as his body became colder and colder. He must get this job done before his mental capacities started to flee from him.

He pulled out his flashlight, turned it on, and started looking for the diesel fuel caps. There were at least two for a boat this big. He walked along the deck until he saw the water intake, and then he saw one of the fuel caps. He knelt down beside it and his heart froze. On the cap was written "Diesel" so there was no doubt this was what he was looking for, but the cap was a type he had never seen before. There was no way to open the cap from the deck. It was a smooth recessed cap of stainless steel, without any slot that he was use to finding on fuel caps. He ran over to the other side of the boat and found the second fuel intake. It had the same cap. He couldn't get the fuel caps open, he couldn't pour sugar in the fuel tanks. Mondo walked back and checked the windows; all were locked. Through the red light from his flashlight he could see the alarm sensors at each window. He hurried back to the cockpit and looked at the large sliding door. It was locked. He knelt down and looked at the base where the door ran on its runners. He could see the alarm pads. There was no way that he could get into the boat without setting off alarms that would pierce the silence of the night or trigger a silent alarm somewhere back at the compound. Mondo was standing there in the freezing cold, his naked body numb, and his mind starting to shut down. There was no way into the boat and he couldn't for the life of him think what to do next. He knew that all of their lives depended on what he came up with in the next five minutes.

The girls walked on in silence, Amy holding the flashlight as they made their way along the rock cliff that should lead them to a little cove and the dinghy. Each girl was trying to focus on the next step but all three were thinking of Mondo, and what he was doing. They all felt despair when he left them and started heading for the dock. Each girl was still too trapped in the emotions of the last few weeks to feel comfortable without him.

His words about making sure they didn't pass the cove stuck in their minds. They walked slowly, deliberately, taking each step in the glow of the red flashlight. They walked on for what seemed like a long time, each girl starting to fear that they had walked too far.

Amy turned the light off and stopped.

"Let's sit down for a minute," she said.

The fog still hung low, making it hard to see very far in the distance. They could hear the water below them slapping the shoreline, but they couldn't see it. The night felt evil to them. It was as if Edwin Hawkins was reaching out to them in the dark and fog, filling their minds and hearts with fear. They knew Edwin wouldn't let them go, that he would use whatever powers he had to capture them. They sat there huddled close to each other, too afraid to move.

Mondo knew his mind was starting to lose control, his thought process was starting to slow down as he stood there freezing, thinking, forcing himself to rethink what was obvious. There was no way to get into the boat and no way to get the fuel caps off. His teeth were violently chattering and his extremities burned. If only he had a heater. Some source of heat to buy just a little time. Suddenly Mondo had a thought; was it possible? He forced himself to move. He looked over the side of the boat, first on the dock side then on the other side away from the dock, and there he saw it. The tell-tale signs of exhaust from an onboard heater. The dark soot stains around the vent thru-hull fitting told him that this was what he was looking for. Mondo knew this was the onboard heater exhaust vent. What came out of that vent was carbon monoxide gas, an odorless and tasteless deadly poisonous gas. He focused his light on the vent, then he reached down and wiped his finger across the soot that surrounded the vent. It streaked off in his hand.Mondo leaned over the side of the boat, bringing his lips up close to the vent, and spit, then wiped it clean. He spit again then brought his backpack down and cleaned as much of the soot away as he could. His mind was running but hypothermia was starting to shut his body down, slowing his thought process as well, making even the simple act of moving his fingers difficult. He spit one more time and cleaned the vent as well as he could with his backpack. The soot stains were gone. He stood up and reached for his flashlight, and pulled the red lens cover off. Reaching down, he covered the exhaust vent with the plastic flashlight lens cover, then taped it in place with a piece of duct tape. Standing up, he tore off three more pieces of duct tape, then he reached down and completely taped the plastic lens cover to the side of the boat. The exhaust vent for the heater was completely sealed.

Standing there naked in the freezing darkness of the night, the fog hanging low surrounding him, Mondo thought that maybe all of their lives depended on a few pieces of duct tape holding tight. There was nothing else he could do. He slipped back into the water and swam for shore and his dry clothes.

The girls sat in the darkness and fog for what seemed a very short time to them, but it was over ten minutes.The sound was faint at first. Each girl heard it, each one straining in the silence to hear a little better. It was like a low howl, a groaning on the wind. The sound grew louder as they listened. It was a sound that none of them had ever heard, a sound so foreign to the human ear that it filled them with fear. The groan became louder, it seemed to be coming towards them, filling the night with a howl from the very edge of hell itself. The girls looked at each other, then all three jumped up. Amy flipped on the flashlight and all three started running for their lives. It sounded like the very voice of evil was coming through the night after them. No one who had heard this evil howl had ever lived to tell about it.

Mondo dressed quickly and started making his way for the cove and the girls. He was seventy-five feet away from the dock after getting dressed when he first heard the sound. It was faint at first, then it started to increase in volume.

The sound floated through the darkness, and it filled his heart with terror. He had never heard such an evil noise before. It was as if something from hell itself was on his trail. Mondo flipped on his flashlight and started running for his life. The sound was getting louder and it seemed to him that it was calling his name in the darkness. He changed his direction so he wouldn't lead whatever was making this noise to the girls. He ran on as fast as his cold legs could carry him, heading for the gate. This was evil that was after him, evil like he had never heard before. His thoughts raced back to what Sharon Jackman had told him just a few days ago.

"There's evil over there, Mr. Mondo."

Mondo ran like he had never run before, he charged headlong, the beam from his flashlight bouncing and careening through the forest. His only hope was to reach the gate. The evil that was after him might have to stop there, maybe. The sound was getting louder, getting closer to him. He knew that whatever was making this noise was after him, not after the girls. He had become the hunted. He could hear the sound following him through the woods as he fled. Mondo ran, but evil floated faster. He suddenly felt it, the night air becoming so cold all at once, a breeze suddenly kicking up the dirt around him. Mondo glanced over his shoulder but he could see nothing. The fear that he felt was starting to cripple his ability to run. The gate couldn't be too much further, he thought. He forced himself to race on. He turned again and looked behind him, then he looked up and he could see it against the night sky. A patch of darkness was descending towards him. Suddenly his entire brain exploded with a sound so strong that it dropped him to his knees, and the flashlight flew from his hand. He struggled to block the sound out as it filled his entire mind with terror, he tried to bring himself up from his knees, tried to start running again, but he couldn't. The evil groan was robbing him of his mental capacities, he couldn't think. He lost control, he vomited, he tried to bring himself up from his knees, tried to run, but darkness descended on him. He collapsed to the ground and couldn't move, then he couldn't remember.

The girls found the cove. In their fear they almost ran right off the cliff into the water thirty feet below, Isabella shouted first. "Stop!"

The light from Amy's flashlight was peering out into a dark void. They found the rope tied to the tree, just as Mondo had told them. They grabbed it and carefully climbed down to the water. There was a small shelf of dry land, four feet wide, that the three of them stood on. They stood there listening to the howl of evil. It was no longer coming their way. Each girl was terrified that the sound was after Mondo.

Amy looked at Mondo's watch. It was two-thirty. They had to wait for him. None of them wanted to leave him, couldn't imagine leaving him behind.They sat there on the little dry ledge thinking, praying, hoping to God that all of them including Mondo could get through the night alive. The girls sat there for over half an hour waiting. Finally it was Amy that spoke what they all had been fearing.

"We need to leave Mondo and row back to Smokin'Joe."

She paused.

She looked at his watch. It was three-ten.

"Now," she said.

CHAPTER 29

Edwin awakened the moment the girls left the compound. He knew something was wrong but he couldn't be sure what it was. He dressed and walked outside, then entered Marshall's cabin. Marshall was still chained to the bed as they had left him. Then he walked to Christy's cabin. It was now fifteen minutes after he had awakened, and she was gone. He raced over to the cabin that held Amy and Isabella; they were also gone. It was eighteen minutes after the girls and Mondo had fled the compound when he awoke Mr. Chein, who awakened the crew they had on the island and told them all to be ready. Each minute Edwin and Mr. Chein wasted was one more minute for Mondo and the girls to escape.

Edwin and Mr. Chein ran into the surveillance room on the second story of the main house.

"Dock cameras show nothing, Edwin," Mr. Chein said.

"Gate sensors, what do they show, is it closed?" Edwin asked.

Mr. Chein reached over to the joy stick sitting in front of him on the desk and rotated it to the right, as he stared at the computer screen..

"Gate is closed. We have to assume it's locked and has not been compromised."

"Dock sensors, have any been tripped?"

Mr. Chein rotated the joy stick.

"None. No sign of any intrusion on the dock, boat looks good."

"They must be on the island, I hope anyway. Whoever opened the cabins and freed the girls must have a plan to get them off. There are no boats at the dock. I wonder what they are thinking?" He brushed his hair back with his hands, staring at the computer.

"Mr. Chein, have the dock cameras pan out as far as possible. I know they can't detect much in the dark and fog but they might be able to see some motion if someone was anchored off of the docks."

Mr. Chein rotated the joy stick, zooming the cameras out into the darkness off of the main dock. At that moment Mondo was fifty feet away from the dock climbing out of the freezing water. He was out of the field of vision for the cameras.

"Cameras panned out to maximum, I'll set the audio alarm, if the cameras see anything we'll know about it. Also, Edwin, the crew are dressed and ready awaiting your orders."

Edwin and Mr. Chein sat in the surveillance room. Mr. Chein didn't know what the next move should be. Edwin did, and it terrified him. He knew he had the power to send the Seeker out but he feared to use it. He could release his evil watcher into the night, his eyes to see what he couldn't see. The price was very high, and he didn't want to pay it, but he would. Too much was at stake.

He turned to Mr. Chein.

"I will be in my room. Do not let anyone leave the compound until daylight, I repeat, no one may leave until daylight. That includes you, Mr. Chein."

He closed the door behind him, knowing that Mr. Chein was able to handle any situation that might come up in his absence.

Edwin hurriedly walked to his room downstairs in the main house, opened his door, then locked it behind him. He went to his closet, and removed a few boxes, then slid open a false panel that was built into the floor. It exposed a hiding place that held his most powerful magic. He reached down and pulled out a cedar box six inches high, eighteen inches long and twelve inches wide. The box had a sliding lid on its top. He put the box down on the floor, then walked over to the light switch and turned the lights down low. In the darkness he could barely see what he was doing, but he didn't need the light. He had done this many times before. Many times since he received this power he had been forced to call out the Seeker.

Edwin walked back to the cedar box and knelt down beside it. He slid the lid back and pulled out a small piece of fabric. It was pure black with no patterns on it, just a silky piece of material nine feet square. He then reached into the cedar box and took out a small black stone jar. It was four inches high and three inches around with a large cork inserted into its opening.

Edwin laid the silk fabric out on the floor, then put the stone jar at the edge of the material. The jar was ice cold in his grasp. Next he stood and removed all of his clothes, shoes and socks as well. He stood there completely naked, fear running through his mind. How much of a toll would it take this time to call forth the Seeker?

Edwin sat down on the fabric, his knees brought up tight to his chest. He slowed his breathing and focused his mind. Instantly he went into a trance. His mind emptied, his heart rate plummeted, his extremities grew cold, then numb. He blocked the pain out as he looked into the darkness of his mind.

"Yes, come to me, Seeker, for I am Yehla, I am the one who calls you from your rest. I am your master and I call you to do my work."

His mind was pushing, forcing its way through the darkness to where he knew he must go. His breathing was slowing even more, his mind locked in battle deep inside itself.

His feet started to twitch and shake, then his entire body started to sway back and forth, like a cobra before its charmer. A strong spasm set in, racking his feet and legs. His body was slipping out of his control. He reached out with his right hand for the black jar, picked it up, and opened the cork lid. The spasms grew stronger, reaching deep into his groin, then the spasm reached his abdomen. Upwards towards his brain the pain raced. Edwin poured some white chalky substance from the jar into his left hand. The spasm reached his heart, then his lungs. He couldn't breathe, he was losing control. At the very moment when the spasms reached his brain Edwin flung the chalk up into the air over his head. The fine powder hung suspended in space, then as the spasm reached his mind, the powder slowly descended over Edwin. His body tried to scream, to move, but nothing happened. The powder drifted down over him, engulfing him, coloring him a chalky white. As the last of the floating powder reached the floor Edwin's mind was gone.

The Seeker flew out into the night. Its eyes were now Edwin's eyes, its sense now Edwin's sense, its mind Edwin's mind, its soul dark and evil. The Seeker, evil black magic from days of old, flew out of the room, leaving the shell of Edwin Hawkins' body crumpled over on the black fabric. The Seeker exploded into the night. It hovered over the compound, then raced skyward until it was three hundred feet above the ground. It stopped, paused, smelled the air, sorted out its bearings, then ever so softly it started to sing. It was the haunting song of evil. It filled the dark, silent night. It was the beginning of the hunt.

The Seeker floated slowly, following its song as it started to move.

It left the compound behind and started spiraling outwards in ever bigger circles, expanding its range, its song now leading it towards its goal, towards the hunted.

The roadway came into view. The Seeker looked at it, sang a little louder, tasting the air for what it sought. It was after humans as always, but tonight it could not kill. It must gather to itself what it sought and bring it back alive. This was the first time that it ever had to return with its prey alive.

Its song grew in intensity and so did its abilities to search. It circled through the night tasting, hearing, sampling the night air. It could taste its prey. It could feel the fear that drove the hunted on, trying in vain to escape. At the docks it circled to its left. It sang louder, driving its fear deeper into the hunted.

In an instant the Seeker turned away from the water and into the woods; a choice was made without even recognizing it. It now could see its prey, the form of the hunted running, racing through the blackness of the night. The light that it carried bouncing, flashing about, as it tried to find its way through the darkness to escape. There was no escape. The Seeker slowly started to unfold itself, started to spread itself out into a web, a net of blackness and power.

Slowly it started to descend, its web extended for the capture. The human ran wildly through the forest, as fast as the Seeker could remember humans able to run, but it was of little use. At fifty feet above its prey it took a huge breath and exploded a single note out into the night. The prey stumbled, dropped the light and fell to its knees. Slowly the Seeker continued its descent, its icy cold tentacles reaching outward and downward. Again it exhaled its song, filling the night with a groan. The prey sensed it was doomed, knew there was no hope, but still it struggled on, trying to get back to its feet. The Seeker finally reached down and touched the human with its net, wrapped its icy tentacles around him, took one long last breath and sang out its note directly at the man. The prey was captured. It collapsed onto the ground unconscious, as close to death as the Seeker dared take it.

The Seeker raced back up into the night carrying the limp body of its prey. It circled over the compound then landed inside, dragging the human over and leaving it at the foot of the steps going into the main house. Like a cat leaves a mouse for its owner. Then it raced high into the air, giving out one more piercing scream, this cry so different from the song that it sang to hunt. One last note of terror that filled everybody in the compound with dread as the Seeker descended through the roof of the main house, sending an icy chill into every corner of the building, filling all that felt its touch with fear and trembling. It crashed into the limp lifeless body of Edwin Hawkins, melted into his mind, and his dark soul. Edwin's body jumped, rolled over and then lay still, deathly still. The Seeker had returned home, it had done its job.

CHAPTER 30

The girls clambered into the dinghy, Christy sitting in the bow, Isabella in the stern, Amy pulling on the oars with all her might. She dug the oars into the cold water as if all of their lives depended on it. The fog continued to hang low like a veil sitting upon the water. Even as they put distance between themselves and the island, the fog hung with them; it was an evil fog. The blackness of the night made any sense of direction impossible for them. They could still hear the evil howl that came from the island, the sound drifting in and out of the night.

Amy couldn't hold the compass and row at the same time.

"Christy, here, hold the compass, push the illumination button on the right side and point with your arm to 095 degrees. It's the only way we can find Smokin'Joe."

She handed Christy the compass, turned it for her so she could read it. Then Amy started rowing again, Christy's right arm pointing the way to safety.

Mondo was on all three of their minds and hearts. Was he still alive? What could make such an evil sound? They knew that whatever they had heard was searching for them. They were its prey, not Mondo. Somehow he had become the hunted instead of them. All three knew that they owed their lives to Mondo. Amy's muscles hurt but she continued to dig with the oars. Christy was faithfully pointing the way. Isabella, sitting in the back, was too shocked by all that had recently happened to think much beyond the moment.

Amy rowed on through the night; she had no way of knowing how far they had to go. They were completely surrounded by fog and darkness, not one light or star could be used for a point of reference. She continued to pull on the oars, not stopping, not giving in to her aching muscles and back. Amy had this terrible feeling that something was wrong with the compass, that her continued rowing would lead them right back to the dock and the large powerboat with Edwin Hawkins waiting for them.

Amy trusted Mondo; if he said to row 095 degrees then that was what she was going to do. She rowed one and a half hours without stopping before she could make out the shore and the faint outline of buildings. She turned the dinghy away from the fish farm and found Smokin'Joe anchored in the cove.

Amy rowed the dinghy up alongside Smokin'Joe and all three of them clambered aboard. Amy tied the dinghy line off at the transom, then they all climbed down below.

Soon Amy had lights on and the heater going. She also had the stove lit, making hot water for tea. Christy and Isabella sat on the settee close to each other, their thoughts sharing the horror of the evening. Mondo had rescued them, but at what price, they all three feared?

They drank their tea in silence, feeling the warmth and comfort, the safety, that Smokin' Joe offered them at the moment.

It was starting to get light outside. The clock on the main bulkhead said five-thirty. They remembered Mondo telling them to leave for Campbell River if he wasn't back by five. None of them could even think of leaving him behind. They finished their tea in silence, each girl lost in her thoughts of the night and of their time on West Penderville Island as Edwin's captives. The clock on the bulkhead slowly continued to move. Soon it was five-forty-five, then six. The girls made eye contact, looking deep into each others' faces, all three of them searching for the next thing they should say. Each one thinking the same thing, but none wanting to be the first to speak; just a little longer they all hoped, just a few more minutes, he will be coming soon.

At six-fifteen Amy stood up, walked over to the chart table and started the engine. Neither Christy nor Isabella said a word.

"We need to leave," was all she could say.

Amy climbed up the companionway steps and walked out onto the deck. She walked to the stern and cast off one side of the line that held Smokin' Joe close to shore. She pulled the other end of the long line in and let it fall to the cockpit floor.

"I have to go forward and pull the anchor," she whispered to the girls still below as she walked by the hatch.

Amy reached the bow and unhooked the short line used as the anchor snubber. She reached down with her right foot and hit the anchor windlass button. The anchor chain slowly started to come in, making so

206

much noise in the silence of the morning. Chain clanking against chain as it rolled up and over the bow roller, the electric windlass ever so slowly pulling the anchor from the muddy bottom.

The fog was starting to dissappear in the morning light. Amy could see the fish farm, but she couldn't see West Penderville Island, and that was all right with her. The anchor was almost up when the chain came to a sudden stop, causing the clutch to slip. She instantly took her foot off of the windlass button only to watch about twenty feet of chain run back out into the water.

"Shit," she muttered to herself.

Amy hit the switch again, and slowly the chain came up. She could see the anchor rising up from the deep. The anchor was almost at the surface. Then again suddenly the chain went tight, the clutch slipped and the anchor and more chain fell back into the water.

"Goddamn it," Amy screamed. The anchor was caught on something. She was starting to panic. What if she couldn't get the anchor free?

Again Amy hit the windless switch, but this time she had the snubber line ready. As the anchor just started to break the surface, just as she could hear the clutch start to slip, she threw the chain hook around a link of chain. The clutch started to slip and a few feet of chain ran out before the snubber came up tight and held the anchor. The anchor was up at the surface of the water. It had a thick rope or cable stretched tight across it, the ends of the cable running off and down into the deep water of the sound. The anchor was up but Smokin' Joe was trapped by this cable and Amy didn't know how to free it from the anchor. She stood there staring at the situation, not having any idea of what to do.

Out from the fish farm she could hear an outboard engine start up. She looked over and a small aluminum skiff was leaving the dock and heading her way.

Sharon Jackman pulled along side Smokin' Joe.

"I'm Sharon Jackman, a friend of Mondo's. Where is he?" She said as she glanced around.

Amy slumped into a sitting position on the bow.

"He's still on the island. He told us to leave him if he didn't get back by five, it's... "

Sharon interrupted.

"He's still on the island?"

"Yes, he is, I don't know what to do, but he said to take Smokin' Joe' and head for Campbell River."

Sharon looked at the fouled anchor.

"You caught one of the old cables that used to hold the fishing dock. I'll help."

Sharon reached down and took a strong piece of rope from the bottom of her boat, then knelt down and reached over into the water and tied it to the cable. She wrapped the other end around a cleat at the bow of her boat.

"Let some of your anchor chain out, slowly or you'll sink me."

Sharon put the outboard in reverse and started pulling at the cable while Amy let some of the chain out. Sharon suddenly felt the cable release the anchor, pulling her bow down. She ran forward and released the line from the cleat and let the line run overboard.

"You're good to go, head for Campbell River. I'll keep an eye out for Mondo, go," she said.

Sharon knew that Mondo must be in trouble, but she also knew that he wanted these girls safe, and if that meant leaving him behind then so be it.

Damn, Sharon thought to herself, her intuition about him was right.

CHAPTER 31

Slowly consciousness returned to Mondo. He couldn't see and he couldn't hear anything. His body ached and he realized that he was lying against a wall with his hands bound together and held up above his head. He tried to move but his hands moved only a foot or so before they came to an abrupt stop.

It dawned on him that he was tied up just like he had seen the girls. Mondo was chained to a wall. There was no escape. He tried to open his eyes, but couldn't; they were taped shut.

Panic tried to overtake him, but he held it back. He knew that he was in big trouble, but panic was a deadly enemy and he couldn't allow himself to lose control.

He forced himself to think back as much as he could. He remembered the noise, a piercing sound that seemed to engulf his entire body, then explode inside his head. That was when he fell, and lost control. After that it was all a blank until the moment that he awoke here.

He had no idea if he was alone. He couldn't hear a thing. He couldn't tell if it was day or night. It took all of his inner strength to fight back the creeping panic.

He wondered if the girls made it. That was his only hope, maybe they made it to Campbell River and the cavalry would return with them. Maybe? Maybe he was in a secret dungeon and even if they returned they would never find him. The terrifying thought entered his mind that maybe somebody was going to leave him here like this to waste away and die.

Mondo slowed his breathing and started counting. He heard someone by the time he reached the number eighty-four.

"You have caused me a great deal of effort and trouble."

The tape was ripped from his eyes. Instantly he burst into tears. He couldn't see, he was blinking and blinking, trying to regain his focus.

Slowly, he could make out the forms of two people, one sitting, the other standing.

As his tears cleared away and his vision returned he could see that the man sitting down was in a wheelchair. Next to him was the asian man.

"You have caused me great pain and for that you will die. It is only a matter of time before I get the girls back. I have my crew out now—you will not deter my plans."

The man looked old, weak, and feeble.

"How does it feel to know that you are about to die, that for all intents and purposes you are already dead? There is no hope, and no way out," the old man said.

"Who the fuck are you?" Mondo spat out, even though he knew he was looking at Edwin Hawkins.

"Good question," he laughed. "My assistant here is Mr. Chein. I am Edwin Hawkins, though I have been known by a few other names in my time."

"What the hell are you doing? Why did you kidnap Isabella and Amy? Who are you, Edwin?"

"My, so many questions for one about to die. Should we tell him of our plans, Mr. Chein, or just let him die in ignorance?"

A smile grew on Mr. Chein's face. Mondo knew this guy was not to be messed with. Mr. Chein had an air of complete confidence about him. Mondo thought he would rather be staring down a gun barrel than looking at Mr. Chein.

"I think that the soon-to-die usually are granted one request. Maybe we should tell him a bit of our plans."

"Very well."

Edwin readjusted himself in the wheel chair. He looked like he was not accustomed to sitting there.

"I don't have the time or effort to answer all your questions, nor the desire for that matter. The girls are mine. They are my great-granddaughters. Their great-grandmother was deceived, she failed, and history was changed. World War Two was to end so differently. It would have ended so differently, if Goodness had not once again intervened, this time saving humanity from self-inflicted nuclear annihilation. Did you know that Adolph Hitler was only three months away from testing the first nuclear weapon when Berlin fell to the Allies? Think of how

210

different history would be if Germany had those three extra months! With German rocket capabilities the entire world would have exploded into a nuclear holocaust followed by a nuclear winter that would have lasted for decades, maybe centuries. The death and destruction would have shaken humanity to its very core. A new world was waiting to rise from the insanity of the old. From this destruction my son and his chosen believers would have risen to start anew. We were to build our city, our fortress, and we would have built it, and we would have survived, for Yehla was with us. But! With no son to lead, with Goodness still being the Goddess that she always has been, all things changed." He paused, shifted his weight in his chair, looked at Mondo, then continued.

"Now Amy and Isabella will each bear me a son as their great-grandmother should have over eighty years ago. Goodness will not be able to interfere this time. Goodness has grown weak, she has fought too hard to protect mankind. Because," he laughed, he spat the words from his lips.

"Because she loves mankind, she has used her strength up fighting for human survival. She had hoped that in time mankind would grow in wisdom and be able to learn. The more Goodness fought for humanity, the harder she struggled to protect and nourish mankind, the more she was betrayed. Humanity took her gifts for granted, always wanting, never satisfied. The more Goodness showed of herself and her riches, the more people wanted, more and more. They have sucked Goodness dry and she has nothing more to give. Mankind has created the bed that he will soon perish in. Goodness is tired. She can no longer fight for you. A new end awaits humanity, one just as deadly, just as final as nuclear war."

"You're mad," Mondo said.

"Mad?" Edwin laughed.

"You're an old man. You... you're going to father children?"

It was Mondo's time to laugh, fear was gone from him.

"You couldn't get out of that wheelchair, let alone father children."

"You are so stupid. You have put me here. The effort it took me to track you down, to capture you and to bring you back here has put me in this chair. I am over one hundred years old. My body already is starting to heal itself. Tomorrow I will be out of this wheelchair, in three days I will be completely renewed."

Mondo slumped back against the wall. He was mad. Mondo thought, but he believed every word that Edwin had spoken. This guy was the evil that had descended on Penderville Island.

"Now," Edwin continued, "I have granted your last request, the dying man's last wishes. Now you will fight for your life."

He nodded at Mr. Chein who smiled, turned, and walked out the door.

He returned in five minutes, carrying a small box, with Marshall Sanbourn standing by his side.

" I believe you two have met. Well, now one of you will kill the other. Here, right now, one will die, one will live for another day or until I have changed my mind."

Mr. Chein opened the box and took out two identical knives, each eight inches long.

He closed the box, walked over and unchained Mondo's hands from the wall. He dropped one knife between his legs.

Mondo grabbed the knife and got to his feet rubbing his wrists, trying to get feeling back into them.

Mr. Chein walked back to Marshall, handed him a knife, then grabbed Edwin's wheelchair and pushed Edwin to the back corner of the room.

"The rules are very simple, gentleman, kill or be killed, that is all."

Mondo realized Edwin was going to sit there, with Mr. Chein standing by his side, and watch him and Marshall fight for their lives.

Mondo glanced around the room. It was rectangular, about thirty feet long and twenty feet wide. Edwin and Mr. Chein were at the far back wall. There were no windows, one door, only one way in and out.

Mondo had no feeling for Marshall one way or the other, but it was beyond his comprehension that he would have to kill him with this knife if he was going to live.

Marshall didn't feel the same way. He was bigger than Mondo and he felt confident in his abilities to put Mondo down. He even thought that maybe if he impressed Edwin enough he might be able to join his ranks.

What Edwin, Mr. Chein, and Marshall didn't know was that all through high school Mondo had studied martial arts. After high school, during the two years he went to college he studied hard to achieve his black belt in karate. His sensei had always told him, never use your skills. Always use your mind; self defense is always the mind first, strength and skill are the last resort when all other means have failed. It looked to

Mondo that at this moment all other means had failed.

Marshall had a smirk on his lips.

He was over-confident. Good, Mondo thought, his first mistake. They each started slowly circling the other, Mondo sensing the balance of the knife in his hand. Even though Mondo would have to rely on his training, he would have to use his mind as well. Even if he killed Marshall he was still in big trouble. He had to get out of here somehow, escape from this island. Killing Marshall, if he had to, was only the first step. He knew he couldn't take Mr. Chein. One look had told him that.

Marshall stopped circling, and held the knife out in front of him, clutching it tight in his right hand. Mondo could read his face. With a sudden forward lunge Marshall brought the knife up to where Mondo had been just a second before, slicing wildly through the empty air. Mondo side stepped to his right, leaving Marshall exposed and off balance. Mondo, with his split second reflexes, couldn't bring himself to drive his knife upwards and into Marshall's chest. The moment disappeared before he could think again.

"Tricky shit," Marshall said."You're gonna die right here, Mondo." Before he finished his sentence, Marshall swung towards Mondo and slashed again with a deadly upward slice. Mondo side-stepped to his right once again.

Let him think I always move to my right, Mondo thought.

He remembered his sensei telling him to out-think his opponent, make them think they understand you.

Marshall slashed again as Mondo jumped back out of his reach. They circled each other. Mondo was keeping his distance, working his way around the room, Marshall more in the center following Mondo. Again and again Marshall rushed at Mondo slashing wildly, no form or control, just rage and anger. Mondo constantly worked his way back and out of the reach of the knife, trying to stay alive one second at a time. So many times Mondo could have taken Marshall; almost every one of his attacks left him open and off guard.

Mondo waited.

"*Use your mind*," he said to himself.

Mondo worked his way next to Edwin and Mr. Chein. Neither of them seemed concerned that he was so close to where they were. Overconfident, Mondo thought to himself.

Marshall again charged, slicing madly, rushing at Mondo. He side-stepped him again, but this time he reached out and grabbed Marshall's right hand. Marshall's momentum made it easy for Mondo to pull him forward and cause Marshall to lose his balance. In one strong fluid movement, Mondo pulled Marshall forward and hurled him right into Edwin's wheelchair. Marshall slammed into Edwin, knocking him backwards, sending the wheelchair crashing against the back wall. Edwin started to tumble out as the wheelchair bounced back from the wall and tipped over on its right side. Mr. Chein took his eyes from Mondo and started to reach for Edwin as he fell. In that moment Mondo turned and drove his knife right into Mr. Chein's chest.

Mr. Chein gasped, his eyes bulging from his face. In the next second Mondo pulled his blade clean and brought it down and across Edwin's face, slashing him. Blood poured from both men. Mr. Chein reached out for Mondo with lightning reflexes, grabbing his throat, and brought a knee up into Mondo's groin. Mondo's body exploded in pain, the knife fell from his grasp. Mondo, using all of his strength and training, pushed himself back and away from Mr. Chein. Edwin was trying to stand up, a look of disbelief on his face. At that moment Marshall charged again. Mondo side-stepped him, to his left this time; it was the only thing that saved his life. Marshall swung the knife to the right where he thought Mondo was going to move. Mondo, in pain and almost out of breath from Mr. Chein's kick, brought his right hand up hard and crashed it against the side of Marshall's head. As Marshall started to fall Mondo brought his knee up high and plunged it into Marshall's solar plexus. He gasped, all of his air forced from his lungs. To Mondo it was all reflex now; no thought process went into what he did.

Marshall was falling, folding over on himself. Mondo brought both of his arms up, locked his hands together and brought them crashing down on the back of Marshall's neck.

The knife dropped from his hand, he hit the floor with a hard crash, and didn't move.

Mondo turned and saw Edwin standing, blood pouring from the wound across his cheek and neck. Mr. Chein was trying to come at Mondo but he tripped over the wheel chair and fell into Edwin, knocking them both down to the ground. Mondo knew Mr. Chein was dying. The asian man was struggling, trying to get up, a look of complete bewilderment on his face, then he collapsed.

Edwin rolled to his right and seemed to leap to his feet, blood rushing from his face and neck. It looked to Mondo that his jugular vein was cut. Marshall was out cold, he wasn't going anywhere.

Mondo turned and ran to the door, hoping it wouldn't be locked. It wasn't.

He flung the door open and slammed it closed behind him. He was in a long corridor with steps at his right. He took off, leaping up the steps three at a time. He was running so fast that at the top of the stairs he rushed right into one of the guards. The surprised guard raised his shotgun, but Mondo was upon him before he could level the gun. Mondo pushed the gun barrel up and away with his left hand as the guard fired into the ceiling. Mondo slammed his right fist into the guard's face, and then brought his right knee up into the man's groin. The guard lost his grip on the shotgun. Mondo wrenched it out of his hands, and using the butt of the shotgun, hit the guard hard along side of his head. The guard fell to the floor. Mondo tightened his grip on the shotgun and ran out the front door and up the dirt roadway.

There was no time for stealth. He had to get away as fast as he could. At the top of the ridge he could see Penderville Sound and the dock. The next moment a bullet smashed into the roadway three inches in front of him. Mondo leaped to his left and dove to the ground, rolling up behind a large rock. Another bullet smashed into the rock inches from his face.

Mondo had no idea where the shooter was. He couldn't guess what direction and he knew that if he moved he would be shot. He glanced out over Penderville Sound and for the first time in this whole ordeal he thought that he really might die here. The shooter was out there just waiting for him to make the next move.

Sharon Jackman had had enough. She watched as Smokin' Joe motored out of Penderville Sound and on towards Campbell River. Then she turned and rushed into her house. She grabbed the .30-'06 hunting rifle that her father had given her and loaded it. She threw an extra box of cartridges in her jacket pocket and ran out the door to her aluminum skiff. She had been afraid for too long. The Jackman family had been here for a damn long time and she wasn't going to let her fears stop her from doing what she knew was right.

She started the engine and headed across Penderville Sound for West Penderville Island. She pulled into the little cove that Mondo had tied his dinghy up to last night. She had just finished climbing up the steep cliff when she heard a muffled gunshot. It sounded far away, but it was a gunshot. She took her rifle off safety, and started walking towards the dirt road. She was walking in the woods, following Mondo's footsteps from the night before.

Suddenly she heard something from her right. She looked up and saw Mondo racing over the top of the hill coming towards her. Her heart leaped with joy; he's alive! The next instant she heard the loud crash of a gunshot and saw Mondo rush off to his left and dive behind a large rock. Another shot blew part of the rock away just inches from his head.

Sharon had a good idea from the sound that the gunman was up the hill and to her left, across the road from where Mondo lay.

"*God, kid, stay still,*" she thought to herself.

She crossed the dirt roadway and walked into the woods alongside the road. Her hope was that the gunman was concentrating on Mondo so much he wouldn't be thinking of anything else.

She reached the top of the ridge twenty feet into the woods and froze. Her years of hunting and the instinct it brought her told her to stop and listen. She could make out the rocks that Mondo was hiding behind. She stood there for five minutes. No sound, not even her breathing could be heard. The forest had an eerie quietness to it.

The shooter made the first mistake. He hacked up a cough and spit to the ground. To Sharon the sound echoed through the woods. He must be about thirty feet ahead of her and closer to the road. She knelt down and aimed her rifle, trusting her instincts to guide her.

Suddenly, Mondo jumped up and fired two shots from his shotgun, then turned and started to run towards the cover of the forest. The shooter rose to his feet, and took aim at the fleeing Mondo. Sharon fired, the slug catching the shooter in the chest, flinging him off of his feet and spinning him sideways. One shot was all it took.

Sharon raced out into the roadway and down the hill after Mondo.

They were both running as fast as they could. Mondo heard something behind him, turned and saw Sharon running after him. He knew then that she had fired the last shot. She had saved his life. He let her catch up to him. Mondo was all smiles.

"This way," she blurted out. She was completely out of breath, but still running fast.

Mondo followed her as she ran off the road, and he knew they were going to the cove. Mondo glanced back, looking for more trouble, but he didn't see any. They reached the skiff, jumped in and cast off.

"I'll drive, you shoot." He said.

All the way back across Penderville Sound Sharon kept the rifle pointed at West Penderville Island. Mondo pulled up to the fish farm dock and turned the motor off.

He looked at her, and smiled.

"You saved my life, you know."

"You're damn right I did." She burst into laughter.

Mondo looked at where Smokin' Joe had been anchored.

"Did the girls get off all right?"

"They left around six-thirty or so. They waited for you Mondo, they didn't want to leave you."

"I need to get to them."

"Take this boat, you'll catch them."

Mondo looked hard at Sharon.

"You're the salt of the earth, Sharon. I'll leave the boat in Campbell River."

He leaned forward and kissed her forehead.

"That's the first time I ever kissed a woman holding a rifle."

Sharon climbed out onto the dock, a big smile on her face.

"There's enough fuel in there. Get the girls, and get to Campbell River."

Mondo started the engine, pulled out from the dock, spun the skiff around and headed out.

Sharon walked up to her front porch and sat down with the rifle across her lap. She felt better with it in her grasp.

CHAPTER 32

Amy knew Smokin' Joe well. Once the anchor was up they headed out of Penderville Sound as fast as they could, Amy at the helm.

"Get me those charts," Amy hollered at Christy who was standing down by the chart table. She brought the charts up into the cockpit. Amy sorted through eight different charts before she found the one that she wanted.

"Look," she said to both girls who were now standing by her at the wheel.

"We need to head down this long narrow channel, then make a bee-line for Campbell River. It's about fifteen miles once we get through the narrows."

"I remember some of the landmarks, Amy, I've been out here twice," Christy said.

"Good."

Amy looked at Isabella. She was so shaken by all of this. Amy was worried. She knew Smokin' Joe was going as fast as she could, but the boat was only going seven knots. It would take them over two hours before they would be safe in Campbell River. Amy remembered the large fast powerboat that was tied up to the dock at the island. If they came after them in that boat they wouldn't have a chance. Amy couldn't think about it and she didn't want Isabella or Christy to know about her fears. Just keep going, she thought. Each minute away from Penderville Island is one minute closer to safety and salvation.

All three girls were completely drained emotionally. Christy was so relieved to have her sister free from that mad man. Isabella and Amy were now so close to each other.

Mondo was on all three of their minds. Amy couldn't stop thinking about him. Had he died to save their lives? What a terrible concept. She loved him so much, for such a long time, but this morning when they had to cast off and leave him behind, her heart broke.

"I just can't believe Mondo didn't make it back, I am so afraid," Amy said as tears ran down her face.

Christy and Isabella both hugged her, all three girls standing close, all three of them touching, feeling the physical support that they each needed.

"He seemed like a hero to me," Isabella said.

Amy realized she had said little about Mondo to her.

"Yes, he is so much more than a hero. I'd marry him today, I could be Mrs. Mondo."

She would have laughed, but her heart was so full of fear for him.

They made it through the narrows. Two more hours, Amy thought.

The two crew members from West Penderville Island had their instructions. Wait until daylight. Don't go outside until the sun has come up. They didn't know the reason and they didn't really care, but they both knew to heed Mr. Chein's warnings. Neither of them left the compound until after seven o'clock.

Their job was simple. Find the girls. They must have left in a boat. If they were on the island they would have been found by now. These two knew the drill.

One cast-off the lines while the other had the engines up and running. Once away from the dock, the driver took a run up Penderville Sound to the end of the channel. Nothing. He turned and started racing for Campbell River. That was the only direction the girls could go.

The driver was occupied with steering and his navigation.

The other crew person had one job and he knew it well. He loaded his shotgun with a deer slug, then made sure that the high powered rifle that he had used to capture Marshall and Christy was loaded and ready for action. If they couldn't find the girls on the water they were to proceed to Campbell River and contact Mr. Chein.

The day before they had observed the sailboat that was anchored next to the fish farm. This morning they noted that it was gone. They knew that was their target. That boat wouldn't be able to get away from them unless it had a huge head start.

The powerboat swung out of Penderville Sound and into the narrows. The shooter thought about how easy it had been to capture Marshall and Christy. Their little red boat sunk in over three hundred and fifty feet of water. No one would ever find it. He had to make sure no one ever found the girls. They could cause trouble if they made it to the police.

The powerboat raced out of the narrows and into Seather Sound. Both crew members could make out a small boat on the horizon.

"Looks like our friends," the driver said.

The gunman didn't say anything, didn't have to; he knew that there was no escape for the sailboat.

Amy was constantly looking over her shoulder as they headed for Campbell River. It seemed like every minute she glanced back and was relieved to see nothing behind them. The last time she looked back her heart froze. There was a large powerboat, too far away to tell if it was the one at the docks, but it was coming fast and coming their way.

There was nothing more she could do. Smokin' Joe couldn't go any faster.

The driver of the power boat flipped on the transponder switch as he rotated a small joy stick on the dash board. In front of him a compass rose appeared on a computer screen and changed course as he rotated the stick. He dialed in the boat in front of him like he was lining up the sights of a gun barrel. The transponder sent out a narrow but very powerful radio beam, its purpose to disrupt any VHF radio communication. It created a static void that no radio signals could penetrate.

Amy reached for the VHF radio microphone in the cockpit. She hit the transmit button only to hear a shocking amount of static.

"Damn," she said.

She played with the radio gain, trying it in all positions, nothing. Her radio was useless.

Isabella and Christy followed Amy's stare behind them. All three girls were silent as they focused on the speeding powerboat coming their way.

"Flip the heater on. It's freezing," the gun-man said. He didn't know why he hadn't thought of it earlier.

The two men on the powerboat could see Smokin' Joe. They knew their prey was at hand.

"Just like before," the driver said. "I'll pull up to their stern and you

221

fire into the boat. That should stop them. If not, fire again with the deer slug. They must be returned alive."

"It will be harder to stop the sailboat. Its engine is down below, and more protected," the shooter said.

"Yeah, well, shoot that sailboat enough times, they'll stop."

Now the powerboat was less than a mile behind Smokin' Joe.

The girls were doomed and they knew it. There was nowhere to run, nobody to call. It was just them and this racing powerboat out on the water. The nearest land was over half a mile away.

None of the girls said a word. Each knew there was nothing that they could do. Amy thought about the flare gun. Big deal, what would that do? All three couldn't bring themselves to imagine that they would be caught and returned to the island. That maybe Mondo was dead and in an hour they would be back under Edwin's control, this whole escape for nothing.

If the driver and the shooter could have looked over the side of their boat they would have seen that the plastic flashlight cover that Mondo had duct tapped over the exhaust vent for the heater was still in place. Carbon monoxide gas was slowly filling the cabin of their boat.

The shooter took the high powered rifle and walked up to the bow, closing the cabin door behind him. He knew he was still too far away but he wanted to shoot at them so bad, just to scare them. He raised the sights over the boat and turned the barrel to the left. The shot would be fifty feet away from them, but the sound would hit them like a cannon.

He fired.

The gunshot exploded over the open water. The sound crashed into Smokin' Joe and the girls. Each girl screamed, that was all they could do. The shooter fired two more rounds, each shot driving the girls closer to panic. They were trapped, they knew it; they were going to go back to the island, and back to Edwin Hawkins.

Terror filled each one of them.

The shooter walked back into the cabin and closed the door behind him.

"That will give them something to think about," he said.

The driver didn't respond. The gunman looked at him. Something about the driver didn't seem right, but he couldn't tell.

By now the powerboat was less than a quarter of a mile away from Smokin' Joe and still racing full speed towards the girls.

Amy was paralyzed with fear. There was absolutely nothing she could do. She grabbed the radio microphone again and tried it, but only static.

The girls stared and waited for the inevitable, their capture. The powerboat was still going very fast when it started turning to their left. It seemed to be swinging out so it could come up alongside Smokin' Joe. They tried to see into the cabin but they couldn't see anybody. The power boat started to swing further away from them. Just when the girls thought it would slow down and pull alongside of them, it passed them by and kept going. Each girl was too fearful to even think of what was going on. The powerboat left them behind, racing towards the island about a half a mile away, leaving all three of them silently waiting for the boat to swing around and come in for the capture.

As the large boat got further away from them it became harder to judge the distance between it and the island. Suddenly the powerboat lurched upwards, flew into the air, and seemed to stop in mid motion before it exploded into a ball of flames and came crashing down onto the island.

"Yes! Oh my God, what happened?" Amy shouted, all three of them wondering the same thing.

Twenty minutes later they saw another boat racing out from the narrows and heading their way. It was much smaller than the burning powerboat. It looked like a small skiff but it was too far away for them to see much. Each girl's heart once again filled with fear.

Isabella and Christy stared at the small boat racing their way. Amy just kept looking forward, concentrating on driving. Had they just escaped from the large powerboat to be caught again?

"It's Mondo!" Christy shouted.

Amy spun around and there was Mondo, racing towards them in a small aluminum speed boat.

All three girls burst into tears.

"Mondo, Mondo, oh my God, Mondo!" All of them were shouting his name, jumping up and down. They were going to make it. At that moment Amy knew she would love this man for her entire life.

Mondo was standing up, waving his hand wildly in the air.

Amy backed off the throttle and put Smokin' Joe in neutral.

He pulled up alongside. He was still the most beautiful man Amy had ever seen.

Everybody was in tears, Mondo too.

He jumped up from the skiff and swung himself aboard Smokin' Joe. He reached down and tied Sharon's skiff off to a cleat. Then he wrapped his arms around all three of them.

"It's okay. We've made it," he said.

CHAPTER 33

By noon, Edwin Hawkins knew that his plans had completely failed. Mondo had escaped, the girls had escaped, and something was wrong with the powerboat. His most trusted advisor, Mr. Chein, who had been with him for over twenty years, lay dead downstairs.

His time on the island was over. All of his plans and efforts, the time and money that he had spent to create this island stronghold, were now worthless. It was because of one man, a man he hadn't even considered in his plans. Mondo would pay. Edwin knew that this setback would not stop his plans for the future.

The police would arrive soon, he had no doubt. There was the disappearance of the speed boat that Marshall and Christy were taken from. The dead shooter, the kidnapping of the girls, there was no way to explain what had gone on here. He would disappear and leave West Penderville Island forever.

He also had two other people to think about, Marshall Sandbourn and the one surviving crew person, the person who let Mondo escape from the house. He had both men downstairs chained to the wall. He would deal with them later.

Edwin started walking towards the dock. He had heard the gunshots. It was only a few minutes before he found the body of the shooter. No signs could be left for the police, no evidence at all.

The shooter was sprawled out in the woods. Edwin surveyed the scene. Blood was splattered everywhere. Edwin pulled a small jar from his pocket and very carefully opened the top and poured a liquid on the dead shooter, one thin line poured from his head to his toes. The liquid started to smoke, then a sickening stench rose up from the body as the smoke burst into flames. In ten minutes, Edwin knew, nothing would be there. No bones, no clothes, nothing. Once the shooter was consumed, the flames would reach out for more. Soon the trees would ignite, quickly spreading through the forest. West Penderville Island would burn. He grabbed the shooter's rifle and walked back to the compound.

One problem taken care of, a few more to go. He walked down to the basement room where his last crew person and Marshall were chained. He left the door open behind him when he walked in. Both men were terrified. He had seen that look many times before, the look of the soon-to-be-dead. Both men knew they were going to die. He turned and looked at Mr. Chein's body. Poor Mr. Chein, such a wonderful and loyal helper he had been all of these years.

What a sad, sad day, Edwin thought. His strength was so exhausted from his efforts with the Seeker, then having to deal with the wound that Mondo had inflicted. He knew the knife cut would have killed a mortal man.

The crew person would die, there was no doubt in his mind. It was Marshall that he had to think about. Could he use Marshall to replace Mr. Chein? He knew that no one could replace Mr. Chein.

Both men were against the wall in chains, just as Mondo had been a few hours ago. Edwin said nothing as he raised the rifle and shot the crewman dead, his blood splattering over Marshall.

He looked at Marshall.

"You will live, for now. Don't betray me."

He walked over and unlocked Marshall.

"Get up, we must deal with Mr. Chein."

Marshall could hardly stand, his entire body filled with fear and relief. He knew he should be dead.

"Get Mr. Chein, bring him upstairs, now."

Edwin walked over to the dead crew person and poured more liquid on him from the little jar. The burning stench started to fill the room. It was all Marshall could do to throw Mr. Chein over his shoulder and make it outside before he started to vomit.

"Lay him there." Edwin pointed to the couch in the living room upstairs.

"What a sad ending to a great man," he said, as he poured the liquid on Mr. Chein. Edwin took one last look around the room, then walked outside, followed by Marshall.

Edwin carried nothing but a small cedar box with him.

"Go into the storage shed. You will find gasoline, you will find flares. I want all of the buildings burning. I want all of West Penderville Island

226

to burn. Once the buildings are burning, start the surrounding forest on fire."

Edwin turned and started walking towards the narrow little path and the back gate of the compound.

"What about me?" Marshall was so filled with fear he could hardly get the words out.

Edwin turned around and looked at him.

"I told you that you will live. Once all is burning, follow the pathway that I take, follow it to the water.I will await you at the waters' edge. Hurry, do your job."

Marshall didn't move. He kept his eyes focused on Edwin. Once Edwin disappeared down the trail, Marshall started running to the shed.

The main house was already in flames. Marshall could see smoke rising from the other side of the ridge on the road to the dock. He ran into the shed, grabbed two five gallon cans of gas and put a handful of flares in each of his back pockets. He dragged the gas cans one hundred feet away from any of the buildings. Next he grabbed one of the cans and poured gas on each of the outbuildings and ignited them with a flare. All the buildings of the compound were up in flames. Then he grabbed the second gas can and ran wildly, pouring the gas over the trees and shrubs that surrounded the compound. His entire focus was on getting no gasoline on himself. Once he had poured out the contents of the gas can he threw a flare into the saturated forest. The flames exploded with an intense heat and a rush of air that seemed to pull the breath right from his lungs.

Soon the entire forest, except for the pathway area that he would have to use as an escape, was up in flames.

Marshall ran for his life. He charged down the pathway, trying not to trip. The air was filled with smoke and the stench of gasoline. He ran away from the heat and flames toward his only salvation. Suddenly he could see the water before him through the trees. Onward he ran, blindly, fear driving his every step. He came to the end of the level pathway. The trail veered to his right and down. He took the steps three at a time, leaping down towards the water. He could see Edwin sitting in a boat with a large outboard engine on the back. Marshall ran past a small boat house that was perched on the side of the rocks, and jumped into the water, then swam the twenty feet out to Edwin. He pulled himself up into the boat and collapsed in the bottom.

Edwin put the motor in gear and they raced out from the burning island, flames reaching high into the sky. Edwin's island fortress was burning to the ground.

Marshall lay in the bottom of the boat, his breathing hard and labored. He didn't move. Edwin looked down at the pathetic Marshall Sandbourn, gasping for air like a fish out of water. Marshall would live today. Edwin had no idea about tomorrow.

CHAPTER 34

One hour after Smokin' Joe and her crew pulled into Campbell River, Amy and Isabella were in jail. Christy and Mondo couldn't believe it, couldn't believe that after all they had been through, the girls were locked up for violating Canadian Customs and Immigration laws.

"Until we get this all sorted out these two girls will stay in jail," a skinny immigration official said. The man was arrogant, with an attitude that no public servant should be able to get away with.

Mondo had taken an instant disliking to him the moment they had been ushered into his office. Mr. Johnston was a little man, with a little man complex, doing a job that made him feel big. The more Mondo had to sit and listen to him, the more that he and Christy had to deal with this bureaucrat, the angrier he got. Mr. Johnston was skinny, short, and balding, about mid-forties, with glasses and a small goatee. The guy wouldn't make it in the real world for one day, Mondo thought. Neither Mondo nor Christy would have given him a second thought, but he was the official who had the girls put in jail. This little man had Amy and Isabella behind bars, and now he was trying to justify his actions.

Mondo's blood was boiling. he couldn't take any more of it. He jumped out of his chair and leaned forward menacingly over the man's desk.

"Take it easy, Mondo," Christy said, grabbing his arm.

"You idiot!" Mondo screamed. "Do you have any idea what we have been through? We came here for help, not harassment."

"You will shut up, you… you… American!"

That was it. Mondo snapped. He reached over Mr. Johnston's desk, grabbed him by his shirt, yanked him up out of his chair, and looked deep into his eyes. The look on Mondo's face told the official he had messed with the wrong man. Mondo held him there for only a few seconds, enough time for him to know that Mondo was in complete control of his wellbeing. Mondo was beside himself, his normal mellow demeanor pushed over the edge.

"I want them out now!" he screamed as he threw Mr. Johnston back into the chair. The little man slammed into his rotating chair, spinning to his right before the entire chair flew backwards, sending him and his chair crashing into a big heap on the floor. Mondo started to run to the back of the desk to continue his assault when Christy once again grabbed his arm.

"Stop it, Mondo, please."

Ten minutes later Mondo was in a jail cell. Only Christy was free to come and go.

After they hauled Mondo away, Christy was forced to sit outside in a waiting area for over twenty minutes. She was in the local Royal Canadian Mounted Police district office. The entire department was ablaze with activity. The story that these four had just told was like nothing ever heard in Campbell River, and there was confirmation that West Penderville Island was on fire.

"Ms. Wilson, would you please come into my office?" Christy looked up into the face of an older, gray-haired lady in a bright police uniform. Christy hoped this woman would be easier to deal with than Mr. Johnston. She didn't want to end up in jail with the others.

The name on the door, written in small black letters, said Captain Harriet Smothers.

Christy followed her into the office. Captain Smothers closed the door behind them and pointed towards a chair in front of her desk. Christy sat down.

"I am sorry for the treatment your friends have received from Mr. Johnston. Frankly, a few of us here are rather glad that ...well...," she paused, looking for the right words. "Let's just say that some of us think Mr. Johnston may have had it coming," she said as she was sitting down in her chair. "The guy is a real jerk. Please tell Mondo we are rather proud of him."

Once she sat down she leaned back in her seat, and smiled to herself. When she regained her official demeanor, she continued.

"We are trying to verify your story. Your sister and Isabella LaMartina did enter this country illegally, that is a fact, and there is nothing that we can do about it. The law is very specific regarding this issue. Your friend Mondo could be in big trouble for assaulting a public employee in the pursuit of investigating a crime. Depending upon what charges will be filed against him he could be here for weeks. I suggest you find yourself a hotel room for a few days. Nobody will be out of jail before then."

Christy could see sympathy in the lady's face.

"Can I see my sister?"

"Normally, no, but, well, I think so, follow me."

Christy followed Captain Smothers out of her office and down a long hallway. She could feel every eye in the entire department on her. They came to a large locked door. Captain Smothers inserted her key, opened the door, and they passed through.

Amy and Iasbella were sitting in a small lounge area. This wasn't what Christy thought a jail cell would look like. The two girls jumped up and ran to Christy and hugged her. Then they looked at Captain Smothers.

"Ladies, let's all sit down." She motioned with her hand to a large table with six chairs around it. They all sat and looked at Captain Smothers.

"I don't know how soon I can get you out of here. I don't think you should be here, and I will do my best to get you out. It will take a few days for sure. As for your friend Mr. Mondo, he could be here for a long time. Assaulting a public official is not taken lightly around here."

Amy and Isabella both looked at Captain Smothers, then at Christy.

"What?" Amy asked.

"Mondo is in jail. He attacked the immigration official who decided that you two should be in jail. That guy is a complete jerk," Christy said, then she looked at Captain Smothers, who continued.

"Is there any way that we can verify any part of your story? Anyone who can help us sort this out?"

The three girls sat there for a long time saying nothing. None of them could believe that this was the welcome that they received once they found safety.

"I met Sharon Jackman," Amy said. "She told me she met Mondo, I think she could help."

"Sharon is great, she's a wonderful person. If she can vouch for you, then I think I can go before the judge and try to get you all out on bail."

"Bail? Bail! We just want to go home," Isabella said.

"Sorry."

Captain Smothers stood up, leaving the girls sitting there. She walked to the door then turned.

"Christy, knock on the door when you want to leave. There is a phone on the far wall. Each of you can have one call." Then she let herself out.

Isabella stood up and walked over to the phone. She picked up the receiver.

"Yes," a voice said.

"I want to make a call, please."

"Your name? Okay, go ahead."

Isabella dialed her dad's cell phone.

"Sunny here."

"Dad, it's me."

"Isabella. Oh my God! Where are you? Are you all right? What ... Where did you go?"

Sunny was driving down 405, heading towards Long Beach.

"Dad, I'm okay, we are all okay, except we're sitting in jail."

"What? For God's sake, in jail! Where, what happened?"

"Dad, it's way too long of a story. We are in a little town on Vancouver Island called Campbell River. I think we might be here for a while."

"Campbell River, goddamn, Isabella, what did you do?"

"Dad, we didn't do anything."

"Isabella, I'm coming up there, I'm flying up today, if I can. I'll get your butt out of jail."

"Dad, you can't just come up here and break us out, this isn't the wild west."

Sunny started laughing.

"Isabella, dear, that was the old days. It's much easier with a lawyer than a gun. I'll get my business taken care of. I'm coming to get you out. I love you."

"Dad, I love you so much."Isabella hung up. She felt so relieved that she had been able to call her dad.

Sunny hung up from Isabella, and punched in another number. The phone was answered on the second ring.

"Sanders, check something out for me. I think Ace Air owes us a few favors. I want a jet to take me up into Canada, and I want to go now. Let me know if they'll fly me up there, okay, great."

Sunny hung up.

Whatever had been on his mind before Isabella's phone call

evaporated. His daughter finally needed him.

"Should we call dad and mom?" Amy asked her sister.

"Forget it, they don't even know we're gone, they'd just worry."

Isabella walked back over to the table, but she didn't sit down.

"You're not going to use your phone call?" She asked looking at them both.

Both Amy and Christy just shook their heads no.

"Make a call for me, please."

"Okay."

Amy walked over to the phone and picked it up. She got the same person that Isabella talked to. Isabella punched in the number for the Orca Whale Research Center. Johnny Mason had been in her heart a lot lately.

The phone was picked up by someone that Isabella didn't know.

"Johnny? He's out on the boat. You can leave him a message."

Isabella hesitated, what did she want to say, how could she explain anything.

"Yes, please tell him Isabella LaMartina called. I'm in Campbell River I really want to talk to him. Tell him he can reach me at the Campbell River police station."

The voice on the other end hesitated.

"Police station, do you work there or something?"

Isabella felt like asking the woman if it was any of her damn business what she was doing in the police station, but she didn't.

"Just have him call the station, tell him I'm in jail."

Ten minutes later, Johnny Mason was speeding back to the whale research center. The intern who had taken Isabella's call had called Johnny on the VHF radio. When she told him that a lady named Isabella had called for him and that she was in jail in Campbell River, Johnny didn't hesitate for one moment. He spun the Zodiac around and headed for base. He was already thinking of which ferry he could catch, one that would take him from Salt Bay Island to Vancouver Island.

"I'm coming, Isabella!" he shouted.

Mondo couldn't believe that he was in jail. He had never been arrested before in his entire life. He was mad at himself for losing his composure; it was wrong and he knew it. Still, that little shit just pushed him over the edge. How could he be of any help to the girls when he was sitting in a jail cell? Damn, he was dumb.

Christy stayed with Amy and Isabella for over an hour. The girls took comfort in the fact that Isabella's dad was coming, and that he had said something about getting them all out of jail and having lawyers. Isabella didn't mention that he was a mobster.

Finally Christy left the jail and walked the four blocks to the Harbor View Bed and Breakfast. It seemed like a life time ago that she had stayed here, wondering what her next move should be. Well, she thought, here she was again, wondering what she should do now. Everybody was in jail but her. It was beyond belief.

Johnny Mason caught the two-fifteen ferry to Vancouver Island. He hoped his ancient 1974 Volvo wagon could make the trip without breaking down. If it did break down he would leave it on the side of the road, he didn't care. Isabella called for him, she needed him and he was coming, come hell or high water.

Sunny LaMartina turned his car around, made a phone call to cancel his meeting in Long Beach, and drove home. He walked into his living room, kicked his shoes off and grabbed his phone. He looked up his attorney's number and called him. Sunny had been paying the guy big bucks for years, and by God he could finally start earning some of it.

His attorney called the Campbell River police station five minutes after he hung up from Sunny's call. After a ten minute conversation with Captain Smothers, who was very sympathetic to the girl's plight, the attorney called an associate of his in Victoria, Canada. Once the attorney in Victoria realized who he was talking too, and realized how important Sunny LaMartina was, he knew this case was his top priority. Anything that he had been working on before he would pass to one of his associates in his office.

While Mondo, Amy, and Isabella sat in their jail cells, wondering how this whole affair was going to pan out, a small army of friends, loved ones, ones who hoped to be loved ones, and ruthless attorneys who didn't care who loved them, were all on their way. The whole damn cavalry was

234

heading to Campbell River.

CHAPTER 35

Ten o'clock the morning after Smokin' Joe and her crew had arrived in Campbell River, Sunny LaMartina was waiting in the police station to see Isabella. He had been waiting for over fifteen minutes and had just about had enough. He sat there concentrating, trying to keep himself under control. He was in a small waiting room, sitting by himself.

Suddenly the door behind him opened with a rush of cold air. He turned to see a young man rushing through the door, out of breath. He looked like he had slept in his clothes, and finished running the Boston Marathon, all at the same time.

Johnny Mason ignored the man sitting in the waiting room and ran up to the desk. No one was there. He glanced around, then slammed his hand down on the small desk bell that had a note taped under the glass counter that said 'please ring once'.

Johnny hit the bell eight times before someone came out from behind the corner.

"Slow down, young man," Captain Smothers said.

She wouldn't normally answer the front desk, but whoever was on duty must have run off to the bathroom.

"I want to see Isabella LaMartina."

Sunny perked up instantly.

"Are you family?" Captain Smothers asked.

"Ah, well no, but listen, I've come a long ways and... I love her and I want to see her, please."

"You love her, do you?" Captain Smothers said, holding a straight face even though it almost killed her.

"Yes, I do, I know my rights, and I want to see Isabella."

The bravado that Johnny was trying to force looked very thin to Captain Smothers, but she had to admire this young man's guts.

"Please take a seat, I believe there are now two of you waiting to see her."

Johnny turned around and noticed Sunny for the first time. Johnny didn't know what to think; his sudden expression of love seemed stupid.

Sunny studied him, a part of him wanting to hug this kid. Anybody who could feel that strongly about his daughter, to stand up to the Police Captain the way he did, just might be all right. Johnny walked over and sat down next to Sunny. He felt awkward, didn't know what to say.

"You're waiting to see Isabella?"

Sunny fought hard to keep his smile back. Be a gangster, he told himself.

"Yeah, she's my daughter."

Johnny swallowed hard. Boy, did he feel like an idiot.

Five minutes later Captain Smothers walked out from behind the counter, smiled and said. "Gentlemen, please follow me."

They walked down the hallway where Christy had been led the day before. At the doorway Captain Smothers reached up on the wall, grabbed a metal detecting wand and scanned both of the men. Satisfied, she unlocked the door and let them enter.

Amy and Isabella were sitting on the couch looking through some magazines. When Isabella looked up she couldn't believe it. Both her dad and Johnny were standing there. She jumped up and ran into her dad's arms, hugged him, then turned and hugged Johnny, long and deep. Sunny stood there, realizing once again that Isabella was no longer his little girl.

"Oh, I can't believe you're both here, how did you meet each other?"

"We didn't," Sunny said. He extended his hand out to Johnny, who grabbed it and shook it.

It felt like Christmas for Isabella; her heart was jumping out of her skin. Amy walked up and stood next to her.

"This is Amy. We have been through a lot together lately."

"Amen," Amy replied.

They all walked over to the table and sat down. Sunny started telling them that he had lawyers, damn good lawyers, working on all of this and that they should be able to leave soon.

"What about Mondo?" Amy asked.

"Who?" Sunny replied.

All this time Johnny just sat there not saying a word, feeling like a little fish in a big pond. If he only realized how happy Isabella was that he was sitting there with them.

So they told Sunny and Johnny the whole story. How Mondo was Amy's boyfriend, about Christy and about Edwin Hawkins, and the island. Isabella told them how Mondo had discovered where they were being held and how he had rescued them all alone.

"Dad, we owe our lives to Mondo. We would never have gotten off that island if not for him."

"Well, I can guarantee you that when we leave this damn jail, Mondo is coming with us."

Sunny couldn't believe the story that he was hearing. It wasn't possible. If he didn't know Isabella better, he'd think she was making the entire thing up.

Isabella was trying to smile at Johnny without being too obvious. Johnny was just sitting there not saying a word, totally oblivious to Isabella's feelings. Finally Isabella stood up and walked over next to him. He looked up as if he were looking into the eyes of the executioner. He loved Isabella, but he didn't know how she felt, his nervousness melting his insides into a puddle of mush.

Isabella smiled, then reached down and brought his face up to hers. She kissed him right then and there, she didn't care if her father was sitting next to Johnny. When she brought her lips away from his she could read his face so well. Tears were gathering in his eyes. He wiped them with the back of his hand. Johnny had just kissed an angel. For the first time in his entire life, Johnny Mason had fallen completely in love.

"Can we continue with the story?" Sunny asked, but he had to laugh to himself. He was going to get to know this kid a lot better, real soon.

After listening to the girls' story for twenty minutes, they all sat there in silence. The girls were exhausted reliving the entire ordeal that they had been through. Sunny's mind was thinking fast. He was going to call the lawyer in Victoria, tell him that he needed to get Mondo out as well.

It was after twelve-thirty when Captain Smothers entered and said that they would need to leave. She let Sunny and Johnny know that they could come back for another visit later in the afternoon.

Out in the hallway Sunny stopped Captain Smothers.

"I'd like to meet this Mondo fellow if I can. It sounds like I owe him a lot".

"Right now I can't let you do that, but I will try to arrange it for this afternoon. But yes, I think you owe this young Mr. Mondo fellow an awful lot. Sounds like he saved those girls' lives."

Outside the police station, Sunny started walking to his car. Johnny was following a few steps behind. He didn't know what to do now. He stopped walking. Should he follow Isabella's dad or what? Sunny walked five more steps before he realized that Johnny wasn't next to him. He turned and looked at the young man. The poor kid was scared to death.

"Come on, I'm buying lunch."

Sunny's attorney in Victoria wrote down all the information about Mondo, as Sunny sat in his rental car talking to him. His lawyer in Los Angeles had given Sunny the Victoria lawyer's name and number just in case.

"I want Mondo out as well, I want everybody out. I want them out yesterday, but I will settle for today. You got that?"

"Yes sir, Mr. LaMartina, by today."

The lawyer hung up. He would get those kids out of jail if he had to drive up to Campbell River and break them out. He knew that if he could do a good job for a client like Sunny LaMartina, he would be in fat city for a very long time.

Sunny and Johnny drove three blocks to a restaurant. Sunny pulled into the parking lot, and turned the car off, but made no effort to open the car door and leave. He looked at Johnny, who felt like he was staring into the very eyes of death itself.

"So you love my daughter?"

Johnny wanted to evaporate, but he could go nowhere.

"Sir, I loved your daughter from the first minute I ever met her. Yes, I love your daughter."

"Relax, kid, I'm not going to tear your head off."

They walked into the restaurant. Johnny was feeling better. Maybe Isabella's dad wasn't going to kill him after all. Sunny was liking this kid more and more.

Mondo sat in his jail cell. He wasn't in a nice little lounge area like the girls. He was in an eight by twelve foot cell with bunk beds and a stainless steel toilet. At least he had the cell to himself. He knew there was no way that he could get himself out of this mess. He would just have to wait it out. He wondered what Christy was doing. Did she end up in jail also? Mondo just wanted to get the hell out of Campbell River and be with Amy, and to put this whole crazy adventure behind him. It seemed so long ago that he was thinking about sailing to Alaska.

Captain Smothers made a few calls to her superiors in Vancouver. She explained that this was turning into a complete mess, and that if the story leaked out to the press it could be an international nightmare.

She also explained that Sharon Jackman, who had lived around here practically forever, could vouch for their story.

"I think you need to go over Mr. Johnston's head and let these kids out. Even if they can't go home, at least let them out on bail."

She was sitting in her office, phone lodged on her right shoulder, drawing little circles with her left hand on a piece of scratch paper.

"Yes, I know, I know that he assaulted Mr. Johnston, but for heavens sake, the man needed it. It was getting impossible to even work with him. Okay, please see what you can do."

She hung up. She hoped this could all be figured out very quickly.

At three o'clock that afternoon she received another call from her superiors in Vancouver.

"Yes, I understand, very good call. Thank you."

All charges had been dropped.

Amy and Isabella were led down the hallway to the men's holding cell. They walked in ahead of Captain Smothers and up to Mondo's cell.

"Hey, sailor, looking for a good time?" Amy joked.

Mondo jumped up and grabbed the bars. God, he wanted to hug and kiss her.

He saw Captain Smothers standing a few feet behind the girls.

"Break me out of here, we can do it," he laughed.

"All charges have been dropped, even your assault charges. Seems like somebody hired the right lawyer to handle this. You're free to go."

Mondo grabbed the bars and shook them, his excitement barely under control.

Captain Smothers led them outside into the waiting area. She gave each of them a small brown envelope that held their personal belongings that were removed from them when they were booked. Mr. Johnston could not be seen anywhere.

The three of them walked outside wondering how to find Christy and Sunny. It didn't take long before Sunny drove up with Johnny in the car. He saw them standing in front of the jail and pulled right up to them. He rolled down his window, and yelled, "Hey, let's get the hell out of here."

"Sounds good to me," Amy replied.

Mondo just shrugged his shoulders and followed everybody into this stranger's car.

"How are we going to find Christy?" Amy asked.

"Call the police station, that Captain lady seemed really nice. Ask her to tell Christy that I rented a suite in the Holiday Hotel, down by the ferry landing.I think we need to celebrate," Sunny said.

CHAPTER 36

It was after eleven that night when the entire group made their way back to Sunny's suite. They all had the time of their lives. Sunny was the big spender. He wouldn't let anybody pay for dinner or drinks; he paid for it all.

Back in the suite, Sunny ordered two bottles of champagne from room service. After it arrived he toasted everybody, and especially Mondo, whom he thanked over and over for rescuing the girls. It was a great time for all.

Mondo and Amy were tired, Smokin' Joe was waiting for them, and they had been waiting for each other for a very long time.

It was after midnight when they finally left. Christy walked with them. They escorted her back to the bed and breakfast, then turned away and started walking the short two blocks to the boat.

"What a fun night," Amy said. She snuggled her head deep into Mondo's shoulder. Mondo had his arm around her waist, pulling her to him. The night was cold and dark, with scattered clouds covering the sky.

There was nobody out. Only a few cars had passed them since they left Sunny's suite. The marina came into view. They walked down the ramp towards Smokin' Joe, which was tied up at the far end of the walkway. It was so dark that even the sparsely placed dock lights seemed to have a hard time penetrating through the night. They walked on, holding each other close.

Fifty feet from Smokin' Joe, Mondo caught a movement out of the corner of his eye. Before he could even think he pushed Amy away from him and jumped into a self defense position. Knees bent, hands out in front of him, ready for whatever would attack. Only a cat walked down the walkway.

"Jesus, I must be paranoid," he laughed as he started to pull Amy to him. Suddenly he heard a voice behind him.

"You had better continue to be paranoid."

Both Amy and Mondo spun around to see an old lady walking towards them. Mondo was still in attack mode, but he was trying to calm his body down. The lady walked up to them. When she had spoken she was only ten feet behind them.

"How did you..?"

"How did I get so close to you? The real question is why?"

"Okay, why?" Mondo asked.

His apprehension was back, his body on high alert. Every fiber of his being was ready for an attack, yet here was an old woman standing before them. Something told Mondo that this wasn't right.

"Are you afraid of a little old lady, Mondo?"

Amy had been standing off to Mondo's right, two feet away. She walked over next to him and said. "You scared the hell out of us. Who are you?"

"I am somebody who knows what you have been through. I have watched you both from afar. I tried to keep you safe from Edwin."

At Edwin's name Amy blurted out. "Who the hell are you? What do you want? What do you know about Edwin?"

Mondo put his arm around her.

"It's all right, calm down."

There they were, standing on the dimly lit dock at one o'clock in the morning with not another soul around, except for this old woman who knew Mondo's name and, worse, knew Edwin's.

"I have a gift for you. It's from a friend that you don't know, but she knows you. She wishes you success in your upcoming struggle."

"What upcoming struggle?" Mondo snapped.

Mondo couldn't believe this. He was shaking deep inside himself. It felt like he suddenly caught hypothermia, he felt a chill to his very core.

"My gift is from one who has watched your struggle with Edwin Hawkins, and all that he has used to capture and control the girls. He will not go away, he hasn't been defeated. You escaped from him and his island, but he will come after you. Here, this is my gift."

The old lady walked up to Mondo and reached into her jacket pocket. She pulled out a long gold chain with a thick medallion attached to it. She didn't say a word, just reached up and put the chain over his head, letting the medallion fall to where it hung right over his heart.

"This will protect you. It is a weapon that you may need. You will know what to do with it if the time comes."

Mondo was too stunned to say anything. There was something about this old lady that wasn't real.

She turned and started walking away.

"Hold it, who are you?" he asked

She turned, smiled.

"I am a friend of a friend, goodness knows you."

Then she started walking down the dock. Amy and Mondo stood there watching, feeling the panic that the name of Edwin Hawkins brought to both of them.

"You know, Amy, whoever that lady was, she wasn't from around here," he said with a smile.

"I know, Mondo," Amy half heartedly laughed.

They walked back to Smokin' Joe, opened her up, and climbed down below.

Mondo felt the weight of the medallion and the chain around his neck; it felt very heavy for its size. He got the heater going and sat down at the chart table, Amy by his side. Mondo reached up and pulled the medallion over his head.

It was pure gold with a blood red stone in the center. The entire medallion was the size of a silver dollar.

"Look here," Mondo said as he put the medallion into the light.

They both stared at the writing that was inscribed upon the medallion. It was written in a text that neither had ever seen. The back side had a picture on it. There was a line drawn across the middle of the medallion. It looked like a picture of the horizon with a partial sun rising up from the center line and a partial moon descending down from the same line. The large blood-red gem went through the entire medallion. It was laced with a twisted gold wreath that appeared around its outer edge.

"This is gold, Amy."

"God, Mondo, what is this about? What did she mean about Edwin?"

"I think we both know what she meant about Edwin. It's not over."

That night they lay in each other's arms. The passion drained from their bodies. Amy seemed to be asleep, Mondo was wide wake. He never thought for one minute that he would have to contend with Edwin

Hawkins again. It seemed to him that he had rescued the girls and it was time to get back to all of their lives. Now as he lay in the darkness of Smokin' Joe, hearing the wind blowing against his little ship, he realized that he would have to seek Edwin out. He couldn't allow Edwin to pick and choose the time of his next attack. If Edwin was coming back for the girls then he would have to be on the offense. He couldn't give Edwin any advantage.

The next morning they all met at Sunny's suite as planned. It was after ten when they finally made it to the restaurant and started breakfast. Everyone was happy. Christy was so excited about getting back to Malibu and her shop. Isabella and Johnny couldn't wait to return to the whale center and continue developing their relationship with the whales and each other. Sunny was resolved to letting Isabella go; he wouldn't hold her back any more. He would give her his blessing to do whatever she really felt in her heart that she wanted to do.

As breakfast continued it soon became obvious to everyone that Mondo and Amy were being very quiet. While the others were full of excitement, Amy and Mondo could not hide the concerns that they felt. Both of them tried to be light-hearted, making an effort to join in, but it was painfully obvious that something was really bothering them.

It was Sunny that finally called them on it.

"Do you two want to tell us about it?"

"About what?" Amy replied.

"Whatever has got you two so down. I thought you both would be happy as hell after spending a night together on your boat."

Amy blushed and Mondo laughed.

"That's not the problem."

"Okay, what is?" Sunny replied. Amy and Mondo stared at each other, finally Amy let out a deep sigh.

"We met an old woman last night on the dock as we were walking back. She wasn't real." Amy said.

"What do you mean, not real?"

Sunny had become the question man for the group, but he was only repeating what they all felt.

"Trust me, she wasn't from around here. She gave Mondo a medallion. She told us that it's far from over with Edwin."

At his name Isabella gasped. She slumped in her chair, hardly able to catch her breath, then she reached over and grabbed her dad's hand.

"Here is the medallion she gave me." Mondo pulled it off of his neck and passed it around. When it got to Sunny he held it, felt the weight of it.

"This is pure gold, kid," he said

"I think this is a lot more than just pure gold. The lady said this was a weapon that I might have to use."

"Against Edwin?" Sunny asked, although he already knew the answer.

"Jesus, I can't go through this again," Isabella said, her voice almost shrill.

"What do you think of these markings?" Sunny asked.

"I don't know about the markings but I think it is ancient. I think this is power beyond this world, or at least beyond the world as we know it."

They all sat there in silence taking it in. Nobody touched another bite. Christy and Isabella were both reliving their ordeal with Edwin, both looking back into his face full of evil.

Isabella burst into tears. She squeezed her dad's hand.

"I can't do this, I can't live with this."

Sunny put his arm around her, brought her close to him.

"You won't have to, love. Let's get back to my place. We need to rethink the rest of our lives."

Edwin Hawkins was living in one of his houses located near Vancouver, Canada. It was a nondescript house on a nondescript street in a suburb of Vancouver. Marshall Sandbourn was with him. Edwin was filled with rage, his emotions completely overshadowing his reason. He wanted revenge and he wanted to make it as painful and as slow as he could. He would get the girls back. That was his destiny. What he burned for was to destroy Mondo. Edwin had spent years putting his island fortress together. He and Mr. Chein had thought of everything except one man, a man who had never even appeared to him in his deepest of meditations. That fact surprised him. In the back of his mind he wondered if Mondo could have protection beyond this world. That was foolish, he knew. Yet how could he have escaped from his meditations? He would find out, and then he would take pleasure in killing Mondo. He would enjoy every moment of his agony. It would not bring Mr. Chein back. That was a loss beyond anything Edwin could ever have imagined. Mr. Chein his faithful servant and friend, his confidant for over twenty years, was now dead, cremated in the flames that still burned on West Penderville Island.

Edwin would start his plans immediately. First he would have to locate the girls, then Mondo. He was in a hurry, he was afraid that if he took too long his emotions would lose the fury that he felt, afraid that he might start listening to his mind and not his anger. He wanted revenge. Edwin wanted blood and he wanted it now. Mondo would die and the girls would be his again. He had plenty of places to bring them to. This time he would make no mistakes, and the girls would never be found again.

CHAPTER 37

Back at Sunny's suite everybody was scared. Even Sunny was wondering what the hell to do next. He pulled Mondo off to the side and they walked out onto the deck. Then he closed the sliding door behind them. A few minutes later Isabella opened the door and started to join them.

"Sorry, honey, go back inside and let the others know we're having a meeting out here, okay?"

Isabella glanced at her dad. She knew what he meant. Keep everybody inside while Sunny and Mondo figured out the next move.

"Jesus kid, do you think we really have to go after this guy?"

"Sunny, if he is going to come after the girls again, then we have no choice. We have to hunt him down and we have to make sure that he goes away for good."

"What do you mean by that?"

"You know what I mean."

"Can you do it, kid?"

"No, I can't, but I will. I've seen what this madman is capable of. You wouldn't believe the fortress on the island. He had Amy and Isabella chained to a bed, in total darkness. This guy is like nobody I've ever met or even read about. None of us can live with his shadow hanging over our heads, we can't and the girls can't."

Sunny knew Mondo was right. There was nothing else they could do but make Edwin Hawkins go away forever.

The two men stared out over the beautiful waters of the Strait of Georgia, barely able to make out the snowcapped mountains on the mainland. Neither spoke for a few minutes, each lost in his own thoughts, trying to figure out what to do.

"Sunny, don't you have connections that can help us track him down?"

"I got connections everywhere, I'll make some calls."

Just then Johnny opened the sliding glass door and stuck his head out, looked hesitantly at Mondo and Sunny, then walked out onto the deck and closed the sliding door behind him.

"I might be able to help."

"Yeah, how's that?" Sunny replied.

"When Edwin showed up at the Whale Research Center I didn't trust him at all. I wrote down his car license plate number. I thought it was dumb back then, but maybe it can help."

He pulled out his wallet and handed Sunny a piece of paper.

"Johnny, this is our first step. This may be more important than you know, thanks."

Johnny smiled at Sunny's compliment. Sunny was about the most intimidating person Johnny had ever met.

Sunny and Johnny walked back into the house, leaving Mondo with his thoughts.

Amy had been waiting for a chance to talk to him alone and she took it when she saw Sunny and Johnny enter back into the suite. Amy walked out to Mondo, gave him a kiss on his cheek, then sat down beside him.

"Christy is totally freaked out about this. Actually, Mondo, so am I."

"I am too, Amy."

If she had been hoping to get some support from him, she didn't. It made her realize just how much they were suddenly up against. The fact that Edwin Hawkins could once again enter into their lives was something that none of the girls thought of once they left West Penderville Island. They thought it was all over. Edwin was defeated, we've made it, so long Edwin, hope we never see you again. Now as they sat in Sunny's suite, everybody's thoughts once again focused on Edwin. It was inconceivable that this was happening again. Each person was lost in their own thoughts, their own fears, and Edwin Hawkins was once again in the center of all of their lives.

Sunny spent twenty minutes in his bedroom on the phone. All of his calls were to Los Angeles. Tracking the license plate number down, if it went anywhere, would take very little time. Sunny hoped to have a call back by early afternoon. He was also looking for something else; he had to come up with a safe place for the girls. They all needed a safe house. That had to be his immediate goal. Once that was taken care of, he and Mondo could start working on a plan. It took Sunny three phone calls to put the safe house together.

Unfortunately, he should have made only two, for Edwin Hawkins had connections as well.

All eyes looked at Sunny when he came out of the bedroom. Mondo and Amy were back inside as well.

"We're checking out of here. I have a safe place we can go and nobody will find us there. It belongs to a friend."

"Dad, what do you mean, a safe place? As in safe from Edwin?"

"That's it, honey, safe from Edwin. We can't assume anything. He could be putting plans together now. Here is how I see it. We put you three girls in the safe house. Johnny, you head back to the whales. Sorry, kid, but that's the safest place for you there is. Mondo and I keep tracking Edwin down until we find him and take care of him."

"How long is that?" Christy asked, her voice showing her fear.

"We need to take this one day at a time right now, one step at a time," he said.

"Sunny, how long?" Christy pressed.

She shouldn't have.

"Listen, people, this is not a game! You've been through this with him once. I'm on the outside of all of this but I can see the fear, the terror that he put you all through. This is over only when Edwin Hawkins is dead. Now let's go."

It took them ten minutes to check out of the hotel and to assemble in the parking lot.

"Dad, I'm going to ride with Johnny. Where are we going?"

"We're heading to a ski area. A friend has a house there. It's called Twin Ridges. We have to drive down to Nanaimo, take a ferry over to Vancouver, and then it's about two hours north from there. We can't get separated."

Sunny looked at Johnny, looked at his old beater Volvo wagon.

"You sure that thing can make it?"

"Yes, sir."

"Well, Isabella, you know my cell phone number. We'll stay together, but if we get separated, call me."

"Sure, dad."

Mondo, Christy, and Amy piled into Sunny's rental car and they headed out of Campbell River, following Johnny's Volvo. Sunny figured if it broke down he might as well be right behind them to help. Mondo knew Smokin' Joe was safe until he returned.

It was a two-hour drive down Vancouver Island to where they caught the ferry across the Strait of Georgia and into Horseshoe Bay, just north of Vancouver city limits. Once on the mainland, they headed north towards the world-class ski area of Twin Ridges.

Johnny's Volvo seemed to be doing fine, Sunny still following close behind. It was a quiet trip in Sunny's car. there wasn't much idle conversation. Mondo was thinking about how he could help track Edwin down. What could he use, what skills could he offer Sunny in trying to find Edwin? He couldn't think of one. Sunny was thinking as well. He knew that he had started the ball rolling with his phone calls. He knew that each person he called could be trusted. At least that was what he thought. His people would have to come through for him. If his people couldn't, then he would have to make another round of calls and that meant more people would know what Sunny wanted. The more people involved, the harder it would be to keep a lid on it, and if the lid pops off everything goes to hell real fast, he knew.

Isabella and Johnny were pouring their hearts out to one another as they drove along, each freely admitting how they felt to each other. Isabella was amazed that Johnny had been in love with her for such a long time. She had no idea. She told Johnny how much she loved him. As they drove, sharing their innermost feelings with each other, the fear of Edwin Hawkins disappeared.

Two and a half hours after leaving Horseshoe Bay, they pulled off Canadian Highway # 99 into a small ski village. Sunny pulled his car in front of the Volvo and started leading the way.They turned onto Wood Duck Lane, then up a steep incline for three blocks, turned right and pulled into a cedar-sided ski chalet at the end of a dead end street. The house had a fantastic view over the ski area and down the valley. Snow hung on the upper mountain ridges but only a few inches of snow were left around the chalet. They all climbed out of their cars, stretched, and followed Sunny up to the door. Sunny punched in the code on the electric lock system, then disarmed the alarm.

Soon Mondo had a fire blazing in the fireplace. Amy had put some music on and everybody was settling in. All eyes were on Sunny; even Mondo was completely out of his league. Whatever happened next, it was going to be up to Sunny.

Edwin was one hundred and twenty five miles south of Twin Ridges Ski Area. He had received his first call regarding Sunny early that afternoon. Edwin's network was working. He knew who Sunny was, recognized his name, Isabella's gangster father. So they were seeking him out, coming after him, they were smarter than he had thought. Edwin sat in his small kitchen thinking about the best way to proceed. The chess game was about to begin. His best move would be to have Sunny and Mondo come to him. He would set them up, bait them with just enough information to bring them into his trap. It would be easy. With Mondo and Sunny out of the way, he would once again take Amy. One girl would be enough this time; Mr. Chein had been right about that. Amy would bear him his son and she would disappear from the face of the earth forever. Edwin knew about the safe house, knew right where they were staying. His plan was twofold: capture Sunny and Mondo, then Amy.

What would he do with Isabella and Christy? He felt little for Christy. She meant nothing to him, but Isabella... Edwin still burned with passion for her. His thoughts drifted back to that afternoon on the island when Isabella had stepped out of the shower, how she had kissed him with such desire, how she had whispered in his ear to make love to her. He should have taken her right then. He had been a fool once, he wouldn't be a fool again.

Edwin's mind was divided by his need for Amy, his lust for Isabella, and his desire for revenge.

By late afternoon Edwin had received two more phone calls, and his plan had started. He had located two gangsters who had a complete dislike for Sunny LaMartina. These gangsters now lived in Vancouver, barely escaping Los Angeles and Sunny with their lives. They would enjoy taking care of Sunny. Edwin assumed that Mondo would be with him; it only made sense. The girls would be left alone in the safe house while Sunny and Mondo came to hunt him down.

Edwin was having a hard time controlling his excitement. Soon he would take Amy, seduce Isabella, kill Sunny, and delight in the slow agonizing death that he had prepared for Mondo.

Marshall would get the girls, he could do that. Neither Amy or Isabella had ever seen Marshall. That would make it easy. If Christy got in the way, Marshall would be able to do as he pleased with her.

With two more phone calls, Edwin had baited his trap. Sunny would receive a call within the hour telling him where to meet tonight to get the address of Edwin Hawkins. Also, Edwin thought, he would sweeten the deal by letting Sunny know that he could obtain a handgun as well. Edwin knew Sunny didn't bring a gun with him when he arrived from Los Angeles, and he knew that Sunny would feel very naked without a weapon.

The plan was in motion, the game had begun. A game that Edwin was so certain of winning that he didn't even bother to meditate and see into the future. *Why*? He thought.

CHAPTER 38

By six o'clock that evening Sunny received the call that he was waiting for. A trusted friend of a trusted friend had located Edwin. Sunny couldn't believe his luck. Edwin was still in Canada, and he was staying near Vancouver. He was less than two hours away. Sunny learned that Edwin was scheduled to fly to Singapore late tomorrow night.

He knew that they would have to act fast before Edwin could leave. They would have to take care of him now. It would be impossible to track him down once he made it overseas.

Sunny was told that he could purchase whatever weapons he wanted, all clean and non-traceable, just bring cash. Sunny felt good, he trusted who he was talking to. Tonight he and Mondo would put Edwin Hawkins down for good, once and for all.

Marshall was given directions to the ski chalet and was told to leave Vancouver by nine that night. His instructions were very simple. Bring Amy and Isabella back alive. He could do whatever he wanted with Christy. It was the last part of his instructions that thrilled Marshall the most. He knew exactly what he was going to do with Christy. He armed himself with all that he would need: a handgun and a large roll of duct tape.

Johnny was told that he needed to leave tonight. Sunny didn't trust him alone with Isabella. She may be his grownup daughter, but he wasn't going to let the two of them spend the night together while he and Mondo were away. Sunny felt that the girls were safe and he didn't need Johnny around. If all went as planned, Isabella could be back at the Whale Research Center by late tomorrow night. If all went well, tomorrow night Edwin Hawkins would just be a memory, a dead memory. Johnny left by seven o'clock that evening. He didn't go very far. He drove around Twin Ridges for a while before he found what he was looking for, the road that led above the ski chalet. He drove until he had a good view of the chalet and pulled his car off the road and parked. Johnny would wait until Sunny left, then he would go back and see Isabella. He knew that she needed him, he knew that she was terrified of the thought of Edwin Hawkins. Johnny was going to stay close until it was safe. He loved her too much to do anything less than that.

It was a few minutes after eleven p.m. when Marshall Sandbourn's car and Sunny's car passed each other just a few miles out of Twin Ridges Ski Area. The two cars passed in the dark, neither occupant even glancing in the direction of the other. Sunny had planned his timing out the best he could. He was to meet his contact at two this morning, and he gave himself an extra hour.

Marshall was excited. He couldn't get Christy out of his mind. He would show that bitch how to treat him nice. Marshall pulled off of Highway #99 and onto Wood Duck Lane. He drove up to the chalet, then realized he was on a dead end street and had to pull into the driveway. He quickly backed out and drove down the street and parked. There was nobody around. Marshall sat in his car. In a few minutes he would walk up to the chalet and take a look around.

Johnny watched as a car pulled into the chalet's driveway, backed out and drove off. He tried to follow the car's headlights, catching glimpses of it as it drove past hills and houses following the twisting road. After watching for five minutes Johnny became concerned when the car didn't pull out onto Wood Duck lane. It had stopped somewhere near the chalet. Johnny's nervous mind started running. He would have to check it out.

Marshall gave himself fifteen minutes to gather his thoughts and his composure. He grabbed the pistol and put the duct tape in his jacket pocket. He climbed out of the car and looked around. There wasn't another soul to be seen anywhere. He kept himself in the shadows as best as he could. He walked up two blocks until he could see the chalet. It was off by itself, the last house on the dead end street. Marshall stole into the darkness and started making his way through the forest.

"I'm going to get in the hot tub, anybody want to join me?" Christy said.

"I don't have a suit, plus I'm getting pretty tired," Isabella
256

answered.

"What about you Amy? Want to take a hot tub?"

"I don't think so, sis. Besides I don't have a suit. For that matter, you don't either," she laughed.

"I know, but there's no one around. You sure you don't want to go, either of you?"

Isabella stood up.

"I'm going to bed, goodnight."

Amy sat on the couch for a few minutes, then decided that she was too tired to take a hot tub.

"Enjoy your hot tub, sis. I'm going to bed."

Amy got up and headed for the upstairs bedroom.

Christy dimmed the lights in the house, then walked outside to the hot tub. She flipped the lid back and checked the temperature. One hundred and two degrees, perfect.

She went back into the house, slid out of her clothes, walked back outside and climbed into the tub. The heat soaked through her tired body as she relaxed, laid her head back, and stared up at a million stars.

Marshall couldn't believe it when he watched Christy walk outside naked and climb into the hot tub. God, this was going to be easier than he thought. Christy hadn't even closed the sliding door behind her. Marshall was thirty feet away from the back stairs that led to the hot tub deck and Christy. He was invisible in the dark shadows. There was no moon, but the stars shone bright enough that he could make his way through the forest without any trouble. He reached the bottom of the stairs without making a sound. Christy was now only fifteen feet away. Slowly Marshall placed a foot on the bottom step and shifted his weight on it, testing it, making sure it made no sound. He took another step, then another. Soon he was hunched down two steps below the deck. He was looking at the hot tub, watching Christy's silhouette, her head leaning back against the cushions. She was looking away from him. Marshall could hardly control himself. He pulled himself up onto the deck and, bending low, made his way across the deck towards Christy. Marshall didn't make a sound. He was right behind her and she had no clue.

In one fast motion Marshall swept his left hand down around her mouth and hit her with his right hand. Christy tried to scream, but the blow forced her head underwater. A strong hand was keeping her under. She couldn't breathe. She struggled, trying to drive her head back above the water. Terror filled her mind, her lungs were about to explode, she was going to drown right here. Marshall could feel her struggle, feel the strength that she reached out with to fight her unseen attacker off. He wasn't going to let her drown, but he was going to take all of the fight out of her, right now. Marshall could feel pain as Christy dug her fingernails into his arms, then slowly he could feel her strength go, her right hand starting to fall away from his. Marshall jerked her head out of the hot tub, removing his hand from her mouth just for a moment, letting her take one breath before he clamped his hand tight around her mouth again. Christy had no fight left in her. With his free hand Marshall reached into his pocket, pulled out his roll of duct tape, and quickly ran it twice around Christy's head, sealing her lips. She couldn't scream if her life depended on it. Marshall pulled her out of the hot tub. Christy couldn't believe that she was staring at Marshall Sandbourn. Her knees went out and she started to collapse on the deck. Marshall pulled her to him and held her naked body tight against his. Christy knew she couldn't resist, she couldn't do anything to stop Marshall.

"So nice to see you again," Marshall whispered as he ran his hands down her body.

"Do everything I tell you to and you might live to see tomorrow."

Then he threw her over his shoulder and carried her back into the chalet. He placed her face down on the couch and forced her hands behind her. He taped her hands tight and let her lie there. She flipped herself back over and looked up at Marshall, and saw evil in that smile.

Marshall didn't say a word. He just stood there leaning over her, sensing her fear, and loving it. Then he knelt down and whispered into her ear.

"If you make a sound, I will kill you."

Marshall looked around, then quietly walked into the downstairs bedroom.

Isabella was sound asleep. She had no idea that anything was wrong until Marshall grabbed her by the hair, jerked her head up off the pillow, and wrapped duct tape around her mouth. She tried to scream but the tape sealed her lips closed. She started to kick out at Marshall but he hit her with the back of his hand, sending her head snapping back into the pillow. He grabbed her hands and wrapped them in duct tape. He pulled the covers back, grabbed Isabella, and dragged her up out of bed and into the living room. He threw her down on the couch next to Christy. Marshall was beside himself. One more girl to go; he couldn't wait.

He knelt down next to Isabella and whispered in her ear.

"Move and you're dead, try to cry out and you're dead, lie here and don't make a sound." He brought the pistol up and pointed the barrel right between her eyes.

Marshall could see the complete paralyzing fear that she felt.

He stood up and walked away from the couch. He checked out the other rooms downstairs, then quietly walked upstairs. He looked in one bedroom. It was empty. Then he checked the next and there was another sleeping girl. This was Amy, he knew.

Marshall pulled out the duct tape and tore a three foot piece off. He walked over to her and knelt down beside her. She looked so cute, so helpless, so vulnerable. This girl was not to be his, he knew. He admired her sleeping innocence, then grabbed her hair and yanked her head up and off the pillow, wrapping the tape around her. Amy instantly awoke, her eyes wide open with fear. She tried to push her unknown attacker back, tried to force him away with her right hand, but it did little. Marshall grabbed both of her hands and wrapped them tight in duct tape. Then he threw the covers off of her and looked at her beauty. He put any thoughts that he had about her out of his mind. He reached down and pulled her up and over onto his shoulder. She started to kick him, pounding on his back with her hands. He turned back towards the bed and threw her down on it hard, then, leaning over, her put the gun barrel right in her face.

"Do that again, and you're dead."

He grabbed her and carried her down the stairs and threw her on the couch. All three girls were sitting there, two of them completely naked, all three in complete shock, verging on hysterics. Marshall could read the girls' faces. He was in complete control, and they knew it.

Marshall walked over to the wall and turned the lights on a little brighter. He walked back to the girls and stood in front of them, then he pulled a chair out from next to the television and sat down, holding the pistol tight in his right hand.

"My, my, I'm going to enjoy this," he said

CHAPTER 39

Johnny carefully made his way down from where he had parked the Volvo. He had to make his own trail, climbing through stickers and dense forest. The thorn bushes ripped his shirt and caused painful cuts on his arms and wrists. He made his way in the darkness down to the front of the chalet. He stopped ten feet from the door and listened, he couldn't hear a thing. Johnny had a real bad feeling and he couldn't shake it. Something told him that he needed to be very careful. He stood there for five minutes, trying to think of what to do next. One part of him wanted to walk up and ring the door bell to see that everything was all right, but he knew better. Johnny looked around. He needed a weapon. Slowly he started making his way alongside the chalet, working his way back towards the rear of the house. He saw a pile of firewood with a large tarp thrown over it. Holding the tarp in place were three lengths of metal pipe. Johnny walked over and picked one up. It was three feet long, and made of three-quarter inch steel. It felt heavy in his hand. Johnny kept the pipe and continued walking.

He came to the back of the chalet and looked up. He could see a light on in the house. Johnny stood still, trying to listen, trying to hear anything, but he couldn't hear a sound. Slowly he made his way to the steps and paused, then he carefully started making his way up. When he got close to the deck he knelt down and listened again. Now he could hear someone talking. It was a man. There shouldn't have been a man in the house. The hair on Johnny's neck lifted and he felt a cold chill run down his spine. He crawled onto the deck and made his way over to the sliding door, which was open a foot. He didn't dare look around the glass door into the room. He just lay there, his head inches away from the open door, listening to the harsh voice of a man inside.

"Don't think for one minute that Mondo or Sunny are coming back to rescue you three. In a few hours they will both be dead. The fools are walking right into a trap."

Marshall had removed the tape from the girls' mouths. They wouldn't dare scream out for help; there was nobody to rescue them. Marshall was loving every minute of this. They were all alone in this ski house, trapped with him, and the girls knew it. They were all his for the night. If he heard anything from their lips, he wanted to hear them beg for mercy.

None of the girls said a word, they just stared at him.

"Christy, I'm sick of your bad attitude. I'm going to teach you some manners." He got up from his chair and walked over to her. He pulled her up off of the couch. She was limp in his hands. She would have collapsed if he didn't hold on to her. He had such an evil smile. He stared into her face, then pushed her and she fell backwards on the couch, then he walked over and leaned down in front of Isabella.

"I'm gonna give you a treat next, my dear," he said.

He looked over at Amy and didn't say a word, his manner implying what he had in store for her as well.

The girls' hands were still duct taped tight. None of them could free themselves.

Marshall put the pistol down on the television, then walked back over to Christy. He pulled her back up and brought her face to his. He grabbed her head and forced his lips on hers. Let the others watch, it just turned him on. Christy, in pure terror, without even thinking, brought her knee up hard into Marshall's groin. His body exploded with pain, he threw her back on the couch, and turned away from her as he fell to one knee.

Johnny heard the man's painful cries, and dared to look around the door. The man's back was towards Johnny and he was down on one knee.

"You bitch!" the injured man screamed.

At that moment Johnny jumped to his feet and charged. It was the bravest thing he had ever done in his life. Marshall heard him coming and glanced back as Johnny came rushing in with the pipe held high in his hand. Marshall swung to his left, reaching for the gun on the television. Johnny brought the pipe down hard on Marshall's back, driving him to the floor. Marshall struggled to get up. He knew he could take this skinny kid if he could only get to his feet. Marshall was up off his knees, trying to stand, when Johnny brought the pipe down hard alongside his head. Marshall's brain exploded with pain, his vision blurred as he went down on both knees again. He kicked out with his right foot as he was falling, catching Johnny in the left leg. Johnny went down as well. He tried to get up, but Marshall was ahead of him. Just as Marshall was about to grab the gun off of the television, Isabella launched herself at him, driving her shoulder into his back. The force of her blow sent him flying into the television, knocking it over, sending Marshall and the television crashing into a pile on the floor. The gun went flying across the room.

Johnny got to his feet, and charged Marshall, smashing the pipe down hard directly across his head. Marshall's skull fractured under the blow and he started to collapse. Johnny was so full of adrenalin and fear that he grabbed the falling Marshall, and with all of his strength hurled him towards the sliding glass door. Marshall's impact shattered the glass, sending thousands of small shards everywhere. He tumbled out through the broken doorway, his momentum carrying him as he stumbled and fell head first into the hot tub. Marshall tried to reach out and pull himself up, but his arms wouldn't respond. Frantically he tried to force his arms to move, tried to tell his legs to kick out, but his body was detached from his brain. Slowly Marshall Sandbourn's vision darkened, then narrowed into a long dark tunnel before he made one last struggle to force his body to obey his mind. It refused. Marshall Sandbourn drowned in the hot tub, his skull shattered by the steel pipe.

"Johnny, oh, Johnny," Isabella moaned, as she pulled herself up from the floor. Blood ran down the side of her head where she had hit the television after Marshall sent it flying.

Johnny ran over to her and ripped the duct tape from her hands. He cradled her head against his chest before he felt the wave of nausea sweep through his body.

"Help your friends," he managed to say before he threw up and collapsed. Isabella crawled over and freed Amy and Christy from the duct tape.

"Hurry, get the gun," Christy said, then she ran over and grabbed it herself.

Johnny was out cold. Isabella knelt down and wrapped her arms around him. Amy and Christy looked at each other, then ran back into their bedrooms and grabbed something to wear. Only Isabella stayed at Johnny's side, her near-nakedness meaningless as she gently cradled Johnny's head.

"Johnny, wake up, Johnny."

Tears streamed down her face as she looked at the man she loved lying there. Johnny opened his eyes and gazed up into her beautiful glow. Slowly a smile grew upon his lips.

"Hi Isabella, I love you."

She buried her head in his chest, her tears soaking his shirt.

By the time Christy and Amy got some clothes on and came running back out into the living room, Johnny was fully awake and sitting on the couch. Both sisters hugged him, tears flowing down their cheeks as they thought about how much they owed this man.

"You saved our lives, you know that?" Amy said as she sat down beside him. Christy put the gun on the couch, then hugged Johnny. Johnny had never been a hero in his entire life. He couldn't think of a thing to say.

Amy walked outside and looked in the hot tub. Marshall was dead, his head buried down at the bottom of the tub. She walked back inside and sat down on the couch.

"Remember what he said, about Mondo and Sunny heading into a trap? We have to warn them."

"I'll try my dad's cell phone," Isabella said.

She jumped up, ran into the kitchen and called her dad's number. After five rings she got his voice mail.

"Damn!" she shouted.

"I have an idea. Stay here, I'm going to check out this guy's car," Johnny said as he stood up and started to walk outside. He saw the gun lying on the couch and hesitantly he reached over and picked it up. He had never held a gun before. He didn't say a word as he held it for a few seconds before he laid it back down on the couch and walked outside.

Amy swept up the broken glass and put it in a big pile off to one side of the room. Then, with Christy's help, they found a spare blanket in the hallway closet and duct-taped it over the frame of the shattered glass door.

Johnny came back in through the blanket in ten minutes. He sat down at the table.

"I found the guy's car with this map in it," he said waving a peice of paper in front of them.

"I had to break a window to get in. Look at this, it's a computer printout of directions on how to find this place. We can use these directions and go backwards, and find out where he came from. Maybe it's the same place that Mondo and Sunny are going to?"

"It's something," Amy said, as Johnny handed her the map.

"I can keep trying to call my dad's cell phone. God, I wish he had it turned on, but he probably doesn't want it to go off at a bad time, if you know what I mean."

"So what do we do? Should we all jump in Johnny's car and follow the map?" Christy asked.

"No," Amy replied.

Everybody looked at her. She had spoken with such authority that she reminded them of Sunny. Was Amy now in charge? Was anybody in charge?

"It doesn't make sense for us all to go. I'm going, " Amy said.

"What!" everybody else exclaimed.

"No way," Johnny said.

"Listen, you've got the gun, I think we are safe here now. We can't all go, it's too dangerous, and it doesn't make any sense. I'm going. Johnny, I'll drive your car."

"Amy, you can't go by yourself, you just can't," Christy was saying, holding back tears once again.

"I'm going, and that is all there is to it. Mondo and Sunny need help, I can warn them, we don't all need to go. It makes sense that only one of us goes. Johnny, get me your car."

He walked out the front door and started trudging back up the hill. If he had the directions he would take off right now, but he hadn't thought it through well enough. He had given the directions to Amy.

Johnny pulled the Volvo up in front of the chalet and walked inside. Amy had dressed again and was ready to go. She stood by the front door, holding the gun in her hand.

"Johnny, you saved all our lives tonight. Here, I hope you don't have to do it again."She handed the pistol to him, walked out the front door, climbed into the Volvo, and sped away.

CHAPTER 40

"I don't like this," Sunny said softly.

The street was dark, no light shined from any of the shot-out street lights. The top of the gate was heavily reinforced with barbed wire and had a large *no trespassing* sign, right next to the *large beware of dog* sign. Both were nailed to the wooden gate of the junk yard. It was one o'clock in the morning. Sunny and Mondo were parked one hundred feet from the gate. Sunny didn't like the whole setup, and he had learned a long time ago to trust his instincts.

"You need to do this?" Mondo asked.

"How else can we get Edwin's address?"

"Don't you have connections?"

"Yeah, that's how we ended up here."

The meeting was arranged for two in the morning. The call said to pull up to the gate and someone would open the door, pull in and bring cash.

"Shit, what was I going to do, charge it on my Visa?" Sunny had asked.

It was Sunny's idea to get here early and wait to see what happened next. He had saved himself more than a few times in the past by arriving early and seeing something go down that made him walk away from the whole setup. He had learned to look ahead, or he would have spent a lot more time in jail.

At one-thirty a car drove by them. Both Mondo and Sunny slid down in the seat, letting the headlights shine on just another empty car parked on a quiet dead end street. After the lights passed they sat up and watched as a Lincoln pulled in front of the gate and three men got out, each armed with a rifle. Two men disappeared into the shadows on either side of the gate as the third stood out front. Someone opened the gate from the inside and the Lincoln drove through, then the gates closed behind the car. The third man followed the others into the shadows. They were waiting for

Sunny and Mondo.

"It looks worse than I thought, kid. Might be time to head out."

"How can we find where Edwin lives if we don't follow this through?"

"Damn good question."

"There are five people at least. We have to assume that they don't care about our health. As a matter of fact they just may want us to disappear and never bother Edwin again. What do you think?"

"I think I want to turn around and leave, but I know that we can't. We have to get this information about Edwin."

"Right."

Mondo followed Sunny out of the car. The car interior lights remained dark when they opened the door. Sunny had unscrewed all the inside light bulbs as well as the light bulb for the trunk. They walked to the back of the car and opened the trunk.

"Here," Sunny handed Mondo a can of grizzly bear spray and a length of pipe.

"Sorry, kid, it's all we have."

Sunny grabbed another can of bear spray and a length of pipe, too.

"I'm taking the guy out on the left side of the gate. You take the one out on the right. Be careful of the guy who was standing right in front of the gate. Once we get the three guys out of the picture we go to the back of the junk yard and work our way in."

"Okay."

"Kid, be careful."

"Yeah."

Mondo knelt down, then started to crawl on his belly over dirt and grass, through gravel and mud. He was now fifteen feet from where he thought the gunman he was after should be. Mondo crawled closer. He could hear nothing. All was dark except for the two lights at the gate. It was way too quiet.

Mondo lay there wondering what it would be like to get hit with this pipe. He wondered if it could kill.

Suddenly, a match lit the darkness. It was only ten feet away, off to his right along the fence. The flash lasted only for a second, but Mondo could see the glow of a cigarette from the gunman's hand. Ever so silently he crawled towards the cigarette glow, and still the gunman had no idea he was there. As he got closer he could make out the gunman, his silhouette barely discernible in the shadow. Mondo grabbed the pipe hard in his right hand and waited. The goon finished his smoke, dropped the butt, and ground it in with his heel. He turned and looked away from where Mondo was hiding and glanced at the gate. Mondo leaped forward. The gunman heard him and started to spin, but Mondo was there. The metal pipe came crashing down on the gunman's head, and he slumped to the ground without a sound.

Mondo grabbed his rifle and searched his body. He found a small .38 special tucked in the man's boot. Mondo took the pistol and checked the rifle. The safety was off.

He couldn't see the third guard, but he remembered where he had seen him last.

Slowly, carrying the rifle and the pistol, leaving the pipe and the bear spray, he crawled forward. He crawled another fifteen feet before he saw the third gunman. He was hiding just inside the shadows, of the fence keeping himself out of the light. Mondo suddenly wished he had the pipe. He couldn't shoot the guy. He doubted he could shoot anybody. Even if he could it would make too much noise and give both him and Sunny away. He lay there in the silence, straining to hear, wishing he could see what Sunny was up to. He looked at his watch. They were late for their appointment. Soon the people inside the junk yard would know something was wrong; they would start to get suspicious and then more alert. It would make things much harder for them.

Suddenly Mondo saw the gunman lurch to his left, looking away from him. Something had caught his attention. Mondo leaped to his feet and charged. The gunman must have heard him because he started to turn back, raising his rifle. Mondo wasn't sure if he could get to him before the man could get a shot off. Mondo was going to be too late, he still had six feet to go and the rifle was just about level with him. He dove, putting everything that he had into his leap, while the gunman struggled to flip the safety off. Mondo crashed into him and both men went down, Mondo landing on top. The gunman tried to punch out, but Mondo hit him with the pistol on the side of his head. The gunman dropped his hands and collapsed. Sunny came crawling along the fence up to Mondo.

"Great job, kid. Grab his rifle and let's go."

They kept to the shadows, walking along the tall fence, looking for a way to get in. In the darkness it was hard for them to see much. They knew they had little time. Those guards wouldn't be out forever. They walked in silence, keeping close to the fence. They came to the back of the junk yard, followed the fence around to the left and kept walking. Through the chain links of the fence they could see a small light shining from the second story of a large building. They couldn't see anybody in the windows, but somebody was up there waiting for them. Half-way down the fence on the back side they came to a drainage culvert that ran right under the fence and into the junk yard. It was a two-foot wide pipe. There was a metal screen on the end of the pipe to keep anything and everything out. Mondo reached down and felt around the screen. It was old; he felt the rust flake off in his hand.

"Give me your pipe," he whispered to Sunny, who was still carrying it, even though he had a rifle with him.

Mondo reached up, grabbed the pipe and smashed it into the center of the screen. The rusted metal started to give way. Mondo hit the screen four more times before he had completely removed it from the pipe. The culvert was fifteen feet long and came up inside a metal grate in the junk yard.

"Let's go," Mondo said.

"Shit, kid, I can't do that. I get claustrophobia."

"Tough." Mondo turned and crawled into the pipe. Sunny stood on the outside of the fence. He watched as Mondo climbed inside the pipe, watched his feet as they disappeared into the blackness of the drainage culvert. Sunny saw the grate cover pop up and watched as Mondo dragged himself out into the junk yard. Mondo looked back at Sunny, then started walking towards the light.

"Damn," Sunny whispered to himself as he started crawling through the pipe.

Mondo moved carefully and slowly, waiting for Sunny to catch up with him. They stood at the bottom of a run down looking building. Large double doors wide enough for a car to drive through were in front of them. There was an outside stairway five feet to their right that led up to the office with the lights on.

"Which one you want, kid?"

"I'll go inside. Be careful, Sunny."

Mondo slowly opened one of the large doors and slipped into the dark building. Sunny made his way over to the stairs, gripped the rifle tightly, and started climbing. Mondo couldn't see a thing in the dark. He stood there for a minute trying to get an idea of what lay before him. As his eyes adjusted he could make out a stairway leading upstairs in the far corner of the shop. There were boxes, metal tools, and car parts lying all around the floor. He knew he couldn't trip over anything or that would be the end of it.

Sunny was three steps away from the second story landing when suddenly the outside lights flashed on and the back door swung open. He was momentarily blinded by the lights. When he could see, he looked up into the barrel of a 12 gauge shotgun.

"Drop the gun, Sunny."

Sunny did as he was told.

The gunman kept the shotgun pointing directly at him.

"Come here."

Sunny walked up into the light. He had never seen this guy before. Sunny was thrown into the room, the shotgun just inches away from his back. The light was blinding for a few seconds. Sunny had to squint to look around, then he saw something that caused his heart to fear. Sitting at a small table were Johnny Talbot and Michael Lomax, two people Sunny never wanted to see again, ever.

"Sit down, Sunny, you're late."

"Traffic," he said, as he sat down across the table from both men. The shotgun guard positioned himself back against the wall a few feet from the door.

Sunny had dealt with both of these men in the past. They used to operate out of Los Angeles before they pissed Mr. Concenta off and then they were given a choice, leave or die. Sunny didn't think they were going to give him the same choice.

"You're a damn idiot, Sunny, for showing up."

"Yeah, well, you got something that I want."

"That's right, we do. Seems you want the address of Edwin Hawkins. It took some doing on our part to find it," Michael said with a laugh.

"Right, why don't you give me his address, and I'll be leaving you three."

All three men laughed.

Johnny Talbot answered.

"You don't get it, Sunny. When you leave here it will be in pieces. You had your fun at our expense and now it's time for you to die. Get it, Sunny? We're going to chop you up in such little pieces they will never find you."

Mondo was slowly making his way up the stairs. He tested each step, sounding out any squeaks or noises that it might give off. When he reached the top step he was standing directly in front of the door. He could hear everything that was being said. He reached down and tried the door handle. It twisted in his hand. The door wasn't locked. Mistake number one, he thought.

"You shit! That was a long time ago. I got more money than you can ever dream of. Tell me what I want to know and you can retire in Bora Bora forever, live like a fricking king," Sunny said with no hint of fear in his voice.

Both men laughed.

"Well, Sunny, that's a thought, but I think I want to see you die too much. What do you think, Mike?"

"It's tempting," Mike said as he stood up and leaned his body over the table, looked at Sunny, then hit him with his right hand and sent him flying backwards off his chair. In that moment of noise and confusion Mondo threw open the door.

Mike and Johnny were both on their feet, their backs towards Mondo, staring down at Sunny. The shotgun-wielding guard was staring right at Mondo. The guard started to bring his shotgun up when Mondo fired two shots from the pistol. The shots were right on. The shotgun dropped from the guard's hand as he clutched his mid-section, then slumped back against the wall, sliding to the ground. Mike and Johnny spun around, staring at Mondo and the pistol.

Sunny jumped up and ran over to Mondo, grabbing the pistol out of his hand. Mondo leveled the rifle at the two gangsters.

"You assholes!" Sunny shouted, "You could have lived like kings, but now it's your turn to die."

Sunny walked over to Johnny, put the pistol to his head, cocked back the hammer, and stopped. Johnny's knees gave out from under him, and he fell to the floor.

"I want something that you bastards know, want to make a deal?"

"Anything you say, Sunny," Mike said.

"I want Edwin's address and I want to know where you were going to meet him and how much he paid you to set us up."

Mike looked down at Johnny, then back at Sunny, who pointed the cocked pistol at his head.

"Okay, Sunny. We don't know Edwin from Adam, he came to us. He paid us ten grand to make you disappear."

"Before or after I died?"

"He was going to pay us when we did the job, seems he didn't trust us."

"No shit."

"Yeah, we were to meet him at this address."

Mike reached into his pocket and pulled out a notebook that he handed to Sunny. Sunny reached out to grab it, taking his eyes off of Johnny on the floor. In an instant Johnny reached into his back pocket and brought up a small handgun, but before he could get a bead on Sunny, Mondo fired. The rifle shot exploded through the quiet of the night as Johnny flew backwards, rolled over twice, and didn't move.

"Stupid shit," Sunny said.

Sunny looked back at Mondo and gave him a wink, then looked at Mike. Mike was terrified.

"Let's go, asshole. You're taking a ride in the trunk."

CHAPTER 41

Sunny walked over to the back wall and flipped the outside lights off, then he put the pistol to the back of Mike's head.

"Walk."

They walked down the back stairs and out to the drainage ditch. Mondo climbed through first, pushing the rifle ahead of him. Mike, then Sunny, followed. Carefully they made their way back to Sunny's car, keeping themselves in the shadows, taking nothing for granted.

Sunny opened the trunk, pointed the gun at Mike and told him to climb in. Mondo read the fear that was written all over Mike's face.

"Listen, asshole, you play it right and you might live tonight. Tell me what you were supposed to do to get paid," Sunny said, the gun inches from Mike's forehead.

"We were told to drive to the address in the book. It's down on the waterfront. There's a manned security gate there. At the gate we were to tell the guard that Little Red Riding Hood was expecting us. I swear to God, that was what we were to say. From there I don't know. I guess the security guy would tell us what to do next."

"Did you meet any of these people?"

"No, it was all arranged over the phone by a connection that Johnny knew. He put this all together."

Sunny stared at Mike, smiled and cocked back the pistol.

"Honest to God. Sunny, don't shoot me, it's the truth."
Sunny released the trigger.

"You stay in the trunk, you be a good boy and if what you say is true I'll let you live. Now what car were you suppose to take?"

"The van parked inside the junk yard. It says Acme Marine Refrigeration on the side. I swear to God, Sunny, it's all true."

"If it's not, I'm personally going to make sure you don't see the morning."

Sunny slammed the trunk shut.

"I'll drive the van," Mondo said.

Mondo turned and headed towards the junk yard. He opened the gate and walked in. He had no trouble finding the van and the keys were in the ignition. Mondo drove out of the junk yard, climbed out of the van, closed the gate behind him, and pulled up next to Sunny's car.

"Let's get out of here. We'll drive until we find someplace to pull over and figure out where the hell we are going."

"Good idea," Sunny replied.

They drove down the street, turned left and started following the route that they had driven to get to the junk yard.

Three miles later they pulled into an all night diner, parked in the far corner of the lot, and Sunny climbed into the van. Mondo had a map of Vancouver spread out on the front seat.

"What's the address, Sunny?"

"It's Front Street, Pier Eleven."

Mondo looked on the back of the map, found Front Street in the index, and flipped the map back over.

"Here's Front Street," Mondo pointed as he slid the map over for Sunny to look at.

"Good, we'll follow the signs for the Port of Vancouver. Here's what we'll do. We'll stash the rifles in the van. Then I'll park my car when we're a few blocks from Pier Eleven. I'll find some dead-end quiet place to park so asshole in the trunk won't hear anybody and start making a racket. I'll ride with you, we'll be Mike and Johnny looking for Little Red Riding Hood. Jesus, this sounds stupid."

"I know, that's what makes me believe the guy," Mondo said.

They started following the map and street signs, and twenty minutes later they entered the Port of Vancouver. Another two blocks and they came to a sign that pointed the way to Pier Eleven. Sunny found a large empty parking lot, pulled his car to the back and parked. He walked to the back of the car and put his head down near the trunk.

"Listen, asshole, make a sound and you're dead. Get comfortable, and if it all pans out like you said, I'll let you go home this morning."

Sunny climbed into the van and they followed the signs for Pier Eleven.

Three blocks later they pulled up to a manned security station, with a steel gate blocking their way. A large guard with a pistol strapped to his side walked out from the security building and up to Mondo.

"Little Red Riding Hood is expecting us," Mondo said.

"Is that right?"

"Yeah, that's right," Mondo said with an attitude.

"Okay, drive down until you see a construction office on your right. Lights are on, somebody's waiting for you."

The gate rose and Mondo drove the van through. The dock area was dark except for a few lights that shined on top of the tall cranes that were used to lift containers on and off the freighters that used Pier Eleven. The parking area was deserted.

"I'm Mike, you're Johnny. Let's hope these guys have never met us. I have the pistol just in case. We get the money and we find out where Edwin is," Sunny said.

"What makes you think they'll know where Edwin is?"

"Because they have ten thousand dollars of his."

Mondo parked the van in front of the construction building and they both climbed out. Sunny took the lead position. They walked up the steps, knocked once and walked in.

A dark-haired man was sitting behind a desk, crunching numbers on a large calculator.

"Ya, what do you want?" the man said.

"We want to find fucking Little Red Riding Hood because she owes us ten grand," Sunny answered.

The man stood up, smiled, and reached for a brown bag that was sitting next to him. He threw the bag at Sunny.

"This means that the job was completed successfully?"

"Absolutely, some people just disappear, never to be seen again."

"What about Mondo?" the man asked.

"Who? Listen, we were paid to take care of Sunny LaMartina and we did. Who the hell is Mondo?" Sunny said, playing his part beautifully.

"Somebody we thought may have been with Sunny."

"Sorry."

Sunny looked in the bag. It was full of crisp one hundred dollar bills. He didn't bother to count it, it looked like ten grand.

"Okay, thanks, we're out of here."

Sunny started towards the door, then stopped and turned back to the dark-haired accountant.

"What if we happen to find this Mondo guy, what then?"

The accountant had already sat down, but at the mention of Mondo's name he turned and looked at Sunny.

"If you happened to locate Mondo, I have someone who wants to take him off of your hands."

"Yeah, for how much?"

"How much does it take?"

"Do you have the cash here? If we happened to have him, like maybe we have him in the trunk or something like that, how much would he be worth?"

"There's more than enough cash on site, do you have him or not, asshole?" The dark haired man said as he stood up and walked from behind the desk, pointing a pistol at Sunny.

"Listen, man, we did your job, put that thing away."

The man walked up to Sunny, then looked over at Mondo. The moment he took his eyes from Sunny, Sunny hit him with a hard right, knocking him backwards and sending him sprawling on the floor. The pistol went flying from his hand. Sunny pulled his pistol and pointed it at the man's head.

"I don't like guns pointing at me, got it, asshole? Now we do have Mondo. He's in the damn van and I want twenty-five grand for him."

"Greedy bastard," the accountant said as he stood up. "I don't have that much money here."

"Well, tell me who does, and where he is, that's how I see it coming down."

The man didn't say a word. He turned and walked back to his desk and picked up the phone. Both Sunny and Mondo followed him. Sunny reached over and hit the speaker phone button just as the man finished dialing. He looked up at Sunny, saw the gun pointed at him and didn't say a word.

"Yeah." They all could hear the voice on the speaker.

"It's me, Sammy. Listen, I got a little problem. Our friends are here, they said all went as planned. But if we want Mondo we need twenty-five grand, which is more than I have here. Should I send them over?"

"Edwin's not here. Don't ask me a question like that."

"Well, it's your call. I don't give a shit if they put Mondo on a ferry and send him to China. What's it gonna be?"

278

The man on the other end of the phone paused for over thirty seconds before he said, "Send him to the nursery. I'll make sure Edwin is notified. I'll bring the cash."

The man hung up the phone and looked at them both.

"You're fucking around with the wrong people."

"Yeah, thanks, just give us directions, asshole."

Amy didn't even look at the directions that Johnny had given her until she was fifteen miles out of Twin Ridges ski area heading for Vancouver. She pulled the Volvo over at a small roadside restaurant, flicked the inside dome light on and looked at where she was heading. The directions were printed out from a web site called "findyourway. com". It showed the chalet and the route that Marshall had taken. Tracing the map backwards showed Marshall had started in Burnaby, a suburb of Vancouver. Amy studied the map, made herself remember the first two exits she would have to take, then she pulled back out into the darkness and continued driving south.

She had given little thought to what she was doing before she left the chalet. The need to warn Mondo and Sunny was all she could think about. It had all made sense to her back then, it seemed the only thing to do. Now as she drove by herself into the glaring lights of Vancouver she felt her bravado disappear. The only thought that caused more fear in her heart was the thought that maybe she was too late. What if the trap had already been sprung? Once again she had to fight the fear that Mondo was dead.

Amy hit city traffic a few miles north of Vancouver city limits. Even for such a late hour of the night the city was alive with cars and pedestrians. She pulled off of Highway #1, the main route through Vancouver, and took #7 towards Burnaby. Fifteen minutes later she found Loyd street, the cross street she was looking for, and turned right. The map was becoming harder to follow. There were now too many side streets and she feared losing her way. Amy pulled the Volvo over three different times to double-check the map and her location. The suburban streets were now empty and that made driving easier, but it made Amy feel more vulnerable. She stood out now, she couldn't blend in, there was no one to blend with.

The house that was highlighted on the map was now only two blocks ahead. Amy pulled the car over, turned off the lights, and sat in the silence trying to gather her thoughts. She looked at her watch. It was two-thirty in the morning. She looked around the neighborhood. It seemed like a regular suburban middle-class American town. Neat little houses all with neat little yards all in neat little rows. What the hell was Marshall doing in a place like this? She asked herself, but she already knew the answer. If somebody wanted to become invisible, a neighborhood like this was perfect. Amy checked the map again, re-read the house address. The house should be on her left. She started the Volvo, turned on her headlights and drove two and a half blocks, passing the house and driving another hundred feet before pulling over and parking. She parked behind a large pick-up truck, which hid her car from any traffic that was coming towards her. Amy turned around and looked back at the house. Was Edwin Hawkins in there? Did he live there? She had a hard time controlling her fears as she sat there in the darkness, parked on that side street, with a map in her hand to go by and nothing else.

A terrifying thought entered her mind. What if Edwin was waiting inside that house for her? What if she had walked right into a trap that was meant for her? What if Mondo and Sunny had just been bait? Amy had to stop herself from starting the Volvo and driving away, fleeing from her fears. She knew she couldn't leave, she had nowhere to go. It seemed to Amy, looking back, that Marshall was too eager to tell them about the trap that Mondo and Sunny were heading into. Why even mention it? Maybe to drive fear into them, that was possible. Why leave the printed directions in the car? Amy had no answers for her questions, only time would tell.

Amy locked the car and sat there feeling fearful and stupid with no idea what to do next. The coldness of the night was starting to numb her fingers and toes. She looked around the neighborhood. The houses were all large and had garages, though many had cars parked in the driveway. Amy studied the house that the map said Marshall had left from. There were no lights on inside, no outside porch light, no cars parked in the driveway. The house looked fast asleep. It looked harmless, and that was what scared her so much.

Amy watched as headlights suddenly came around the corner and started down the street towards her. She slid down into the seat as the headlights flashed on her car then suddenly turned away. She sat up and looked behind her as a car was pulling into the driveway of the house that she had been watching. The garage doors suddenly opened and the car drove inside and the doors closed behind it.

She watched as a few house lights went on. After five minutes the lights flicked off and the garage door opened and the same car backed out into the street. The car started to turn in her direction and Amy slid herself down in the front seat. The car headlights flashed over her. Without even thinking she scrunched herself down further in the seat, her left foot momentarily hitting the brake pedal. Amy had no idea that her brake lights flashed for a second, but the driver of the car did. He was looking right at Amy's car, thinking to himself that he had never seen an old Volvo parked in his neighborhood before, when her lights flashed. The driver didn't slow down until he was around the corner, then he pulled over and parked. Edwin Hawkins slowly climbed out of his car and started walking back towards the Volvo.

CHAPTER 42

Edwin was twenty feet from the car when he knew that Amy was in it. His senses told him so. He couldn't see the Volvo because it was parked behind a big truck, but he knew that she was there. It was fate, he told himself. She had come to him because she was meant to be his.

Edwin walked up to the front of the truck and sat down on the bumper. He took two deep breaths and focused his mind.

"Open the door and come out, Amy. It's okay. It's safe. You need to look around."

Edwin said this in his mind a few times, directing all of his energy and thoughts toward the Volvo and the unsuspecting Amy. He heard the car door open, heard her climb out of the car. He could see the reflection of the inside light come on then quickly go off as Amy closed the door behind her. Edwin was having a hard time keeping his excitement under control. He felt the vial of powder that he had put in his jacket pocket before he left his car. Edwin always traveled with a few of his special poisons. He never knew when they would come in handy. This powder would instantly immobilize whoever inhaled it, and they would take over an hour to recover.

Amy stood beside the Volvo, convinced that the best thing she could do was to walk across the street and look around. She suddenly felt a new sense of confidence and she didn't stop to ask herself why. Amy had taken two steps away from the Volvo when Edwin came around the back of the truck and ran up to her. She turned around at the sound of his footsteps but there was nothing she could do. Edwin flung the powder in her face. Amy gasped at the sight of Edwin, inhaling deeply. She went limp, and would have collapsed on the ground except that Edwin grabbed her and held her tight.

"Amy, my love, so glad that you have returned to me."

Edwin knew that even though Amy couldn't move or speak, her mind was normal and functioning. Only her eyes showed the fear and terror that she felt. Edwin lifted her over his right shoulder and carried her to his car. He laid Amy on the back seat and drove away.

Mondo drove the van out of Pier Eleven, past the security guard and towards Sunny's parked car.

"Okay, you got it? We head east on HWY 1 through Surrey, towards the United States border crossing at Sumas. We turn off on Route 6A. What we want is High Springs Nursery. If we get separated I'll wait for you at the turn-off for Route 6A. Don't lose me," Sunny said.

"Got it."

Sunny looked across the seat at Mondo. He really liked this kid. He held up the bag with ten grand in it.

"Kid, I think this bag has your name on it."

Mondo laughed.

"Great, save it for me."

Mondo pulled up next to Sunny's car and Sunny climbed out, carrying the ten grand. He started his car and Mondo followed him as they headed out of the parking area.

The drive through Vancouver and out into the countryside was easy. There was little traffic and the road signs were good. Sunny turned onto route 6A with Mondo right behind him.

Mondo was wondering how Mike was doing in the trunk. Well, at least he was alive, he thought.

Mondo watched as Sunny tapped his brakes twice as they drove past a sign for High Springs Nursery two miles ahead. Sunny drove past the nursery, didn't even slow down. Around the next turn he pulled into a roadside produce stand and parked in the far corner. Mondo followed him and parked next to him.

Sunny got out of the car, walked over to the van, and slid open the side door. He threw the blanket back that was covering the rifles and grabbed both of them. He carried them outside and slid the van door closed. Mondo walked around to the side of the van and up to Sunny, who handed him a rifle.

"I'll keep the pistol," Sunny said.

"Keep the safety on at least until we get to the nursery. I say we hike through the woods and have a look," Sunny continued.

Mondo didn't say a word, just nodded his head slightly, and followed after him.

They crossed a barbed wire fence, then made their way through tall rows of trees, all planted like corn in a field waiting for the harvest.

They came to the back of the nursery and hid in the shadows. A few lights were on in the main house, but they didn't see anybody moving around. It was a large two-story old farm house, with a few barns, a couple of small outbuildings and two greenhouses around it. The nearest neighbor was over half a mile away. They stood there in the silence and cold waiting for something, but not sure what it was.

They both knew that whoever was waiting for them wasn't going to hand over twenty-five grand, and let them walk, even if they had Mondo to give them.

Ten minutes after capturing Amy, Edwin's cell phone rang. That was unexpected. Nobody ever called him; only two people even had this number. Edwin reached over and answered the phone.

"Edwin, sorry to bother you, something's come up, I hope I handled it right. Sunny's been taken care of. They have Mondo but they want twenty-five grand for him. The accountant called and I had to make a decision, so I told them to bring Mondo to the nursery and we'll pay them. I couldn't risk them letting Mondo go free."

Edwin sat there sorting his thoughts out for only a moment.

"Fine, you did good. I'm on my way. Keep them there, don't let anybody leave. I think that it might be time to renegotiate the value of Mondo. It might be time to use these two guys as fertilizer."

Edwin hung up.

Mondo was in his grasp. Edwin glanced at Amy, who was still out in the back seat.

He was amazed at how quickly things had turned around for him. An hour ago he was wondering if Marshall was going to come through. Now he had both Amy and Mondo. The hell with Marshall, he had served his purpose, he thought.

Edwin changed directions and started heading for the nursery. His other business could wait.

Twenty-five minutes later Edwin drove into the nursery, pulled up to the front door and parked. Amy was just starting to stir. The outside porch light flipped on and two men walked out to meet him.

"Bring her upstairs, put her in my room. One of you stay with her until she comes around, then call me."

They dragged Amy out of the back seat and one of the men threw her over his shoulder and carried her into the house.

Mondo watched as they carried Amy out of the car. His knees went weak. Sunny reached over and put a hand on his shoulder.

"Goddamn it," Mondo whispered.

They watched as the front door closed behind them. A minute later a light went on upstairs.

"That's where I have to go, Sunny."

"I know. Let's wait five minutes. You head for the balcony, maybe you can get upstairs and into the room that way. I'll drift off into the shadows and try to keep you safe."

"How the hell did they find her? What about..." Mondo stopped in mid sentence and looked at Sunny.

Sunny realized what he was going to say. If they had Amy, what happened to Isabella and Christy? Sunny's face went pale, even in the darkness Mondo could see the change.

"God, Mondo, how did we screw up? What about my daughter?"

"I don't know, I doubt they killed her, why would they? They didn't before. Listen Sunny, we need to end this tonight. I never want any of these girls to ever have to look over their shoulder again wondering about Edwin Hawkins. This isn't over until he's dead. Not captured, not arrested, dead. Dead, Sunny!"

Sunny didn't say a word, he knew Mondo was right.

They stood there in the darkness for only a few more minutes, then Mondo started to climb over a low split rail fence. Sunny grabbed his shoulder. Mondo turned and looked at him.

"Kid, be real careful, I mean real careful. Before this night is over, that house is going to be full of dead people. Make sure you're not one of them."

Sunny turned away. He didn't want Mondo to see the tears that were welling up in his eyes. What if Isabella was dead? He couldn't answer that, but he could swear to God in heaven that this was all going to end tonight.

They both climbed over the fence and started towards the house.

286

Sunny watched as Mondo made his way to the back of the house, and hid under the balcony. Sunny carefully walked to a small outbuilding fifty feet from the front of the house, knelt down, sighted down the rifle barrel and waited for the fireworks that he knew were about to begin.

Mondo tried to steady his breathing, but it was impossible, he was so filled with fear. He was standing in the darkness under the balcony and there was no way that he could reach it. It was too high and he didn't know what to do. He doubted he would last five seconds if he tried to get through the front door.Mondo knew time was wasting. Every second seemed to pull more effort from him, seemed to cast more doubts about his chances to make it through this night alive. He looked around him again, then saw a large wood plank leaning up against the foundation of the house. Mondo walked over and picked up the plank and carried it to one of the upright beams that supported the balcony. He leaned the top of the board against the beam, then put his weight on the back of the plank, trying to get it to dig into the ground. He knew that as he climbed up the plank it would try to kick out at the bottom. If that happened he would come crashing down in a loud bang and that would be the end.

Mondo suddenly realized that he couldn't carry the rifle with him. He needed two hands to walk himself up the steep incline of the plank. Damn, he cursed to himself, he had no choice but to leave his weapon behind. He took one last look around then climbed up the plank, both hands holding tight underneath the board as he pulled himself up. He reached the balcony, quickly released his grasp on the plank, and grabbed the balcony decking. He hung there not making a sound, his feet on the plank and his hands locked on the decking above him. Mondo slowly pulled himself off the plank, swung his feet around, and pulled himself up on the deck. He crawled over to the wall and pulled himself up into the shadows.

Amy's body was starting to respond to her mind, and she was terrified. She could move her hands and feet, then slowly she could feel her body awakening as if coming out of a bad dream. She sat up and looked around. She lay on a bed. The lights in the room were turned down low. A large man, her guard, was sitting in a chair two feet away from her, a pistol in his hand. He smiled at her menacingly, but didn't say a word. Amy slumped back down, her nightmare continuing.

She remembered Edwin attacking her, remembered turning around at the sound of footsteps and seeing him there. She had walked right into his trap. She had delivered herself to Edwin just as she had feared.

Amy lay there in despair, thinking that maybe she was destined to bear Edwin's child. It all seemed beyond her ability to resist anymore. She would go with Edwin, give herself to him, if it meant that Mondo would live.

CHAPTER 43

Mondo was on the balcony, still hiding in the darkness, wedged tight against the wall. The light coming from the window three feet to his right cast slanting shadows onto the decking. He could see the silhouette of somebody crossing in front of the drawn curtains. What was going on in there? Whose outline was it? How many guards were in there? Was Amy in there? Where were Isabella and Christy? How long before Edwin would whisk the girls away, never to be found again? So many questions.

Where were Isabella and Christy? How long before Edwin would whisk all the girls away, if they were alive, never to be found again?

Mondo had to shake all of the questions out of his mind. He stepped out from the the wall behind him and into the dim light coming from the room. A shot rang out a second later. The wood siding exploded just inches from his head. He dove over the railing down into the courtyard as another round grazed his left leg. Mondo landed hard on a patio umbrella, smashing through, crashing onto a metal table, bending it over before he hit the ground. Fortunately for him the table had taken most of his impact. The gunman lost track of Mondo as he fell. Before he could find him, Mondo picked himself up and ran to the back of the house. He didn't slow down. He crashed right into the back door.

Sunny saw the flash from the rifle coming from a parked car off to his right. He spun his rifle around, but not before the shooter fired another shot. Sunny sighted in on the gunman's silhouette and fired. The shot caught the man in the chest, flipping him backwards like a rag doll. Sunny knew his shot hit home.

The wood door exploded as Mondo hit it with his full force, his shoulder driving the door back, shattering the hinges and causing the entire door to fly into the room in front of him. It saved his life.

One of the guards that Edwin had stationed downstairs turned the moment he heard the door give way. In a second, he brought his gun up, firing. Two bullets hit the floor in front of Mondo. The next second, as the gunman brought his weapon up to chest height, Mondo hurled the flying door at him. Two bullets hit the door as it flew through the air. Before he could pull off another round, the door caught him squarely in the chest, knocking him off balance. As the guard stepped backwards trying to keep his feet underneath him, Mondo leaped. The gunman tried to bring his weapon up, tried to put Mondo in his sights, but he couldn't as he was falling backwards. Mondo reached out and knocked the gun hand up and away. The next instant he smashed his right hand into the side of the gunman's head. With his left, Mondo hit the shooter in the nose, the palm of his hand driving the nose cartilage up and backwards, breaking it instantly. A wave of pain so intense struck the gunman that he dropped the gun and started to fall to his knees. Mondo slashed out with a flat right-hand chop to the falling man's throat. He could feel the soft flesh of the gunman's Adam's apple as his hand struck home. As the gunman collapsed a thought rushed through Mondo's mind, just for a second, before he cast it away. Had he just killed this man with his bare hands? Mondo remembered what Sunny had told him: be careful, a lot of people are going to die in that house tonight. Mondo forced the thought out of his mind. There was room for only two thoughts tonight; find Amy and kill Edwin.

Mondo grabbed the gun. It felt awkward in his hand. He had never believed in guns, but he had been on the wrong side of the barrel too often tonight. If anyone was going to start shooting at him, he was going to fight back.

He raced upstairs, diving around the corner as he hit the dimly lit second story hallway. Gunfire erupted over his head. In a split second Mondo fired off two shots. His aim was right on as a second gunman staggered back. He collapsed to the floor, tried to get up, struggled, and then didn't move. A surreal picture entered Mondo's mind. He could see himself floating over the dead man's body, except it was him lying dead on the floor, not the gunman. Mondo knew that only this weapon had saved his life. He had been forced to protect himself and cause another's death. He prayed that after tonight he would never have to do that again.

Mondo stood up. He knew what room Amy must be in. She was at the end of this hallway. He started walking down the hall towards the door, all of his senses alert, his mind ready for any action that would save his life or Amy's. He stopped ten feet from the door. His instinct told him not to go further. Whoever was behind that door knew he was coming. He must have heard the shots. Mondo studied the door, then looked to his left and saw another door. He opened it and closed it behind him, leaving the door open just a crack. It was a broom closet; it went nowhere. Mondo started to turn around and walk out of the closet when he suddenly heard the bedroom door open, the hinges creaking ever so slightly. He could hear footsteps stepping out into the hallway, and then slowly they started shuffling down the hall toward the closet door. Mondo held his breath. He knew he would live or die, depending on what happened in the next few seconds. The steps stopped two feet in front of the closet door. Silence, then he could hear the shuffle of shoes again. His breath was about to explode from him with or without his control. At the very last moment, when he was going to have to breathe regardless, just as the shoes walked to the doorway, he kicked the door open. It caught the gunman by complete surprise. Amy screamed but managed to get out of the way of the flying door. The gunman raised his gun and fired one shot. His aim was off. The bullet hit the door jamb inches from Mondo. Mondo reached out and grabbed the shooter's right hand, locking his fingers on the gun barrel. The gunman brought his right foot up, catching Mondo in the stomach, the kick forcing air from his lungs. Mondo couldn't let go of the barrel. He was dead if he did. The gunman brought his left hand up and hit Mondo along the head. Mondo rotated his wrist, bending the gunman's hand over, causing the hand muscles to contract, shutting off blood supply to the fingers. It took only seconds for the man's hand to weaken. The gun flew from his hand. Mondo took his eyes off the shooter for only a split second, following the path of the falling pistol. He kicked out at the gun hitting it before it reached the floor. The gun flew into the air spinning, then over the second story railing and down to the floor below. Taking his eyes off of his opponent was a mistake. With lighting speed the gunman brought his right hand out flat aiming at Mondo's throat. Mondo turned his head to the right just before the blow landed. The pain charged through Mondo's neck, causing his mind to explode. He felt his knees start to buckle. He couldn't go down. If he did, he and Amy would die. Mondo pushed back, falling away from his attacker, as Amy tried to run past the gunman. He turned and grabbed at her arm, taking his eyes off Mondo. In one second Mondo was back. This was it, he knew, time to win or time to die. There was no second round. Mondo charged the gunman, who was just turning back toward him. Mondo brought his right fist up with all of his power. He hit the gunman under the chin in a sweeping uppercut, knocking the gunman back, sending his feet off the floor. Mondo didn't stop. He kicked out his right foot, snapping the man's head back so hard that the shooter flew backward, crashing into the wall, smashing a large hole in the sheetrock. Dust covered the shooter as he charged Mondo moments later, this time with a five inch knife in his right hand. The blade swung through the air, catching Mondo on his upper right arm. Pain shot through him as blood started to flow. Mondo never took his eyes from the knife.

"Run, Amy! Run!" he shouted, not even looking at her. The gunman smiled. He knew victory was at hand. The knife was always his favorite weapon. He charged, Mondo stepped back and swung his right foot out, low and hard in a sweeping motion. The knifeman's weight was squarely on his advancing right foot, the foot that Mondo swept out from underneath him. The man's momentum carried him forward. He was off-balance, he struggled to put his weight back over his right foot, but it was too late. As he started falling forwards, Mondo reached out and locked his fingers around the hand that held the knife, while the falling knifeman's weight still drove him forward. Mondo, using all of his strength, turned the knife hand around and plunged it into the man's chest. The man gasped, and fell to his knees, took one long look at Mondo, gasped for another breath and collapsed. Mondo turned and started running after Amy.

He jumped down the flight of stairs, taking four at a time. He ran out into the living room, reached down and picked up the pistol, then looked up. There stood Edwin Hawkins holding Amy in front of him. Edwin had Amy from behind, his right arm up to her neck, a six-inch knife blade inches from her jugular vein. Edwin had Amy's left arm locked behind her. She looked absolutely helpless. It looked like Edwin was completely supporting her body. If he let go, Amy would collapse on the floor. Edwin had the most evil smile on his face Mondo had ever seen. Hatred burned from Edwin Hawkins. He wouldn't kill Amy unless he had no other choice, but Mondo was about to die.

"It is time to lose, Mr. Mondo. Shall I cut her throat now or in ten seconds? What does it matter? She is dead, and before she falls to the ground you will be dying as well."

Mondo dropped his hands to his side. He didn't say anything.

"Giving up so easy, Mr. tough guy? I thought you would try some of your chop, chop, hero moves. Too bad nothing can help either of you."

Mondo dropped the gun. It could do nothing and he knew it. Each second seemed like an hour, Amy standing there so close to him, and yet even closer to death. Edwin was out of reach, too far away for Mondo to do anything. He knew that Edwin was beyond his powers to beat. He couldn't fight evil.

"What will it be? Shall you die or shall you watch her die? I hate to spill her blood, but I want to see you watch as the woman you love dies, bleeds to death, gasping for air, trying to scream out your name to save her, but you can't do one damn thing. How does it feel to be so helpless?"

Mondo could see the knife wavering just inches away from Amy's throat.

There was nothing that Mondo could do. Except...

Slowly he reached up to his collar and in one motion ripped his shirt open, exposing the medallion that the old lady on the dock had given him. Edwin's face froze, the smile disappearing from his face, his hand losing its grip on Amy, his knife hand starting to fall away from her throat.Amy could feel his grip loosen, could sense his right hand dropping from her throat. With every ounce of her strength she kicked back and up with her right leg catching Edwin directly in the groin. Edwin started to fall backwards, bringing his hands down to protect himself. In that instant, Amy leaped forward, broke free from his grasp and scrambled across the floor. She stood up trembling, next to Mondo.

"Where did you get that?" It was not just a question, it was a demand.

"You, you are the wearer of the medallion?" Edwin gasped out.

"Then let us see your power."

He threw his arms forward, a blaze of flames extending out from them. An all consuming blast of fire raced toward Mondo and Amy, pure destruction was coming at them. The medallion glowed, burned hot on Mondo's chest, then just as the flames were going to reach them the medallion formed a bubble, a circle of white light that surrounded both of them. The flames from Edwin's fire hit the white light of the bubble and hissed, turned into steam and dropped to the ground as water.

"My God!" Edwin screamed.

Edwin reached into his cloak and brought forth the very essence of his evil black magic. He pulled out a small jar with a large cork lid in it. This was the same powder that he had used to call the Seeker. He pulled the cork out and flung the contents of the jar at Amy and Mondo. The chalky white powder floated through the air. It started spinning and spiraling around itself. The powder growing, increasing in size. It started to take shape, a form was growing out of the white dust as it spun toward them. Ten feet away from Amy and Mondo the powder grew into a three dimensional hologram. A beast was being born. It was appearing out of the dust, a hideous beast was taking shape, coming right at them, transforming itself from the powder into a life size apparition of evil itself. The dust congealed into a monster from hell. The beast landed five feet in front of Mondo and Amy, its eyes blood-shot, its face hideously deformed. Large teeth extended over its semi- human lips, drool dripped from its mouth, the claws on its fingers over three inches long. The beast stood naked before them. Death and destruction was standing there in front of Mondo and Amy. There was nothing they could do. This was power beyond anything that they could defeat.

Suddenly the medallion burned red hot on Mondo's chest. It scorched his flesh, then it turned into pure light, casting forth a ray of golden brilliance. It blinded Mondo and Amy, and they flung their hands up to protect their eyes. The beast roared, brought its scaly hands up to its eyes to protect itself. The light hit the beast, causing it to scream in pain, then it started to disappear, to wisp away, particles of beast turning back into white chalky dust. Mondo looked through the beast and saw Edwin standing there. He grabbed Amy's hand and charged. He ran right through the beast. The body of the evil apparition dispersed into vapors of white dust as they rushed through. Edwin hadn't moved. Mondo let go of Amy's hand one second before he hit Edwin, tackling him in the mid-section. Both men flew over backwards, falling over the couch, sending furniture flying.

Amy turned and looked behind her. She saw the beast starting to transform itself back from wisps of vapor and powder, back into its hideous physical self. She watched in horror as the beast grew, the vapors of evil coming together, forming themselves back into the living beast of destruction. The beast landed five feet from Amy, snarled at her, and started walking her way.

Mondo landed on top of Edwin. Edwin was struggling, trying to push him off. Mondo reached down and grabbed the chain that held the medallion. With one tug he broke it off of his neck, and crammed it into Edwin's mouth. The medallion broke teeth as it entered; Edwin couldn't stop it. The power that came from the medallion instantly spreading its poison into Edwin Hawkins.

With a shriek, an ungodly scream of agony, Edwin easily threw Mondo off of him and rose to his feet. The beast had stopped in its tracks a foot away from grabbing Amy. Edwin clawed at his throat, dragging the gold medallion out and casting it to the ground. Edwin looked at Mondo, fear and terror filling his face. His lips were turning a dark blue as if his oxygen was cut off. Edwin clawed at his mouth, gagging, reaching deep into his throat as if trying to remove something. His face began to contort, to change, to lose some of his human features. Mondo and Amy stood paralyzed as they watched Edwin's face start to drip layers of flesh, like a wax figure held too close to a flame. Edwin tried to scream, but his deformed lips couldn't make a sound. His entire face and head were melting, then suddenly his head burst into flames. Edwin fell to his knees, still clawing at his mouth, his fingers becoming blackened bones where flesh had been just moments before. His entire upper torso was smoking, flaming, melting into a pile of burning stinking flesh.

The beast screamed behind them. Mondo and Amy turned and watched as the beast started to melt away as well. The beast's entire body beginning to transform into the white chalky powder. Then the powder erupted into flames. The beast, now a burning wisp of white powdery vapor, screamed out. It suddenly screamed out again and raced across the floor and dove into the melting, burning body of Edwin Hawkins. As the beast slammed into Edwin, both flew backward, sending a burning gel of flames and smoke up and outward. Edwin reached out, his arms flailing as he slowly sank into a burning, smoking puddle. The burning gel landed on the couch and the floor, instantly igniting them into flames. Suddenly the whole room seemed to explode into flames. The carpet, the couch, in one minute the whole living room had become a burning inferno.

"Quick," was all Mondo could say. He grabbed Amy's hand and rushed backward, away from the flaming bodies that had been Edwin and the very creation of evil itself. They ran back into the kitchen, the flames racing after them. It was as if Edwin was reaching out from death with the last of his power to consume them. Mondo and Amy leaped over the body of the dead shooter, then ran outside through the empty doorway that Mondo had broken down earlier. They raced out of the house, ran thirty feet across the lawn and collapsed in each other's arms.

They both looked back. The entire house was ablaze. Never could fire have spread that fast on its own, never could it have consumed what it did with such a furious appetite.

By the time Sunny made his way around to them, Mondo and Amy were standing a hundred feet from the house. Sunny walked up and wrapped his arms around them both, bursting into tears.

He looked at Amy, afraid to ask the question that burned in his mind.

"What about Isabella?"

"She's fine. She's at the chalet with Christy. Johnny saved us."

Sunny's knees went out from underneath him and he collapsed on the ground, tears flowing freely from one of the toughest mobsters there was.

"Let's get the hell out of here," Mondo shouted.

They all turned and started running back for the parked cars.

It was another fifteen minutes before they passed the first fire engines and police cars responding to the fire. The police drove right by them on the other side of the freeway, never even giving Mondo's van or Sunny's car a second glance. By the time the fire department arrived there was nothing to do but watch it all burn to the ground.

The nightmare was behind them now, and they all knew it. Edwin was defeated, consumed in the fire, along with whatever evil he had planned. Mondo and Amy knew that they were alive only because of a little old lady that had appeared that night on the dock. Who was she? Amy and Mondo thought they knew. She was the mother goddess herself, or at least someone sent by her. She had given them the medallion that had saved their lives and destroyed Edwin and his evil. The medallion was gone, lost in the burning house. Mondo knew it would never be found. It wasn't his to keep, it wasn't for this world. It was to be used only when all else failed against the powers of evil. Mondo hoped that it would never be necessary for anyone to ever have to wear that medallion again.

296

An hour after reaching Vancouver, Mike was let out of the trunk, sore, scared, but alive. He never said a word to anybody about what happened that night. Two days later Isabella and Johnny were back at the Whale Research Center. It was impossible for them to hide their feelings for each other, so after a day they didn't even try.

Sunny and Christy flew back to Los Angeles together, and they are still seeing each other. Who would have ever thought?

Mondo and Amy finally made it back aboard Smokin' Joe and slipped out of Campbell River. Smokin' Joe was last seen sailing northbound, on a beam reach across Queen Charlotte Strait on a Sunset Run.

THE END

The author and his wife live on a small island
in the Pacific Northwest.

CPSIA information can be obtained
at www.ICGtesting.com
Printed in the USA
FFOW03n0931190814
6937FF